MY
HUSBAND'S
LIES

BOOKS BY LIZ LAWLER

The Next Wife
The Silent Mother
The Nurse's Secret

I'll Find You
Don't Wake Up

MY
HUSBAND'S
LIES
LIZ LAWLER

bookouture

Published by Bookouture in 2023

An imprint of Storyfire Ltd.
Carmelite House
50 Victoria Embankment
London EC4Y 0DZ

www.bookouture.com

Copyright © Liz Lawler, 2023

Liz Lawler has asserted her right to be identified as the author of this work.

All rights reserved. No part of this publication may be reproduced, stored in any retrieval system, or transmitted, in any form or by any means, electronic, mechanical, photocopying, recording or otherwise, without the prior written permission of the publishers.

ISBN: 978-1-83790-915-5
eBook ISBN: 978-1-83790-914-8

This book is a work of fiction. Names, characters, businesses, organizations, places and events other than those clearly in the public domain, are either the product of the author's imagination or are used fictitiously. Any resemblance to actual persons, living or dead, events or locales is entirely coincidental.

For Diane, Bernadette, Teresa, John – who love flying.
Cabin crew prepare for take-off.

PROLOGUE

She cast a furtive glance over her shoulder. There was no one behind her. The sound of hurrying footsteps on the pavement had ceased. They had probably disappeared into a bar.

Where she stood, the narrow street was dark, the shops and cafés closed with only a few lights on in upstairs windows. The owners getting their sleep far enough away from the bars that were still open, the music muted by the shut windows and doors.

Her eyes trained on the opening to the alleyway.

Doubts flooded her. Why had he contacted her now? Because he now knew the truth? She certainly wasn't going to make the first move. Once bitten, twice shy. She would let him speak first.

She counted off the seconds as she waited in the shadows. It was a minute past midnight. Why choose such a late time? Less chance of being seen, she supposed. For him.

A grubby little thought took hold as she saw her reflection in a dark shop window. The silvery-white material had a metallic hue. She wished she had worn jeans and a jumper. Not a dress and heels. And not new underwear. Try as she might to convince herself that she was there only to set the record straight, she had prepared for not only meeting him, but for whatever might be on offer. She had spent a silly fortune on a plane ticket, new clothes and perfume, when this might just be a quick hello and goodbye to give an apology.

She glanced at her watch. He was five minutes late. He'd probably changed his mind or forgotten. Or he only meant his message to be taken in jest, added to a Christmas card that arrived six days late. Not a serious invitation, just an impulsive add-on to sound genuine. It rankled that he was so blasé in assuming she would see it as a joke. Giving her a time and a place. He hadn't even felt the need to check with a phone call or a text if she was coming.

She was a fool. A silly, immature, thirty-year-old fool.

Stepping out of the shadows, she peered along the empty street, deciding what to do. She could leave before he saw her there waiting for him. Which was only fooling herself.

He wasn't going to appear. Acting rashly, out of wounded pride, she had come here. Never again would she be so foolish. She would go back to the airport and wait for her return flight, and not allow herself to cry. There was no reason to cry. She had weathered the worst already. Nothing new had happened. It was a blip. Twenty-four hours in her life that no one need know about. Not even him.

Her body felt suddenly weary. Her year of remonstrations against the unfair treatment. The anticipation of seeing him ached her stomach, leaving her feeling empty. She heard the rush of traffic on the streets ahead. She would hail a taxi, go back to the airport, and wait for her morning flight. To hell with him. She had only been trying to help.

She raised her face and felt the cool wind passing through the passage. Why couldn't he have suggested to meet in the summer? She could have stayed and swum in the sea, with or without him.

She shivered and turned towards the opening to the main street, preparing to move, when a figure stepped into her path. Her heart skittered with fright. She gave a small yelp, followed by an embarrassed laugh. 'You scared the life out of me,' she exclaimed.

She half-smiled. Then felt confusion at the sight of the brick in their hand.

She edged a step back, trapped against a wall. She involuntarily squeezed her eyes shut as the brick sped towards her. A solid weight connected with her head.

Dazed, she stood transfixed, feeling a clamp of pain. Pressure pulsating in her eyes, her ears, through her nose. The taste of blood in her mouth. A flow of liquid was dribbling down her forehead and into her eyes. She gasped and toppled to her knees.

She needed to put her hands over her head. Or lie down and pretend she was dead – then they might go away.

She sensed their presence. It was still there. It wasn't over yet. Air whooshes across her face as she hears the clear sound of a sickly crunch.

That was me... she thinks, feebly. It's over...

CHAPTER ONE

The clanking noise started up the moment Kate switched the boiler back on. She had no hot water, no heat, and was now going to be late for work. She had stressed to the woman on the phone that she had to leave at one o'clock. If an engineer didn't turn up soon, she would have to leave it for Mark to sort out.

She raced down the stairs to put the kettle on. She'd have to make do with a strip wash. Twenty minutes later, standing in her underwear, she shivered as she pulled on her bottle-green uniform. She dragged a brush through her tangle of hair and tied it in a ponytail, then took a moment to assess the damage. Not her best look for sure. Her Celtic skin was almost white against the blue of her eyes. Today she looked all of her thirty-seven years, brought on by yesterday.

Yesterday, when she met baby Andrew. Eleven months old and chubby and tiny baby teeth still pushing through, with blotchy skin and hands and feet that were way too cold. Emergency care couldn't come fast enough. With every minute she spent treating him, she felt her stomach knotting tighter. By the grace of God, he was stable this morning. Her call to PICU had been reassuring – not out of the woods, but at least on the right side of living.

When she had patients like Andrew, it always showed in her face and would take a few days for the stress to disappear. While in the thick of it, she would take control, stay calm, tell others what to do. It was when she left the department that fear of losing the battle hit home.

She had experienced the light of life vanishing in these little bundles of innocence, and it was then she prayed her hardest to let her patients live. A few lines on her face was a small price to pay.

She pulled on socks and trainers, slipped her lanyard over her head. She quickly texted her mum, forewarning her she might have to take Jacob back to hers after school. The house was too cold for them here. She texted Mark as well, telling him the boiler was on the blink, adding a frozen face emoji.

In the kitchen, she spooned coffee into her travel mug. From the bread bin, she grabbed a raisin bagel and shoved it in her fleece pocket. She'd eat it on the way. A fleeting thought reassured her: there was an electric blanket in the airing cupboard. She'd get Mark to put it on the bed if the boiler couldn't be fixed. She'd shower at work after her shift and then snuggle into Mark's warm back when she got home, imagining putting her cold feet on his legs with glee.

His face stared out at her from a photograph on the windowsill. She'd taken it secretly during the renovations of the house. Mark and Robert sitting up on the roof drinking beers, thinking that she didn't know. Behaving like lads until they saw her car. It was a memory she cherished, now more than ten years ago.

It was through Robert she met Mark. Her car wouldn't start when she returned to it after shopping. Robert came to her rescue, charming and chatting but showing little interest in the dead vehicle. His friend joined him with barely a glance at her, got her to open the bonnet on her Mini Cooper. Under the hood, he quickly got the car started again. Then he grinned at her. A beautiful proud grin. And she was instantly captivated.

The ring of the doorbell jolted her. The repair man – just when she had to leave. In the hallway, Barney barked at the disturbance to his sleep. She shushed him. She decided she would leave the engineer in the house alone and give him her mobile number so he could let her know how he got on.

Kate stared in surprise at the two men standing on the doorstep, one a youngish man in a suit and tie, the other gruff-looking and older, wearing an open collar shirt and zipped jacket, holding up a small black wallet in his hand for her inspection. On a laminated card embossed in blue was POLICE, and below a photograph of the man. She felt a wave of fear wash over her. Her mind racing. Jacob. Mum. Mark.

'Mrs Jordan?'

Kate stared at the police officer. Before she could answer, the younger man spoke.

'Or is that Doctor Jordan?'

Kate, still in a daze, responded. 'Yes, that's me.'

'Married to Mark Jordan?'

She nodded, her heart thumping in her chest. It was Mark... But why weren't the airline officials standing there? Her mind rushed for answers. She hadn't watched any TV or listened to the radio. She'd been busy trying to fix the clunking noise in the boiler. Had the landline rung while she had her head in the cupboard? Her mouth trembled. Did everyone in the country know something she didn't? Had a plane crashed?

She let out a half sob, startling the younger man. 'Are you all right?' he asked, stepping forward.

'Is he dead?' she uttered in dread.

He instantly shook his head. 'No! No, of course not!'

Kate gulped back her tears, moving backwards along her hallway. The two men followed, and Kate didn't try to stop them. Backing into her kitchen, she sat on a bench. She rested her arms on the table and sank her head onto them for a few moments until she was back in control.

When she sat up, there was a glass of water in front of her. The younger man sat opposite, watching her worriedly. 'I'm sorry for alarming you. I'm Detective Sergeant Raj Sharma, and with me is Detective Constable Ryan Kelly. What made you think we were here to tell you that?'

It embarrassed her to think of the sob she gave at the front door. She smiled weakly. 'Mark's an airline pilot. Two official-looking men on my doorstep... I foolishly thought the worst.'

He gave a nod of understanding. 'I'm sorry you had a fright. We're aware your husband is a pilot, so I should have thought about that. We're here to speak to your husband, but clearly he's not home.'

Her heart began hammering again. Only this time, she would not lose her cool. 'You want to speak to Mark?'

'Yes.' He pulled out his wallet and leafed through the pockets for a card. 'If you could tell him to contact this number as soon as he returns. We would like to talk to him today if possible.'

'I'm not sure what time he lands,' she lied, for no other reason than she felt she had to. She knew Mark's roster. Knew where he would be, when he would land, reasons for delays, every day. On her phone she had an app for tracking flights in real time. He was due to land at Bristol Airport at 14:25. He'd be back home by half past four, unless there was traffic.

The detective stood up. 'Right. Well, you have my card, so I'll wait for his call.'

Kate heard the front door shut and sat numbly in the chair, her stomach doing somersaults. Something was seriously wrong. They had come as a pair, not the ordinary police but detectives no less. Something had happened. They wanted to talk to Mark today. He had been away for three days, so whatever it was had probably happened during that time.

She grabbed her iPad and opened a new tab in Safari. She typed 'local news Barcelona'. Tapped on 'Barcelona – latest news, breaking stories and comments'. Below a photograph of Barcelona Airport runway, the headline read:

BRITISH TOURIST FOUND DEAD ON STREET IN BARCELONA

She tapped on the headline:

Catalan police are eager to speak with a British man who was seen with the woman. Guardia Urbana *are treating this as a murder investigation.*

CHAPTER TWO

On autopilot, Kate led the boiler engineer upstairs to the cupboard on the landing, briefly explaining the problem. On autopilot she rang work to say she wouldn't be going in, citing the emergency with her boiler and exaggerating the extent of the problem by adding that there was a potential fire risk. She felt bad about letting them down when there was no reason to think Mark was in trouble. The police needing to talk to him could be about anything, something relating to the airport, security, or even an unruly passenger. But instinctively she felt she needed to be home when Mark returned.

From a shelf in the airing cupboard she found the electric blanket. Pulling the duvet and sheet from her bed, she spread the blanket across the mattress and plugged it in. She remade the bed, then tidied around the room.

She felt compelled to open Mark's work wardrobe where his dry-cleaned uniforms hung. The shoulder loops on his shirts to attach his epaulettes, the four gold stripes, marking him captain, on the sleeves of the airline jackets. She closed the cupboard, trying not to think about the dead woman.

The knock on her bedroom door startled her. A cheery look greeted her.

'Up and running again. I've had to order a new valve 'cos that's where the problem's coming from. It'll be all right until then, but as soon as it's in, I'll replace the old one.'

Kate saw him to the door, and watched him drive off in his van. With the heating back on, the house would soon be warm. She would close the curtains to keep out the cold and the dark. Four o'clock and the sky was already black. Mark would be home soon.

It was another two hours before he arrived. He came into the kitchen and sighed, placed his case down, and walked to the sink. He poured a glass of water and drank it thirstily. He had yet to notice her, as he wouldn't be expecting her to be there.

'That was a hearty sigh,' she quietly said.

Mark turned, surprised. 'You're home!'

Kate nodded. 'Boiler was on the blink. Had to get an engineer in. The house was like a fridge earlier. It's warming up now.'

'And work?'

'Told them it was on the verge of exploding so I couldn't come in.'

His eyes rounded. He wasn't buying it. As a specialist registrar in emergency medicine, Kate didn't just take a day off. It would have to be for something much more serious than a faulty boiler. Maybe for a life or death situation, not because the house was cold. 'What about Jacob?'

'He's at Mum's. She thinks the boiler's still broken. I haven't let her know it's fixed. He's sleeping at hers tonight.'

His face fell. 'Oh... I was really looking forward to my hug.'

He looked drawn. She walked towards him and put her arms around his shoulders. 'You'll have to make do with just mine.'

He pulled her tight, and held her close. She felt the tension in his body. It made her anxious.

'The real reason I stayed home is because the police were here. They've left their number. Said they need you to ring them today. It's probably nothing to worry about, but I thought just in case.'

Mark gave a shuddering breath before relinquishing his hold. He looked shaken, his voice hesitant. 'I already spoke with them. They were at the airport, waiting to greet me. I have to go to the police station in the morning to be questioned under caution.'

Kate inhaled sharply, feeling stunned. 'Oh my God! Are you serious? They want to talk to you under caution. Did they say why?'

He nodded. 'Yes. A British woman was murdered in Barcelona last night.'

'But why do they need to question you?'

She saw the look of confusion on his face, his worried eyes. 'She was on my flight. A passenger.'

Kate was baffled. There was a tone of outrage in her voice. 'What! That's not enough reason. They can't bring you in for that!'

'Of course they can, they're the police!' he snapped. Then quickly apologised. 'Sorry. I didn't mean to shout.'

His sharp response showed how stressed he was.

She let him know she wasn't offended. Only concerned. 'Hey, I'm sorry for getting aerated. It's just me with my worry hat on.'

He smiled, indulgently. Her 'worry hat' was an expression he used when she got upset over something she couldn't change. He would tell her to take it off, otherwise she would wear it out.

He took a steadying breath. 'They're interviewing me because they say there is a witness who saw me there.'

'Saw you where, Mark?' she asked anxiously, feeling panic bubbling within her, already knowing what he would answer.

'With this woman,' he replied in a low voice. Shaking his head in bafflement. 'On the street where she was found dead.'

CHAPTER THREE

Robert Brennan was helping the police with their enquiries. This was not the actual phrase used by Detective Raj Sharma, but Robert couldn't think what else to call it. He was at a police station in Bristol volunteering information and answering questions. He had no idea whether it helped. They weren't telling him anything. They were asking questions about what he did yesterday in Barcelona. Robert had given an account from when they landed yesterday to their departure this morning, and given the names of the cabin crew and the captain, the hotel they stayed in, the café where they had coffee, the bar where they ate and had a beer. All mundane matters that weren't very interesting.

'And are you the second captain?' the officer sitting next to Sharma asked.

Robert had removed his blazer and the epaulettes on his shirt, leaving them in his car, wearing only his overcoat into the police station so he didn't draw attention to his uniform. 'I'm the first officer. I sit in the right seat on the flight deck.'

'And in Barcelona, were you all together for all of the time?'

Robert thought it a nonsensical question, and raised his

eyebrows at the older, detective. He looked like a man who'd been around the block a few times, and suspected DC Kelly would kick himself afterwards for his schoolboy error.

'I think that would be impossible given that none of us were glued together, and each had our own hotel room.'

Robert knew what they were asking, but he wasn't going to give answers to unclear questions. He would choose how he answered carefully, and throw in a little ambiguity where possible.

Detective Sergeant Sharma looked at him enquiringly.

Sharma now raised his eyebrows at Robert, sharing in his sense of humour. 'Yes, I can see how that would be impossible. It would present a sticky situation.'

Robert smiled, quite liking the man. He took a sip of the bland coffee from the cardboard cup in front of him and felt a sting from the graze on his knuckles. The brown plaster needed loosening so he could flex his hand. He had examined it this morning and had squirted on some antiseptic cream to keep it from becoming infected.

Officer Kelly noticed his slight discomfort. 'You hurt yourself?'

Robert nodded. 'Yes, I took a tumble while out running and scraped the back of my hand along the pavement.'

'Was that in Barcelona?' he asked.

'Yes. I enjoy sprinting once or twice a day. Short distances don't take up much time, but allow me to keep fit.'

'So there would have been times when you weren't with the other crew members?'

'That's correct. Which answers your other question. We were not all together all of the time.'

'Do you know what your colleagues were doing with their time?'

Robert shrugged. 'I can take a guess. Of the three cabin crew, Martin Samworth was probably in his room watching films. Olivia Vaughn seems never to get enough of revisiting the Sagrada Familia – I think she's hoping to be there the day it's finally completed – and I imagine she would have looked after our new cabin crew member, Kerry Hall, who is only just out of training.' He gave a sigh before continuing. 'That leaves Captain Jordan. He's a creature of habit. Usually straight to his room, then a meet up for an early beer. He reads a lot. Has a fascination with engineering, particularly the problem of carbon emissions. So studies a lot while away.'

Officer Kelly exchanged a glance with Detective Sharma. Robert wondered if they were going to mention the woman murdered last night in Barcelona. So far, they'd skirted around the topic of a serious incident, and they hadn't asked if he had witnessed anything. Their interest was in what the flight crew were doing individually when out of sight of one another.

'Did you see Captain Jordan yesterday evening?'

The question came from Sharma, and Robert was instantly alert. The mentioning of Mark specifically was a red flag.

Robert answered truthfully. 'Yes. Briefly. Getting in the lift.'

'And at what time was that?'

'Eight thirty, give or take a minute.'

'And do you know where he was going?'

'I imagine to his room.'

'I see. So you saw him on the ground floor?'

'Well, yes. Otherwise I wouldn't have guessed he was going to his room.'

'Did you see him at any time after that?'

Robert gave a truthful answer to another poorly worded question. 'Yes. At breakfast this morning in the hotel restaurant.'

Sharma gazed into the corner of the room. He made a striking figure with his handsome face and lean form. Robert could see he was thinking. When he looked back at Robert, he had another question.

'Did you see Captain Jordan between eight thirty yesterday evening, the time he got in the lift, and when you saw him at breakfast this morning?'

Robert gave a sigh and raised his eyes to the ceiling. When ready, he spoke bluntly. 'I went to my room after seeing Captain Jordan take the lift. I came out of my room this morning to join the rest of the crew for breakfast.'

Sharma regarded him with a speculative expression, as if trying to guess if Robert knew something more. He then rose from his chair. 'Thank you for your time, Mr Brennan. We'll be in touch if we have any further questions.'

Outside the station, Robert pulled up the collar of his coat, feeling the bitter cold on his neck. He fished out his phone from his coat pocket and stood still on the pavement to read the messages. He'd missed two calls from Mark and had received one text message.

Do you know any good solicitors?

Robert did. He messaged back the name of one that Mark could count on.

He put his phone away and started walking in the direction of the car park on Rupert Street, thinking about what he'd said to Sharma. He hadn't lied, but he wondered if the detective had picked up on any deception by omission. If Sharma had asked him if he stayed in his room until the following morning, Robert would have given a different reply. But as the question never came, he was under no obligation to volunteer the information. He had a feeling that Mark was going to need an excellent solicitor. He didn't need Robert to add anything that would make matters worse. The police were thinking Mark was involved in a serious incident that happened only last night. Mark was going to need all the support he could get.

For the crew to be met at the airport meant they didn't even get to go home first, that their interviews with the police couldn't wait until tomorrow. They clearly had evidence for them to be acting so fast. He wondered what the cabin crew were asked, but wasn't tempted to call them and find out. He was better off keeping his own counsel. There were Kate and Jacob to consider. Kate would be worried. She loved Mark, but would she be able to support him?

That was the trouble Robert foresaw for both of them. Kate had trust issues, which Mark thought she was over.

Robert would do all he could to ease the situation for them. That's all he could do for the moment. Be there for them, and be there after, whatever the outcome. He had promised a long time ago that if anything happened to Mark, he would watch over his family. Mark should feel reassured knowing Robert would keep that promise.

CHAPTER FOUR

Kate pulled on a pair of jogger pants and a warm hooded top. She was shivering despite her hot shower and the warm house. The thought of Mark being questioned by the police about a murder had put her in a state of shock.

Mark came into the bedroom, placed his cabin bag on the bed, and began his ritual of unpacking the unclean clothing and replacing with clean, ready for the next trip. Perching on the bed, she watched him. She would describe his look as unfussy. His character wouldn't suit being styled. He had been using the same barber since she'd known him, and he kept his brown hair as short as possible, more out of necessity than for appearance's sake. He didn't notice the lines at the corners of his eyes, and stuck with soap to wash with. So long as his skin and eyes were healthy, he was satisfied. But as she looked at him now, his face was pale.

She wondered if the rest of the crew knew what had happened, if they were present when the police approached Mark? What would Robert say about it? He probably spent nearly as much time with Mark as Kate did. She'd never queried their friendship, accepting they were like chalk and cheese, completely different from each other. Yet it somehow worked. Kate hadn't seen him in a while, but she was surprised he hadn't called Mark, checked he was okay. Maybe he wasn't aware. Mark might not want anyone to know about it.

Mark hung his jacket in the wardrobe. With or without his uniform on, he was noticeable, he carried himself with a purpose, like someone in authority. Kate never doubted that, if her life was in danger, she could rely on him to save her.

He needed her now, though, and she was no lightweight in a difficult situation. She needed to think of practical ways to help.

Her eyes rested on the Ziploc bag holding underpants and socks, and the few items of casual clothing he had worn while away.

'Mark, I have an idea. Keep your unwashed clothing in the bag.'

He looked at her, perplexed.

She nodded encouragingly. 'Trust me. You don't want them washed. We're forgetting about DNA. That's what the police will be gathering. Everything you wore while away, even shoes, can prove you weren't there.'

She smiled brightly, hoping the suggestion would lift him, but his deep brown eyes remained troubled.

'Good advice, but I'm not sure it will help.'

Kate could feel questions forming in her head, and had to prevent asking the one question she didn't want to tumble out. Were you there?

'Kate, I was on that street on New Year's Eve. I was there in a bar where all the crew hang out. I had a drink with them on our first night stop. Next day, we flew to Paris. And yesterday, it was back to Bristol for a quick turnaround back to Barcelona. But last night, I was not on that street. Last night I stayed in the hotel.'

Kate let the information settle in her brain. It was not

great news, but neither was it all bad. For starters, the witness may have seen him on the street on New Year's Eve, and misremembered that it was then and not last night. The city would have been packed with people out celebrating. Perhaps this witness saw the woman standing in the crowd, close to Mark, and assumed they were together. Then by chance sees the woman again last night standing with a man resembling Mark, it's his image they're seeing in their mind. Not a different man.

DNA could still prove to be their friend. Mark's DNA could be on the woman's clothes if in direct contact in a crowd, but so would the DNA of other people. But last night there would be the DNA of the killer.

She reached across the bed and took the Ziploc bag. 'Look, at least if the police ask for your clothing, you can give it to them unwashed. Don't offer, in case they think you swapped them with different clothing.'

She stood up from the bed. 'Are you hungry? I can make us something.'

Mark was regarding her quietly. He looked tired, with shadows beneath his eyes.

'What?' she asked.

'I just wondered if you picked up on the lie I told. New Year's Eve when I called you? You asked what I was doing and I said I was staying in. I was outside the bar when I was talking to you.'

Kate had picked up on it, but wasn't going to say anything. She was a little surprised, and couldn't understand why he couldn't just say he was out. She was not a possessive wife, someone who needed to check up on their husband's activities. They were grown-ups, both holding down responsible jobs, their colleagues and friends not always part of each other's lives. She would have thought it quite normal for him to be with his crew on New Year's Eve.

'It's okay,' she answered. 'It's no biggie. I'm sure you had a reason.'

His expression was regretful. 'I wish I hadn't, though. I just felt it might sound mean to say I was out when you were on your own at home.'

His comment puzzled her. It made her sound like a needy wife, though in reality she was extremely self-sufficient. She never minded his job. She was occupied with her own job when he was away. Any free time was used to give the house an extra clean, cook meals she could freeze to save having to cook every day. It allowed her, if she liked, to walk about with a charcoal face mask on, or do her legs and underarms with a hair removal cream instead of a quick job with a razor. His nights away were her catch-up time.

Kate didn't say any of this. His intention had been to be kind, she knew.

Later that night, after brushing her teeth, she climbed into bed beside him and was relieved to find him fast asleep. He needed to be rested for tomorrow. She couldn't get her head around the day's events. The speed of the police. Both the Spanish and British. Spain must have been in contact straight away, or maybe Interpol. She didn't know how it worked, but however it worked, it was an efficient system.

They were there when he landed. If they hadn't come to the house, Kate would have gone to work none the wiser.

Of course, they may have suspected she knew something. It might have shown on her face if her husband rang and confessed to something and asked for her help. It was possible they envisaged finding her with packed suitcases ready to scarper.

His bags of clothes were quietly worrying her. Maybe she should have kept quiet and let him put them on a wash. He said he wasn't there at the time of the crime, so there should be no reason to worry.

It's just... supposing he was there for something that had nothing to do with a crime, there for another reason and too scared to tell her.

She flipped over onto her left side so that she could release the breath she was holding. His low snore reassured her she hadn't disturbed him.

How peacefully he was sleeping. It had to mean something good that he wasn't restless. She nuzzled her forehead against his back trying to push off her worry hat. Trying not think of the witness who saw him there. They had to be wrong. It was probably dark. Mark never lied to her. It's just with the police acting this fast... she couldn't help but worry that he might not be telling her everything.

CHAPTER FIVE

Kate cast her eyes around the clinical space, over wall-mounted plastic boxes of gauze, cannulas, bandages, her mind a blank. She couldn't remember what she came for. She stared at her gloved hands, hoping for a clue.

'Kate?'

Kate turned and looked into a pair of blue eyes shining with concern.

'Are you okay? I thought you got lost.' Eva, a third-year student nurse, smiled.

Kate pulled herself together and nodded. 'Yep. I just can't remember what I came in for.'

'Pink cannula,' Eva replied.

Kate retrieved one from the box in front of her and followed Eva back to the cubicle. The small, ninety-year-old woman was groaning. She needed morphine. The cannula put in by the ambulance crew had tissued – the puffiness in the crook of her elbow was caused by saline fluid leaking into the surrounding tissue because the cannula had punctured through the vein.

Kate quickly inserted the new cannula, taping it securely. She picked up a syringe of saline and flushed it. Then checked the label on the second syringe before administering slowly 1 mg of morphine.

Kate suspected a fractured neck of femur, and was instigating initial management: analgesia, bloods, intravenous fluids, diagnostic X-rays, ECG. Patient referred to orthopaedics, then to a ward to await a theatre slot.

A few minutes later, the pain eased from the patient's face. She reached out a veiny hand to clutch Kate's. 'Thank you, my dear. The pain was so shocking.'

Kate smiled at her kindly. 'I'm glad you're more comfortable.'

The small wrinkled face smiled back. 'I had red hair like yours once. Had a will of its own.'

Kate was aware of her untamed hair escaping the claw clip. She needed to use a dozen hairgrips to keep back the curls falling in her face. She winked at the old lady.

'My husband says I remind him of a cocker spaniel.'

The woman found energy to chuckle. 'There's many who would pay dearly to achieve those waves, my dear. I'm sure he's very proud of you.'

Kate was touched by the kind words, and gently squeezed the woman's hand before leaving her with Eva.

In the glass-walled office, she checked her mobile phone. Nothing from Mark. Until she heard from him, she couldn't relax. It was half twelve. Was he still at the police station answering questions? He knew to ring as soon as the interview was over. She had left him a message in capitals on the back of an envelope propped up against the kettle. Hard to miss.

She got up from the office chair. She needed to freshen up in the staffroom. Her skin felt overheated, like her blood was too warm. She woke in the night in a lather of sweat from the electric blanket she left switched on, and still felt like she was trapped in a hot room with the energy sucked from her.

In the staffroom toilet she drank greedily from the cold tap and cupped hands to splash water onto her face. She ran her wet fingers through her hair to smooth it back and cool her scalp. Feeling better, she checked her phone again. Mark had texted.

Finished at police station. See you later at home.

She breathed a sigh of relief, and quickly replied.

How did it go?

She stayed in the staffroom a further five minutes, waiting for the screen to light up, but nothing came back. Putting her mobile away, she returned to the department.

It was staggeringly busy. Every cubicle filled, ambulances in every bay outside waiting to offload, and she'd been told the waiting room was like a refugee camp with people bringing in folding chairs from their cars for somewhere to sit. Kate needed to pick up the pace and focus. Thinking about Mark wasn't going to help anyone if she made a mistake.

It was half two when she was next able to take a breather. She downed a bottle of water, followed by a lukewarm tea, followed by an urgent trip to the loo to pee. She washed her hands quickly, eager to see her phone. And hallelujah, there was a message.

I'm picking Jacob up. I let your mum know. See you soon.

Kate was flummoxed. Where was his answer to her question? She sent it again in capital letters.

HOW DID IT GO?

Then, impatient, she rang him, but he wasn't picking up.

She tried again, listening to the rings until her call went to voicemail.

Her jaw clenched in frustration. What was the matter with him? He must know she was waiting to hear from him. So why couldn't he just tell her what was going on? Not for a minute did she think him capable of murder. But she resented the horrible feeling of not being able to completely trust him.

Her stomach curdled with a buried jealousy that still had the power to hurt. Damn him for putting doubts in her mind. She wasn't going to accuse him of being unfaithful with every woman he spoke to or passed. If he was there, it was probably an innocent encounter.

This stupid worry might be for nothing.

The doubts in her head settled into a dull noise. Picking at a scab that had already healed over would only make it bleed again. Pessimism was not part of her character. For a good while she wasn't a person with a glass half full. She'd had to work at becoming that person again. Three years ago, she chose to start afresh. There was no reason to change a positive attitude. No reason to start doubting him. No reason to stop loving him. She trusted in him.

CHAPTER SIX

Kate was still waiting for a reply when her shift ended three hours later. As she was about to drive away from the car park, she saw Sophie. Kate stared through the windscreen, dumb-struck. She had an overwhelming urge to wind down her window and call out a hello.

They talked as colleagues now. Sophie kept a respectful distance at any gathering they attended, and Kate shut her ears to any mention of Sophie's name. She was just another doctor in the hospital where they both worked. Their special closeness ended three years ago, after Sophie came to talk to her, and after Mark had already confessed to his part in it.

Mark called himself several names. Foolish, mindless, self-ish. He was drunk, it was a mistake. While Sophie's criticism of herself was harsher. She thought her punishment should be for Kate to never talk to her again, until she realised that what was worse was Kate never feeling the same about her again.

Kate tried not to think about the past. She knew every detail, the full extent of that episode. A near miss. An opportu-nity that never went all the way. He had extracted himself from the situation, a mistake for nearly putting his penis into another woman's vagina.

Kate cringed at her vulgar thought, never thinking of it so graphically in her mind before. She had taken responsibility for the mitigating circumstances to help her stay strong in her marriage. She had let him go to the party alone, while she should have pushed herself to go with him, not grabbed the excuse of tiredness. He wouldn't have asked her to go alone, not if it was his friends hosting it. Her friends loved him and she knew they would give him a good time, her best friend, Sophie, especially. The only reason for encouraging it.

Gorgeous, flirty Sophie, who she had been best friends with since med school, who ate men like Mark for breakfast, who treated them like gods until she grew bored. But they never resented her for it because, somehow, she always found a way for them to feel it was them who ended it. She would then become their friend and would actually do some good. The half dozen exes that Kate had met adored their partners, as if it was Sophie who helped them find the right ones.

Sophie blamed herself entirely. Said it was she who followed him into the bathroom, who pulled him close for a kiss, who grabbed his hands to touch her. Mark was just standing there.

A narrow escape. The door had been unlocked. A guest opened it. The moment broken. A close call.

Kate never let on about the images in her head that came with that close call, the serious bruise to her heart as she saw Mark's mouth on Sophie's, his hands massaging her breasts. She never allowed her imagination to create further images of what might have happened if the door was locked.

It had taken time for that bruise to fade. The foundation of her marriage had been rocked. To know that her husband had been attracted to someone else. It had taken time for her to move on. She hated that worry over Mark had dredged it all up again now.

She watched Sophie drive away. Her mind returned to Mark. Did he have any idea how worried she was? How worried she'd been since the police visit yesterday? She wasn't a mind reader, so why hadn't he reassured her as soon as he could today? Phoned or texted with at least a hint of how it had gone? Did he think it kinder to leave her in the dark, that it would be better not to tell her bad news while at work?

She inhaled sharply. The coolness she had been craving all day swept over her in a rush. It made the hair stand up on the back of her neck as she felt a sensation of threat. It had to be bad news. Had he been charged and was avoiding telling her?

She put her hands on the steering wheel and put the car in first gear. She would drive slowly and give herself time to calm her thoughts. She was overreacting. Mark wouldn't have picked Jacob up if something bad had happened. He'd more likely have met her from work so that he could tell her in person before she got home. His radio silence had to be for another reason.

She concentrated as she approached the roundabout, taking the second exit onto the A37 towards Pensford and home. The village was ideal for Mark's journey to Bristol Airport and Kate's to the hospital in Bath. They had roughly the same commuting time. It couldn't be better. The four-bedroom cottage had needed renovation when they bought it. They envisaged the project taking a year, but it wasn't until Kate was on maternity leave, when they finally finished and could sit outside and appreciate what they had.

Her stomach churned as she wondered what waited for her at home. She'd know the minute she walked indoors if good or bad. Mark had better be ready to talk. And she had better not find that his less than forthcoming responses today was down to petulance. Although there were many things she loved him for, on occasion he could be damn well arrogant if he thought something stupid. Like when Jacob fell while sucking a lollipop at a birthday party just before Christmas, and the stick went up into the roof of his mouth. Mark, first on the scene, castigated the birthday boy's mother for letting five-year-olds run around with hard-boiled lollies.

Kate had taken over and removed the stick, persuading Mark to wait in the car while she rinsed out Jacob's mouth. Not wanting him to say anything further to the embarrassed mother.

Keeping the details to himself may be more indicative of a bruised ego. The police officers dented Mark's pride by meeting him at the airport and thinking he was not trustworthy enough to contact the police by himself. Being the captain, the pilot in command, he was used to being trusted with the lives of hundreds of strangers every time he strapped himself into a cockpit. Mark would have thought that enough to make him an upstanding citizen.

Like her, he had dealings with the police from time to time, but always in the course of their work. A disruptive passenger, an accompanied patient, the police were their allies, their security, always for them and with them, never against them. They had never come to their home in pairs, and never as detectives, or given them reason to feel afraid of them. Which was how Kate was feeling since yesterday. For the first time in her life, Kate was afraid of the police.

CHAPTER SEVEN

The house was toasty warm when Kate stepped inside. She hung up her fleece, passed Barney asleep in his basket, and reflected that he was sleeping a lot more than usual. His yellow fur showed his age. She had acquired him before she met Mark, the last of a litter that somehow got foisted on her from her local shop. The wily shopkeeper must have seen her coming. She went in for bread and came out with a golden Labrador.

Kate smelled the floral scent of soap powder from the clothes on the airer in front of the radiator and breathed a sigh of relief. Mark had washed his dirty laundry.

Jacob's soft voice floated in to the hallway. 'Daddy, I want it green, not red.'

She headed to the kitchen, knowing Mark was about to have a battle trying to serve their son pasta with tomato sauce. She spotted a pan of still plain pasta on the stove. From the fridge she took a jar of green pesto and quickly mixed Jacob a fresh bowl.

'I forgot,' Mark mouthed, while Jacob happily picked up his fork.

Kate kissed the top of her son's head and waited until he

looked up at her. 'That wasn't polite, Jacob. When you ask for something, you say, please, and then thank you.'

He swallowed his food, then nodded solemnly. 'Sorry, Daddy.'

She felt her heart lurch at his sombreness. He was such a gentle boy, and sensitive to criticism. She rarely had to tell him off. She needed patience sometimes, though, like when he was completing a task, as it had to be perfect in his eyes. He found it difficult to leave what he was doing when in the midst of a project. Every dinosaur had to be facing the same way across the floor. Farm animals separated from sea creatures, bugs separated from lizards and snakes. It had to be correct. He knew a vast number of animal names and wouldn't be fobbed off if she gave one the wrong name. In their plastic forms, a brachiosaurus, diplodocus, brontosaurus, all looked similar to her. But not to Jacob.

She worried he spent too much time alone and sometimes wished he had a sibling. In his first term at school the reception teacher had no worries. He made friends easily and loved learning.

She hadn't seen him since she dropped him off at school yesterday morning, his first day back after Christmas. It was a long time to be without him. She'd have a quick shower and then sit with him.

She slipped off her shoes before making her way upstairs.

* * *

Mark placed her dinner on the table and joined her to sit down and eat. She took a mouthful and murmured her appreciation. He made the best tomato sauce, using garlic and onions and basil leaves. She ate contentedly and finally allowed herself to unwind. Glancing at Mark's face, she could see that he seemed relaxed.

She tucked Jacob into bed at seven o'clock and came down the stairs to find the kitchen clean, and tea poured for her. She curled up at one end of the sofa and sipped her drink. Finally, they could talk.

'So,' she said, in a deliberately light tone. 'Don't keep me in suspense. On a scale of one to ten, how rude were you to Sergeant Sharma?'

'I wasn't rude, Kate.' He glanced at her and she tensed at the seriousness in his voice. He sat straighter and laced his fingers across his chest, his thumbs tapping together. He sighed. 'The police will contact me when they want to speak to me again.'

Kate felt her throat dry. She placed her cup on the blanket box beside her and worked her way to sitting up properly with her feet now on the rug. 'Do they think they'll need to speak to you again, or was it just mentioned casually?'

'No. It wasn't said casually,' he said, without taking his eyes off her. 'It was to inform me it would be happening.'

'Why?' she asked, feeling the dryness in her throat turn scratchy. 'What do they have to make them think they need to talk to you again? Is it this witness? What did they say they saw? I mean...' She bit her lip to keep it from quivering, and emitted a shaky breath. 'It couldn't have been you.'

He nodded at her bleakly. 'That's what I said. That it was a case of mistaken identity. The witness described a man with dark hair, slim build, about six feet tall, mid-thirties to mid-forties.'

She stared at him. The description fit him, but then it would fit a thousand other men who were in the area that night. 'That's ridiculous,' she said in a derisive tone. 'They may as well have said tall, dark and handsome. It could be any man between thirty-five and forty-five who happened to be tall and have dark hair.'

'There's something else,' he added grimly.

She felt a shiver at the finality in his voice. She was afraid to ask what the something else was. She watched the stranglehold he had on his fingers. The knuckles were turning white. Whatever it was, he was finding it hard to tell her.

'I knew her,' he stated quietly. 'She worked for the airline a year ago. Because I knew her, they suspect me. I could see it in their eyes. They're going to question me again, I know it.'

He unlaced his hands and slumped back, closing his eyes. 'It wasn't me, Kate. But in the meantime, I'm grounded. I'm not allowed to fly.'

CHAPTER EIGHT

Kate carried her barely touched tea out to the kitchen. She placed the cup in the sink and clasped her hands on top of her head, trying to think what to do. The reality of the seriousness of the situation hitting home. These things didn't happen to people like them. Her husband had never been in trouble with the police in his life.

She heard Mark in the hallway. Through the doorway she saw him turning the airer around against the radiator so the other side would dry.

'Why did you wash them? I thought we were going to keep them unwashed in case the police asked for them.'

She could feel the tension coming off him in waves. He was probably more anxious than he was letting on, probably angry and frustrated as well for being put in this position.

His expression turned sour. 'They didn't ask for them.'

'Did you mention them to your solicitor? To see if it might help?'

He shook his head. 'No.'

Kate sighed. He was behaving stubbornly. He probably washed them as soon as he got back from the police station in an act of defiance. Helping the police was the exact opposite of what he wanted, which was to sabotage his situation in the face of being thought guilty for one second. She was aware he had a stubborn streak, but this behaviour would work against him. He needed to use any advantage he could to resolve the matter.

'Mark, you're not thinking straight. It's been a shock, but come on... They'll soon realise they don't have evidence against you.'

Her words seemed to reach him. The stiffness in his shoulders dropped. He lowered his head and placed his hand against his forehead. 'I can't believe she's dead,' he said quietly. 'A beautiful young woman. I just wish I'd never gone. I should have requested the time off and stayed at home with you.'

Kate went up behind him and rubbed her hand across his back before reaching her arms around his chest to hold him. 'You know... you can be a numpty sometimes,' she said in a low voice. 'The hotel will show you checking in with all the crew. It will show you never left until you checked out yesterday morning. There'll be security cameras inside and outside the hotel, and CCTV on the streets as well. Same as in the UK, they're never too far away. They'll have their own surveillance system, and when they check it, they'll see you weren't there.'

He sighed heavily. 'I hope you're right. I hope it's as simple as that. Her poor parents. What must they be going through?' He turned and hugged her. 'What a start to the new year? A bloody nightmare! I should never have gone.'

She eyed the decorations above their heads, still hanging from the ceiling. She could take them down now. It might help to have the house back to normal.

Mark planted a kiss on her head. 'I'm going to take a bath. Use some of those bubbles you say relaxes you. See if they work.'

She watched him walk up the stairs, hoping what she had said would prove true. Tomorrow or the next day, she hoped, the Spanish police would realise he wasn't on the streets when the murder took place, because he was in his hotel.

She fetched the containers in the cupboard beneath the stairs to put away the decorations, and grabbed a stool from the kitchen to stand on, continually thinking of other ways that could help Mark's situation. Did he phone down to reception for any room service? Use any channels on the TV that had to be paid for? Use the gym or swimming pool? The crew always stayed in the same place in the Gothic Quarter, and she'd joined him for a trip last year. The staff knew him well from all the times he stayed there. They could vouch for his whereabouts.

She reflected on all the people she could call on for advice. She had friends who were doctors, nurses, people who worked in hospitals. She knew one nurse was married to a judge, a physiotherapist who was married to a police officer who was quite high-up in anti-fraud. One of the porters in the department was a retired custody police sergeant. Duncan would probably know everything about where Mark stood if she spoke to him. She was sure he wouldn't mind, and he certainly wouldn't gossip. But should she go down that route just yet? Should she speak about something so serious happening in her personal life when it might not be necessary? It might make Mark look guilty when he wasn't. Or it might look like she was questioning his innocence.

She curbed the unwanted thought. He just happened to be in a city at the same time as a woman he once knew, who happened to be murdered, and happened to be unfortunate enough to resemble a description given by a witness.

She wished she had someone to ease her anxieties. At one time that person would have been Sophie. If she hadn't chased after Mark, Kate would still have her as a friend. Her actions had hurt Kate to the core, because she didn't pause to consider what she was doing to Kate.

Sometimes, Kate wished she had never been told, if only to have kept hold of her best friend. Sophie would understand how she was feeling now, and would help rationalise her fears. They had been good for each other. Sophie had called Kate her moral compass. Kate kept her good, but Kate never thought herself better than Sophie. Sophie made her laugh more than any other person. She wondered what Sophie got from her? A friend who was quieter, less adventurous, and a bit prissy at times. Sophie always said she would have to confess if she ever did something Kate would disapprove of. In that, she was telling the truth.

Kate hopped down from the stool, annoyed with herself for still trawling the past. She felt guilty for questioning Mark's loyalty when she had no reason to. He wasn't a womaniser, or someone who couldn't keep his eyes in his head. Just because he described the woman as beautiful didn't mean he was involved. He was describing a woman who was dead.

She felt instantly ashamed. The woman was dead! Mark was being questioned for a murder! And all she had done was bleat on about what happened in a bathroom three years ago. Thank God Mark couldn't see into her head. He'd feel very much alone. What was happening to him would only become worse if he felt she wasn't by his side. She needed to get a grip. Mark needed her to be strong. Anything from the past overshadowing that would tear him apart.

She was not about to let him down.

CHAPTER NINE

The following two days passed more easily for her, with Mark taking Jacob to and from school. There was no need for her to rush about in the mornings. Kate could concentrate on her job, knowing Mark was at home. Yesterday, Jacob made a complicated dinosaur farm that required Mark to keep safe four precious dinosaur eggs from being eaten by an unknown source. Jacob's giggling, along with his brown-coated teeth, hinted at where the chocolate mini eggs were going, while Mark pretended to be shocked for not guarding them properly.

She loved seeing their closeness. Mark loved being a father, his conversations with Jacob always gentle. Can I share this with you? Can I show you something? Would you like to know how?

They avoided discussing what was happening to Mark. Kate refrained from looking up anything on the internet, but it was hard not to be curious. She descended the stairs fresh from a bath, in cotton pyjama shorts and a T-shirt. She joined Mark in the sitting room and put her feet on his lap. He smiled at her lazily.

'Is he asleep?'

She nodded. 'Out like a light.'

His hand stroked the arch of her left foot. He raised it in the air and pressed his lips against the sole. She felt the pull of him already, and sighed contentedly. She held her breath as his lips inched up the side of her calf. All she wanted was what she had right now, her son asleep upstairs, her husband close by. She wanted him inside her, and feel the weight of him against her. She groaned. He lifted his head and teased her with a smile.

'You feeling impatient, Doctor Jordan?'

She bit her lip and nodded, before whispering, 'Very.'

His eyes were on her. 'Here? Or in bed?'

'Both,' she answered with a small sultry grin.

* * *

Kate woke feeling every inch of her body had been loved. She resented leaving the warmth of the bed, wanting to stay in her husband's arms. But she felt a stir of worry. Today would not be as easy as the previous two days. The outside world was going to interfere again. Mark had a meeting with the airline, followed by a meeting with his solicitor. The severe winds shaking the trees in the landscape felt like an omen of some sort.

She parked with ten minutes to spare and couldn't hold off any longer from finding out if there was any further news. She picked up her phone, typed 'Murder in Barcelona' in the search field, then panicked at her choice of words, as if someone would know what she typed. She even looked around to see if anyone was watching. She was on her own in her car and behaving like she had committed a crime.

She pulled herself together. Her search was completely legitimate in light of her husband's predicament. She wasn't looking at anything she shouldn't have been. Of course she would want to know what the police had discovered. She concentrated on the screen on her phone. A newsfeed of newly published content had materialised since the third of January, the day she looked on her iPad and first read of the murder of a British tourist. She tapped on an article at the top of the screen.

A woman has been pronounced dead at the scene in a popular tourist area. An eyewitness spotted the woman standing on the street shortly before midnight. The woman, who has not been named, was found lying on the ground by patrons leaving a bar at close to one o'clock in the morning, and immediately called for an ambulance. The incident took place in a narrow pedestrian street outside a patisserie, while the owners above the shop slept undisturbed. Police officers confirm no arrest has been made, and that they are working with British police to gather information.

Kate's head snapped up. The last sentence was about Mark. It felt more real knowing she had inside information that the reporter lacked. She could add to that sentence – they are working with British police to gather information on a man believed to be a British airline pilot.

Kate gulped air and closed the article, and then tapped another newsfeed. A photograph of the murdered woman appeared on the screen. She was definitely beautiful. In a head and shoulder shot, wearing the airline uniform of cabin crew, her blonde hair smoothed back from her face showed a smiling young woman with bright red lipstick and perfect white teeth.

The headline was intended to evoke the reader's emotions.

BEREAVED PARENTS ARRIVE TO TAKE THEIR DAUGHTER HOME

The parents of Fleur O'Connell arrived in Barcelona this morning to take part in the difficult identification of their daughter. The couple were met at the airport by an embassy official and ushered into a people carrier where they were taken to an unnamed hotel. A close family friend spoke to a reporter in Manchester, and has said Mr and Mrs O'Connell were at a loss to understand why their daughter was even in Barcelona on her own. They spent New Year's Eve with Fleur and she made no mention of taking this journey. Their thirty-year-old daughter was said to have been in good spirits when her parents last saw her. Her parents were looking forward to her moving back home in the new year, and were pleased she'd been accepted onto a teaching course.

A post-mortem is expected to be carried out later this week to establish the cause of death. While the police continue an ongoing investigation, they are asking the public for any information they might have that would be useful in establishing Fleur's last movements. They would like to hear from any taxi drivers who may have seen her, or people who were out that evening taking photographs in the area. While the investigation continues, the police have cordoned off the scene of the crime, and have asked the public to kindly not leave condolence flowers.

Kate turned the screen off on her phone. She shouldn't have read anything. It was better knowing less. Fleur O'Connell wasn't in Barcelona on New Year's Eve, so the witness couldn't have seen a man with her at that time.

Kate breathed raggedly. It felt like a whole other world coming fast towards her, getting ready to break her world apart. She didn't know how she could cope with this when she had no control over anything that happened. And things would get a lot more scary. She suddenly felt the need to be home where she could lock the doors and close the curtains until it went away.

But it wouldn't go away until the police found nothing to pin on Mark. She needed to be smart. Think about how the police used technology. They could track someone's movements by their mobile phones. It would tell them if someone was on the move, where they went, and how long they were there. Mark's phone would have been in his room, or with him if he went to the bar or the gym. Calls and messages would be logged. If only he had called her from his room at the time it happened, it would prove he was there and not somewhere else.

She pondered on that. Why couldn't he have called her, or she called him? This one time when it mattered. A log of a call from his phone to hers at around midnight as they spoke to each other while they lay in their beds? She wished with all her heart it was so. Mark was being investigated for something he did not do. In a country that wasn't his home. How did that even work? Did the UK extradite its own nationals? Was it possible he could be taken to Spain?

Kate had to sit with her fist against her stomach to stop her fear from spilling out. She was used to dealing with emergencies and tragedies and having to think fast on her feet in what sometimes felt like a storm. In this, it felt more like an avalanche coming down on her, with no cover or chance to move her family out of the way.

She shouldn't be here, spending time with others. She should be home trying to find every possible way to prove him innocent. At work, she would have no time to think.

She switched the engine back on, pulled her seat belt back around her, looked to her left and then to her right, and saw Eva frantically waving at her.

Kate wound down her window. Eva started speaking rapidly the moment she knew Kate could hear her.

'Sorry for coming to find you, Kate. I knew you were here and thought you probably didn't know yet what's happened, otherwise you wouldn't still be in your car.'

Kate found her inner calmness and gave her full attention. 'What's happened, Eva?'

'Major incident, Kate. Scaffolding collapsed. A dozen roofers have fallen with it.'

CHAPTER TEN

Kate lost count of the number of times she cracked her ankle or knocked her thigh or bashed her elbow or caught her wrist as she scurried around equipment, around drip poles, around beds, using her feet to raise them or lower them or take the stubborn brakes off the wheels, using her elbows to turn on taps, to shut them off, bouncing bone on metal. She was walking-wounded by ten o'clock and they were not even halfway through with the patients in resus.

The three men had woken this morning, strong and fit, and were now fighting for their lives from head injuries, spinal injuries, thoracic trauma. They were young – in their twenties and thirties. A team of doctors, surgeons, anaesthetists, emergency care nurses, radiographers surrounded them. They changed from men arriving in hi-vis vests over work clothes, with tools in pockets, wearing knee pads and thick socks and heavy boots to patients with tubes protruding from their throats, cannulas in different colours with plastic taps inserted in their necks, cannulas in their arms being fed with bags of fluids, with syringes of therapeutic agents, and wires connecting them to multiple machines. Young men, whose parents wouldn't recog-

nise them, who would be terrified and left with these images of
their sons even if they did fully survive. This first sight of their
sons would render them petrified.

Kate stepped out of resus and walked through the rest of the
department, and while it was busier than ever, more noisy,
looking ransacked from the amount of equipment pulled out of
cupboards and drawers left discarded in haste to treat the
patients, the overall tension was containable. The staff were still
breathing, still doing, still effective. Twelve patients arriving in
the emergency department at the same time could be counted
as normal on any other day. It wasn't the number that was the
concern, it was the severity of their injuries all presenting at the
same time. Scattered throughout the department, eight other
roofers were being treated.

Out of twelve men, only one walked away uninjured, as on
the ground when the scaffolding gave way.

Kate spied him helping Eva, holding his mate's arm up so
she could inspect it. The entire armpit, spreading to the side of
the chest, and the inside of the arm down to the elbow, was a
deep, almost black, navy blue.

Kate slipped through the gap in the curtains to see how Eva
was getting on. Eva gave a small smile. 'Gary's helping me with
his friend, Will,' she said.

Gary stood at an awkward angle straining, as he was short
and the patient's trolley was elevated high. Kate pressed a foot
pedal to lower it. She sucked air through her teeth as she gave a
wincing smile to the patient. 'Wow, that's some bruise you've
got there.'

Will opened his eyes wide and shook his head, as if to
convey his disbelief at surviving what must have been a horri-
fying experience. 'A scaffolding pole saved me,' he said in a
fatigued voice. 'As I was falling, reaching out for anything to
grab hold of, I swung my arm wide so I could land on the
bastard while praying it didn't give way. I was hanging by my

armpit two storeys up for God knows how long. And I weigh nineteen stone!'

Gary exhaled sharply. 'Christ, Will, your arm's like a roll of lead. I need to rest it down. It's knackered me holding it up for just a few seconds.' He nodded at Kate. 'How does someone as small as you manage a lump like him?'

The lump he was referring to was indeed like the missing link. Huge broad shoulders and chest, covered by just a ripped vest, exposed the beefy muscles at the top of his arms as wide as decent-size tree trunks.

'Ignore him,' Will replied, then cheekily winked at her. 'He's yet to realise that not all small people are as weak as him.'

Kate played the game and stood taller. 'I don't think five foot two is that short.'

Gary, Will and Eva looked at her and then at each other, Will nodding his head in her direction, his eyes opened wide as if to indicate she was deluded. Eva was the first to giggle, followed by cackles from the roofers. Kate felt a smile tug at her lips, and then a release of laughter that took away all the stresses of before.

Checking that Eva was happy, and that the attending doctor assigned to Will had organised X-rays, scans and bloods, Kate left the merry trio, feeling uplifted. She detoured back to resus and the lighter atmosphere and the less harried expressions on the faces of the doctors and nurses reassured her.

She would take a ten-minute break and check to see if she had any messages. Hearing Mark's voice, though, would be better. She wanted to feel their closeness and seal it around them. To keep her strong, and him safe.

Kate went outside carrying a mug of coffee, into a gust of wind that billowed out her top. Flattening it down, she found shelter at the side of the building, where it was quiet enough for her to phone Mark. She leaned against the wall and took sips of coffee while she waited for him to answer.

'Hi.'

Kate jolted at the brisk tone. 'Hi back. This a bad time?'

He sighed heavily in her ear.

'Mark, is everything okay?'

She could hear him breathing down the phone, huffs of impatience, before picking up the sound of his tut. His tone was blunt. 'Kate, it will be better if we talk at home. I'm with my solicitor at the moment. I've popped outside his door to answer this.'

Kate felt a drag in her stomach. 'Okay, you go,' she agreed, with just enough time to say the words before he cut her off.

She felt numb. In moments, she felt her jaw quiver and a tight ball form in her stomach in reaction to his hurtful attitude. Especially after the warmth of last night. She was every bit as affected as he was by what was happening to him. The situation was constantly on her mind unless she was dealing with emergencies like today. And now he made her feel like a nuisance for taking up his time, when all she wanted was to help and let him know she was thinking about him.

She shoved the phone in her pocket and wrapped her hands around the cooling mug. She gulped the contents and eased the ache in her throat. Her emotions were all over the place and probably, she accepted, so were his. They were reacting out of fear. He was probably losing patience with the whole damn world at the moment. Her phone call may have interrupted some vital point in a conversation between him and his solicitor. Maybe Mark lost his chain of thought at hearing his phone ringing.

She breathed deeply, feeling his sting lessen and her composure return. She needed to finish this day and just get home and wrap the big lug in her arms, and maybe give him a kick on the shins to let him know she had feelings too.

CHAPTER ELEVEN

It was gone seven when she let herself in, and her shoulders slumped in disappointment at finding the house quiet. It meant Jacob was in bed and already asleep. It was past his bedtime, but she'd been hoping he'd be up. She eased off the trainers that were meant to let her feet breathe. She'd been on them nine hours and was grateful she was not on duty tomorrow. She could stay at home all day and not do a thing, except be with Jacob.

She crept tiredly up the stairs and felt instant joy as she spied one wide-awake little boy staring at her from his bed. Kate went into the room and navigated her way around his toys before climbing onto his bed. She kissed his face, nuzzled his hair, and held one of his small hands.

'So, Mister Snackosaurus, what are you doing awake?'

He grinned impishly. 'Waiting for my snack, of course.'

'You'll be getting no snacks at this time of night, my laddie. Your tummy, no doubt, has had enough.'

He nodded. 'We had a big dinner. Jacket potatoes as big as an ostrich egg.'

'Wow, as big as that!' she gasped. 'I'm impressed. And did you have a nice day with Nana?'

'Uh-huh. She said I got my knitting in a pickle.'

Kate hoped he'd not been in her mum's knitting basket. 'How's that?' she asked.

'Because my loops kept coming off the sticks.'

Kate was relieved. 'Oh, I see. Nana's teaching you to knit.'

'Uh-huh. We're making a blanket.'

Bless Mum, Kate thought. She would love the idea of teaching her grandson something Kate would never have thought to do. 'Just keep practising and you'll get it right. And what about Daddy?'

Jacob gave what could only be described as a soulful sigh. 'He's hunting,' he replied in a voice that suggested this was a sad thing.

Kate inwardly smiled. Giving him a goodnight kiss, she got off the bed. 'It's Sunday tomorrow, and I'm not working.'

'I'm happy, Mummy,' he replied.

Kate went in search of Mark in case he hadn't realised she was home. From the doorway, she saw the disarray of the room. The suitcase he packed on Tuesday was open on the floor, the contents in a bundle beside it. He had tipped out the contents of his leather shoulder bag on the bed. Airline paperwork, spare chargers for his phone and iPad, his sunglasses case and pencil case. Some chewing gum and throat lozenges, and lots of little pieces of paper, mainly receipts, smoothed out.

He hadn't sensed her presence yet. He had his head in the wardrobe, searching the pockets of his airline jacket. On top of the chest of drawers, his wallet had been emptied of his driving licence and bank cards and some more receipts.

Jacob was right. His daddy was hunting.

'Do you need any help?' she enquired from the doorway, and he swung around startled.

'I didn't hear you come in,' he said in a surprised voice.

Stepping away from the wardrobe, he closed it. 'I thought you were going to ring when you were leaving. I would have had you something ready to eat.'

That had been the plan. She'd texted him at four to tell him she'd be late and would let him know when she was leaving.

'I was so tired, I forgot.'

He came towards her with an expression of sympathy. 'I heard it on the news. You poor thing. And those poor men. God, I'm surprised they're not dead. They think it was damaged in the storm in the night – I don't know if you heard it. I thought the tiles on the roof were going to lift off.'

Kate could have remarked to being otherwise occupied in the throes of passion to have noticed anything outside, instead replied, 'Yes, I heard it. The winds were still bad driving to work this morning.'

'Why don't you have a bath and I'll fix you an omelette or something?'

It seemed like he was blocking her from entering the bedroom and trying to usher her straight to the bathroom, as both were now standing in the doorway.

'Can I take off my clothes first?' she asked pointedly, to get him to move out of the way so she could come through the door.

He stepped back. 'Sure. I just thought...' He shrugged. 'I'll just tidy these things.'

She undressed and pulled out some clean pants from her drawers while Mark shoved his belongings back in the cases. She was burning with curiosity, but would wait until after her bath to ask him what he was looking for.

She joined him in the kitchen as he slid an omelette onto a plate. On the table a poured glass of red wine waited for her.

Mark placed the omelette in front of her and handed her cutlery. 'Eat it while it's hot,' he encouraged.

Kate picked up the glass of wine and drank down half of it. Her stomach was churning too much to start on the food. Mark was hesitating to tell her something. She could feel it in the air between them. The bottle of wine on the worktop was two-thirds gone, and it was unusual for him to drink that much on his own. She couldn't wait any longer. She needed to know.

'What were you looking for in the bedroom?' she asked.

He was leaning against the worktop with his glass in his hand. He shook his head. 'Nothing.'

'Nothing,' she repeated. 'Nothing at all for you to empty out your cases and be searching in your jacket in the wardrobe?'

He shrugged and stared at her, open-eyed. 'Just sorting out bits and pieces. Checking for any receipts so I can claim back. The usual, you know, collecting up expenses I've incurred to do with work.'

Kate didn't know, and she wasn't sure if she believed him. He didn't usually tell her about such things. 'And how did it go today with your meeting at work?'

He tilted his head to the side, exposing the strong column of his neck. The blue shirt he wore was formal wear, as were the trousers. The sleeves of his shirt were rolled up and Kate's eyes fixed on the light covering of hair on his forearms. She had touched his skin only hours ago, they properly held each other, yet it seemed like it hadn't happened.

'They were sympathetic,' he replied. 'And understood why I'm presently grounded. It was more of a welfare chat.'

'And the meeting with your solicitor?'

'Eat first, and then we'll talk,' he replied.

Kate pressed her feet on the floor and pushed the bench back from the table. 'I can't eat until I know what's happened. You said on the phone it would be better if we talk at home. Well, we're at home, Mark. I want to hear now.'

CHAPTER TWELVE

The kitchen was the largest room in the house and the hub of their family life, for every activity – eating meals, after-school snacks, drawing and painting, and drinking wine at the banquet table with two benches either side that fit under the table when not in use. Made from vintage scaffold boards, Kate loved it. It never seemed to look cluttered, and it could take a fair amount of knocking without fear of it being damaged. Now it was acting as a barrier with Mark one side of the kitchen and her the other.

He reached for the bottle of wine to pour some more in his glass.

'Dutch courage?' she asked.

He turned to face her, and she saw at once the cornered look in his eyes. He hauled in a breath and bowed his head, and Kate felt her knees sag.

'You might want to sit back down,' he said.

Kate stayed as she was. 'I'm fine with standing. I'm stronger than I look, Mark.'

He raised his head at that, and smiled softly. 'I've never doubted it, Kate. You're the strongest person I know. Which is why I know you'll be able to handle what I've got to tell you.'

He waited till her eyes were looking in his before he told her. 'My solicitor thinks the police are going to arrest me. They found out something which I didn't think they would. I was absent from the hotel for about an hour.'

She gave a small gasp. 'But you said you stayed in. Why did you lie?'

He shrugged. 'It was foolish. I shouldn't have. My room key card gave that information. The electronic lock keeps a record of when the door is opened, and connected to a system in reception for security. So for the police, it was just a matter of checking that and then looking at the hotel cameras.'

Kate was being swept up in the story, which she wanted to slow down. Something didn't sound right. How would the solicitor know all this? She thought the police only revealed what they had to. 'I don't understand,' she said. 'How does your solicitor know this? I would have thought the police would want this kept under wraps until they had you in front of them.'

'They have had me in front of them, Kate.'

'Yes,' she said forcefully. 'But that was Wednesday, when they didn't mention any of this.'

His eyes had flickered away, and Kate felt her stomach wrench.

'You're right, they didn't mention it. But today, they did.'

His voice had assumed a worried tone, and Kate didn't want to hear it. Everything he was telling her now was something he'd kept back from her previously. He hadn't told her he was seeing the police today. He hadn't told her he left the hotel. He told her he was in the hotel all night. She couldn't understand why he would lie? What reason did he have to hide the truth?

An image of Fleur O'Connell came easily to mind. The pretty young woman had reminded her of someone straight away. The same type of smile and bold red lipstick. She could have been a younger Sophie with that smooth blonde hair.

Kate couldn't summon the energy to shout at him. Instead, her voice was placid. 'Where did you go?' she asked.

'Nowhere,' he replied in a low voice, possibly to keep her speaking calmly.

She shook her head in despair. 'Nowhere, that's your best answer, is it? You went nowhere when you left the hotel and you were looking for nothing in the bedroom?'

'Kate! I had nothing to do with this woman's death.'

Kate felt a desolation sweep over her. How could she trust anything he said if he avoided telling her where he went? He was absent for about an hour, so he said. Which meant the police had found that out. Which meant it was the period of time he was away that interested them most. They wouldn't be looking at him otherwise. He skipped past that part of the story quickly. Fleur O'Connell was murdered around midnight. So clearly her husband had been walking nowhere at around midnight.

'Kate? Look at me, please.'

She lifted her gaze and tried to ignore the pleading in his eyes. He had lied to her, and she didn't know why. He wasn't even trying to explain. He preferred not to tell her than keep her trust. He must realise she was doubting his word. He had given her reason not to believe him.

Tears filled her eyes. He stepped towards her.

'No, Mark,' she cried, holding out a hand to stop him coming closer. 'I don't want your comfort! I can't be comforted while you're not telling me the truth. Everything feels like a lie. It feels like I'm falling, and I need to stay on my feet for Jacob's sake.' She shook her head sadly. 'Tomorrow, I think it would be best for me and Jacob to spend the day with Mum.'

His expression made it clear he was stunned. She wanted to yell at him and demand how he expected her to react. This conversation could only end one way. He had no right to be shocked. She thought she could trust him with her heart and soul. She'd wanted to be home to prepare for anything bad. She hadn't expected it to come from Mark. To discover how easily he could lie, to have her belief in him shift beneath her feet. She couldn't be near him. She had to walk away.

CHAPTER THIRTEEN

Kate slipped out of Jacob's bed without disturbing him. She didn't want him confused by finding her sleeping beside him. Her bedroom door was open and the bed looked undisturbed. She found Mark sleeping on the sofa, wearing his clothes from the night before, with his hand resting in Barney's basket, which he had pulled beside him. It reminded Kate of how she would sleep with one arm in Jacob's Moses basket to feel for him moving in the night when he was a baby.

She knelt down to stroke Barney's head and was alarmed by his feeble response. His eyes opened and found her. He slowly raised his head for a moment, before laying it back down. She felt her breath hitch in her throat. Was her beloved dog quietly dying? She tapped Mark's arm to bring him awake, and he quickly sat up, alert.

'How is he?' he asked, gazing keenly at the dog.

'He's not very responsive,' she replied. 'How long has he been like this?'

'This sleepy?' He shrugged. 'To be honest, I'm not sure. It was only a sixth sense last night that made me check on him before I went to bed. He was asleep in the hallway and I had to encourage him to go outdoors to spend a penny. And only on reflection, I realised he's not been under my feet the last few days.'

Kate felt riddled with guilt for failing to notice, for acknowledging Barney was sleeping more, but doing nothing about it. He might have been ill. Mark sensed how upset she was and tried to reassure her.

'I've been listening out for him all night. I promise you he hasn't shown any signs of distress. I spoke to the on-call vet last night, and she said to call if he showed any sign of discomfort. She's checking Barney over this morning at nine o'clock. I was going to wake you shortly as I know you'll want to go with him.'

She nodded, thankful that Barney hadn't spent the night alone. 'I'll get dressed,' she said.

'I'll make you a coffee,' he replied, nearly bumping into her as he stepped over Barney's basket. She moved out of the way awkwardly, and felt utterly sad that her reaction was to step away from him, when it should have been natural to want his embrace.

In the bedroom she dressed quickly, then hurried back down the stairs to pull on her trainers. Mark made her coffee not too hot so she could gulp some of it, and had her phone, bag and car keys ready to hand her.

'He's in the car, nice and comfortable. Don't drive fast, and ring me if you need me.'

Kate nodded hard. 'Will do.' She couldn't bring herself to look in his eyes and see his evasiveness. She'd rather deal with polite conversation instead.

An hour later she was home again, having been given lots of useful advice from the sympathetic vet. At thirteen, Barney was a senior citizen. For a Labrador it put Barney at the higher end of the scale. He could still enjoy life. Unless he deteriorated sharply, and Kate thought it was time for him to go.

Mark stood in the driveway as she reversed back. She felt a sweet sadness that she was bringing Barney home to be cared for until his time came. She greeted Mark sadly. 'He's just old, and needs more sleep.'

He hugged her tight and then let her go, telling her he would sort Barney and the car out. She went indoors to find Jacob in his pyjamas, making a get-well card for Barney and knew Mark would have put in place these little measures to help prepare Jacob if Barney hadn't come home. She sank beside him on the bench and praised his drawing of a rainbow over a yellow shape with a round head and four legs.

'Did you have breakfast?' she asked.

'Uh-huh,' he responded, using his new informal reply, no doubt picked up from listening to Nana on the phone.

'Well, how about I make some scrambled eggs? They're Barney's favourite too.'

He raised his face, and she saw his anxiety give way to a fixed grin, meaning he was holding back tears. She encouraged him to let go. Flinging his body into her arms to have a cry would soon sort him out.

At lunchtime, Mark came and found her lying on the sofa beside Barney. 'I can take over if you want to visit your mum?'

She appreciated that he hadn't avoided mentioning her intended plan to stay at her mum's, and looked at him properly. 'Thanks, but I'd rather be home. But if we get a knock at the door, I hope you'll understand if I don't answer it and don't let Jacob see.'

He answered in a voice heavy with emotion. 'I don't want either of you there if that happens. I don't want that memory in your heads. I'll make sure it's done quickly. I'll go quietly. And, Kate, I know this doesn't make any difference, but I'm sorry.'

She dropped her gaze and carried on stroking Barney until Mark left the room, then swallowed the tight ball in her throat. It was killing her to feel this distance between them, but she didn't know how to bridge the gap when they weren't speaking the same language. How could he not see that saying sorry was treating her like a fool, when all he had to do to mean it was to tell her the truth? Which he had not yet done. The longer she waited for that to happen, the more she thought the very worst.

CHAPTER FOURTEEN

Eva placed a croissant and mug of milky coffee in front of her, and Kate turned in surprise.

'For me?'

Eva nodded. 'You look like you need some sugar. Your hands were shaking when you were drawing blood.'

'Probably,' Kate explained. 'I've not had much sleep, been keeping an eye on my old dog.' That she was living on her nerves would remain private. Every noise she heard outside yesterday evening had made her flinch, expecting it to be followed by a police knock at the door.

Eva smiled sympathetically. 'You work too hard. I don't know how you manage. I'm glad I'm training to be a nurse. I couldn't handle the pressure of having to make big decisions like you do.'

'You get used to it, Eva, and after a while some things become second nature as your instincts get sharper. You just have to be careful not to let experience take things for granted, to always look at a patient with a fresh pair of eyes.'

Kate picked up the mug of coffee and drank it gratefully. She was struggling to get through the shift, and this gift from

Eva was just what she needed. She had checked her phone throughout the day and read all the updates on Barney without sending back replies, and ignored the text sent hours ago with a repeat of the same words as yesterday.

I'm sorry.

He might well be sorry, but Kate wasn't going to chat with him just for him to have nothing to say again. She was beyond that, and was going to tell her mum that she would have visitors to stay in the shape of her, Jacob and Barney. She couldn't stay in the house and feel the gap between her and Mark get bigger, while he chose to ignore it by being attentive, his behaviour just the same, while he avoided what was standing between them. The truth, that he knew what Kate didn't, keeping her in the dark. Kate couldn't stand that type of deception, using normality to camouflage a problem, as if she wouldn't see through it.

She ate the pastry, drank the rest of the coffee, and rose to her feet. Forty-five minutes to go before she finished for the day. Time enough to see one more patient.

While picking up a new casualty card, she heard the red phone ringing. She placed the card back and stood with Sister Lewis to hear the pre-alert details of the incoming patient. Kate recognised the paramedic's voice.

'We have a male, no name or age, possibly mid-forties. Estimated time of incident 14:30, believed to be a victim of a hit-and-run involving a car. Large scalp wound to back of head. Blood pressure ninety over sixty, pulse hundred and ten, respiratory rate twenty-four. Pupils equal and reacting. GCS score twelve. ETA six minutes.'

Kate headed to resus, followed by Sister Lewis and Eva. While they set about checking the suction unit, ECG monitor and defibrillator were working, and tested the brakes on the bed,

Kate checked the emergency airway trolley, ensuring she had a laryngoscope working and the appropriate size endotracheal tubes including a large one. They were ready with seconds to spare when the doors pushed open and their patient arrived.

Kate took in at a glance the bright orange head blocks with straps immobilising the head, oxygen mask obscuring the face, and rigid cervical collar around the patient's neck. The paramedic, taking the lead for the patient, suggested Kate go at the foot end for the transferring from stretcher to bed. Kate did as she was told before coming back to the head end to take over and receive an update.

'Ten centimetre gash at the back of the head. Has a second dressing in place as seeping. No witness to the incident, so no history of mechanism of injury.'

'How do you know it was a car in a hit-and-run?'

'A farmer. Said he would have seen the roof of a van or high vehicle over the hedge. He heard a car driving, and then a thud. By the time he got out of his field, the lane was empty apart from the man on the ground.' The paramedic then added his own view. 'Likely the driver thinks they'll get away with it. A country lane with nothing but fields around. Lucky the farmer found him.'

In the short time that Kate was listening, Sister Lewis had bared the patient's chest to attach ECG leads, and placed a blood pressure cuff around an arm. Eva removed the man's shoes, and the little green dinosaurs on the navy-blue socks struck Kate as familiar.

Kate stared at the white bandage stretched across his forehead, and the oxygen mask covering his mouth and nose. She leaned closer to get a look at the face beneath the mask and couldn't believe what she was seeing. She could hardly raise her voice. 'It can't be you. It's not you. You're at home.'

Her words alerted her colleagues that there was something wrong. Someone shouted her name. 'Kate!'

The spell was broken. Her voice was urgent and uncontrolled. 'Mark, open your eyes for me. It's Kate. Mark, can you hear me?' Her movements frantic as she switched on a pen torch, she yelled at those around her. 'I need the trauma team now! He needs an urgent CT! Mark, can you hear me? Mark!'

She felt a hand on her shoulder and shrugged it off, then someone pulled at her arm. People were blurring her vision, getting in her way. Eva was speaking loud in her ear, and now they were trying to pull her away from him. She slapped at the arm around her waist. Didn't they understand? She had to stay! She was the doctor. She had to save him. Her distressed cries continued until the quietness of the room made her aware she was in an office, with Eva watching her carefully.

The door opened and her consultant, John Brown, appeared. He hurried to her and hunkered down to hold her hand. His familiar face, with large nose and hooded eyes, looked right at her.

'Mark is in expert hands. He's got your best colleagues in there with him and I'll be with him too. You can help us by being strong. And I promise, I'll let you know as soon as possible how he's doing.'

He went to stand and Kate grabbed his hand. 'John, please let me just speak to him. Please, I just want to say I love him.'

He nodded. 'Be quick, Kate. He needs looking after.'

When she returned to his side, Mark was regaining consciousness. His eyes were struggling to focus on her. 'Kate,' he whispered in a horribly weakened voice. 'Please, please, believe me... Lost it... must find it...'

The urgency in his voice tore at her. 'Find what, Mark?'

'My watch... parrot on the door... green.'

His slow, infrequent breaths made Kate quickly hush him. 'I believe you, Mark. I'm here, so don't worry about a thing.'

She felt her shoulder being tugged. She managed to kiss him

on his forehead without leaning on him. 'I love you,' she whispered.

Then she watched his eyes roll back in his head, a second before the monitor started beeping and flashing.

'Move away from the bed, Kate. He's showing bradycardia,' John instructed loudly. Kate couldn't move, forcing the consultant to shout at the team. 'Get her out of here, people! He's peri arrest!'

Kate's eyes were wide with shock. Someone yanked her back from the bed. She could no longer see Mark. The team had closed around him, ignoring her completely, acting on the commands of the consultant.

She allowed Eva to walk her out on trembling limbs and sit with her. Kate waited to be told Mark's heart had stopped.

CHAPTER FIFTEEN

Kate was sitting in a trance by Mark's bed the following morning when a nurse came to find her. 'You have a visitor, Kate.'

Kate found it hard to focus. The rhythmic hissing sound, rising and falling in volume from the ventilator, was hypnotic. She struggled to stand after sitting for so long in an uncomfortable chair, and got to her feet feeling stiff and dishevelled and weak. She glanced anxiously at the patient.

'We're watching him, Kate. Nothing's changed. Heart rate's good. You can stretch your legs and go for a little walk.'

Kate nodded faintly. 'You'll call me if anything changes?'

'Of course. So nothing to worry about.'

Nothing to worry about, Kate repeated the words in her head. Yesterday, her husband's heart had stopped, following what they thought was a moderate brain injury. The paramedic recorded a GCS of twelve. John had found her after the emergency was over and said Mark's heart returned to a normal rhythm on the first shock. He gave his opinion on the cause of the cardiac arrest – given that Mark had no history of heart problems, was a non-smoker, drank moderately and was fit –

was that a concussed brain will correct the amount of blood by signalling to the heart a tighter control over heart rate, according to research. Reducing the heart rate would prevent blood flow to other organs, but not to the brain. So, in theory, it was likely the brain was protecting itself. In Mark's case, his heart rate went too low.

All Kate could think about was the possibility it could stop again.

She let herself out of the intensive care unit to find the police officers who came to the house waiting in the corridor. She could only recall Sergeant Sharma's name.

'Doctor Jordan,' he said. 'I'm sorry to hear about what's happened to your husband. I wonder perhaps if we could talk. DC Kelly has fetched us some coffees, and there's a bench just along the corridor where we can sit and is quiet. It's not too far,' he added as if Kate was a visitor and didn't know the layout of the hospital of where she worked and where they could sit. It was the kind of thing Kate would do if she thought someone was in shock.

'I don't mind a little walk,' she replied. 'I need to stretch.'

There was room on the metal bench for them both to sit, and Kate put the lid of her coffee on the space between them. She sipped tentatively in case it was too hot, but the temperature was fine, allowing her to quench her thirst. She then rested the cup in her lap. 'Have you found the person responsible for this?'

'No, not yet. We're looking at the closest cameras in the area. There are a lot of country lanes that the driver could have taken before reaching a main road. We're also checking for any abandoned vehicles. Do you know why he might have been on foot walking down that lane? It's two and a half miles from where you live.'

Kate shook her head. 'He enjoys walking in the country, usually with our dog, but the dog's getting old. Mark might have felt the need to stretch his legs. He's got a lot on his mind, as you know. It's not unusual for him to go walking, but I didn't know that he was out walking as I was here. He prefers it to running.'

'And how was his state of mind before yesterday?'

She looked at him pointedly. 'Functioning quite well, considering what's hanging over him.'

He nodded. 'I mention it because it was clear during our last interview with him that he was finding his situation stressful. We stopped for a ten-minute break to allow him to compose himself.'

Her mouth opened in surprise, and for a moment she couldn't speak. 'Are you saying he was crying?'

His head tilted to the side. 'Not quite, but close. He was very distressed.'

Kate sat numbly, staring into space, remembering how she was with him after he told her they might arrest him. She hadn't wanted to hear the worry in his voice. And now hearing how he'd been... In the ten years they'd been married she could count on one hand the times she'd seen him come close to crying. When her father died suddenly from a heart attack, Mark had known him only a year, but the sadness had brought him close to tears. At the birth of Jacob, the first hold of his son showed them in his eyes. Then hidden tears that he denied himself, as he comforted her instead, when she miscarried eighteen months later with their second child. The last time, when he thought she might not forgive him over Sophie. Hearing he was distressed in the way Sergeant Sharma described, brought an ache to her breast right over her heart. He must have felt so alone.

'I'm sorry to have told you this, but I felt you should know,' Sharma said.

Kate turned her head and looked at him. Focusing on what he was saying. 'Why do you think I should I know?' she asked him.

He shifted in his seat so he was facing her. 'The driver responsible should never have left the scene. Failure to report an accident is a criminal offence. In this case, likely to carry a prison sentence and loss of licence. A common reason for leaving the scene in a case like this is having no insurance or tax or driving an unroadworthy vehicle. Or it could be due to drinking – wanting to sober up before handing themselves in. Or panic – they flee before thinking things through. Sometimes it happens from shock. When they knock a person down, especially if they think the person is dead, their automatic reaction is to drive away. Where pedestrians are involved, drivers are likely to report themselves to the police later.'

'And is this what you think is going to happen?'

'I'm hoping for that to happen.' He paused and rubbed at his chin before continuing. 'Your husband will have been under enormous strain. Waiting to be arrested can sometimes be worse than the actual event. He will have known that this is where we were heading.'

Kate released a shaky breath. She lifted the cup from her lap, and Sharma had to take it from her badly trembling hands.

His expression was sympathetic. 'I'm sorry. I know this is hard. The lane left plenty of room for him to stand out of the way where they found him, even though it wasn't wide enough in some places for two-way traffic. A farmer heard a car, but didn't think it sounded like it was speeding. Then he heard a thump. I mentioned your husband's distress, his state of mind, to see if it might have had any bearing on what happened to him yesterday.'

Kate gasped, feeling overwhelmingly let down. Her husband was in a medically induced coma, and they were saying it was his fault. And when he woke up, they would arrest him.

Her gut was twisting in knots, forcing her to her feet, forcing her to lose control. She bitterly lashed out. 'My God!

You've got him guilty of a murder he didn't commit, and now jumping in front of a car because of his guilt. So nice for you to tie it all together. If he dies, you'll close your case with him called a murderer. My God, what sort of man do you think he is? He has never committed a crime in his life! I don't care what your witness saw, because he wasn't there. And you won't prove it!'

Kate turned on her heel and walked blindly as fast as she could to get away, ignoring his calls for her to wait. She wouldn't wait to hear another damn word out of his mouth.

She was flushed and panting by the time she reached the ICU doors, but instead of pressing the button to be let in, she backed into the wall and slid down onto her bottom, where she sat in stunned silence trying to blank Sharma's insinuations from her head.

Mark would never have taken that way out. He would never have left his son like that. He would have fought to prove his innocence. He would have done that. He wouldn't do what Sharma was suggesting.

Kate cried out in anguish, wanting to rush back and find the detective before he left and denounce him in front of his constable. His opinion was wrong! And nothing would force her to think otherwise.

CHAPTER SIXTEEN

The quietness of the corridor left her undisturbed. Kate didn't have the willpower to stand up and go back in to her husband. She rested her head in the palms of her hands, still hearing Sharma's words.

Your husband will have been under enormous strain.

She pressed her hands into her forehead, trying to drive the words out.

There would have been a warning sign. She would have sensed it, felt it in her bones, in the very fabric of her being. He was preparing to be arrested. He knew what it would entail. He hadn't wanted for his son to see his father being reduced in his eyes. He hadn't wanted that memory in her head.

I'll make sure it's done quickly. I'll go quietly, he'd said.

She moaned softly. Mark's words hadn't meant taking his own life, she was sure of it. He was referring to being arrested. He'd go quickly and quietly with police officers, not out of her and Jacob's lives!

A pair of boots stepped into her field of vision, and Kate recognised them. She raised her head and stared up at her mother. Grace Shortman could not have taken a more apt surname when she married Kate's father. Her diminutive figure, less than five feet tall, suited the name perfectly.

Kate struggled to her feet and fell into her mum's arms, sobbing for dear life. Grace held her and soothed her like she was a child. Kate let it all out, every drop of emotion in her falling tears, while her mum took care of her and shushed her until her crying exhausted her into silence.

Grace looked firmly into her daughter's eyes. 'Go home, and sleep. And when you're rested, you can come back. I'll watch Mark for you, like I do Jacob. I won't let anything happen to him while you're not here.'

Kate smiled tearfully at her. Standing in her woollen slacks and winter coat, her rubber ankle boots and furry hat covering her grey curly hair, promising something she couldn't control. They could only hope nothing bad would happen.

'His heart stopped, Mum!'

Her look stayed firm, but her voice softened. 'I know. But it's beating again now. How is he? And in layman's terms, please.'

Kate nodded. 'They've put him in a drug-induced coma to help rest his brain. He's on medication to help reduce swelling. He's on a machine that's breathing for him. They're regularly scanning his head. He's surrounded by equipment, most of it attached to him, so it looks scary. But he's not in any pain.'

'Does he have any brain damage, Kate?'

Kate pressed her lips firmly together. 'It's too early to say.'

'Well, no news is good news,' she replied determinedly. Her stoic response was exactly what Kate needed to hear. 'Now, you get off home. I'm here now.'

Kate couldn't decide. She couldn't think clearly about what to do. Her brain was in a fog from the fear and worry and exhaustion. 'It's ICU. They're only letting in next of kin. I'll need to introduce you.'

'Well then, do that. Then get your coat and go home.' Her

mother pressed the buzzer on the wall. 'Before I forget, Marge and Len phoned. They said you called them. Poor things can't fly home. Marge just had a hysterectomy. I told them you'll keep them informed.'

Kate would. She had phoned Mark's parents last night just after nine, conscious of the time difference in Australia and not wanting to waken them too early. It had been a difficult call, trying to support them while unable to offer complete reassurance. She wouldn't mention to them anything about Spain or the police. They didn't need to know about that unless absolutely necessary.

She had used her time by Mark's bed to email his employers to let them know what had happened and had received a reply this morning expressing their sympathy and offer of support. She couldn't imagine what form that support would take.

'How's Jacob, Mum?'

'He's fine. I haven't told him anything. He thinks you're both at work.'

Kate nodded resignedly. 'Best I tell him. Not sure when though,' she said, thinking of all the grim things in the way. She couldn't promise him that his daddy would be coming home, because even if he got well, he had the police to face. His daddy might not be coming home for a long time.

Kate didn't know how she was going to get through this. The only adult support she had was her mum. She had no one else she could call on to childmind, and ferry a small boy to school and back, and make his dinner, and mind Barney and the house. Kate couldn't think about it. She already felt overwhelmed. She had a husband in ICU who faced being charged with murder when he woke up. It was enough to break the strongest of minds.

She needed to sleep, even if only for an hour. Turning maudlin wasn't going to help anything. She had Jacob to think of. If she fell apart, he'd have only his nana to care for him. And as much as her mum was willing, she wasn't strong enough to mind him full time. She managed the pickups from school and helped in the holidays and at weekends, but Kate was conscious of her health and her more frequent use of inhalers. She couldn't ask her to do more.

It was down to Kate to sort out the immediate problems, and there would be plenty now with Mark not being at home at all. She already squeezed her thirty-hour week over four days between Mark's days off and her mum helping, and even then, it was a juggling act.

Kate just wished she had a magic wand to wave all this away. She could have her life back the way it was before all of this happened, before this shitstorm landed in her lap.

But it wasn't a magic wand she needed. It was coming up with a better story that gave Mark his life back. It was Mark who needed a miracle.

CHAPTER SEVENTEEN

The ringing of the doorbell raised Kate's head off the pillow. Shuffling into slippers, she padded downstairs to answer it. Robert was standing there, with someone next to him whose face was hidden behind a huge bouquet of flowers. Kate was so surprised to see him, she simply stared.

He stepped forward and brought Kate into his arms. 'I'm so sorry,' he said softly. 'We heard what happened to him, and the entire crew are devastated. They all send their love and said if there's anything they can do, just ask. Anything, Kate. We all want to help.'

Kate stepped back and stared at the welcome sight of Robert's handsome face. He had flown with Mark many times as first officer, and was Mark's best friend. She hadn't seen him since Mark's fortieth last July, and had wondered if it was because of that brief awkward moment when alone with her in the kitchen. She hadn't mentioned it to Mark, and put it down to Robert's drinking. A lapse in his thinking for a moment, forgetting she was Mark's wife. It wasn't the same situation as Mark and Sophie's. It wasn't intentional on Robert's part. She had put it from her mind immediately, and only the reduction of his visits caused her occasionally to think of it. It was lovely to see him now. He was Mark's best man, and her friend of ten years, too.

The rustle of cellophane reminded Kate there was another visitor. With a warm smile on her face, the woman handed the flowers to Kate. 'Hello, I'm Olivia. These are for you, from everyone.'

Kate clocked her nervousness, and how pretty she was. Dark hair swept back in a neat bun showed her green eyes and perfectly formed ears wearing delicate studs.

'Gosh,' Kate replied, then laughed lightly, feeling the weight in her arms. 'They're the biggest bunch of flowers I've ever had in my life. Thank you so much.'

She beckoned them to follow her. 'Come through to the kitchen, make yourselves at home while I put these in water.'

The surprise visit flustered her, and she looked aimlessly around for something to put the flowers in. She thought she should make some tea, and probably get out of the dressing gown she put on after showering, before climbing into the bed. Suddenly, she felt panic, and stopped still, having no clue what time it was. Was it still morning, or had the day drifted into afternoon? She glanced at the wall clock, saw it was quarter to twelve, and quickly excused herself. Dropping the flowers on the table, she rushed from the room, up the stairs to her bedroom for her phone and gave a relieved sigh at seeing nothing from the hospital or her mum.

Kate took off the dressing gown and hurriedly dressed in jeans and a jumper, clothes she would be comfortable to wear at the hospital. She zipped across the landing to the bathroom and splashed her face, brushed teeth, and pulled her hair up into a messy bun, using clips to keep it off her forehead. Grabbing toothpaste, toothbrush, deodorant, she rushed back to the bedroom and shoved them in her bag with some clean under-wear. She was ready to go back downstairs to her guests.

Olivia was pouring boiling water into a mug when Kate returned to the kitchen. Robert was nowhere in sight. 'He's in your downstairs loo,' Olivia informed her, smiling a little awkwardly as if embarrassed. 'I hope you don't mind me doing this, but I couldn't have you wait on us. I'm sorry for even intruding, but Robert offered me a lift in to Bath. I thought he'd be dropping me there, then going to the hospital.'

Kate wondered if she was Robert's girlfriend. If so, she was a vast improvement on the last one, who hardly said a word other than when she spoke to Robert.

'You're not intruding at all. Thank you for what you're doing.'

Olivia gave a relieved look. 'He's having coffee and I'm having tea. Can I add you to the list?'

Grateful to have the task taken from her, Kate smiled. 'I'd love some tea, please. I'm parched.'

Kate then noticed the flowers. Olivia had found her largest vases and made two arrangements, one for each end of the table. 'Oh my goodness, they look stunning.' She felt overwhelmed, and her voice quavered. 'You found vases and made tea. It's so kind of you to do that.'

Olivia's eyes expressed deep sadness. 'It was nothing. I'm glad to help. Captain Jordan is our favourite. We all like to fly with him. He makes everyone feel valued. He has everyone's respect, because while he's friendly, he's always professional. When he's in charge, even on a difficult flight, we know he'll land us safely.'

The sound of the toilet flushing and the door closing helped Kate to collect herself and concentrate on her visitors.

Then Robert's change of subject on returning to the kitchen made her feel guilty, and to worry again.

'Barney's getting old, isn't he? Didn't come out of his basket for his hello like he usually does.'

Kate hadn't checked on Barney since arriving home this

morning. Out of sight and out of mind after what happened to Mark yesterday. She had forgotten all about her beloved dog.

'Looks like he's being spoiled, mind. The chicken and rice is almost gone from his bowl.'

My kind mum, Kate thought. Her bed in the spare room and Jacob's were made, and the breakfast dishes washed up and put away to leave the kitchen clean before she left the house to take him to school.

'He's getting very old, and sleeps a lot now,' she said to Robert.

'Do you mind if I go and say hello?' Olivia interrupted politely. She glanced at Robert, then back at Kate. 'He's anxious to hear about Captain Jordan. After what's been happening to him. He drove very fast to get here,' she added in a subdued tone.

Kate inwardly jolted at realising they knew about Mark's situation with the police. Robert read the surprise on her face.

'Kate, nobody's talking about this. We only know because they interviewed us about it. Olivia and two other cabin crew. No one for a minute believes he had any involvement whatsoever. It was just bad luck him getting caught up in this business in the first place. So don't be worried he's being talked about. In our eyes, he couldn't be more innocent.'

Kate swallowed past the lump in her throat, seeing a confirming nod from Olivia, and felt marginally less alone. She wanted to ask Robert questions now it was out in the open, and hear everything he knew about Mark's movements while they were away. Anything to shed light on the situation and give her some hope.

Olivia quietly left the room, leaving Robert and Kate to talk.

Robert drank from the mug, while Kate's remained on the table. She eased into the conversation by remarking on Olivia. 'She seems nice. Is she your girlfriend?'

He chuckled and shook his head. 'No. I don't mix my love life with work.'

She held his gaze while asking the next question. 'And Mark? Is he the same?'

Robert put down the mug, any amusement in his eyes now gone. 'Kate! Why would you even think that? Mark doesn't mess about behind your back. He never has.'

She dropped her gaze to hide her embarrassment. 'He refuses to say where he was when this woman was murdered.'

She had to look at him when she heard no response. His expression gave nothing away.

'Say something, Robert.'

Robert looked away, before he gave a weary sigh and met her look. His voice was low and soft. 'I'm fucking disappointed, Kate. That you would think the worst. One slip up in ten years and you have him pegged as a murderer. I expected better of you, and it hurts.'

Kate felt herself flush all over at the strong rebuke, and at finding out Robert knew of the problem in her marriage three years ago. When had Mark told him about it? Tears stung her eyes as she hung her head, feeling utterly disloyal because her husband's friend showed more faith in him than his wife. She hoped Mark never got to hear about it, that what she'd said was just between her and Robert.

She felt her fingers being gently squeezed and saw Robert taking hold of her hand. His face was full of regret. 'Kate, I should never have said that to you. That was awful of me and I'm sorry. I think you're brilliant and lovely and Mark's a lucky man to have you. And I shouldn't be so quick to judge you. You have the right to question your husband's loyalty after getting hurt. It's only natural to feel cautious about it happening again. He'd be insane, though, ever wanting to look elsewhere.'

His penetrating gaze made her face warm again. She eased her hand from his and rubbed her forehead gently, hoping to make it appear natural and not the conscious act of breaking physical contact.

'Are you okay?' he asked.

His eyes were sincere, and Kate let herself relax. He had defended her husband at the expense of hurting her, and was now trying to make amends. If she read more into his gaze than should be there, it was up to her to ignore it.

She dipped her head amicably. 'I needed to hear it, Robert, especially from you. Mark couldn't ask for a better friend, and neither could I. Tell me about Barcelona. Anything that might help prove his innocence.'

He talked, but there wasn't much he could tell her apart from where the murder happened.

She got up from her side of the table and smelled the flowers nearest to her. 'This is you,' she stated, arching an eyebrow. 'Only the best and priciest will do. I dread to think what you have parked in my driveway. The last time we spoke, you said you were getting a Lamborghini?'

He gave a shamefaced grin. 'Nothing so fancy. You'll be surprised to know I drive a humble Mazda these days.'

Kate's mobile rang, silencing the reply she was about to give, as the urgency to get it out from the back pocket of her jeans galvanised her into action. She jabbed her finger at the screen.

'Hello?' she answered tentatively.

'Doctor Jordan?' A female voice that Kate couldn't identify. 'Yes.'

'Oh good. Kate, it's me. Rachel from the ward.'

Kate had an image of the nurse now in her head and knew who was calling. 'What's happened?' she asked sharply and urgently.

'Nothing with Mark,' Rachel replied. 'It's your mum. She's all right now, but she had a bit of an asthma attack. Probably from the heat of the ward, she thinks. She's had a nebulizer, which definitely helped, and feels fine. But she's thinking of driving, and I just felt a little concerned.'

Kate heaved a sigh, grateful it was not more serious. What did she do now? Ideally, her mum should go home and rest, which meant Kate would have to pick Jacob up from school, so she wouldn't be able to visit Mark, which she had to. Her mind was buzzing. There was no one else to sit beside him, and even if there was, she needed to see with her own eyes how he was doing.

'Thanks, Rachel. I'll call Mum and speak to her, and hopefully see you later.'

Robert was standing up and clearly concerned when Kate came off the phone, which she barely acknowledged because her eyes were on Barney. He trailed behind Olivia, giving a small wag of his tail as his eyes lit up at seeing Kate.

Clutching her chest to keep herself from choking, the fatigue and stress and fear washed over her. It was all too much. Kate went down on her knees to hug Barney. She pressed her face into his fur and gave in to the feeling of hopelessness as she burst into tears.

CHAPTER EIGHTEEN

Robert and Olivia did what they could to console her, sit her down, and get her to tell them the problem. Robert gave her a hug after she was calm again, and Olivia fetched a cool flannel for her face. Kate looked at them gratefully. The bout of crying and then their listening had helped, but she now had to think about the time. She hadn't phoned her mum yet, to put a stop to her collecting Jacob. It was a quarter to two, so she had to do that now.

Her visitors stayed with her while she made the call, telling her mum not to worry, she had it all sorted. She could go home to rest instead of minding Jacob. It was not a problem at all. After convincing her, and feeling reassured she was okay to drive, Kate hung up.

She turned to her visitors, needing them to leave so she could get on with everything she had to do.

'Thanks, both of you. And sorry for the waterworks. You must be worn out after visiting me.'

She laughed lightly, but neither of them joined in. Robert looked like he needed to say something and kept glancing in Olivia's direction, as if trying to give a signal. Kate wondered what was going on. She didn't wait long to find out. Robert had a plan.

'Look, let me and Olivia pick Jacob up from school. Then you can go to the hospital and be with Mark. We'll bring him back here and make sure he's fed.'

Kate was shaking her head before he'd even finished speaking. 'I can't ask you to do that. And anyway, it's ages since he's seen you, Robert. You might feel like a stranger to him.'

Robert held up a hand. 'It's not been that long and it will take less than five minutes for him to remember me. I'm the only one who can do the dad's voice in *The Croods*.'

Seeing his earnest expression, Kate felt hysterical laughter building up inside herself. Then Olivia added her equally preposterous input. 'And I like dinosaurs.'

Kate stared at the two of them and wondered if she was mad to consider it. Then Robert took over. 'We need you to ring the school to let them know, and we need the address. And a quick rundown of the dos and don'ts, what he likes to eat, any allergies, that type of thing.'

'And a car seat,' Olivia added. 'If you give us your car keys, we'll get it out of yours and put it in Robert's.'

They were thinking practically, and keeping safety in mind, and Kate could feel herself calming to the idea. It was only for a few hours, and Jacob would probably enjoy seeing some new faces.

'If you're sure—'

Their vigorous nods stopped her talking, causing her to smile and making her mind up.

'Two things,' she stressed. 'Jacob doesn't know his father's in hospital. He thinks he's at work.' Then looking pointedly at Robert. 'No driving fast. I mean it.'

He nodded solemnly. 'I promise. Now go see your husband. And stop worrying. Any problems, I'll text you.'

Kate was amused when she saw the Mazda parked next to

her ten-year-old Volkswagen and Mark's Volvo estate. Robert's idea of a humble car was a far cry from what she'd been led to expect. The sleek cherry-red vehicle looked like an expensive weekend toy. It suited Robert. While for someone like Mark, it wouldn't do at all. Mark wouldn't dream of buying anything that he couldn't fit camping gear, bikes, a dog, a five-year-old, and everything else that went in a car for a weekend away.

Her mind became occupied with her concerns as she drove back to the hospital. In a short while she would be with Mark, and hopefully see him improved and giving her a reason to be less fearful. She wanted him back exactly the way he was, with nothing changed in his brain. She would cope with anything else if that could happen. As bad as it was being investigated for murder, it paled in comparison to losing a part of him.

Kate couldn't bear to think about it. She was better off thinking about the other situation, no matter how unpleasant, to give her something to focus on. She mustn't just let it slide and do nothing. And who knows what she might find? Was there evidence to prove his innocence that no one else had found?

Robert had given an account of Mark's time in Barcelona. He explained the route and the distance from the hotel to the bar they all went to on New Year's Eve, which was on the same street where the woman was killed. How long it took them to walk there. Kate felt an urge to walk in Mark's footsteps to see for herself where he went and what he did.

One of those receipts he smoothed out on the bed might have a time and date for a bar near the hotel where he stayed. That would show he couldn't have been on the street at the same time that Fleur O'Connell was being murdered, because he was too far away.

He hadn't told her where he went when he left the hotel, but that didn't mean she couldn't find out. She could show his photograph at every bar and café that was open at that time of night, and maybe get lucky and find someone who recognised him. Someone might even have had a drink with him. It occurred to her that drinking could be the reason for him not telling her where he was. Perhaps he wanted to keep it secret as his judgement and safety could be called into question by the airline.

She pondered another idea. Could he be a secret gambler? Going out that time of night, feeling restless to place a bet, needing the thrill from gambling? She was thinking in extremes, hypothesising for any explanation. But gambling? Really? He didn't even bet on the Grand National. Drinking too much in a bar was more likely, even if he'd never been known for it.

It was a better reason than where her mind was trying to stray. She shocked Robert by even thinking that Mark would be interested in other women. But maybe Robert was wrong and Mark did occasionally play away from home. An image of Sophie swooped into her head, followed by an image of the dead woman, Fleur O'Connell. Mark might have been with a woman, not Fleur O'Connell but someone else, for about an hour or for however long it took for him to meet, then cheat, maybe even paying for the pleasure of her company.

Kate squirmed at the graphic images that leapt into her mind. He would never want her to know about it, which could be why he wouldn't give her a reason for leaving the hotel. He would have to admit it to the police to save himself. Had he done that? He either had, and they didn't believe him, or hadn't because he hoped the police would find the actual murderer, and where he was and what he was doing didn't have to be revealed. As much as she wanted to reject this motive for staying quiet, if she was to prove him innocent of murder, she would have to consider the possibility for their son's sake. She would rather Jacob have a cheating father than one who went to prison. Jacob need never know if his father behaved immorally, but she could not protect him for all of his life from knowing that his father was sent to jail.

The weight of that knowledge would mark him. The impact of an incarcerated parent left children at a higher risk of depression, guilt, low self-esteem. She wanted none of that for Jacob. It would destroy his sensitive soul. She would rather find out that Mark was cheating – even if it broke her heart. Anything to prevent her child from suffering would be worth it.

A car horn blared and she jolted in shock as she saw she had veered into the oncoming lane of traffic, and quickly pulled to her side of the road. Her hands were shaking as she gripped the steering wheel. She slowed down her speed and took steadying breaths, and berated herself for her stupidity. She should be concentrating, not letting herself get in a state.

She was grasping at straws and she knew it. Trying to find a plausible explanation for his absence from the hotel, she imagined only the worst-case scenarios. Nothing innocent, such as him taking a simple walk. She was labelling him a sex addict. She didn't understand why. She had never sensed a seediness about him. He was a passionate lover, but had self-control if she wasn't in the mood. He wanted her to participate, not just open her legs.

A psychologist would tell her, she suspected, that she had dormant issues. Suppressed emotions she unconsciously avoided because she didn't know how to deal with them. It wouldn't surprise her, as why else was she looking for the bad in him, sabotaging his excellent character? Did she want him to bleed? To forever atone for one small sin?

He had shown his love and commitment in a thousand ways. So what more did she want? Was there something she wanted to change about him? She didn't need to think very hard. She already knew the answer.

He wasn't a perfect man, but he was perfect for her. She wouldn't want to change an imperfect thing about him. Without shades of grey, he wouldn't be Mark. He wouldn't be her husband, and Kate loved the sum total of her husband's personality, not just the black-and-white certainties that were easy to love.

Lack of information was undoing her faith in him, and tainting her mind. Mark was not a philanderer or a murderer. His situation was as Robert said – just bad luck at his getting caught up in this business. He would have a good reason for keeping quiet about his whereabouts. It would be for an honourable purpose, which only he knew about.

Kate had to believe in that. Otherwise, everything he meant to her would turn to ashes.

CHAPTER NINETEEN

Robert watched Kate's little boy aligning his dinosaurs and felt a little left out. Olivia was doing a brilliant job of keeping Jacob happy all on her own. She was a natural with kids and astounded Robert with how much she knew about these plastic toys. She was on the same level as Jacob with her knowledge of dinosaur names. Whereas Robert's knowledge of the Jurassic era came entirely from films.

He was happy to have Olivia with him, though. Jacob was clearly at ease and was talking more than Robert had ever heard him speak. He'd thought him always a very shy boy. Robert left them to play in the sitting room. He'd make himself useful by looking in the kitchen for something to cook for Jacob's tea.

In a cupboard, he found a packet of dry spaghetti and chose a large saucepan from a hanging rail of pots and pans to boil some water. He had a vague memory from last summer of Kate having a problem with getting Jacob to eat something, and decided he'd better ask first if Jacob liked spaghetti.

In the sitting room, Jacob was giggling. Robert waited until it passed before interrupting. 'Jacob, I'm making some dinner. Is there any food you don't like?'

'Uh huh,' he replied. 'I don't like red, thank you.'

'Do you like spaghetti?'

He nodded enthusiastically before turning shyly away.

Robert felt his heart tug. He was such a mixture, this child, of brightness and vulnerability. Mark was a lucky father to have such a beautiful son. Back in the kitchen Robert went to work, and an hour later his efforts paid off. Robert's chicken broth, parmesan-grated carbonara passed Jacob's inspection and he ate it enthusiastically. Olivia gave Robert a well-done-you relieved smile. Robert was happy to see the boy fed. The three of them cleared their bowls, and while Robert washed up, Olivia and Jacob fed Barney. She whipped up some scrambled eggs and mixed it with a small amount of the leftover pasta. She and Jacob sat on the floor watching as Barney slowly ate it.

They were working together as a team. The three of them were keeping Kate's home life stable, and he wished there was some way they could stay longer and do more. He'd discuss it with Olivia when they were alone. Otherwise, he didn't know how Kate would manage. He knew Grace would do her best, but hearing today of her asthma attack, Kate wouldn't want her mum overburdened. He'd think of something to make it work. He cared too much for Kate to see her struggle. She was the reason he'd never married. He'd lived life to the full, had plenty of female companionship over the years, but none who made him want to commit. Mark found the only one Robert could ever consider. Mark's good luck and Robert's misfortune.

Today was the first time he'd seen her since the summer and he'd wondered if there would be any awkwardness, but she'd been as lovely as always. His one – and only one – faux pas during Mark's party still embarrassed him. He'd made it perfectly clear how much he liked her. Almost went in for the kiss, until she gently pushed him away, laughing politely that he had had too much to drink. That she never told Mark was clear in the way Mark was unchanged in their friendship.

There was a part of him, though, that hoped she acknowledged his behaviour was not all down to drink. The thousands of thoughts that had gone through his mind over ten years had not lessened. He should have managed his feelings by now and started his own family. And he should never have wished Mark away, as he had occasionally, because right now those wishes were coming true. His wishes turning to reality made him feel guilty because what he desired wouldn't feel right unless it happened in other circumstances.

They hadn't got divorced. Mark hadn't died suddenly from an illness. Kate still loved her husband. And Robert... the bottom line was Kate was forbidden fruit. She was not free to be with someone else.

Olivia startled him when she placed Barney's empty bowl beside the unwashed pots. She saw his slight flinch. 'You were in a world of your own there for a minute. What deep thoughts are you thinking?'

He raised soapy hands from the water, shook his head, kept his voice low. 'Just wondering how Kate's going to manage. I can help out tomorrow, but Thursday, Friday, Saturday I'm away.'

'Well, I've got a whole ten days off,' Olivia announced, surprising him.

He glanced at her. 'Are you suggesting you could help for that long?'

The idea didn't seem to worry her as she nodded calmly. 'I don't see why not. Unless Kate objects, of course. I've got nothing planned, and he's a dear little boy. I think any of us would help Captain Jordan's family at a time like this. Look at you? Cooking and washing up, and fetching their boy from school.'

'Yes, but that's because I've known Mark for fifteen years and Kate for ten. I'm godfather to Jacob. I helped renovate this house.'

'I didn't realise you knew them so well. If you don't think

it's a good idea to offer help, I won't be offended. It's just a thought because I have the time.'

Robert felt his trouser leg being gently tugged and looked down to see Jacob standing next to him. 'Do you know when Mummy's home?' Jacob asked, looking suddenly unsure. His eyes were wide in a solemn face.

Robert hunkered down to be at eye level with him, and pretended not to notice he was transferring soapsuds from his hands to his face. It did the trick of distracting Jacob from his worry.

'You've got bubbles on your face, Uncle Robert,' he said, laughing.

'Who me?' Robert replied in extreme surprise. Then he pretended to be cross. 'It's that Fairy Liquid bossy baby. He always puts bubbles on my face when I wash up.'

The suggestion from Olivia that they take Barney outside for a wee helped further the moment of uncertainty. The informal word had enormous appeal for Jacob, making him laugh out loud. His mummy called it Barney doing his business.

Robert gamely grinned up at Olivia. She had a knack for saying the right thing. Kate would be relieved to leave Jacob with someone like her. If Kate let her lend a hand, it would calm some of his guilt about wanting to be Mark for so long.

To have what he had. A wife like Kate. A son like Jacob. A life like Mark's.

CHAPTER TWENTY

Mark looked unchanged from the morning apart from the clean white sheet. The old one had drops of blood on it from when they inserted a third cannula. Throughout the night, Kate's eyes kept returning to the red spots, finding them strangely comforting. Perhaps it was because blood signified life.

She was waiting to speak to the consultant. She wanted his opinion more than anyone else's, although what he could tell her that she didn't already know from looking in Mark's medical notes would be very little. The induced coma would have hopefully offset any intercranial pressure. The propofol sedation acted by reducing the electrical activity of the brain, which in theory reduces the metabolic and oxygen demand. What she was hoping for was an indication of how long they would keep Mark in a coma.

The ICU nurse, Rachel, was still on duty. She measured the hourly urine output and wrote it down on a chart. Just one of the many vital body functions being monitored and managed while Mark was attached to a respirator, a breathing tube in his throat, to deliver breaths to his lungs while they kept him asleep. Every time Rachel attended to her patient, she spoke to him as if he were awake and listening. Her voice was warm and natural. She even spoke to him about Kate.

'I'm just going to make Kate a cup of coffee, Mark. She doesn't like the hospital tea, not that I can blame her. We all like our tea to taste like the tea at home. So I'll be back in a minute.'

Kate was grateful for her care and hoped she was on duty every day while Mark was there. Across the department, she spotted Julian Sullivan and got up from her chair, relieved she would get to speak to him before she went home. He was the consultant anaesthetist in charge of Mark's care. An expert in airway management, used to dealing with difficult intubation, difficult laryngoscopy, difficult ventilation. Necessary skills in ICU as most of the patients there were on ventilators.

He met her halfway and gave her a tight hug, momentarily frightening her it was bad news. But he smiled when he released her. 'Had to do that. You looked so afraid. Come and sit down and let's talk.'

He guided her behind the nurses' station to give a modicum of privacy. He was wearing his trademark dark-blue scrubs, his salt and pepper hair looking recently cut. Kate smiled at him nervously.

'How is he, Julian?'

He gave her a moment to settle, and she saw his attentive and kindly gaze. 'I'd like seventy-two hours, to be sure. There's no raised ICP showing on the CT. He's not had any seizures. If things remain the same overnight and tomorrow, we'll look at Thursday to wake him. How does that sound?'

It sounded alien to Kate. Her medical world, so familiar, was handing her uncertainties, robbing her of her confidence in medical science. Perfect obedience from machines and drugs couldn't guarantee a perfect outcome. Only when they woke him would she find surety.

'I'm scared,' she admitted. Her body trembled with emotion as she confessed her greatest fear. 'If he's not the same, if he loses who he is, a lifetime of learning stripped away... I don't think I could bear it for him. I'd rather he slipped away... for his sake. With no fear.'

Julian put some tissues in her hand as she gazed at him through a blur of tears. 'Am I the worst wife ever?' she asked.

He shook his head sadly. 'No. You're just thinking of the heartbreaking reality that sometimes happens – seeing a loved one losing capacity you don't want them to bear.' He reached for her hand to comfort her and waited until she dried her eyes before giving his advice. 'The mind is powerful and can achieve what seems impossible. It can work through obstacles. Do you understand what I'm saying?'

She nodded, sniffing back tears. 'I do. We must give him the chance to do the best that he can before I pronounce him gone.'

'Exactly,' Julian agreed. 'And, if you don't mind me saying, you're racing too far ahead, when he hasn't even had the opportunity to join in. Fear is what's causing you to imagine the worst, and I get that. But worrying about things that haven't happened yet will stop you coping. Remind yourself, kindly, as a doctor, of all the times you thought a patient's life was over, only to be proved wrong – you sent them home fighting fit. Do you see what I'm saying?'

She nodded again. 'I do. And thank you for reminding me of that.'

They stood up and he hugged her again. 'Be kind to yourself,' he said softly in her ear. 'That's the best thing you can do.'

She took a deep breath, pulled her shoulders back, and nodded. 'Thank you.'

She returned to Mark to say goodnight, then quickly departed, trying to avoid noticing all the beds she passed with relatives sat beside them. She almost raced along the corridors of the hospital, needing to be out of the building fast. Every familiar step she took had been part of her normal world two days ago. Now she felt like an outsider who didn't belong. She felt unconnected to the role she had always served, to the events of only days ago, when she was a doctor treating the very sick. The three young men in resus needing critical care after falling from a roof seemed to have been in another lifetime, so little connection did she feel to that memory.

One week ago to the day, Tuesday morning of the third of January, her life was hectic but normal. It was Jacob's first day back at school after Christmas, and she had a boiler to fix. From then on, everything spiralled out of control. The magnitude of Mark's situation, that seemed ludicrous at the time, became clear overnight. Her mind, in overdrive, was persecuted by past events. A wall of uncertainty grew between them. Then more heartache – at having to know she would be having to make a decision about Barney when it went past being able to manage him at home. Yesterday, which she had given very little thought to, a car hit Mark in a country lane. Somewhere there was a person who, maybe too frightened or too selfish to report the accident, had no idea about her suffering this week. Their involvement was just one part. They couldn't know that something had already crashed her life.

If she went back to last Tuesday, she had only to carry the sadness of baby Andrew. With his chubby legs and tiny baby teeth pushing through, a little bundle of innocence she prayed would live. The memory of him made a sudden and painful impact on her.

She had not lost all connection.

In floods of tears, she walked through the car park, her sobs muffled by a woollen scarf covering her mouth. She didn't notice anything else around her until a concerned voice shouted her name.

'Kate!'

Her head rose sharply, her hands grappling to use the scarf to dry her face before the person was upon her and saw the evidence of her distress.

It was too late to hide. Sophie was standing in front of her, her face contorted with worry. She took in the sight of Kate and gave a mournful cry.

'Oh, Kate! So many times I've wanted to ring you. I only just heard about Mark. I rushed up to ICU, but they said you'd just gone. Kate, if there's anything I can do, please let me help.'

Kate wanted to respond, but her throat was too constricted to speak. She had locked up her feelings about Sophie for so long, she was unable to determine how she felt at this moment. The best she could do was nod, her head moving of its own accord like a nodding dog on a car dashboard.

The unexpected meeting was lasting too long. She was noticing Sophie looked tired, slightly older, a sadness showing in her eyes, a quality of vulnerability that had never been there before. Kate couldn't risk seeing the intimacies of her any longer. She made a gesture of farewell, a small wave of her hand. Sophie may have construed it as a hostile sign to stay away.

Kate averted her eyes, walking away, knowing it must seem rude. But she couldn't think of any other way to escape. Exhausted and disorientated, she didn't need this sudden intrusion into her life. She already had enough to cope with. Sophie had to stay buried in the past. Kate was not ready for her in the present.

Not yet. Not now. Maybe not ever.

CHAPTER TWENTY-ONE

Barney was standing on the gravel managing to balance while taking a pee when Kate pulled into the drive. The sight lifted her spirits. He looked stronger than he had in a while.

Jacob appeared on the doorstep, not realising her car was there, his interest occupied in carrying a plank of wood outside with the help of Robert. Olivia had a breeze block in her hands. Kate watched as the three of them made a ramp up the two stone steps to the front door. Barney, now finished with his business, was trying out his new ramp. They clapped his success.

Kate climbed out of the car. Jacob raced towards her full of chatter. She picked up on several topics, his yummy dinner, bubbles on Uncle Robert's face, and the highlight of the evening, causing him the most excitement: 'Olivia knows the names of every single dinosaur in the whole world. Even more than me,' he exclaimed, totally star-struck.

'Does she?' Kate replied, laughing and swinging him up in her arms to hug him. 'Well, that's just brilliant. We're going to have to invite Olivia here more often.'

Olivia came to greet her. 'I've had the best time ever.' She beamed. 'I'm in absolute awe of Jacob's knowledge. I have learned so much. Contrary to what Jacob believes, I think it's him who knows every name. I can't even pronounce half of them.'

Robert smiled at Kate over Olivia's head. 'I'm just the chef and bottle washer, so you can ignore me.'

Kate soaked up the lively atmosphere and followed the group into the house. It was warm and inviting with lamps she never turned on, lighting corners in the sitting room. They replaced cluttered surfaces with some flowers from the kitchen in more vases. They had switched the rugs in the hallway to opposite ends. Kate didn't have to ask why. The longer stretch of rug normally at the bottom of the stairs now covered the distance from the sitting room to the front door to make it less slippery for Barney. Her other rug was now joined by a mat from the kitchen, making the entire hallway safe. They had stacked the shoes properly on the wooden shoe bench, out of the way.

On the kitchen table, a jigsaw puzzle was in progress. She recognised it as a Christmas present to Jacob from his Nana Marge in Australia. A makeshift raised dog-bowl station was set on two more breeze blocks, with Barney's bowls on a non-slip drinks tray she vaguely remembered having in the cupboard.

Kate felt like twirling at all the improvements and didn't know who she had to thank. Slightly giddy, she was overcome with gratitude. 'How did you know? It's unbelievable. The vet's only just suggested we do all this. How did you know?'

Robert's amused eyes looked toward Olivia, his explanation simple. 'She likes dogs, apparently.'

Kate didn't know what to say. Instead, she gave Olivia a hug.

Collecting her emotions, she turned practical. It was way past Jacob's bedtime.

'Jacob, say goodnight to Olivia and Uncle Robert. It's bedtime.'

He sweetly did as he was told, and even thanked them. Kate was one proud mama as she climbed the stairs. He was quick into bed and almost asleep by the time she tucked him in and headed out the door.

Downstairs, Robert had made her a mug of tea. Olivia was looking in the fridge. 'You must be hungry. We were wondering what we could make you to eat.'

'I'm just going to have toast,' Kate replied. 'But I'm in no rush, and I can do it. You two must be wanting to get home.'

'We don't,' Olivia answered. 'In fact, we have something to put to you. We'd very much like to help with looking after Jacob, and Barney, of course. Robert would like to take Jacob to school tomorrow, and I'd like to stay, if it helps. That way you don't have to worry about leaving Captain Jordan, and can visit him for as long as you like.'

The offer astounded Kate. Her eyes went from Robert to Olivia and back again. Her immediate instinct was to refuse. She didn't know Olivia from Adam. It would be far too trusting to leave her child with someone she had literally never met before. Having her help out for a few hours while Robert was in attendance was a decision made quickly while emotional. It had gone well by all accounts, but accepting Olivia's offer to stay was something else entirely. She would need to think about it. Talk it over with Robert first when Olivia wasn't around.

Olivia must have sensed some concern as she excused herself to use the bathroom. Kate grilled Robert the moment she was out of earshot. 'I don't know her, Robert, or anything about her.'

He glanced at Kate and spoke frankly about Olivia. 'She's a natural with kids, that much I do know. She's the one they call for if they have any onboard children travelling alone. Judging by today, Jacob certainly seemed happy.'

Kate pondered the idea. The suggestion would solve so many problems, and she could always check with a few of

Mark's other colleagues about Olivia. Having her stay would take the pressure off her mum. It might even allow the possibility of flying to Barcelona for a day. It would only happen if Mark's condition was stable, so only a thought for now, but something she would do if she could.

Losing his watch might mean something important for him to mention it so urgently. If she didn't find it in the house or his car, a parrot on a door was her only clue. She needed to figure it out.

When Olivia returned from the bathroom, Kate gave an answer to her guests. 'Yes, please. Yes, thank you. You'll have my mum to help as well. Grace has the room next to Jacob's when she stays here, but you can use it, Robert, and Olivia can have the other bedroom. They're both made up, though yours, Robert, needs fresh linen. Mum slept in it last night.'

'Kate, let us sort ourselves out. You just concentrate on what you need to do,' Robert said firmly.

'But—'

'No buts.' He held his hand up, showing his palm, telling her to stop and eyed her sternly. 'Play ball. Else we're out of here.'

Her mouth fell open. She was shocked for as long as it took to see he was holding back laughter. 'Ha ha. Very funny. If you're lucky, I'll put a mattress on the floor for you, so you'll feel the draught coming through the floorboards.'

Robert folded his arms. 'There are no draughts. I made sure of that by filling the cracks with sawdust when you and Mark were happy to leave gaps. So there.'

Olivia and Kate both laughed, while Robert gave a good impression of being offended. The whole last hour had lifted Kate's mood. She drank her tea and listened to their plans, giving an occasional nod to something she needed to agree. Robert was going to drive Olivia home to collect some clothes and then bring her back. With Kate's permission, she would drive Mark's car to take over the school runs when Robert had to leave. She had a clean licence and was insured. Robert would spend the night, and stay again on Sunday. It was clear they had already talked things through, which made their offer that much more genuine.

Kate would be in bed before they returned with Olivia's things, so she fetched a front door key for them to let themselves in. Robert said he'd warm up the car, leaving the two women alone. Kate gazed thoughtfully at Olivia. She seemed too lovely to be on her own. Curious to know, Kate asked if she had anyone.

Olivia gave a small sigh. She had a wistful look on her face. 'I have a son. He's five. Only he's not with me.'

Kate frowned in consternation. Olivia shrugged, however, her expression open and friendly.

'It's okay, Kate. I'm fine with it. I don't mind you knowing.'

It was as well she didn't mind, because Kate needed to know her better. It would stop her asking the usual questions of someone single, like whether they wanted children. Kate should ask about him, though, otherwise it would seem as if she had no interest. 'Where is your son?'

'He's with his father. And he's a great dad,' she said with admiration. 'With my job and all the travelling, it makes more sense for him to live with his dad. He's in the right place, and who knows what might happen in the future? I hope that one day we'll all get to live together.'

It sounded to Kate like this hadn't happened before. Olivia and her son's father living together? She noticed the absence of a wedding ring. Olivia hadn't called him her husband, referring to him as her son's father. Kate wondered if it was due to financial circumstances that the boy was with his dad. Cabin crew basic salary was low, she knew. It would be hard to raise a child on that wage.

Robert came into the kitchen through the back door, making

them both jump. 'Sorry, I shut the front door and didn't want to knock in case I woke Jacob. You have the key Kate gave us,' he added to Olivia. 'So let's be going so we can get back at a reasonable time. I'm on breakfast duty for a five-year-old in the morning, don't forget.'

Olivia gave a groan, mocking him. 'Oh my God, that's all we're going to hear from now on. I think you're going to regret having him here, Kate.'

Kate didn't think so. She'd been entertained by the two of them since arriving home. They'd given her a fun time, free of worry for a while. She was glad to have them. They gave her energy by being there, and even some hope, where before she was low on both.

She sat in the quietness after their departure, thinking of this change of good fortune. Robert turning up couldn't have come at a better time. It would make her life ten times easier.

CHAPTER TWENTY-TWO

Kate had a missed call from her mum and a text message. She read the words.

Out in the corridor.

Kate sprang up from her seat, heading for the exit. She felt guilty for not thinking to call last night and see how her mum was after her asthma attack in the morning. She completely forgot. Feeling genuinely contrite, she hurried out of the department to see her mum.

Grace Shortman was using every inch of her nearly five-foot frame to stand tall. Her cheeks were flushed, her eyes bright like she was on the verge of crying. Kate felt weak with sudden alarm and a wave of nausea tilted her stomach. She dragged in a lungful of air before she could speak.

'Mum, whatever's the matter?'

Grace's nostrils flared as she too breathed in, like a small snorting bull. 'Well, Kate, thank you very much for letting me know that you have replaced me. I arrive to take my grandson to school and find not only a stranger in your home, but a stranger taking care of your son!'

Kate flushed with guilt. Her mum had made an unnecessary journey, and was clearly upset with Kate's new arrangements. 'Sorry, Mum. I should have let you know. But Robert's not a stranger.'

She gave Kate an impatient stare. 'Robert has an agenda. And don't tell me you're not aware. The silly fool has been in love with you forever and by now should have got his own family. But do you even know this woman? She said she only met you yesterday.'

Kate needed to breathe in before she threw up. The heat on the ward had made her nauseous. Her hand rose of its own volition to flap air onto her face. She could understand her mum's reaction, but surely she could see Kate did it for the best. For her sake, as much as anyone's.

'I'm sorry, Mum. I didn't want to burden you. What with your health—'

'My health! I'm fucking sixty-eight, Kate, not ninety! I get a bit of seasonal asthma, so what? I am more than capable, thank you very much.'

Kate was shocked. She had never heard her mum swear in her life until today, which was testament to how upset she was. Grace was normally the most mild-mannered person on earth. She couldn't defend Olivia with her mum in this state. It would be no good telling her that Robert vouched for her, that Jacob liked her, and that Barney was getting a second lease of life with her being there. It would probably upset her more. Kate suggested the only thing she could.

She gave a shaky sigh. 'I need a cup of tea, Mum. Will you come with me to the canteen?'

For a few seconds, Grace said nothing. Then relenting, she gave a nod. 'Fine.'

In the restaurant, she asked Kate to find a table while she

went to the counter. Returning with a tray, she placed a pale-looking drink in front of Kate. Then a salmon sandwich and a banana.

'I don't expect you've eaten this morning,' she declared in a more softened tone.

She was correct. Kate had left the house at six and hadn't even switched the kettle on, let alone eaten breakfast. But she couldn't face the very weak tea in front of her. Her stomach wouldn't stop rolling since facing her mum. She put it down to nerves, and less the heat of the ward, the constant worry about Mark.

It would be unfair to unload onto Grace. She was in the dark about everything else that was going on, like Mark's parents in Australia. None of them knew that their son and son-in-law was in trouble. Kate needed her mum to be strong with the present situation. She picked up the mug and sipped, and was pleasantly surprised.

'Chai latte,' Grace announced, noticing her reaction. 'You don't like ordinary hospital tea.'

The thoughtfulness warmed Kate. Her mum still loved her. She was just a little upset at not being kept in the loop.

'So tell me how it happened?'

Kate knew what she was asking and didn't prevaricate. 'Robert showed up yesterday with some flowers. I thought the woman with him was his girlfriend at first, but it turns out she's cabin crew and flies with Robert and Mark. Seems to have a great regard for Captain Jordan, said he's everyone's favourite. Then the hospital phoned about you. Robert suggested he would collect Jacob so I could come here. When I got home last night... everything was shipshape. Jacob happy, Barney more lively. They offered their help and I gratefully accepted.'

Grace nodded. 'Okay, I'm sorry for bawling at you. I can see how it happened. What's her name?'

'Olivia.'

'No last name?' her mum enquired. Seeing Kate unable to give one, she gave a weighty sigh. Another black mark against a daughter who didn't even know the surname of the stranger looking after her child. 'Oh well, I'm sure you'll learn it in time. But for now, I'm going to keep helping. I can sit with Mark to give you breaks and keep an eye on the home front. Will that help you?'

'Enormously,' Kate replied, managing to sound positive. 'I will be checking about Olivia. I wasn't just going to take Robert's word for it that she's good with children.'

'Well, good then. We're settled. We all have a part to play. Including Mark.' She looked into Kate's eyes with the reassurance of a practical mother.

Kate was greatly relieved they were back on a firm footing. She never wanted to be out of step with her mum. Grace didn't take prisoners when trying to achieve something. But Kate needed to correct the misconception that she had known Robert's feelings. She hadn't the slightest inkling that he was attracted to her until last year. And then he'd been drinking and would have tried it on with any woman he could kiss. Why would her mum think he was in love with her? What had she seen that Kate hadn't?

She had to ask her. She had to say something, otherwise it might never get mentioned again, and Kate didn't want her mum thinking her callous, or worse, leading Robert on. She came out with it before she lost her nerve.

'Mum, I wasn't aware of what you said about Robert. In ten years, he's been nothing but a friend. Mark's birthday last year is the only time he's ever stepped out of line. He was drunk, and I put it out of my mind straight away. So what on earth makes you think he's always been in love with me? What have you seen?'

Grace pulled a hand across her brow, shielding her eyes.

Kate would love to know what she was thinking or preparing to say. She then gave a small sigh, as if decided.

'I never really saw anything, Kate. He's always been a flirtatious man, and is charming with it. It was Mark who told me. He never said how he knew, but I gather it was from something someone said.'

Kate was blown away. She wouldn't be more surprised than she was now if her mum suddenly started speaking fluent Mandarin Chinese.

'How are they still friends?' she uttered in a shocked voice.

Grace shook her head. 'Oh, I doubt Mark ever mentioned it. How would Robert be able to work with him? Mark told me it was because he was sad for his friend. He didn't like the thought of him pining. It's what makes him a good friend. Other husbands would have viewed a handsome, charming man in love with their wife as a threat. Not many men would have the charity to accept it and still be friends.'

'When did Mark tell you this?' Kate asked.

'The night Jacob was born. Mark and I were in your kitchen, toasting the baby's head. Then Robert's name came up. Mark wanted him to be godfather, but he didn't know if it was a wise choice. I asked why, and that's when he told me. We've never talked about it since.'

'Well, I'm glad you told me now,' Kate replied calmly, for her mother's sake.

Inwardly, her mind was racing. Did Mark think the same as her mum? If so, did he wonder why she never remarked on it, perhaps even thinking she enjoyed being the object of another man's desire? Kate really hoped not. If he'd had any of these thoughts in his head, they must have occasionally affected him. Yet he carried on caring for Robert and loving her.

What she learned today shamed her. How quickly she chose not to trust him. She would never do that again.

CHAPTER TWENTY-THREE

Kate stared at her husband. She had cheated him, really. Despite telling herself three years ago it was a new foundation, she had held onto her distrust, using it against him as soon as she could. She never thought him guilty of murder, but doubted his innocence of some other wrongdoing.

It was unforgivable when she thought about it. In ten years, for only five minutes, he let her down and she'd been hanging on to it. Wearing it on her head like a martyr's crown.

She should have gone for counselling and not buried her feelings. She knew that now. Rather than bring them closer, this unforeseen turn of events had come close to destroying her goodness by allowing the past to take away her trust. Her unconditional love. It wasn't a new foundation she laid, but a hard little wall stopping all the hurt escaping, built slowly with tiny bricks she didn't even know were there. Where was the girl who always saw a glass half full, rather than half empty? Behind a wall, denying herself the freedom to forgive.

Somewhere in a myriad of emotions was the answer to how to fix herself. The girl with the glass half full? Kate wanted her back.

She needed to start with admitting how much she missed Sophie, the only friend she ever truly loved. Flirty, gorgeous Sophie. With her exuberance for loving, she breezed so much happiness into Kate's life. In all the years of friendship, Sophie had hurt her for only five minutes. Where was her magnanimity in accepting the brief failure of a friend?

She had learned much about herself in the last few days. One thing was for sure, if she got the chance, she would push the reset button on her world. She had to plan how to make that happen. In a matter of days, the odds were high that her life would topple further. If Mark woke fully recovered, all the joy would get snatched away by the police. Detective Sharma would be keeping tabs on developments in Mark's condition. As soon as the doctors gave the green light, Mark would be arrested.

That possibility was all too real. So why was she just sitting around doing nothing, when she could do something to help him? The police were going in the wrong direction in pursuing Mark. It just didn't make sense that they suspected him. She was not ignorant about the law or the police. They hadn't just blundered onto a crime scene and picked Mark's name out of a bag. They had evidence. And it had to be more than a witness and confirmation he was not in a hotel. Otherwise, they wouldn't be coming after him so hard or be so ready to arrest him.

She had to do something and quickly, even if it meant leaving Mark on his own. The longer she left it, the less likely she would find something or someone who could help prove his innocence.

First things first – she needed to speak to Mark's consultant about the desperate decision she had just made, and why she was abandoning her husband in ICU. She would ask one of the nurses to bleep him, because by the afternoon she planned to be gone for at least a day. She went to the desk and put her request to the nurse sitting there. Then she sat back with Mark and waited, and thought of all things she would need to do.

Head to a cash machine and draw out money to give to Olivia or Robert for any shopping or petrol. There was food in the fridge and freezer, but they might prefer takeaways. Take the hundred pounds of euros from her bedroom drawer. After that, she'd use her debit card. Get her passport at the same time. Show Olivia and Robert how to set the alarm on the house, show them the electrics box in the under-stairs cupboard. Give Olivia her mobile number and get hers. Write down phone numbers for the vet, for their GP surgery, Jacob's school, her mum. Go through Mark's flight bag for those receipts. Find an up-to-date photograph of Mark in case her phone played up or ran out of charge. Book a flight and hotel.

The first thing she should do was find Mark's lost watch, in case it had any bearing on his situation. Was it lost at home or in another country? She needed to search for it.

It was nearly eleven. She'd like to be home by noon and at the airport by early afternoon.

* * *

Thirty minutes later, her face hot with embarrassment, she gazed at her hands and not the doctor. Why was she surprised that Julian was aware the police were interested in Mark when she had already pictured the doctor giving the green light for the police to arrest him? The consultant would have to know.

But it came as a bit of a shock when Julian emphasised he wouldn't let anyone visit Mark until Kate was back. It couldn't have been clearer who he meant. She felt horribly exposed. In that moment she had a small taste of what it must have felt like for Mark to have stood in front of his employers and tell them the reason he couldn't fly was because he was being investigated for murder. Stripped of autonomy in an instant, powerless to disobey.

She shuddered to recall how unsupportive she was with him, in what was their last conversation before he ended up in resus with his heart stopped. Her coldness when she told him she wouldn't answer the door or let Jacob see when the police came for him. Sharma said Mark would have been under enormous stress. They had to give him time to compose himself. Had her coldness, on top of all that he was going through, caused him so much stress that with or without a car being involved, his heart was already primed to stop?

It was a painful, sobering thought.

She lifted her head high. She could support him by not acting like the wife of a guilty husband. Her defiant stare caused Julian to take note, his expression of sympathy changing to one of admiration.

'There she is. Fire back in her belly to go with the fire in her hair.'

She poked her tongue at him. 'Shut up, Julian. I'm scared witless.'

He stood up when she rose from the chair. 'Try not to worry. I will look after him, and call you if necessary.'

She knew he would do everything possible to get Mark well. She couldn't ask for anyone better than Julian in charge. It gave her peace of mind to know, whatever fate decided, Mark was in the best hands.

'Tell him I love him, Julian, if something suddenly happens.'

His voice was gentle, kind. 'I'll even hold his hand, Kate.'

She walked away from the comfort that Julian provided her, and managed to get outside the hospital before vomiting the sandwich her mum made her eat. She didn't want to contemplate anything happening while she wasn't there. She straightened and wiped her mouth, forced herself to move on.

Quickening her pace. Ignoring the sudden headache and waves of nausea, not allowing the discomfort to slow her down. Her husband was counting on her to make things right. This moment was her reset button.

CHAPTER TWENTY-FOUR

Kate stormed through her home like a whirlwind, jerking wardrobe doors and drawers open to find clothes, spare footwear, a travel pack of toiletries to stuff into an overnight bag. She grabbed passport, euros, phone charger. Snatched photos of Mark from a packet not yet assigned to an album. Then she went through Mark's suitcase and flight bag, collecting loose bits of paper and receipts he'd zipped into a side pocket and transferred them to her own luggage. Job done, she carted her bag down the stairs and dumped it in the hallway, reeling off demands as she rushed past her visitors.

'I need a flight, Robert, today to Barcelona! And a room booked at the hotel where you stayed.'

Robert stood there, raking his hand through his hair. 'What's happened? What's wrong?'

Kate could feel her frustration rising, but having no time to explain the unexpected situation. 'Tell you in a minute, I need to search Mark's car first. My passport is in the bag by your feet. The outside pocket.'

Olivia hadn't moved. Her face looked alarmed. 'Kate, are you ill?'

Her headache growing from the seesawing sickness in her stomach, she breathed in deeply, trying to control it. 'I'm fine, Olivia. I need you to write down your phone number for me, and in the zipped part of my handbag you'll find two hundred pounds in cash. Take it to use for whatever you need. Petrol, food, it doesn't matter, just take it now so I don't forget. I'll write down numbers for you as soon as I've searched Mark's car.'

'I have the keys,' Olivia said, disappearing to the kitchen to fetch them.

'What are you looking for?' Robert asked.

Kate looked at him then, checking his phone for a flight, and realised she hadn't asked him if he knew anything about it being missing. 'Mark's watch. He wants me to find it. I think it has something to do with what happened in Barcelona. Did he mention it?'

Robert was shaking his head, not lifting his gaze from the screen. 'No, never mentioned it.'

Kate studied his face. His lack of curiosity probed at her senses, telling her something was not right. Then he raised his eyes and looked at her with concern.

'Sorry, I was concentrating. Do you want me to help look?'

She rubbed her head and sighed. She was imagining deceit where there was none. 'No, you just get me a flight. Please.'

Olivia put the car keys in her hand, and she shook herself and focused on the last few tasks, telling herself to stop analysing Robert's behaviour. He was helping as best he could. She didn't need to hinder herself by having doubts about his character now. Or judge him for having feelings for her. It couldn't have been easy for him. Kate just wished she had known, so she could have helped him find someone else. Like Sophie used to do with her former suitors. Not that it was too late. Robert was a handsome man. Funny and intelligent. There was someone out there for him. Just not her.

Her search of the car found plenty of rubbish, but not

Mark's watch. Returning indoors, she went in the kitchen for her address book and underlined several numbers with a green pen. At the airport she'd forward them from her phone, but for now she was showing Olivia where they were written.

In the hallway, she showed her how to set the security alarm on the panel by the front door, and then the consumer unit inside the stair cupboard, in case of any problem with the electrics so she would know how to flip the circuit breaker to reset it.

Robert popped his head out of the sitting room. 'Kate, how many nights do you want to stay?'

'Two, just in case.'

He looked undecided. 'I can get you a flight at 18:05 with EasyJet. It'll get you to Barcelona at 21:10. Returning tomorrow with a choice of afternoon, evening or night flight. Alternatively, returning Friday 12:20 or 19:00 hours with Ryanair. Any idea what you'd prefer?'

She shook her head. 'Book me on a flight for tomorrow evening. If I don't get it, I'll have to book one for the next day.'

He nodded.

'What time is it now?'

'One forty-five. I'm leaving here at three. I can drop you at the airport. Then I'll be back on Sunday. Olivia's doing the school runs and will be here.'

Kate glanced at Olivia and saw her nod. 'Give me ten minutes,' she said to both of them. 'I just want to freshen up. Then I'll explain.'

In the bathroom, she ran a flannel under her arms and between her legs before chucking it in the laundry bin. She rinsed her face and brushed her teeth before going to the bedroom to find underwear and put on her travelling tracksuit – a black lightweight sweatshirt with matching pants to wear with comfortable trainers. She spent the remaining minutes searching under the bed, under the bedroom furniture, on the windowsill and surfaces, under items on the floor, but didn't find Mark's watch.

Mugs of tea were on the table when she returned, plus a glass of water, which Kate reached for to quench her raging thirst. She hadn't drunk anything since she threw up. It was no wonder she had a headache.

'You're a lifesaver,' she said to Olivia, knowing who it was she had to thank for looking after her.

Olivia's eyes were concerned. 'You looked like you were going to faint.'

Kate sat down to drink the tea, and Robert and Olivia joined her. Robert pushed her passport across the table. A folded sheet of paper between the pages. 'Flight details and Olivia's phone number. You have mine already, don't you?'

'Yes. Thanks, Robert, for all your help. I don't know what I'd have done if you hadn't turned up.'

He laughed. 'You mean like a bad penny?'

'No! I mean like you. Helping us out like you always do. We'd never have finished this house if not for you.'

He gave a reminiscent smile. 'Never thought it would end up looking so polished. You were right to go with just white décor throughout. Shows off the floor and doors. It almost killed me sanding them down. I wanted to kill you for buying Victorian doors that were painted when you were after natural wood. Did it on purpose, I used to think.'

She smiled back. 'Never did. It's just what they had in the yard that day. And it's not just white paint on the walls. It's All White, number two, zero, zero, five on the can.'

It took a moment for him to understand her meaning. Then a short sardonic laugh came back at her. 'You little snob, Kate Jordan. Name-dropping brands to impress us. Whatever next?'

Kate threw her head back, laughing, and had to catch her breath before she could reply. 'I lied.' She chortled with glee. 'We only have it in the hallway. The rest is Dulux.'

She calmed herself down, grateful for the release of tension. She felt normal for the first time in days. She glanced at Olivia, who was sitting across the table looking amused. 'I don't usually act this crazy. I'm putting it down to my unusual circumstances.'

'Here, here,' Robert agreed.

Kate explained what she was doing. 'Before I forget, can you please remember Jacob still doesn't know about his dad. And if Grace, my mum, calls, don't let her know I'm in Spain. I'll be letting her think I'm with Mark. I'm going now because tomorrow the doctor might bring Mark out of a coma. If Mark is compos mentis, which I'm praying he will be, there's a high likelihood he'll be arrested. Probably not tomorrow, or the next, but in the following days. I have to at least look for some way to prove him innocent. I'm going on a wing and a prayer, but I have to try and find something.'

Olivia rose to her feet and gave a small sigh. 'I have to go. I don't want to be late for your boy. I wish you the best of luck, Kate. And I'll pray for Captain Jordan.'

Kate got up and stepped around the table to hug her. 'Thanks, Olivia. And for looking after Jacob. I'll ring from the airport to say hello to him. You've taken the money, yes?'

'Yes, Kate. And he'll be fine. Please don't worry. I won't let him fret. And your mum's around if need be. It's only for a day or two. Nothing bad is going to happen in that time, I promise you.'

* * *

Bristol Airport had one terminal. Kate checked-in online, had her boarding pass on her phone, and only a carry-on bag, which speeded up her journey through security. She had wandered in and out of Superdrug, Dixons, Accessorize and WH Smith to fill in the time, and take her mind off her barely half-minute call with Jacob, which left her bereft of significance. His playing time took precedence over talking to her. Kate was relieved that he wasn't missing her and was happily occupied. But a twinge of disappointment had passed through her that he was so happy without her.

She shrugged it off and focused on the present as her gate number came up on the departures screen. Proceeding to the stairs she felt fluttering in her stomach, but this time she knew it was down to her apprehension about where this journey would take her.

CHAPTER TWENTY-FIVE

The ornate carving of the ceiling, and the tan, black and cream marble floor, felt instantly familiar as she walked in the hotel door. The receptionist, wearing a buttoned jacket and blouse, greeted her with a smile, and already knew her name.

'Doctor Jordan. Welcome back. How was your journey?'

Kate was impressed, considering she'd only stayed there once before. It could be she was the only guest checking in, and her name was already in the system, but it was a nice personal touch. 'Good, thank you.'

Kate handed her passport to the woman, noticing the name badge on her lapel. 'Am I too late to order some food, Camila?'

'No, you still have ten minutes. Room service closes at eleven.' She produced a menu. 'If you choose something now, I'll order it straight away.'

Kate scanned the menu. 'I'll have a margherita pizza, a bottle of water, and can you do a shandy?'

'Of course. Beer with lemon soda.'

'Wonderful.' Kate sighed. 'I'm famished and thirsty.'

Camila handed her a key card. 'You have a spacious room on the fourth floor, so may wish to take the lift in the lobby.'

Kate would. She was bone-tired. She wanted to strip off her clothes, lie on a bed and do nothing more strenuous than use her hands to eat. The room was indeed spacious. She was in what looked more like a suite. A super king-size bed, bathroom with a tub and separate shower, and a terrace with quality outdoor chairs. Kate stared in surprise, then wondered if Robert had something to do with the upgrade. The email Robert forwarded to her said a double room. She felt grateful to him, for the lift to the airport as well. He'd let her rest her mind while listening to classical music instead of talking.

She slipped off her trainers, then unzipped her holdall and took out the photographs of Mark. She felt an ache working its way through her chest, and a hotness behind her eyes, finding it hard to reconcile the smiling man in the pictures with the man trapped in a bed, a tube in his throat and paper tape keeping his eyelids closed to protect his corneas.

At the soft knock on the door, Kate set the photographs by the bed and opened the door, thanking the waiter for the tray. She'd been expecting a box, but the pizza was on a plate. She carried the food and shandy to the table on the terrace and gazed at the Sagrada Familia. She'd grown up in a city famous for its architecture and Roman remains. Bath was a beautiful city, the sandstone buildings soothing to the eye. When she had visited the Sagrada Familia in daylight last year, she'd found the gothic structures daunting, like a sinister castle in the sky. Gazing at it now at night time, illuminated, it was stunning.

She looked downwards to all the people out on the streets. Barcelona was still very awake. She munched through a large slice of pizza and drank half the shandy, shaking off the tiredness. She didn't have time to sleep. This was almost the time Mark left the hotel. She needed to follow in his footsteps.

Closing the door to the terrace, she put her trainers back on and retrieved a lightweight jacket from her bag. In the pockets she put the bottle of water and fifty euros in notes, before adding a photo to an inside pocket. She was going to see where Fleur O'Connell's murder happened, and en route search for a green parrot.

She'd only been walking a few minutes when she saw a police officer frantically talking on a radio as he crouched over a second officer on the ground. Kate could see the blanched face of the unconscious man and hurried forward to help.

'I'm a doctor,' she said to the officer on the radio, hoping he understood English.

He nodded and then spoke rapidly in Spanish. Kate picked up the word *doctura* while she knelt down and felt for breath against her cheek. She needed his jacket off to get at his chest. He wasn't breathing. Removing the mass of equipment adorning his torso, along with belted sidearms and with every single button fastened on the jacket, would take precious time that he couldn't afford to lose.

She mimicked the urgency of needing scissors to cut everything off. The officer momentarily stared aghast, before unclipping, unzipping, unfastening a uniform familiar to him. Kate couldn't have been faster with a pair of shears. The hairless chest now bared, she interlocked her fingers, placed her hands in the centre of his chest and pushed down and released twice per second.

'Defibrillator?' she asked urgently.

'Yes, yes, we have one!' the officer replied in perfect English. 'I get it now.'

Kate didn't look up to see where he went, keeping her neck aligned with her shoulders and elbows straight. His return no more than a minute later, and the clunking of a plastic box onto the ground, raised her head.

'Open it,' she instructed, hoping he was familiar with the AED.

'I take over from you,' was the answer.

Switching places, Kate opened the lid and turned the unit

on, selecting the option to choose English, listening to the voice prompts: 'Stay calm. Check for responsiveness. Remove clothes from patient's chest. Attach defibrillator pads.'

She had them already placed against the skin before being told.

The officer stopped compressions, hearing the automated voice commands: 'Stay clear of patient. Analysing heart rhythm. Please wait. Do not touch patient.'

Kate could hear praying in Spanish. A voice with rising and falling rhythm. Across from her, the officer was kneeling with hands in prayer. She noticed the thin pale scar across his cheek, the square jaw.

The automated voice sprang his hands apart.

'Move away from the patient. Preparing shock. Shock will be delivered in three, two, one... Shock delivered.'

Kate had to prompt him to carry on with CPR, as he appeared to be in shock.

'Keep going!' she encouraged firmly, while carrying out a head-tilt chin-lift to open the man's airway. They would have to continue for a minute or so before the AED wanted to analyse again.

'I am named Mateo,' he informed her.

He was in his thirties, she guessed, and appeared physically very fit. The sweat dripping down his face was probably caused more by fear than the arduous job of giving compressions.

'I'm Kate,' she said. Then, 'Hold on. Stop for a second.' She held her breath, concentrating on what she could feel, and now perceptibly see. A warmth against her cheek, a slight rise of the ribcage, a soft rebound against her fingertips from the neck. She released a deep breath of relief, and gave a thank you to the sky at the reassuring sound of an ambulance arriving.

Moments later, paramedics took over. Kate got to her feet on legs like jelly. It was only then she realised they had attracted an audience. People from a bar had come out on to the street to watch.

She glanced at what the paramedics were doing, and was relieved to see the ECG monitor showing the heart in sinus rhythm. She then stepped back.

'I need a drink,' she said to no one in particular, and walked towards the bar, only to be embarrassed by a round of applause.

'Kate!'

She turned. Mateo had called her.

'I need where you're staying to get details.'

Kate pointed at the hotel. 'There.'

'Okay, I come there tomorrow morning. Thank you for your help.'

While Kate sat and drank a glass of red wine, it occurred to her she may have inadvertently found a way to assist Mark's situation. Especially if the police officer survived. Mateo might be willing to talk to her about the case they had against her husband.

Fate had intervened on her behalf, putting her there at the right time to help, when only a short while before she'd been planning to go to the site of the murder. She wouldn't go now as she felt too drained. She would sip her wine instead and think about how meeting Mateo might help her.

She hoped he would be able to. She hoped coming here helped save more than one man's life.

CHAPTER TWENTY-SIX

She stopped at the reception desk the next morning to enquire if they had found a man's watch in the last two weeks. It didn't take long for them to check. While his colleague looked on a computer, the man taking charge went through a folder. Both searches came up negative. Kate thanked them and was about to walk away when she noticed the receptionist staring at her curiously.

'Doctor Jordan, is this the same enquiry made by Captain Jordan during his last stay?'

'Yes. He still hasn't located it, so I thought I'd check while I'm here.'

'We haven't found it either. Captain Jordan should have an email from me, Alvaro Fernandez. I'm the deputy manager. I'm sorry we haven't been successful. I searched his room after his departure and didn't find it. I advised him to report it to the police.' His attentive expression gave way to one of surprise at something behind her. 'And as if by magic, they appear.' He smiled.

Kate turned and saw Mateo entering the hotel. She thanked Alvaro Fernandez and moved away from the desk before he gave anything away. She didn't want Mateo alerted to the watch being missing. Though she suspected her visitor might now bring gossip. Connecting her to Captain Jordan was bound to cause talk among the staff. The police had been to the hotel to investigate the comings and goings of her husband.

'Shall we sit somewhere?' she suggested.

'Yes, that would be good. Allow me to buy you some coffee or tea if you prefer?'

The invitation, she hoped, was a good sign. She doubted he'd be here if his colleague was dead. Another officer would have come to get her details.

They sat at a table in the bar to wait for their drinks. The only customers being waited on.

'How are you today?' she asked him.

He wore a bemused expression on his face. His voice, slightly disjointed. 'That is the first time I had to do that to someone. I felt very sick after. Like the heart was in the mouth. I am not so scared to do it again, now I see it works.'

'That's great,' she said.

'Yes, my aunt thanks you greatly. She sends you a gift.'

It surprised Kate when he handed her a white jewellery box. She lifted the lid and saw, nestled on white satin, a rosary with glass beads in green and pinks and golden browns, a crucifix in silver.

'It's beautiful,' she said, looking at him. 'But I'm confused. Why is your aunt giving me a gift?'

He spread his hands and pulled a face, before stating what he thought was obvious. 'You save her son.'

Kate's eyes opened wide. 'He's your cousin?' she said in a shocked voice. 'Mateo, you must have been terrified!'

'I was! But now it is all good.'

A waiter arrived and placed coffees in front of them. Mateo looked more relaxed. She had written all her details on a sheet of paper for him, which would save time for talking about what was more important to her. She took it out of the pocket of her Lycra leggings – which she normally only wore in the gym, but they were perfect today for walking in – and handed it to him.

'This has my name, phone number, address in the UK, where I work, and my professional qualifications.'

It worked. He put the information in his jacket. It should leave plenty of time to talk, as their coffees were still untouched. She closed the lid on the rosary and put it on the table. Maybe it was a gift she could use as a bartering tool. An option to trade prayers in exchange for something good. 'Please thank your aunt for me. I shall treasure this.'

He raised his coffee cup. 'Good health, Kate.'

She raised hers to him. 'You too, Mateo. And to your cousin.'

After a few moments of silence, he asked the expected question. 'What brings you here?'

Kate wasn't sure how to begin. Did she tell him outright, or feel her way in? She went midway. 'My husband's in trouble with the police. I'm trying to prove he's innocent.'

She'd surprised him. He gazed at her, shifting in his seat, a sign of his unease. 'He is here with you in Barcelona?' he asked in a voice several octaves higher.

She shook her head. 'No. He's in a hospital in England, in a coma.'

His head pulled back in shock. '*Madre de Dios!*' he exclaimed in Spanish.

Kate understood. Mother of God.

'Why are you here, and not at home in England with a husband so ill?'

Kate took a deep breath. 'Because he is suspected of committing a serious crime here in Barcelona.'

She watched the penny drop.

'Oh no. No, no, no,' he repeated quietly to himself.

'Yes, Mateo. The police here think my husband murdered a woman.'

He shook his head at her. 'I cannot discuss anything of the investigation. You cannot ask me. If you wish, I can try for you to speak to the inspector, but he will not reveal evidence.'

Kate shivered. The decisiveness in his policeman's voice made her suddenly feel alone. Despite their unique connection, she was now sitting opposite an unwilling stranger. Her mouth trembled, and her eyes welled with tears. It was not intentional. She needed to stay in control. She swiped at her face, then stood up.

His voice stilled her movements. 'What are you hoping to find?'

She took a deep breath to calm her nerves and sat back down. 'Anything that will help. You don't know my husband, Mateo. He would never kill someone, no matter the provocation. I'm going to try to find out why he left the hotel, because there will be a reason that has nothing to do with committing a murder. And now, if you'll excuse me, I have a green parrot to search for.'

She was out of the hotel doors and halfway along the street before he caught up with her. In his hand he held the white jewellery box. Kate took it from him and placed it in her jacket. She hadn't intentionally left it on the table.

He shook his head in exasperation. 'I don't know any place or building with the name green parrot, but I know a bar that has parrots painted on the walls.'

He gave her a white card with the emblem of the *Guardia Urbana de Barcelona* and the address and telephone number of the police force. And on the back, the name of the bar.

'It could be,' he added, 'referring to monk parakeets. Barcelona's little green parrots, thousands of them you will see in palm trees. The bar with parrots on the wall is a gay bar.

Forty kilometres away, in Sitges. I don't think this is the place you want.'

'Thank you,' she said.

She walked away before taking out the map she took from the hotel. Mateo was probably right. She couldn't imagine Mark being gay as an explanation for his absence. A trip to this bar would be a waste of her time. She would make the journey to the crime scene that she could not take last night because of helping save Mateo's cousin.

And hope one good turn begets another.

CHAPTER TWENTY-SEVEN

Kate walked aimlessly for a while, taking in the sights of Catalonia Square, its fountains and statues attracting flocks of tourists. It was a starting point for the main arteries, such as Las Ramblas, Passeig de Gracia, Portal de l'Angel. Kate headed to the bar where the crew went on New Year's Eve, near where Fleur O'Connell was murdered.

The passageways became more compact with tapas bars, cafés, places to eat. She glanced in the windows of an Ale Hop shop, and at the black and white cow standing outside it. She gazed at the many bars of soap in the *Farmacia*, at the boxes of cigars in a *Tabacs*, all the time hoping to find what she was searching for – Mark's watch hanging on a door with a green parrot.

She stopped to take a drink of water. Looking toward the narrow passageways, she saw something flapping in the gentle breeze, tied to a grey metal barrier. She walked towards it and read the blue words highlighted in capitals.

NO PASSEU. POLICIA.

She stood motionless, staring at the flowers in the cordoned off part of the street. A narrow walkway formed with more barriers allowed people to walk past the area where the body was found. Kate tore her eyes away, the queasiness of yesterday returning in full force, making her feel sick. She cupped her hand over her forehead, trying to bring coolness to her skin, before negotiating a path between the people standing behind her.

A further barrier, formed of tourists, forced her to take the walkway. A middle-aged woman in a black dress stared glumly at people passing her shop window. The sign on the door of the patisserie said *CERRADO*. Kate remembered reading the incident took place outside a patisserie, while the owners slept undisturbed above the shop.

She threaded her way around people stopping to look, until she was past them and it was possible to pick up the pace. A minute later, she was at the door of the bar. She entered and noted the vaulted ceiling and bottles of wine lining the walls. Traditionally Spanish, with Catalan tiles in the décor. A long bar on one side, small tables opposite, offered plenty of places where one could eat and drink. She sat at an unoccupied barrel table with two stools, away from the groups drinking.

A smiling waitress appeared almost at once and addressed Kate in English. 'What would you like?'

She hadn't had time to think about what she'd like so chose a glass of white wine and a *patatas bravas*, the only tapas she could remember.

While waiting, Kate took out the photograph of Mark. When the waitress returned, she showed her the photo and recognition sparkled her eyes. 'This is your husband?'

Kate nodded and saw her interest grow. She climbed on the stool opposite, and presented Kate with an earnest expression. 'Last time, I tell him I want a job on aeroplanes. My English is good. He says he is happy to give me a reference. My service to customers is good. Will you remind him for me, please?'

'What's your name?' Kate asked.

'Valentina.'

'Well, Valentina, I will tell him I spoke to you. Can I ask you now for some help?'

'Of course,' she responded with enthusiasm.

'Do you know anywhere that has a parrot on a door?'

Her eyebrows raised in surprise. 'A real parrot?'

'I don't think so. Maybe a painting or a carving?'

'I never hear of this. Only the real birds we have here.' She rubbed her forehead, looking worried.

Kate intervened. 'It doesn't matter. It wasn't important.'

She was relieved, and free now to leave Kate and go back to her work.

Kate sipped the wine, thinking about Valentina's reaction to Mark. She was grateful the waitress was unaware his name was linked to the murder. Kate hoped it never became public. Leaving half the wine and most of the potato dish, she took twenty euros out of her pocket and put it on the table. As she made for the door, a man from a nearby table beckoned her over. His elegant jacket and tie, and long sleek ponytail, gave him an exotic look.

Kate curiously approached.

'You have a map?' he asked.

She nodded, and placed the tourist pamphlet on the table.

He scanned it, then tapped his finger on a street. 'You look for a building with large glass doors with a pale green arch. A parrot is on the door.'

His serious expression unnerved her. She couldn't place his accent. 'Thank you,' she replied. 'My husband lost a watch, that's what I'm looking for.'

His lips curved in a cynical smile. 'Good luck, and watch out for the pickpockets.'

Feeling slightly disorientated, she headed back out onto the streets, unconsciously keeping her hands in her pockets around the jewellery box and her phone, alert at anyone coming too close to her.

Then buoyed by the possibility of finding this place, she followed the map.

Twenty minutes later, Kate stared at her destination, nonplussed. The glass door had a handle in the shape of a pale green parrot. Across the windows, dusty banners stating: *Cerrado Permanentement.*

She peered in at the white walls, her gaze automatically dropped to the floor. No sign of a watch. No sign of life. No sign of what had been here.

She rested her forehead against the glass, then yelped as someone touched her shoulder. She whirled around to be confronted by an old woman holding out a begging bowl. The woman seemed impervious to Kate's fright. Kate's eyes fixed on the few coins in the wooden dish, and pulled from her pocket a paper note to the value of ten euros. The woman bowed before scurrying away.

Her heart rate slowed, and disappointment dragged at her feet, she began the walk back to the hotel. She had assumed finding this place was important. But it was a dead end. Whatever the building had been, the place was now permanently shut.

She glanced at the length of the busy major road that seemed to stretch on forever. Carrer d'Arago, she recalled, was a thoroughfare in Barcelona that went on for miles. It cut through many districts, where she was yet to explore. Along with four thousand five hundred other streets. The realisation of the extent of the task, which she could never hope to complete, gave her a sudden inexplicable urge to scream at the passing traffic like a madwoman. At the God who wasn't listening. A rosary in her pocket hadn't helped. There was no one to hear her prayers.

CHAPTER TWENTY-EIGHT

The hotel loomed up ahead. Kate wasn't ready to face her luxury room. She'd rather tuck away her failure in the comfort of a café. And maybe get very slightly drunk. She carried on walking past the hotel until she came to a taverna that looked quiet and dark inside. She went in and sat on a red plastic stool at the bar, and gazed around at the mismatched furnishings. Pub stools, dining room chairs, and the odd armchair in leather or cloth, went with an array of shapes and sizes of tables. Eclectic artwork, abstract paintings, photographs, and ceramics on the walls, and shelves of old books. Kate found it distracted her perfectly, which was all for the good.

The bartender, in black T-shirt and apron, was watching for her reaction. His white moustache and sprinkle of hair gave him a friendly demeanour.

He gestured at the wall. 'You like? Or not?'

'I like,' Kate said with a smile.

'For that, your first drink is free. It's the work of my children and grandchildren. Not that any of them will be a Goya or Picasso. But they try.' He placed a glass in front of her. 'Red or white?'

'Red. Thank you.'

'You here on holiday?'

'No. I'm here looking for something.'

'Mhm... You looking for work?'

'No. I have a job in England. I'm trying to help my husband out of a situation. But I've not been successful.'

He held his hand out to shake hers. 'I am Paulo. It is a problem for you now?' he asked.

'A big problem, Paulo. My husband may go to prison.'

'Aye yai yai,' he exclaimed.

Kate reached in her jacket for the photograph and placed it down on the bar.

Paulo gave another cry of surprise. 'I know him! I know this man!' His entire face showed amazement. 'This is Mark!'

She watched in astonishment as he rushed from behind the bar and turned the sign around on the door. Closed for business. He went back behind the bar and poured himself a brandy before coming back to her.

'You must tell me what has happened. This man never makes trouble. He is one of the good guys.'

She couldn't speak for a moment. Meeting someone who knew Mark was monumental. 'I'm Kate,' she said croakily. Then she told him about the trouble Mark was in.

His head was bowed by the time she finished. It seemed from his stillness that he had concluded Mark was not one of the good guys. He began by shaking his head from side to side, his chin disappearing into his chest. He looked at her.

'No, no, no, this is not possible. I know when this happened. It happened when Mark was here.' He pointed to the floor around their feet. 'I look for his watch with him here!'

He was shaken. He downed the drink in his hand.

Kate wondered if she was asleep and dreaming. He sounded so sure. It scared her to believe him. 'But they say there is a witness!' she cried woefully, to stop him from raising her hopes.

He stared at her hard. 'I tell you, it's not possible. This person makes mistake. Or lies. Maybe someone pay this person to lie? We call the police. We do it now!'

It was happening so fast, Kate couldn't think. There had to be holes in his story. She latched onto the only thing she could think of. 'But you don't have a green parrot.'

'Aye yai yai,' he exclaimed for the second time, only now with concern for her. 'How much have you had to drink?'

She showed him her still full glass. 'I'm not drunk. I've spent the day looking for a green parrot on a door, because Mark asked me to look for his watch, and said a green parrot was on the door.'

Paulo considered her carefully, frowning hard. Then a weak smile appeared on his face. He pointed a finger in the air. Then tutted mildly, bending down behind the bar, muttering to himself, before surfacing with a bundle of children's drawings in his hands.

'You find your parrot in there. Emilio. *El nino*. Only six. Likes to compete with his papa. Puts his drawings all over the place.'

She found Emilio's drawing. Definitely a green parrot with an orange beak, a good likeness. She fetched out the business card Mateo gave her and showed it to Paulo.

'I shall call him,' she said.

'No, no, I make the call. I am new witness. And I know the chief.'

Kate realised she was nervous. She didn't want to wait to hear Paulo was wrong. But she didn't want to leave either. This place was like a sanctuary. She felt the gift in her pocket, and hoped he was right that the police would listen to him and agree.

* * *

'Go home, Doctor Jordan.'

Kate didn't need telling twice. The short man with jet-black hair and olive skin was issuing an order. She couldn't read his face. She had no idea if this superintendent's opinion had changed. His manner was austere, and Kate felt unwelcome.

Paulo, on the other hand, was unfazed by the high-ranking officer and police guards. He spoke in rapid Spanish, and Kate couldn't tell if it was in anger or just an assertive conversation. She watched bemused as he stepped close to the superintendent and took him by the shoulders, talking right into his face. She expected the guards to step forward, but was surprised when they laughed instead.

Paulo then turned to her. 'Come, Kate, we now go. This is no longer my workplace. We leave Bernardo to do good work.'

Kate rose to her feet. Then Paulo responded to something the superintendent was saying, his tone now easy to interpret. He was vexed.

'*Si, si. No le estoy diciendo nada. Nada!*' he snapped, clicking his fingers in the air. Then, moderating his tone with Kate. 'Come, we leave the man with his headache to sort out, while you get on a plane.'

Outside the building, Kate caught her breath. She had sat more than an hour in a chair in an office listening to the back and forth intense conversation between two men, in a language she couldn't speak or understand. Bernardo was not the only one with a headache.

She was curious to understand. 'Were you a police officer, Paulo?'

He glanced at the building. 'Yes, but now I retire.'

Paulo drove her in a small dusty van from the police station to the hotel, where he then parked.

'I don't come in with you, Kate. We say goodbye now.'

She looked at him, alarmed, not expecting their parting to be so abrupt.

'What happens now?' she asked.

He gave a gallic shrug. 'The superintendent now decides. He has something, that I'm not at liberty to tell you. He has to decide about this evidence.'

Kate's eyes turned fearful. 'How serious is the evidence?'

'Very serious,' he mused. 'I've been in his shoes. You follow the evidence wherever it leads. Right to the door.'

'So, it's not over then?' She shook her head forlornly.

'Not over yet, Kate. But you need to go back and get British police to find the person who hit Mark with a car.'

She was taken aback. 'How did you know about that?'

'I know, because Bernardo knows. The British police tell him everything. They don't catch someone yet. You need to be suspicious of that.'

She looked at him carefully, not entirely sure what he was suggesting. His warning tone was telling her to take him seriously. She was already suspicious, not of the accident, but of everything else that had happened. She wasn't doubting it was all too strange. It's why she came to Spain. To find answers. Paulo had given her plenty.

Kate had a horrible notion of what the evidence the Spanish police had might be. Something that tied Mark to the crime scene. They would need to look no further than the inscription on the back of the watch:

Captain Mark Jordan. Cleared to land.

CHAPTER TWENTY-NINE

With renewed purpose in her step, Kate exited through the doors of Bristol Airport. Climbing into a taxi, she gave instructions to take her to the hospital in Bath. It would be late when she arrived. She was nervous about what she would find. Julian hadn't called or sent any update, so maybe nothing had changed. Kate had no idea what to expect.

She hadn't notified Robert or Olivia that she caught the return flight, as it could be gone midnight before she got home. It might even be morning if she stayed all night in the hospital. It all depended on how things were with Mark.

Drizzling rain accompanied her on the forty-minute journey, making it miserably wet, with trees dripping, and roads and pavements soaked. A sharp contrast to the weather she left behind. The driver took her to the main entrance, and Kate hurried inside, only to stop and slow her pace. She was suddenly afraid to make the five-minute walk. Scared of what she would find.

She trudged along the silent corridor to the intensive care unit. She stood and stared at the door, knowing once she pressed the bell there was no turning back. Then an image of

Mark in his bed forced aside her cowardliness. For everything he was going through, he'd been alone without her. In sickness and in health, she vowed. For as long as he needed her, she would be there. Changed or unchanged, he was her husband.

She glanced around the ward, deliberately leaving Mark's bed till last. Walking slowly to it, knowing her first sight could tell her everything. Kate stood at the end of the bed and noticed the absence of the paper tape on his eyelids. She sensed a slight movement behind her, before Julian put his hand on her shoulder.

'You made it back then,' he quietly acknowledged.

'Yes. Just now.'

'We started tapering the medication at four o'clock. Hopefully, we'll start seeing some early responses.'

Kate held her breath, while her eyes fixed on Mark's face, not wanting to miss even the tiniest flicker of an eyelash.

Julian squeezed her shoulder. 'It could be a while. You know that, don't you, Kate?'

Theoretically she did, but it was many years since her stint in ICU. Her memories of coma patients waking were few. The ones that stuck in her mind were because something happened, like violent seizures, aggressive behaviour, an inability to breathe on their own. She remembered the four stages of recovery, the wait to determine their prognosis. Mark was yet to reach stage two. He was still at stage one, unresponsive.

'I'll fetch you a cup of coffee,' Julian said. 'You just sit and talk to him.'

Kate glanced at him. 'Thank you for looking after him.'

'De nada,' he replied, making a light joke about where she had been.

'It went better than I hoped,' she whispered, conscious of being by Mark's bed. 'I found a witness, a retired Spanish police officer. He runs a bar. He can give Mark an alibi. But he's not the one who gets to decide if Mark is innocent.'

Julian breathed in deeply and gave a long sigh. 'My fingers are crossed, Kate.' He walked away, returning with a coffee a minute later, before leaving her to her thoughts.

Kate pulled her chair close to the bed and held Mark's hand, finding comfort in its familiarity. They held hands when walking, and sometimes when in bed. She couldn't remember a time when they didn't hold hands.

She talked to Mark, telling him this, and about the time he helped her up a hill in the Brecon Beacons, while she moaned it was more of a mountain. She talked about how they met, him fixing her car, their first date, kayaking on the Kennet and Avon Canal from Bath to Dundas Wharf, their wedding night, when she discovered him wearing odd socks, one black and one blue. She talked about Jacob's birth when he held him in his arms and didn't want to let go.

Kate talked throughout the night, sometimes interrupting herself, to tell him about something happening right then, about the nurse attending him and what she was doing. When dawn arrived, she told him what time and what day it was, teasing him about being asleep when it was about time he was awake.

At just after seven, Kate got up from the chair. Her stubborn husband was not responding, stuck in the first stage. She didn't want to consider how long it had been, and what it might mean. She was determined to cover up any trace of fear on her face or in her voice. Mark mustn't pick up her fear, or he might not put up the fight to come back. He might give in to the deepest slumber, where she would never reach him.

She kissed his eyelids. 'I'll see you later, lazybones. I'm popping home to give our son a hug, and then I'll be back, so be warned. I'll be talking dirty in your ear later. No more tame topics for you. You need a shake-up.'

Shoulders back, her spine straight, she walked back through the corridors, forcing herself to stay positive. Everything would be all right. Unaware that her expression betrayed her, the deep-seated fear in her eyes was hard to ignore in a face so white. She looked like a relative who had just received bad news.

She paid for another taxi journey from the two hundred pounds found in the zipped part of her handbag, which Olivia hadn't taken. Kate discovered this only a few minutes ago while sitting in the back seat. She'd have to force it on the woman by the looks of it. She wished now she'd bought her some perfume on the plane. As it was, she was walking in empty-handed with nothing to give her or Jacob.

Back at the house, Kate headed to the kitchen where she could hear them talking, and was amazed to see Jacob eating a cooked breakfast. Skinny sausages and poached eggs. Normally, on a school day, he'd have cornflakes or Weetabix.

He jumped up in excitement and dashed towards her, flinging his arms around her waist. Over his head, Olivia smiled and offered her a cup of tea, using sign language with her fore-fingers to make the letter T. Kate nodded, appreciating her unobtrusiveness in allowing her to say a proper hello to her son. Kate sat with him at the table, letting him talk and eat at the same time. She drank in his happiness and marvelled at his confidence. Her shy little boy was finding his feet.

At the sight of Barney shuffling into the kitchen, Kate blinked back tears. She watched his progress, stopping at her to be stroked, before ambling onwards for his breakfast. In his bowl, already prepared, was what looked like cooked minced beef with chopped carrots. From a beige and blue box on the counter, Olivia pressed out a tablet from a blister pack and pushed it into Barney's food with her finger. She showed Kate the medication that she had given Barney.

A dog and cat image was on the front, with the words: Nutraquin – Everyday support for joints and mobility. On the back: Recommended by vets across the UK and Ireland.

Kate expressed her approval by holding her palm against

her chest in a gesture of gratitude. She saw that Olivia had replaced the breeze blocks and tray with an elevated dog feeder that looked brand new, so she shook her head in amazement and broke the silence between them. 'You, missus, are a wonder!'

With a little shake of her head, Olivia denied the compliment, but Kate could see she was pleased.

Kate looked at the clock and realised she should get ready to leave if she wanted Jacob to be at school on time. But Olivia already had things in hand.

'JJ, when the big hand gets to six, I'll meet you by the front door. Your shoes, jacket and backpack are in the hall. I'm just going to put on socks quickly, so my feet don't rub.'

A quick kiss from Jacob, a rush from the kitchen, footsteps sprinting up the stairs. The big hand hit six, and Kate heard the front door closing, leaving her quietly stunned. She had a vague sense that everything she just witnessed was all for the good. It was just so unexpected. The performance looked like they carried it out every day, instead of happening overnight. She had a Mary Poppins living with her, she mused, administering to everyone's needs. Her behaviour was almost too good to be true. Kate hoped she didn't have a measuring tape that found Kate lacking in practically every way.

She squeezed her eyes shut to push out the mean thought, unhappy with herself for looking for faults. The slight misgivings about her character were down to plain old jealousy, because Jacob had taken to her so well, and a mother's resentment at hearing her son's new nickname. JJ.

It fit, of course. His initials. Jacob Jordan. Kate just wasn't sure if she wanted him to be called JJ. She should check about Olivia as she'd intended, to put her mind at rest. She fetched out her phone to call Diane Atwell. The woman had worked for the airline for donkey's years. Kate had been to her home for dinner. As a cabin manager, Diane was bound to know Olivia.

Kate left a voice message when Diane didn't pick up, asking for her to give her a call back.

Ignoring her sense of guilt, she got up from the bench and washed the few breakfast dishes. There was little to do as Olivia had cleaned the pots and cooker after their use. Everywhere looked more tidy. She dried her hands on a tea towel, then went to check the other rooms.

The downstairs loo had Harpic around the bowl. The small sink looked cleaned. The crusty limescale was gone from the taps. It was an annoyance that Kate continually battled, because of the hard water. Last week she soaked cotton wool in white vinegar and attached it to the spouts with elastic bands. It worked, but not this well. She would ask Olivia her secret.

She opened the sitting room door and gave a small gasp. She felt almost overwhelmed with emotion. This was not the same room as yesterday. She never imagined it could look so good. She stared around, feeling an excitement in her chest. The suede sofas now faced each other, instead of at an ad hoc L-shape, to watch TV. The blanket box centred between them, styled with a pyramid of books, a set of woven coasters, and a heavy glass bowl which she hadn't seen before. She instantly fell in love with it – the smoky-brown colour with thin strokes of gold, the thickness of the base and rim, but most of all its creative irregular shape. Kate wondered where Olivia found it. She wanted to pay her, however much it cost. It looked expensive.

Her delight continued as she noticed the small dark-green armchair, now by the bookcase creating a reading corner, with a side table and the low footstool from the spare bedroom. Then in the second alcove, the rustic cabinet had been cleared of all the random ornaments, and too many picture frames, leaving only a black-and-white photograph of Kate and Mark on their wedding day and a large wooden candle holder with a cream pillar candle in it.

Kate didn't want to go into the room, preferring her view from the door. She admired the way Olivia had placed the cushions and throws and lamps. She wanted to clap her hands. Coming home to find this was a special kind of medicine and gave her the same feeling as Paulo's place. A sanctuary where she could sit and feel safe and let her mind drift away from all the worry.

Barney nosed past her, looking for his bed, which Kate hadn't noticed until Barney settled down on the far side of the sofa.

Her lips curved. It was perfect.

CHAPTER THIRTY

Robert sensed a note of discord between him and the new recruit, Kerry Hall. After behaving nicely to the other crew members, happily chatting to them, her short answers to him were becoming difficult to ignore. Clive, the captain, just raised his eyebrows at her blunt 'No, thank you,' to the offer of a second drink.

It was obvious by the manner in which she was speaking he had upset her, but for the life of him, he couldn't think how. He'd barely passed time with her. The negativity jarred him. He'd just wanted a cup of coffee, to unwind before their departure to Dusseldorf. And now he was feeling like fish gone off. She looked like a nice, sensible, young woman, but maybe she was the unsettled type, prone to dramas, with imagined wrongs, craving a listening ear. He'd have a word with the purser when he got the chance and let him handle the situation.

The opportunity came a few minutes later when she excused herself to go to the ladies'. He edged closer to Martin Samworth. 'Do you know if anything's up with Kerry?'

Martin used his eyes to signal now was not a good time.

Keeping his voice low, he spoke out of the side of his mouth. 'I'll tell you later.'

Robert gave a brief nod and hoped he wasn't going to hear some minor complaint, like she felt slighted because she hadn't been invited to sit in the flight deck for a take-off or landing yet. Or was miffed because he corrected her greeting to the passengers – 'Hello,' or 'Good morning,' rather than 'Hiya,' would be a better way to welcome them.

Considering how new she was, it was surprising that she was showing ill will towards a colleague, especially as he was second in command of the aircraft. He was old school, and expected at least a slight deference towards anyone in authority. The same as he expected of himself, to show he had respect for others.

She returned to her chair and Robert smiled politely. She averted her eyes and engaged in conversation with Martin. Robert would bide his time, and was now more curious than vexed by her behaviour. The purser might have something interesting to tell him. He rose from his seat, deciding a visit to the gents before boarding would be a sensible idea.

A few minutes later, Martin joined him at the handbasins. He was a wiry individual with tightly cropped grey hair, and someone Robert respected. The airline would do well to use his character traits as the standard expected of new recruits. But maybe such things were becoming less important, and perhaps that was how Ms Hall got through the door.

Before speaking, Martin checked the toilet cubicles were empty. He looked troubled. 'Anyone comes in, I'll stop talking.'

'Okay,' Robert agreed.

'She's upset about Captain Jordan, and the interview she had with the police.'

Robert felt his jaw tighten. He rinsed his hands, noting the tiny scabs on his knuckles, and reached for some paper towels.

He let Martin hear the coolness in his voice. 'Really? Well, I hope she's not talking about Mark to anyone else.'

Martin shook his head. 'I don't think she is. She's upset about you as well.'

Robert looked at him pointedly and exhaled a sharp breath. 'You don't say,' he drawled with heavy sarcasm. 'And tell me, how have I upset Ms Hall?'

The slight inclination of his head and down-turned mouth forebode an unpleasant answer. 'This business in Barcelona. She thinks it might have been you.'

Martin's words rang in his ears. As much as he didn't want to hear it, he needed Martin to expand on his explanation. 'What does she mean by that?'

Martin's brow furrowed. He looked burdened. 'Look, I'm just going to repeat what she said, because you need to know. The police asked her if she saw Mark from ten p.m. onwards. She said she did, at around eleven. She saw him in the foyer. What's upset her is, she says she saw you not long after, going out the hotel door. She's got it in her head that you somehow implicated Captain Jordan in this crime.'

Robert had to concentrate to keep an impassive face. Showing his shock would make him look guilty. He needed to assess the damage. Come to terms with the cold, hard fact that this was karma knocking on his door. He sounded bewildered. 'She really thinks it might have been me? Has she told this to the police?'

Martin shook his head. 'No.'

Robert's eyes narrowed. 'Why hasn't she, if she believes this? I don't understand.'

'They didn't ask about you, Robert. They asked about Captain Jordan. Kerry just answered the questions they asked her.'

Robert sighed heavily. 'Christ, Martin. No wonder she's giving me the evil eye. But what do I do? Mark's completely innocent and look what's happened to him. They're going to arrest him as soon as he wakes from the coma.'

He leaned over the sink.

Martin clapped a hand on his shoulder. 'Robert, try not to worry. I shouldn't have told you this before a flight.'

Robert didn't reply. He was thinking about what to do. A dozen scenarios flitting around his head. A vague idea formed. It was a gamble. He talked under his breath, testing the concept. He'd never been able to turn his back on danger. He owed Mark. He had Kate and Jacob to consider. There was really no other choice to make.

He turned and faced Martin, ready to share his decision. 'Mark said a witness gave a description of a man with dark hair, someone tall, mid-thirties to mid-forties. I'm thirty-eight, and two inches taller than Mark. I think Kerry should go to the police. It will help Mark by giving them a second suspect.'

Martin looked appalled. 'And what if they arrest you?'

Robert frowned. That wouldn't happen. He'd always felt he was living on the periphery of his life, waiting for it to start. His wishful thinking had brought him to this. He had to kick himself out of the equation. He had to want for Mark to survive, and to have a chance of being free. There'd be no real satisfaction in winning Kate otherwise.

He had to allow fairness to take a part, because Mark was not the only one who left the hotel.

'Robert, don't be hasty. You really could be arrested.'

Robert just shrugged his shoulders. 'If it happens, it happens.' He realised then how little he was worried – finding it hard to believe that what had happened so far was real. He glanced at the purser. 'Don't sweat it, Martin. They won't find any evidence.'

CHAPTER THIRTY-ONE

After showering and changing into clean clothes, Kate denied herself the opportunity to sleep, and found Detective Sharma's business card instead, requesting an update on the vehicle that hit Mark. She was relieved when he agreed to meet her at the hospital, rather than have her drive to a police station in Bristol.

Sharma was on his own, sitting on the same metal bench in the corridor with two lidded coffees in his hands. He stood up to greet her and waited until she sat down before handing her the hot beverage.

'How is he?' he asked, almost immediately.

Kate gave him an appraising glance, not letting him off with a polite response. 'I'm sure you already know. They're trying to wake him. They haven't had any success so far.'

She lifted her hand to press the corner of her eye before a tear rolled down. She didn't have the energy to deal with tears.

To her surprise, Sharma's gaze locked on her face to show he genuinely sympathised. 'My grandmother had a bleed on the brain. It was traumatic for my father to sit by her bed waiting for a response.'

Kate wanted to be annoyed with the detective, but she couldn't after hearing this. 'How is she now?' she asked quietly.

He gave a little shake of his head. 'She was seventy-seven. There wasn't much they could do.'

Kate glanced at him again. 'I'm sorry.'

Sharma shifted in his seat and emitted a small sigh. 'I'm the one who should be sorry. I shouldn't offload personal history. You have your own difficulties to contend with.'

Kate liked him better. Or at least had come closer to a better feeling towards him, where before there was only distrust. She felt more confident to air her grievances.

'I was in Barcelona yesterday, where I met the superintendent in charge of the murder investigation. Bernardo. I didn't get his surname. I didn't want to ask, as he seemed in a bad mood,' she said with a rueful smile.

Sharma was staring at her agog. Kate continued, not giving him a chance to speak.

'You see, a strange thing happened that you, in fact, might find quite remarkable. I went in to a bar, ready to give up and come home, and in between a free glass of wine for appreciating some artwork and an honest admission of why I was visiting, I found a new witness. Name of Paulo, who is a retired police officer, took me to meet the superintendent.

'Paulo, whose surname I also don't know, not only recognised Mark from his photograph, he was with him on the night of the murder while it was happening. He and Mark were in Paulo's bar. Now don't you find that interesting?'

Sharma looked speechless. Kate felt pleased to have shocked him. He got to his feet and crossed to the other side of the corridor to stand in front of the window. She had finally been able to give him some proof of her husband's innocence. Now she wanted to know what he was thinking.

Sharma eventually turned around to face her. 'I expect you're now hoping for me to reassure you. But your husband will remain a suspect until advised differently. An arrest warrant has been issued by an EU country's judicial authority for the purpose of a detention order. Since Brexit, the UK agrees to facilitate cooperation between EU member states and the UK in relation to law enforcements. Under the agreement, an arrest warrant may be issued for the prosecution of any offence which carries a custodial sentence of at least twelve months.'

Her mouth had gone dry. Sharma wasn't listening. Did he not understand what she had just said? Her husband was innocent while he was standing there spouting about the law!

He sighed heavily. 'Did you not consider the appropriateness of your actions? You went there looking for evidence—'

'Yes!' she hissed, interrupting him. 'To prove him innocent!'

He shook his head slowly. 'No, Doctor Jordan. In Superintendent Perez's eyes, you went to their country to look for evidence to hide his guilt!'

Kate made a sound like a battle cry as she shot up from the seat. She took a step, and then another, towards him, her anger rising in a torrent of rage. She drew her breath in deeply and spoke with ice in her voice. 'I went there because he is innocent. Do you honestly think an ex-police officer, one of their own, would put himself forward if he thought Mark was guilty?' Kate dwelled on what Paulo said. *They don't catch someone yet. You need to be suspicious of that.*

She shook her head in disgust. She squared up to the man in front of her. 'Try this one for size, Detective Sharma. Have you found the person responsible for driving the car that hit Mark? I suppose you're going to tell me you have no information. That in all the looking for this vehicle, no one has spotted it. Tell me I'm wrong.'

Sharma looked away. A note of weary irritation in his voice as he said, 'Without a description of the vehicle, it's a matter of looking at all cars that could have exited that lane, via any

number of other country lanes, before meeting a road with
cameras. It's a case of searching hours and hours of CCTV on
the day, the hours leading up to the incident and the hours after.
Not to mention all the hundreds of places where the car could
have parked before reaching a camera. So far, we have
contacted dozens upon dozens of drivers. We cleared all of
them. So we continue to look.'

'It's a needle in a haystack, isn't it?' she questioned deri-
sively. 'The driver hasn't come forward as you hoped,' she
reminded him, scathingly. Her anger showing no sign of
abating.

'Look, I understand your frustration—'

'Oh, do you? I don't think you do, Detective Sharma. I don't
think you could possibly imagine my level of frustration. To
have an innocent husband a suspect? Frustration is not what
you feel. It's annihilation.'

'I do understand,' he said again. 'It's part of my job to realise
the effect it has on a family when a member of it is being investigated for a serious crime. I'm not immune to the suffering.' He
sighed heavily. 'What I will tell you is, I hope this new witness
can refute the compelling evidence. I will be happy for you if
that happens. I'm not wishing for your husband to be guilty. I'm
wanting justice for Fleur O'Connell. The two things are not
mutually exclusive. But until directed otherwise, we have to
conduct this investigation.'

The conversation had come to an end. Her fired up anger
left her frazzled. She sat alone in the corridor after Sharma
departed, thinking of everything he said. It shook her to hear
him say the Spanish police considered her visit suspicious,
when she thought she might have their support. Perhaps it was
why Paulo pressed her to look more closely at the accident. He
wanted her to find a new angle to prove Mark's innocence.

It was as if Paulo wasn't surprised that they hadn't caught
someone. He was inferring the accident was related somehow to

the murder in Barcelona. She couldn't see how, unless someone put a hit on Mark, which seemed ludicrous. And what would be the point when Mark was already a suspect, set to get the blame? Mark couldn't go anywhere – the stable door was already bolted.

Unless it was to make him look guilty – suicidal in the eyes of the police. If that was the reason, it had worked. No one was thinking the accident was suspicious in terms of him being deliberately targeted. Only Paulo seemed to think it suspicious.

In her mind's eye, she saw Mark walking along the lane, perhaps occupied with his thoughts. He doesn't worry about hearing a car driving normally. He's not thinking he's going to be hit. He just feels it when it happens, when he hits the ground.

She shuddered, imagining the moment of impact. The fear he would have felt. He may even have heard the car drive away, leaving him there. It didn't make any sense to her. Why would the driver risk leaving Mark as a witness, when he might identify the vehicle and maybe even the driver? It made more sense to leave him dead... Want him dead.

Her breath suddenly caught in her throat, her thoughts narrowing on a malignant and twisted theory. Were they intending to leave him there dead? Did they drive away thinking the mission was successful? The British pilot still a suspect, but now dead. Case closed.

And the real killer is free.

CHAPTER THIRTY-TWO

Kate gave consent for the electroencephalogram, a test to record the electrical activity in the brain. Her voice was hoarse after her anger at the detective, but mostly from talking to Mark throughout the night after getting back from Barcelona. She should really be in bed catching up on sleep. She could rest her voice during Mark's painless sixty-minute procedure.

She waited outside the curtains, hovering by the nurses' station. The gap in the curtain drew her eyes. Mark's head, covered in wires and resembling something alien, brought nausea to her stomach, forcing her to look away. Her heart in her mouth, Kate could well imagine her own fired neurons were near to combusting. The waiting to know was torture. She wasn't superstitious, but when she signed and dated the form she realised it was Friday the thirteenth and crossed her fingers. The machine was monitored by a clinical neurophysiologist. She wondered if he would relay the result to Julian before he told her. She was relieved when she saw the consultant coming to join her.

'I think he's just about done. Shall we see?'

Kate nodded.

The neatly bearded Asian doctor acknowledged Julian, greeting him with a broad grin and an informal nickname. 'Hello, Sulli-man.'

'Sullivan, you blockhead,' Julian corrected in a droll tone, causing the other man to titter.

Julian glanced at Kate. 'Forgive him. He thinks he's a comedian. He'd behave impeccably if he didn't know you were a doctor.'

Kate managed a weak smile. 'I'm sure he would. I don't doubt it.'

The hoarseness in her voice had Julian looking at her with concern. 'You're tired.' He then addressed the clinical neurophysiologist. 'Sanji, we're waiting for your opinion. So tout suite, my old friend.'

'You can be hopeful.'

Kate's limbs turned to jelly. Julian must have sensed her state as he put her arm in the crook of his elbow to give her some physical support.

Sanji continued. 'The EEG measures brain voltage in microvolts. I consider the waveforms presenting a good positive. I would predict a level of consciousness to show soon.'

But what about predicted neurological outcome?

The moment the thought popped into her head, Kate resented it. No one could answer that question. And like Julian said, Mark hadn't even joined the party yet. He didn't need the added pressure to perform.

After the doctors had gone, she placed the chair back by the side of his bed and told Mark about her adventure in Barcelona. 'I met your friend, Paulo, and saw all his children's artwork on the walls in his bar. I found your green parrot. Drawn by Paulo's grandson. Paulo said he helped you look for your watch, Mark. Can you remember that? You and Paulo searching for it?'

Kate fixed on his face to watch for any miniscule response, her eyes on him as he did... nothing.

She gave his hand a squeeze. 'Don't you want to open your eyes, Mark?'

'Kate, let me take over.'

Kate turned in surprise, looking up at her mum with big, frightened eyes. Grace pulled a book out of her handbag. *The Concorde Story*. The thoughtfulness made her cry.

'Hey now, enough of that,' she said softly, planting a kiss on Kate's head. 'You need to go home and spend some time with your boy.'

Kate wiped her eyes. She rose from the chair and hugged her mum, not able to argue the suggestion. It felt like a lifetime since she held her child properly. She needed to snuggle him and breathe in his scent to take her mind off this torture.

'Thanks, Mum.'

She picked up her bag and coat, while Grace took her seat. Her mum then reached for her hand. 'I heard you, Kate. I don't know what you're keeping secret, but you're not alone. I'm here for you.'

CHAPTER THIRTY-THREE

Kate felt like a guest at a welcoming hotel. Waited on hand and foot by Olivia, she'd been fed and watered, and spoilt with hugs from Jacob. She was unfurling in the comfort of her much cosier sitting room, lying on the sofa since coming home, appreciating the sense of wellbeing. Olivia had insisted she rest when Kate almost tripped over her feet in exhaustion.

It would be so easy now to fall into a deep sleep, or climb into bed with Jacob and hug into his small back. She felt guilty for not putting him to bed, allowing Olivia to do it instead, but he'd not seemed to mind as she heard him telling Olivia the book he wanted her to read. She briefly worried that he was becoming a little bossy with their guest, and was seeing Olivia as a playmate who will play with him whenever he wants. While Kate was resting, Olivia might be getting tired herself.

A brief look around her home showed that Olivia wasn't idle while Jacob was in school. It was looking even more spick and span than it did this morning, and she had made more small changes. She had replaced the picture in the hallway with a rustic wooden mirror that went much better with the white walls and stripped doors. The landscape painting from John Lewis was now a lovely statement on the large wall in the kitchen. Kate didn't mind at all. Her only concern, Olivia was spending her own money on things to make Kate's home look nice.

She propped herself up against a cushion as Olivia came through the sitting room door, carrying a small tray. 'I've made tea,' she said. 'I'd have brought wine, but I wasn't sure if you were going back out.'

Olivia placed the tray on the blanket box and sat down on the sofa opposite Kate. Kate took the opportunity to thank her. 'Olivia, you've made this room look stunning. I love the glass bowl, and the mirror now in the hall. You must have worked hours doing all this. Plus a lovely dinner tonight! Oh, and I want the secret for how you got my loo taps looking new again.' She laughed. 'Is there anything you can't do?'

A blush crept up Olivia's neck. She ducked her face and tried to hide behind her lovely dark hair, which she was wearing down for the first time since Kate met her. She said in a small voice, 'I can change it back if it's not quite right? You might prefer the way it was? I just thought it might be more relaxing for you.'

Kate couldn't have sounded more surprised. 'Olivia, I love what you've done. I'm absolutely grateful. I'll be happier still if you let me pay you for all these things. Barney's new bowls and supplements didn't come cheap. I don't want you out of pocket.'

Olivia raised her head, looking reassured. 'I'm glad you like it. And really, I spent hardly any money. Less than ten pounds.' She smiled at Kate's disbelieving face. 'Honestly. I promise. They're charity shop buys. They have some fantastic ones in the high street near Jacob's school. I wandered through them yesterday.'

Kate held her gaze. 'Less than ten pounds?' she asked sceptically.

'I cross my heart,' Olivia replied, emphatically nodding, before breaking down laughing. 'Stop looking at me. I'm a terrible liar. I can't keep it up if you keep staring at me.'

Kate kept the stare on her.

'Fine,' she confessed with a touch of petulance that made Kate smile. 'I spent the grand sum of fourteen pounds and fifty pence. Not including Barney's bowls and medication, which is a present for him from me. Now can you please stop asking the price? It's only a token, and it didn't break the bank.'

Still gazing at her, Kate paid a sincere compliment. 'You are a very generous soul. I'm so glad Robert brought you here.'

'Me too,' Olivia mumbled with embarrassment.

Kate drank some of her tea. Then let Olivia know her plans. 'I will go back out. I need to help wake my sleepy husband.'

A shadow passed across Olivia's face. 'How is he? Everybody at work keeps asking.'

'It's taking longer than I hoped for him to wake.'

'Did the accident cause a lot of injuries?'

'To the rest of his body, no. But when it's a head injury, it's difficult to know the outcome – even a minor head injury can lead to serious symptoms. It's a crap situation, to be honest. The whole damn thing. It's like the universe is conspiring against us. When Mark told me that the police suspected him of murder, I was thinking these things didn't happen to people like us. But they do.'

'And they shouldn't!' Olivia answered forcefully. 'The police have got it wrong. Captain Jordan is a good man, he wouldn't hurt a fly.'

Her face looked crumpled with sadness. Kate was grateful for her loyalty. She was definitely on Captain Jordan's side. Kate eyed her thoughtfully and asked, 'What was she like? Fleur O'Connell.'

Olivia stared at her for a moment, her dark brows knitted

together. 'Well, that's another thing that doesn't make any sense. Captain Jordan wasn't her type.'

Kate frowned in surprise. 'You're assuming she was there for a romantic liaison?'

'Well, why else would she be in Barcelona alone, if not to meet someone?'

It had surprised Fleur's parents that she was there alone, as she hadn't mentioned anything to them on New Year's Eve. Olivia sounded like she knew her well. Kate was curious to know something more.

'And you think Mark wasn't her type?'

'Hardly!' Olivia gave a short laugh. Then, catching Kate's look, she exclaimed, 'That's a compliment to your husband. Fleur was attracted to men who were more outgoing. Guys who sweep women off their feet, but have commitment issues. She liked nightclubs, cocktail bars, socialising. Hardly Captain Jordan's style. We're lucky if he comes out for a drink. He's not unsociable, he just prefers a quiet time. Which is why none of us can believe this has happened to him,' she said in a dispirited tone.

Kate's mind was racing. She needed to know more about Fleur O'Connell's past. She wanted details of her friends and all the men in her life, something to point the police in the right direction. If she was in Barcelona for a romantic liaison, who was she seeing? Who might that be? Was there anyone who stood out in Olivia's mind? Kate would start by asking the obvious question.

'Did she have a boyfriend?'

There was a moment of awkward silence. Olivia looked uncomfortable, avoiding her gaze. Kate wondered if the question offended her.

'Sorry. This is a heavy subject. You don't have to answer.'

'It's not that I don't want to answer. It's just... I don't want to say things that might not be true. So please don't take my word for it.' She drew in a breath, then looked at Kate resignedly. 'There was a rumour going around not long before she left that she was seeing someone from the airline. The thing about Fleur is, she had boyfriends. Some more casual than others. She was single and enjoying life, so why not? The rumour, though, is she left because she had to. The gossip circulating at the time – she was stalking a pilot, making his life difficult, leaving a checklist in his jacket. We never heard a name, so it might not be true.'

'What do you mean, a checklist? What's that?'

Olivia sighed. 'You know, what women desire in a man. A list of attributes they want in the person they marry.'

Kate grimaced. It sounded juvenile to her. There was something worrying in what Olivia said. The thought of stalking made her shiver. It put in mind someone unstable. Someone to worry about. She was curious to know if Olivia believed the rumour.

'What did you think?'

'It's hard to say. If she put a wish list in a man's jacket, she was declaring he was the man she wants. I suppose to some that would come across as stalking.' Her eyes grew pensive. 'Fleur denied it. Said it was one date, then he dumped her. She told one of the cabin crew it was a mistake. That she put it in the wrong jacket. She tried explaining it to this pilot. Said it was the only reason she kept approaching him. He apparently refused to believe her, left her crying in a car park.'

'That's sad,' Kate replied. 'Maybe she fixed her sights on the wrong man, someone who was married?'

'It's possible,' Olivia agreed. Then, to lighten the mood, she put the blame on Kate. Giving a theatrical sigh, she said, 'It's the likes of you that cause the problems. All the good ones are married.'

Kate laughed, glad to end on this note. It put her in a good frame of mind for her visit. But also left her with something to think about. She would ask Mark, of course, in the hope her question might prod him awake. Who better to know the goings on of other pilots?

CHAPTER THIRTY-FOUR

'No rest for the wicked,' Robert quipped, as he made himself comfortable in the chair. 'You must have to work long hours in your line of business, Detective Sharma, to catch criminals.'

It felt like a long minute before Sharma responded. 'You have that right, Mr Brennan. It's been a long day already, so perhaps you'll give some straight answers. Makes this nice and quick for both of us.'

Robert intended to. He'd rehearsed what he was going to say. 'Sounds sensible to me. Do you mind if I begin? It might speed up all the back-and-forth questions and replies. I gather you wish me to clarify the gaps in the narrative given previously?'

'You gather correctly. The floor's yours, Mr Brennan.'

'Shall I start at the time most relevant to your enquiries, or would you prefer I begin when I saw Captain Jordan getting in the lift?'

Sharma's pasted-on smile looked grim. Robert could see he was winding him up, and reeled his behaviour in. Being a smart alec wasn't really beneficial, not when the subject was an ex-colleague's murder. It was poor form.

'Sorry, a long day getting the better of me,' he apologised. 'I'll start again. When asked before if I saw Captain Jordan between eight thirty in the evening and when I saw him at breakfast the next morning, my answer should have been a simple no. Instead, I fudged a little, not wishing to raise speculation about my own whereabouts at that crucial time. I left the hotel shortly after eleven. I'm not someone who retires to bed with the television or a book. I prefer to unwind with exercise. As I mentioned before, I enjoy running, which is what I was doing, and I probably took a tumble because it was dark and I misjudged the edge of the pavement. I'd say I was gone for maybe forty to fifty minutes. There was a receptionist behind the desk when I returned. Whether or not he saw me, I don't know. And that's it. Nothing very exciting to report, I know. But then that's often the way with the truth. Plain and boring.'

'And that's how we like it, Mr Brennan. So thank you for that. And perhaps we can continue with some more plain truths. Did you meet with Fleur O'Connell during that time?'

'No. I did not.'

'Did you see Fleur O'Connell during that time?'

'No. I did not.'

'Did you know Fleur O'Connell was in Barcelona that day?'

'No.'

'Did you contact Fleur O'Connell by letter, text, phone call, email, by any means, to give a message or make any arrangement during December and the first two days in January?'

'No. I did not.'

'Mr Brennan, how well did you know Fleur O'Connell?'

Despite not being worried, Robert was still careful with how he answered. 'I knew her well as a cabin crew member. Enough to know she was friendly and chatty, but not well enough to know her personally.'

'How would you describe "personally", Mr Brennan?'

Robert couldn't help himself. He loved being pedantic

when the occasion was called for. At a party when he wanted to bore someone so much they would go away, or at work to silence a nitpicking passenger, or sometimes just for fun. 'I would say "personally" describes oneself. I'm here in person. Or, as belonging to a particular person. The tie you're wearing, Detective Sharma, belongs to you personally. I'm now speaking personally to Officer Kelly. I hope what I've said isn't taken personally.'

DC Kelly was not impressed, while Robert detected a slight twitch of Sharma's mouth. He was right about liking the man the first time round. The detective had a sense of humour.

'Other than knowing her as a chatty and friendly colleague, would you say you knew her in any other capacity?'

'No.'

'Do you recall her leaving the company?'

'Not really. You work with so many people that you don't always know that someone has left.'

'Were you aware there was an allegation of stalking?'

The question caught Robert by surprise. He hung back from replying. He never expected for this to rear its head. Maybe he should have. Sharma would have dug up everything about his past. His mouth turned dry.

'Were you aware Fleur O'Connell resigned because of this allegation?'

Sharma was studying him closely. Robert couldn't produce a passive face at will, not while his mind was turning over past events. Images came to him in fragments. The encounters he thought were in his imagination. Her presence causing a prickling alertness. A wish list found in his pocket – nice manners, loyal, intelligent, good provider, commitment.

She wasn't a threat. Immature and attention-seeking, certainly. But then those sharp little nails had meant to do harm. His face the target. Her lunge making him pull back.

Then her fit of crying because he didn't understand her showed she was unhinged.

'Do you wish me to repeat the questions, Mr Brennan?'

Robert looked at him then. His handsomeness more striking by his remoteness. Keeping him at a distance. His humour no longer accessible. He'd thought this interview would be safe, but Sharma now thought he had motive.

Robert shook his head. 'No. I heard you. Yes, I was aware on both accounts.'

'Were you the one who made the allegation, Mr Brennan?'

Robert felt unable to answer. He should just take his leave. Get up and walk out of the room before it was too late. But he needed to say it, before his own situation got messier. Make a U-turn. It couldn't bring any more harm. His presence had already muddied Sharma's case – thrown doubt on the primary suspect as he had intended. To allow fairness to take a part. He had done that. He was free to tell the truth.

Feeling a slow return of power, no longer pinned by the two men in the room. He locked eyes with Sharma for what seemed like forever.

'No, it was not me. Captain Jordan reported her.'

CHAPTER THIRTY-FIVE

Kate gazed at the relatives by the beds, wondering if Mark's blue language had offended them, particularly his use of the most foul word in the English language. She guessed it would at least prepare them not to expect it to be like in the movies – waiting for a loved one to slowly open their eyes. A reunion with lots of happy crying, and a short time later, with strength returning, they're getting out of bed showing they can walk.

Mark's wake up speech was certainly memorable – the C-word coming out of his mouth first, followed by every profanity under the sun. From an outsider's perspective, he would appear to be a man well-versed with rolling these words off his tongue. In reality, the worst Kate had ever heard him say was 'fuck', usually under his breath.

Kate had ignored the cursing, aware more of his head rising off the pillow, his legs and arms moving, while looking disorientated and scared. It took Julian's hand on his brow to calm him, and Julian's words to soothe. Speaking to him man to man. 'We've got you, mate. You've had a tough time. But you're fighting through. We're here, Mark. We've got you.'

Kate was never more grateful to have Julian by her side. His indomitable presence, continuing to fight for Mark, was a tremendous comfort. Her husband was now sleeping and breathing on his own, the ventilator by the bed switched off. She could hear soft breaths and breathed with him, giving thanks over and again.

Grace had been there to witness it, and it was Kate who comforted her mum. Standing startled and small, clutching the book to her chest, she couldn't stop looking at her son-in-law. 'He's back,' she whispered.

Mark's lovely nurse made them tea. When Grace finished hers, she informed Kate she was going home to give them some time alone. Kate watched her composure return and her dignified exit. She got her strength from her mum. She'd been Kate's rock all her life. Kate would tell her tomorrow about the police situation. She'd need her support more than ever if Mark couldn't come home.

Kate roused to the sound of Mark's voice. Raising her head, she looked at his face. His eyes were closed. She inched up from the chair to get closer, to hear what he was mumbling. Her lips curved in a dampened smile. Her mum would have loved to have heard this first sentence. It was all down to her. 'Only twenty Concordes were ever built.'

Kate didn't feel the need to call anyone. Mark was playing his part. Resting and sleeping through an arduous journey from a prolonged state of unconsciousness. It wasn't like emerging from a long, deep sleep. He was having to recognise the feel of his body again, the touches on his skin, the moisture in his mouth, the heaviness of his limbs, the memories returning.

She would let the moment pass without him being disturbed, the night pass before informing his parents, not wanting to jump too soon at good news. She wanted to give him more time to turn the corner first. See him go from strength to strength before breathing a sigh of relief.

She settled her head back down, feeling the warmth of his skin, daydreaming of hearing his voice, his laughter, his occasional cross tone, his whispers in her ear.

The sounds on the ward woke her in the morning. The telephone ringing, the chatter of staff, the scrape of furniture across a floor – a cleaner pulling a chair out of the way. She sat up and looked at Mark. His eyes were open, staring up at the ceiling. She rose to her feet and moved her face into his field of view. Their eyes briefly met, then he closed them.

She waited patiently. A few moments later, he opened them again. She smiled at him. 'Hello, you. I missed you.'

He was looking right at her, making the connection, with a hard stare in his eyes. Kate's lips curved again. 'I've been waiting for you to wake up, and now you're here.'

His gaze moved from her face to stare back at the ceiling.

She placed her palm against his stubbled jaw and turned his face, but his eyes wouldn't meet hers. 'I know I look terrible.' She laughed. 'I haven't even washed my hair.'

The intensity in his eyes dazzled. She wondered what he was thinking. It must be frightening to resurface and feel so much of everything. She wanted to pull him into her arms and tell him not to be afraid. She lowered her head and softly kissed his lips. 'Don't think too hard about anything. Let your mind relax. Everything will be all right. I promise.'

The emotion in his eyes was impenetrable. He was looking above Kate's head, to the side. So it seemed. Anywhere but at her. She slipped her hand into his, but felt no response. His eyes closed again. She heard him take a breath, and then his voice – low, firm, and clear. 'Go home, Kate. There's nothing for you here.'

Kate inhaled hard, and sat as if someone had cut a string in the back of her legs, her breathing tight. He didn't mean it. It wasn't him talking. It was the effect of all the drugs, the physical and emotional trauma he'd gone through. He wasn't trying to hurt her.

She felt him tug his hand free. His head turned on the pillow. And now he looked at her. She couldn't avoid seeing he was deadly serious. His next words were much more punishing.

'Go home. I don't want you here.'

CHAPTER THIRTY-SIX

Kate stared, mesmerised at the blanket of snow that had fallen overnight. She had lost contact with the outside world. Her work, her everyday life, watching the news, had all stopped the moment Mark came into this hospital. She hadn't considered the weather becoming a problem. She should ring Olivia and tell her not to drive Jacob to school.

The cramping in her belly snatched her breath, forcing her to look for the nearest place to sit down. The plastic chair felt cold through her clothes. There was a chill draught through the entrance doors. She gave a low moan as another wave of pain hit her stomach. She was having a panic attack, she was sure. It was the shock of Mark's words, nothing more. She needed to make her mind go blank, then her body would follow accordingly.

She rocked gently back and forth in the chair, relieved no one was around to witness it. No one was in the café area at this early hour. She would let the pain subside and then get home before the roads became impassable. The cramping in her belly made her groan, making her wonder now if it was a stomach bug. She reached under her jumper and undid the button on her jeans. She was probably full of air from gulping breaths after walking away from Mark.

She tried hard to erase his words, but the sting of rejection wouldn't go away. He probably wasn't even aware of how much he hurt her. He was bound to be depressed with his memory returned, knowing what he faced. The possibility of not going home.

She extended her arms across the round table, trying to ease the discomfort. A second later, she went utterly still. Waiting, hoping for the moment to pass. Please, no, she was not going to be sick. Not here, in a public place on the floor. Trembling all over, she attempted to stand, the churning in her stomach rising into her throat telling her she would not make it to the bathroom. She vomited on the table, the chair and her shoes. Tears watered her eyes as she spat the taste from her mouth. She breathed deeply, hoping to feel better, only to moan again at another rising wave.

Then she heard an urgent cry from behind her. 'What the hell! You poor love. What's happened to you?'

Kate's eyes teared up at hearing Sophie's voice. Her arm went around Kate's waist to steer her away from the smell and the mess to a clean chair. 'Sit. Don't move. I'll be a minute.' She didn't wait for Kate to respond as she rushed away to fetch a wheelchair.

'Don't you have to be at work?' Kate asked, as Sophie wheeled her along the corridor.

'No. I've got the day off. I only popped in to leave a message for one of the registrars.'

It was, perhaps, inevitable that something like this would bring them back into each other's lives at the right time to reset their friendship. Kate found she didn't mind at all. Sophie gently helped her out of her jeans and put her on a patient trolley. Eva then appeared with a grey cardboard sick bowl.

'Sorry for being a nuisance. Can I rinse my mouth, please?' Kate asked.

While Eva fetched a glass of water, Sophie didn't wait for an A & E nurse. She strapped a tourniquet on Kate's arm to get a cannula in. When Eva returned, Sophie instructed her to let the doctor know Kate needed something for the pain and nausea.

Kate reflected that Sophie was still bossy. She shivered under the blanket, then remembered the weather. 'Soph, could you pass me my bag? I need to ring the woman looking after Jacob to keep him home from school. I don't want her driving in the snow.'

Sophie rubbed a gentle hand on her shoulder. 'You silly billy, it's Saturday.'

Kate opened her eyes in surprise. 'Oh yes, so it is.'

Sophie stared at her with a tangible sadness in her expression. 'I've missed you so much,' she breathed. 'I know this isn't the best moment for me to say this, but I'm so sorry, Kate. What I did was unforgiveable. More so, because I never fancied Mark. I was in a bad place at the time, which is no excuse. The lovely man I was dating dumped me that day. It was a first for me. I got a taste of my own medicine, and didn't like it. So I made a beeline for poor Mark. I behaved outrageously. Mark's never even flirted with me. I caught him in a relaxed mood. He'd sank a bottle of wine. I had my tongue in his mouth before he could react. But I'm telling you this now, Kate. He wasn't aroused. You know what I'm saying. He may not even realise that. But trust me, I was. Your husband wasn't attracted to me.'

Kate felt the weight of the truth land in her chest. Sophie had tried to explain it to her all before. She hadn't wanted to know. All that hurt she experienced was because she didn't want to hear or believe what she was being told. Everywhere Sophie went, men looked at her. Why should Mark be any different? It was easier to convince herself that he was attracted like every other man. But what she'd done was judge him for being something he wasn't. She'd turned her back on her good fortune. Withdrawing some of her love. When she should have listened to Sophie and remembered Sophie always told her the truth.

Sophie stood before her, her head slightly at an angle, and complete misery on her face. 'I've never forgiven myself. I know what it would have done to you. To have doubts about Mark. I've never seen a couple more in love, and I damaged that.'

Kate reached for her hand and gave her a watery smile. 'I damaged it, Soph. For not having more faith. But all I saw at the time was me looking like a mum, and you looking like a model. I should have swatted away my distrust the moment it landed. And remembered who my husband is. I'm glad you told me again. Forgiven, Soph. I've let it go.'

A half hour later, a drip hydrating her, the pain controlled, she was feeling better. Her obs done, bloods taken, urine sample given, she wanted to go home. The curtain drew back with Eva's return. She glanced at Kate, then at Sophie. 'I just need to talk to Kate for a moment.'

Sophie understood and made to leave. Kate stopped her.

'It's okay, Soph. You can stay.'

Eva pulled the curtain closed. 'Your urine showed something, Kate. We did a pregnancy test.'

For a doctor, Kate was pretty slow on the uptake. She couldn't have asked a more daft question than the one she asked now. 'What does that mean?'

Eva exchanged an amused look with Sophie. Then gently smiled at Kate. 'You're pregnant.'

Kate held an outspread hand over her face, stunned. Her befuddled brain trying to absorb the news. She was pregnant. She shook her head in wonderment. She hadn't a clue, and yet there were so many. The feeling of nausea and being sick more than once. Her emotions all over the place, not just because of what was happening in her life, but because of what was happening in her body, her changing hormones.

Her mind filled with thoughts of Jacob. He would have a brother or sister to grow up with. Someone to play with. She saw him with another child, talking animatedly as they lined up every toy animal he possessed. She saw herself soothing a crying baby, trying to hush the sounds in the night, while Jacob slept. The image tugged at something inside her. There was Jacob, and a baby, and herself. Where was Mark in this picture?

Her chest heaved in a ragged sob as reality registered in her body. There would be no Mark at home. She looked at Sophie. Her eyes wide with fear. 'What am I going to do, Soph?' Her crying intensified. 'I can't do this without him. We need him. I need him!'

Eva stepped forward to clutch her hand.

Sophie hung back, searching Kate's face with anxious eyes. Then the bond that had always been between them rushed her forwards to take Kate in her arms. 'Breathe. Just breathe. I'm here. I'm here now.'

CHAPTER THIRTY-SEVEN

Kate managed the last spoonful of porridge under Sophie's watchful eye, thinking Sophie should eat something as well. She was shellshocked from everything she'd heard, her face pale. The hospital café seemed the best place to talk. At home, Jacob could hear, and there was Olivia to consider. Kate wanted the pregnancy kept quiet until she knew how far along she was.

She sipped the sweet hot chocolate, feeling comforted by both the nourishment and the sharing of her worries with Sophie. She didn't mind waiting for Sophie's verdict. It was a relief just to talk about it. Kate was happy for her to take her time.

'You're right to think it's probably depression,' she now agreed, as if Kate had only just mentioned Mark's behaviour, and not an hour ago. 'So shelve that worry. It's the rest of it we need to concentrate on. I'll play devil's advocate. According to this Paulo, Mark was in his bar at the time of the murder. We need to determine how long he was there, and whether it's possible he could have been at the place of the woman's murder before his visit to the bar, or after searching for his watch. It would give him an alibi and a witness to the watch being missing. But who's to say he didn't lose it when he was with her?'

Kate reared back, sending Sophie a fierce stare. 'You think he's guilty!'

Sophie's eyes snapped open in mild shock. 'Well of course I don't bloody believe that! Not for a second. I'm trying to look at this from every angle, find any loophole that can trip him up. If this Paulo can say he was there, let's say from eleven to half twelve, he's in the clear. What we really need to look at is motive. What is the reason for this woman's murder? And if it wasn't Mark, why has someone given a description of him? Have you searched thoroughly for his watch?'

Kate shook her head. 'Given the time I had, no. But I think Mark looked for it. And it's what he said in A & E. He lost it and needed to find it.'

'Okay, moving on from that, Mark notices he's lost his watch. We don't know the circumstances. And let's say you're right, and assume that the watch is the evidence the police found at the murder scene. How did it get there?'

Kate shrugged. 'I don't know the answer to that. But it has to be why the police think it's him. The inscription on the back says Captain Jordan.'

'And who would know that?' Sophie pressed.

Kate tugged at her hair, trying to think. 'I don't know. Me, his dad. It was a gift from him. Lots of people, possibly. Whoever he showed. Everyone at his birthday.'

'Who was with him in Barcelona?'

'I don't know all the names. Olivia, who's staying with me, was there, and Robert flew with him.'

'Robert?' Sophie raised her eyebrows. Her voice was ponderous. 'Robert was Mark's co-pilot?'

Kate shot her a look. 'Don't, Soph. Not even in jest. That's not fair.'

Sophie held her gaze. 'It's not about being fair, Kate. It's about how the evidence got there. If it is Mark's watch they have, how was it there? Robert is also tall and dark-haired. He also fits the description given of the man that was seen.'

Kate leaned away from her. 'Robert wouldn't do that,' she whispered in horror. 'You're not saying he would murder someone and blame it on Mark?'

Sophie placed her hand over Kate's. Her eyes were direct. 'If he was obsessed, he might. I was your maid of honour. He was Mark's best man. And you know what I'm like.' She gave a small self-deprecating smile and continued. 'Him, the best looker in the room and single! I, nor any other woman in the room, had a chance. He had eyes only for you.' She sighed heavily. 'Over the years we've met the odd girlfriend, and then I'd catch him unawares, looking at you, and realised they were just a cover. So yes, Kate, I think anyone can be pushed to the limit if they want something badly enough.'

CHAPTER THIRTY-EIGHT

Kate took her time driving home. She needed to clear her mind of the horrible suspicions Sophie tried to raise about Robert before she and Sophie stepped into the house. It was bad enough Sophie thinking it, without putting it in her head. It was not something she wished to consider at all.

She left space for Sophie to park beside her and got out of the car. Sophie looked uneasy, and she wondered if she was remembering the last time she was at Kate's home. Kate linked her arm. 'Come on, you. Come and get reacquainted with your godson. He's grown,' she warned.

They entered the house quietly and heard shrieks of laughter from upstairs. 'JJ, you do that again and I'm putting you in the basket!'

Sophie's eyes lit with amusement. Then a bundle of clothes came flying down the stairs, followed by the sound of running feet and a gleeful shriek. 'You can't catch me. I'm the clothes monster.'

A moment later, lugging a basket of laundry down the stairs, Olivia stopped mid-sentence in her giggling reply to Jacob. 'I can and I—'

Kate smiled at her. 'He giving you trouble?' she asked. 'This is my good friend, Sophie.'

Olivia's cheeks were flushed. She looked young and care-free and suited Kate's old blue dress far better than Kate did. She came down the rest of the stairs, animated, her eyes shining.

She greeted Sophie. 'Hello, excuse the noise. We've been playing out in the snow, and both got soaking wet. He just had a hot shower and used every towel.' She glanced at Kate. 'I had to borrow something to wear. My last pair of joggers are in this wash.' Her eyes then turned to the stairs at the boy coming down them. 'Here he comes. The monster of towels.'

Jacob giggled and flung himself at Kate. Kate lifted him up and smelt his warm soap-scented skin. She turned him to face Sophie. 'Jacob, this is my friend Sophie. She's come to say hello.'

Jacob turned his head into Kate's shoulder. She heard his solemn reply. 'I'm not Jacob.'

'Not Jacob!' Kate pretended to be outraged, and tickled him. 'Where's my Jacob then, if you're not him? What have you done with him?'

Jacob giggled. 'He's here, Mummy. I'm him. I'm JJ. Olivia calls me him.'

Olivia softly gasped. She gave Kate an apologetic look, and mouthed 'sorry'. Kate saw Sophie clock it too. Kate just ignored what Jacob said and tickled him.

Jacob wriggled out of her arms and dashed back up the stairs. Olivia politely excused herself, indicating the laundry in her arms.

Sophie's eyebrows wiggled again, overdramatising as she mouthed, 'JJ'.

'Shut up,' Kate quietly hissed, even though Sophie hadn't said it aloud. Then pulled her into the kitchen where she could make them some tea. The trouble with having a good friend, Kate remembered, was they could read you. Sophie had prob-ably picked up on her surprise as Jacob denied his name.

She pulled two mugs out of the cupboard, then a third one, feeling acutely embarrassed for introducing Olivia like an unpaid servant, letting her stand there with a laundry basket in her arms. Where were her manners? Kate should have taken the damned washing from her and asked her to join them.

She screwed her eyes shut. What must Olivia think of her? She was probably feeling very uncomfortable right now. Staying in the utility room, out of the way, so Kate could socialise with her friend. Kate felt out of sorts; the trying events of the morning, and now this. She should have diffused the matter with a joke, and called Jacob by his new nickname. She was the one who had made this bigger than it needed to be. Not Olivia.

'Soph, stick the kettle on. I'll just be a second.'

Olivia was loading the washing machine. Kate interrupted. 'Olivia, I'm so sorry if I made you uncomfortable. After everything you've done, and with Jacob so happy, I acted ungraciously. You have no reason to apologise. None. It's a super nickname. I think I was a bit of a green-eyed monster for a second.'

Olivia turned. Her eyes were worried. Kate felt awful and started to apologise again, but Olivia stopped her.

'Kate, I'd feel the same way. Us mums are precious about our boys. And so we should be.' She held up her hand to show her phone. 'You've got nothing to be sorry about. If I look a bit off, it's because I just had a call from the police. They want to speak to me again. I've to go to the station today. I don't know what time I'll be back.' She frowned worriedly. 'Do you think your mum would come and sit with Jacob?'

Kate was relieved. Olivia wasn't upset with her. She was curious to know why the police wanted to see her again. She shook her head in bemusement. 'I don't know which one of us is worse. Me worried about upsetting you, or you worried about causing me a problem. Though I think you win this one.' She gave Olivia a warm look. 'When you get back, missus, we're going to have a glass of wine. And I'm going to wait on you for once.'

Olivia beamed. 'I'll be back as quick as I can.'

The situation sorted, Kate joined Sophie in the kitchen. She was reacquainting herself with Kate's home. 'I love it here. Your home is so lovely. It has the same touches you gave to our flat. A bloody lifetime ago that was. What were we there; five years? Then one day you bring a furball home from the shop that chewed the rugs and our shoes. How we kept Barney hidden from the landlord, God knows.'

Kate smiled. 'They were fun days.'

'They were. I just bought a flat in Henrietta Street, you know. You'll have to come and see it soon. It couldn't be a more perfect location with the added bonus that Bath rugby's finest are on my doorstep, should any of them need a check-up.'

Kate laughed. 'You're an eye doctor, Soph. Not an orthopaedic surgeon.'

Sophie considered this irrelevant. 'They get mud in their eyes sometimes.'

Sophie hadn't changed, but then Kate wouldn't want her to. She lived life boldly.

Sophie's expression altered. A glumness coming over her. 'I'm thirty-six, Kate. I don't know what I'm doing anymore. My life should be more than just being a doctor and having the next fling. I feel like I've wasted it, sometimes.'

Kate eyed her curiously, wondering where this had come from. She'd never thought of Sophie as lonely.

Sophie glanced at her then. 'Tell me to shut up again, will you?'

Kate obliged. 'Shut up, Soph. And where's the tea? You haven't even put the kettle on.'

Sophie gave an impish grin, her positive and naughty side reappearing. She whispered, 'If you weren't preggers, we could have had a drink.'

Kate had a lightbulb moment. 'Shit! I told Olivia I'd have a glass of wine with her later.'

Sophie whistled. The sound low, then rising like a warning of disapproval.

Kate knew it wasn't about the wine. She glared at her. 'Pack it in. You're as bad as my mum. I don't know where I'd be without Olivia the last few days. She's given up her time to help me. It's kept Jacob from knowing anything. He doesn't even know Mark's in hospital. Seriously, Soph, Olivia has been really kind.'

Sophie went quiet. Kate wondered what she was thinking.

For the rest of her visit, she behaved. She made a fuss of Barney, reckoning he remembered her. She went, by invitation, to see Jacob's room, and came away with the opinion her godson was a genius. Olivia wasn't mentioned again until it was time for her to go.

'Why is an attractive young woman giving all her time, Kate? Doesn't she have a life of her own?'

Kate folded her arms to stay warm, watching the car drive away, and realised she didn't have an answer. She hadn't given it any thought. Olivia was fond of Mark and respected him, but was that enough reason? Sophie might be right. Maybe Olivia didn't have a life of her own, apart from her work and her hopes. She had a son who didn't live with her. That had to be lonely. And hard. Minding another woman's child and not her own.

Kate was reminded that she hadn't heard back from Diane. She was probably in the air, flying somewhere. She'd give it until tomorrow and then try again. Sophie had got her slightly worried. She didn't like to think Olivia was there out of loneliness. She could get hurt if she became attached to Jacob. Olivia didn't need Jacob in her heart. She needed her own boy to love.

CHAPTER THIRTY-NINE

Kate noticed the silence following Sophie's departure. The last time she was home alone with Jacob was the morning he went back to school. The morning the boiler broke. The day her world was shattered. It seemed inconceivable that so much had happened in so short a time. In twelve days her life had gone from being that of a normal person to one that had her racing to another country to prove a husband innocent of murder.

She stood at the bottom of the stairs with no idea what to do. Mark didn't want her with him, though he may have changed his mind. The only way to find out was to ring the ward. She would have a bath first and wash her hair. At least that way she would be clean if he consented to seeing her.

Making her way upstairs, she checked on Jacob and found him in Olivia's bedroom. He was kneeling by the bed, looking at a picture on the chest of drawers.

'Hey, you, you shouldn't be in here. This is Olivia's room.'

Jacob reached for the picture frame and held it up to her. His voice was concerned. 'Her little boy can't live with her. That's very sad, isn't it?'

Kate took the photo. The boy had brown hair and a sweet

smile. She was struck by the resemblance to his mother, and carefully placed it back on the chest of drawers. It was sad, but she would rather Jacob didn't know Olivia's circumstances. He would worry about her. He worried enough about small matters – spiders being put outdoors, worms not finding their families when they are dug up, snails getting crushed. He didn't like to think of anything getting lost or lonely. She helped him to his feet and moved him out of the room, closing the door behind them.

'She could live here,' Jacob suggested. 'That way she could share me. That would be fair.' His upturned face was earnest.

Kate crouched down to talk face to face. 'Hey you, I'm your mummy. I don't want to share you. You're my Mister Snack-osaurus.'

The idea didn't appease him. His face was full of thoughts. 'I can be both. I've got lots of room in my belly for everybody. I can be JJ for her and Jacob for you. Then she won't leave.'

Kate was concerned. His eyes looked teary. She pulled him in for a hug. 'She's not leaving, silly. Not yet. She's our new friend. And one day she might bring her little boy here to play with you. That would be nice, wouldn't it?'

He nodded against her chest. 'Uh-huh. She could play with us both then.'

Kate felt guilty and was glad she was at home for a change. Jacob needed some Mummy time. He was in just as much need of protection from getting hurt as Olivia.

'How about we get pizza and cuddle up on the couch?'

He settled for that. While Kate had her bath, ordered them pizza, then discreetly rang the ward to send Mark her love so Mark would know she was thinking of him, Jacob played on the landing.

When the doorbell rang, she wrapped her hair in a towel and rushed to the door. The pizza delivery arriving quicker than expected, there was no time to brush it or put Jacob in her bath water. With luck, the thought of it waiting to be eaten might encourage Jacob to let her wash him quickly. She pulled the front door open and stared blankly at Robert standing on the doorstep.

'What are you doing here? You're meant to be flying.'

Robert shook his head and gave a rueful smile, stamping snow from his shoes before coming through the door and closing it. 'Meant to have been, until they grounded me. No warning. They gave the excuse that while police enquiries are ongoing, I'm not allowed to fly.' He gave a short laugh. 'They've put me in the same boat as Mark.'

Kate was shocked. 'Why? When did they decide this?'

Robert shrugged off his coat. 'Probably yesterday, after Detective Sharma interviewed me again. I got back from Dusseldorf and was told they wanted to see me. I was meant to be positioning to Charles de Gaulle yesterday evening to bring the aircraft back this morning, but my roster's been wiped until further notice.'

Kate moved along the hallway in a daze, automatically heading for the kitchen, and filled the kettle for something to do.

'Do you want coffee?' she asked.

'I'd prefer a beer, or wine if you have one open?'

He joined her at the counter and reached down some glasses from the cupboard. Kate looked in the fridge and found a small bottle of French beer, conscious of him driving and not wanting to encourage him to stay too long. She twisted off the cap before he could object.

He turned the bottle around in his hand and eyed it with amusement. 'You think my babysitting duties will suffer if I have anything stronger?'

'No. But your driving might.' She smiled, willing him to change the subject.

He inclined his head, his tone light-hearted. 'Oh, I see. I'm not on duty tonight.'

She spoke in a congenial manner, not wanting to offend him. 'Sorry, Robert, but I'm home this evening. Jacob and I are going to veg out in front of the telly and eat pizza.'

He gave a small shrug and smiled. 'Sounds fun. But no matter. I know when I'm not wanted.'

Kate was conscious of him standing in almost the same spot as he had last year, for almost the same reason – to reach down a glass. She'd backed into him, unaware of his presence, and turned to find his eyes gazing at her, particularly her mouth. She'd felt the slight motion of his hip as he pressed against her. And she was now conscious that she wasn't wearing a bra beneath her clean T-shirt.

Had she invited him to do that? Had she given off a sexual vibe while they stood alone, hearing the boisterous fun outside? Kate had felt sexy that night, but not for Robert. She wasn't blind to his masculinity. The shirt he wore that night was similar to the one he had on now. Button-down collar, tailored, tucked into the waist of a pair of dark-blue jeans, making him wholly male. He dwarfed her in a way that Mark never did, but she'd never felt any sexual stirring. He didn't do it for her. There was no chemistry. She wouldn't be tempted even if she was single. Mark only had to look at her to provoke an instant arousal. It was the knowing look in his eyes of what he wanted to do to her that lit her like a flame and made her hunger for him to begin. The leashed desire in his dark eyes.

She flushed hot at the thoughts in her mind. She was standing in the middle of the room and had forgotten for a moment that Robert was there, letting him see her naked expressions. She pulled the towel off her head to let her hair cover her face and mumbled about fetching a brush. Hurrying up the stairs, she located Jacob and quickly bathed him. She put on a bra and pulled her hair up in a damp ponytail. Putting

Jacob in pyjamas, she descended with him holding her hand to find Robert had answered the door and taken delivery of their pizzas.

She felt awkward and damned Sophie for making her feel on edge. Though really what Sophie said to her wasn't why she was tense. It was being in her home alone with Robert. It had only just occurred to her that there wasn't a time before when Mark wasn't present. She felt self-conscious on her own with him.

Jacob's presence made it easier for her to act naturally around Robert and be a gracious friend by asking him to take part in their meal. He couldn't have refused if he'd wanted to, not with Jacob begging him to stay. Throughout the meal the two of them were like giggling boys, talking all sorts of nonsense. Just a couple of days ago, watching them would have made her smile. But now she was willing Robert to go, and wondering about the real reason he wasn't allowed to fly.

CHAPTER FORTY

Olivia hadn't returned from the police station when Jacob needed his bed. While Kate was upstairs tucking him in, Robert wandered into the sitting room. When she returned, he enthusiastically praised the improvements, making no sign of leaving.

'It looks so much better. When did you find time?'

Kate sat down on the opposite sofa. 'I didn't. Olivia did. She did it while I was in Barcelona.'

The mention of her trip led into the conversation. Kate filled him in on what she discovered, and on Mark's progress since her return. He looked stunned.

'That's great news! Things are looking up. Mark awake, plus a witness. You clever girl. And what news about Mark's accident?'

Kate shook her head. She hadn't given it any further thought since her conversation with Detective Sharma. She passed on Sharma's excuse. 'It's a needle in a haystack. They're still searching for the driver.'

'I don't suppose they will find them. The amount of times I hear of a colleague's car being hit after they've parked it, and nothing gets done. Even in a car park. The police want eyewitness accounts to do the job for them.'

His comment about the police gave her the opportunity to tell him where Olivia was. Robert's reaction was to nod at her knowingly, like he knew this could happen.

'They're probably questioning her again for the same reason I was. They want to know how well we knew Fleur.'

Kate noticed he had poured himself a glass of white wine in her absence. He drank some and then put the glass on the blanket box. He brushed something off his trouser leg, only visible to him. She was tempted to reach for his glass and take a swig.

'It's complicated,' he said, and caught her eye. He held on to her gaze for a fraction of a second longer. 'But I think knowing her will have made things easier for Mark.'

Kate's breathing changed as she waited for him to expand. Was he about to confess to something which would worry her? Hopefully not a declaration of love. Sophie was wrong about him having eyes only for her. Her mum was wrong about him being in love with her forever. They both were wrong. Robert had more going for him than that.

He bent forward to reach for his glass and held it aloft as if in a silent toast. 'You know you should never keep hidden what you know can be found. It's that which complicates things. It's senseless to hide something so easily discovered. It discredits in the worst possible way.'

He stood up abruptly and was suddenly too close to her. The air squeezed from her lungs as he lowered himself to sit sideways on the arm of her sofa and face her. She moved her hand to her lap to give him more room. Her eyes focused on the belt in his jeans. She could smell his expensive aftershave. She heard him sigh and chanced a look at his face. He was gazing into space, his hands wrapped around the glass, the right one bearing small dry scabs across the knuckles.

Then, just as quickly, he stood again. He walked behind the sofa to Barney's basket and bent down. 'There you are, Old Boy. I wondered where you got to. You've been sleeping all this time?'

He sighed more heartily and straightened up, rolling his shoulders tiredly. 'I knew her, Kate,' he then said, and glanced at her expectantly.

Kate swept her hand up her throat, wondering what he expected her to say. He'd used the same words as Mark. I knew her. It was hardly a surprise. She had worked for the same airline a year ago. What she didn't understand was how Robert knowing her helped make things easier for Mark?

He gave her a quizzical look, raising an eyebrow. 'Mark didn't mention it?'

Kate felt a deeper confusion. A moment ago her heart was thumping with trepidation. She had felt afraid of Robert, but now she sensed he was embarrassed. Or feeling awkward. His cheeks were flushed. There was nothing frightening about him at all.

'He didn't say anything to me, Robert,' Kate said slowly. 'If he had, what might I have heard?'

Robert met her eyes. His were unreadable. The atmosphere between them was charged. What wasn't he telling her? Kate had had enough with all this mystery. She wanted her vision cleared and for him to talk straight.

She said it how it was, in a quiet and serious way. 'Robert, if you've got nothing to say. Please, just go.'

She heard his chuckle and shut her eyes, waiting for him to leave. Knowing his character, she shouldn't be surprised by him laughing at her. But making light of it was not the right reaction when she was so much afraid already of what she couldn't understand. Tears squeezed between her closed lids. She felt his hand stroke the top of her head and shrugged him off.

'Don't,' she uttered firmly.

'Sorry, Kate. Didn't mean to wind you up. And, of course, Mark wouldn't mention it. He's not the type to gossip.' The amusement had gone from his voice. He sounded contrite.

She blinked away the tears and opened her eyes. 'Just tell me, for goodness' sake. What wouldn't he have mentioned?'

He hesitated for a moment, then settled his gaze on her. 'She was a problem that Mark helped make go away. She was stalking me, Kate. That's why they interviewed me again yesterday. The good thing is, Mark's not the only suspect anymore. Sharma's got two of us to consider now.'

Kate's heart thumped. It took all her willpower not to jump up and call him a liar. Robert had to be bluffing. The way he said it sounded like Sharma already had the right suspect. So how was this meant to make things easier for Mark if it was him who helped make this woman go away? The answer was it couldn't. It sounded like Robert had made things worse. Had he deliberately offered himself as a suspect to bring something to light?

Kate couldn't look at him because she would reveal the sudden distrust she now felt. She remained sitting in her place, her hands folded over her stomach, and made a small moan at the period-like pain in her lower back. She prayed it was just hormone changes and she wasn't miscarrying. She needed this baby as much as she needed her little boy upstairs. She needed something good to hang onto for Jacob's sake. She needed someone else for Jacob to love if his father was taken away.

Robert was looking at her worriedly as the cramp subsided. The discomfort gave her a reason to get up.

She feigned weariness. 'Bed for me, Robert. Too much pizza and not enough sleep.'

He eyed her shrewdly. Kate managed not to flinch. She did what she would normally do when saying goodbye. She hugged him.

CHAPTER FORTY-ONE

Kate took her time cleaning the few plates and glasses in the kitchen. She needed to go over the story in her head. Robert had not explained how Mark helped make Fleur O'Connell go away, which could imply any number of things. As usual, his need to engage his audience had got in the way of the facts. At a party it was entertainment. He was a clever conversationalist, his wittiness provoking laughter often at himself, making him fun to be with. Tonight it had got on her nerves that he couldn't just tell her plainly. Everything he said seemed like it had to be punctuated with a bit of drama. Maybe it was from his insecurity, his need to be thought of as clever.

She listlessly wiped the countertop, missing some stains. Her mind was growing dark thoughts about Robert. Was he trying to start something with her, with Mark absent from the house? He had sat far too close to her for comfort. Invading her personal space. Or someone in need of attention who talked in riddles to make something more interesting? She couldn't decide. His behaviour had unsettled her.

The sound of Mark's Volvo pulling up outside was a relief. Olivia was safely back. It was an excellent vehicle for driving in snow with winter wheels fitted. With all things mechanical Mark prioritised safety first. There was little he didn't know about brake traction control or hydraulics. While flying was his first love, mechanical engineering came a close second.

She felt a catch in her throat at the thought of him not being able to fly again. Even if this investigation miraculously disappeared, there remained the problem of his health. Heart health. Number one on the list of medical disqualifiers for pilots. Flying an aircraft required a healthy heart. Mark's would be subject to rigorous examination and most likely lead to his licence being revoked. She breathed in deeply to steady her emotions as Olivia bounced into the kitchen, apologising before even removing her coat.

'I'm so sorry. They kept me there for ages.'

'Shush.' Kate smiled at her. 'Get your coat off and put your feet up. I've saved you some pizza and a glass of white wine.'

Olivia grinned. 'Thank the Lord, I'm famished.'

Kate let her eat while she made herself a cup of tea.

'Are you not joining me?' Olivia said.

Kate pointed to the glasses on the draining board. 'Had some already,' she white-lied. 'Robert was here.'

The animation in Olivia's face instantly reduced.

Kate caught the worry in her eyes. 'What's up?'

She picked at the crust of pizza left on the plate. Her lips parted as if to speak, then pressed closed. She unconsciously covered her mouth with her hand. Kate was no psychologist, but she could read this language. Olivia was supressing what she did not want to say.

Kate clued in. 'Is it Robert?'

Olivia nodded. Then put her head in her hands. 'I'm so confused. I'm not sure what's going on.' She glanced at Kate, seeking support. 'I've been asked the same questions about Robert as I was about Captain Jordan. And it isn't sitting well with me, I have to say. While I have a hundred per cent faith in

Captain Jordan's innocence, I can't be a hundred per cent sure of Robert. It felt like I was having to make a choice between the two of them.'

She shook her head. 'It was terrible!' she whispered. 'The police seem so sure it was one of them. On and on. Where was Robert? How did he seem? Did I see him leave the hotel? Did I notice when he injured his hand? I was so bloody scared to say the wrong thing in case I made it worse for either of them.'

Kate joined her at the table and grabbed hold of her hand. 'Hey, you're not alone. I've been in a quandary myself the last hour about whether or not to trust Robert.'

Olivia gave a small gasp. Then squeezed Kate's hand firmly. 'Don't say that! Please! I don't want to think of Robert as a murderer.'

Kate realised she'd said the wrong thing. Her distrust of Robert wasn't anything to do with having committed a murder. She was distrustful of his intentions to help with Jacob were pure, and not an ulterior motive to be around her. She quickly corrected the misunderstanding.

'I wasn't thinking that, Olivia. Far from it. I just found his behaviour tonight a little... not flirty. Maybe a bit intimate. I probably just imagined it. He's been our friend for so long. Mark's friend really, but mine as well. It just made me feel a little uneasy.'

Olivia gave her a frank stare, and tugged her hand away. 'He's got feelings for you. He mentions your name a lot at work. Always adding the prefix "Mark's wife, Kate" like it would make it less noticeable when he mentioned you.'

Kate took an unsteady breath. How was it she was the last to notice? If it had been that obvious? Olivia didn't need unsettling further, but there were things she was unaware of that needed to be discussed. Kate looked at her. 'I found out tonight Robert's the pilot Fleur O'Connell was stalking.'

Olivia's mouth fell open. Her eyes widened. It took her a

moment or two to focus. Either from shock or conscious of Jacob upstairs, her voice dropped close to a whisper. 'Holy crap. That's why they interviewed me again. They suspect Robert.' She shook her head in despair. 'Oh God, you don't think it's true, do you? He wouldn't do that to Captain Jordan? Kate, you need to get him to wake up. He might have answers.'

Kate jolted. Her hand flew up to cover her mouth as she gasped. 'Oh my God. I'm so sorry. I haven't told you how Mark is. He's awake, Olivia. He's talking normally.'

Tears spurted from Olivia's eyes in a silent waterfall, shocking Kate into fetching some kitchen roll.

Her voice was husky. 'That was a shock.' She sniffed and lightly laughed. 'A good one, I'm so relieved.'

Kate took a sip of Olivia's wine to settle her own nerves. It heartened her in one sense that Mark was so well liked, but she had concerns for Olivia's fragile emotions. She supposed her airline colleagues spent so much time together that maybe they were like a family to her, some she was more fond of than others.

'Let's say we put this to rest for now. I don't know about you, but my mind's in overdrive.'

Olivia agreed. 'Yes, please. You need your energy to get your husband well. And I'll need some to build snowmen. Hopefully they'll grit the roads overnight so you can still visit.'

Kate was worried by the sudden thought about Olivia and her circumstances. 'Olivia, you've been here since Tuesday. That's five days. You must be getting tired and you'll end up going back to work exhausted.'

'It's fine, Kate. I'm off until next Friday, but I won't be going back even then. My manager has put all the crew that were on the flight to Barcelona on paid leave as a duty of care. So I can stay, unless you've had enough of me?'

The uncertainty in her eyes formed a lump in Kate's throat. She felt guilty for waiting on a phone call to give the all-clear about Olivia, while still using her. 'I wouldn't have coped without you,' she answered honestly.

Olivia laughed. 'You'd soon get sick of my OCD ways. I'm a nightmare to live with. I'm permanently finding cupboards to put things in. You and Captain Jordan will be searching for your things after I'm gone.'

Kate smiled. 'You can call him Mark, you know.'

She scrunched her nose. 'No. I'm a stickler and like to maintain a certain behaviour. Goes with the rest of my character.'

Kate's shoulders sagged. 'Mark doesn't want to see me. Waking has made him remember what's going on. I think he wants to put a distance between us in case the worst happens. So I don't know how things will pan out tomorrow.'

Her face fell. 'You have to be there, Kate.'

Kate shrugged. 'That's all very well, but he can refuse to see me. I might only be allowed in if I take a patient from A & E, in which case I'd have to be at work.'

Kate pondered the idea. John had texted her a few times telling her to take all the time she needed. She'd think about it and decide in the morning. For now, she just needed to rest.

She went to where Olivia was sitting and gave her shoulders a brief hug from behind. 'Sleep well, Olivia. Sweet dreams.'

Olivia turned her head. 'Always, Kate. And always the same one. A home, with my son and his father.'

Kate held her eyes. There was so much hope in them. She couldn't imagine Jacob not living with her. It must hurt Olivia to see Kate with Jacob and be reminded of her son. She hoped things would work out for her in the future, that her hopes were not just a pipe dream.

She lightly squeezed Olivia's shoulder. 'If I can ever help your situation in any way, please just ask. I'd like to repay you for all your wonderful help.'

Olivia looked overwhelmed and gave a quick nod.

Kate left her then. It was a personal matter. She just hoped

Olivia realised her offer was genuine, because she *was* great with kids. Rarely had she seen Jacob take to someone so quickly. The only thing she'd have to guard against was him liking her too much, which was a small cross to bear. Her little worrier would have them all live together if he had his way. One big happy family.

CHAPTER FORTY-TWO

It felt strange to be wearing her uniform. The quickness of her decision to return might have something to do with it – back in the saddle after only thinking it last night and one phone call with John Brown.

And after a phone call with Julian.

'Sorry, Kate. He's an awkward cuss. He'd rather you didn't visit.'

John put her in charge of Minors. Kate didn't mind, but she thought her consultant put her there as a delaying tactic, so she didn't have to face resus straight away. It was a sympathetic gesture, if so, but not needed. The first thing Kate did was walk in to the resuscitation area and attend to the equipment around Mark's bed, its pristine sheet ready for the next casualty. Mark had died in there before they brought him back to life. She just wanted to make sure it was ready for the next patient to have the same chance.

Eva was working with her, which was a bonus. The mature student, sensing Kate was better off being busy than probed about her personal life, got straight down to business, letting Kate know which patients were a priority. Two hours in, Kate felt like she'd never been away – not in a good way. The word 'Minors' was misleading in the sense that people could think it less busy. In reality, most of the people in the waiting room were waiting to be seen by the staff. So far, she had dealt with a minor burn, a minor back ache, a minor wound requiring six sutures, a shoulder dislocation, a fractured arm, and a broken coccyx – all caused by minor mishaps. The workload had certainly helped her get back into the rhythm.

She was glad John stipulated a short shift. No more than five hours for her first day back. She'd be home in time to have tea with Jacob and bath him before bed. She knew he would be having a good day. Olivia promised snowmen, and now the roads were clearer his nana was there as well. Kate would try to persuade her mum to stay over so they could catch up. She hadn't seen her since Friday and had yet to tell her Mark's first sentence was because of her. She'd like to know that. Kate had a lot to tell her, some of it easier than the rest.

Kate was standing in the changing room when her phone rang. She stared with trepidation at the name on the screen.

Diane spent the first minute expressing her shock over what happened to Mark. Then her relief at hearing he was out of a coma, before asking Kate how she was coping?

While listening, Kate realised she still didn't have Olivia's surname. She wanted to ask about someone whose name she still didn't know. She would have to wing it.

'I'm doing okay, Diane. Robert and the cabin crew have been wonderful. I received the most amazing flowers. Olivia, one of the cabin crew, is staying with me to help with Jacob. They've all been given leave, apparently.'

'Yes, I heard that,' Diane responded in a puzzled tone. 'I understand it's a compassionate leave because of Mark. Very kind of the airline to do that.'

Kate shut her eyes in relief that Diane didn't know the real reason. 'Well, it's certainly helped me having Olivia in my home. Jacob's taken to her.'

There was a smile in Diane's voice. 'Well, that's good. She's a very capable woman. Had an asthma child onboard. Olivia was great with him. But then she's a mother.'

'That's what I wanted to talk to you about.'

'Why didn't you just ask, you daft thing? Totally understandable that you would want to know about her. Here's what I can tell you. Excellent at her job, cool head in an emergency. Obviously CRB checked. Non-smoker, but you probably already gathered that. Has a kid, that lives with her ex. Don't know the circumstances, but it's bound to be down to her job. She's full-time, so she's away more than she's home.'

'So no skeletons or anything that you know of?'

'None that I know of. Do you want me to check?'

Kate gave a reluctant reply. She felt guilty doing this. 'If you would, please. But discreet, of course. I'd hate for her to know I was asking about her.'

Diane reassured her. 'She won't, Kate. Not a dicky bird.'

* * *

Three snowmen stood on the lawn. The one in the middle was much smaller than the other two – a snowman and a snow-woman, judging by their scarves, as one was flowery and the other plain brown. The smaller snowperson was wearing Jacob's hat, so it wasn't difficult to work out this was him with his mummy and daddy. It was sweet. A lot of work went in to building them.

She kicked her trainers off in the hall and breathed in the heavenly aroma of something familiar. Her fingers crossed in the hope it was a roast dinner. Not counting Christmas, she couldn't remember the last time she had a Sunday roast. She and Mark took turns with cooking, but it was usually something quick.

Grace was busy at the stove. The room was like a furnace, with all the windows steamed up. She never used the extractor fan as she didn't like the noise. Kate crossed the room and opened the back door, careful not to make Grace jump while dealing with heavy pots and pans. She was in a world of her own and hadn't noticed Kate yet. The feel of the cold air made her turn, and Kate grinned at her happily.

'Is that stuffing I can smell?'

Grace walked towards her with an odd look on her flushed face. She put her hand behind Kate's head and pulled her in close so she could whisper in her ear. 'We need to talk.' She then stepped back and pointed up at the ceiling.

Kate sighed. She'd hoped to find her mum and Olivia getting along, but Grace had a bee in her bonnet about something. Kate nodded, then carried on talking in a normal voice in case they could be overheard. 'What can I do to help? Lay the table? Or decant the pots?'

Grace stared at her mutinously, her lips pursed in a circle of wrinkles.

Kate met her eyes and mouthed, 'Later.'

Grace gave a stiff nod and turned back to the stove. Kate left her to it. She needed to change out of her clothes. She took a two-minute shower, barely drying herself, and hurriedly dressed in clean joggers and a T-shirt. Then went in search of Jacob and Olivia.

The two of them were sitting on Jacob's bedroom floor with colouring books, sharing a pot of felt tips. Jacob was in his pyjamas, Olivia in a pair of Kate's pregnancy pyjamas that were well worn and not at all flattering.

Olivia glanced up and caught sight of Kate. She raised her eyebrows and gave a sigh of relief. She spoke quietly in a kind of code so as not to disturb Jacob from his busy drawing. 'Made sense to have our baths as already wet from the snow. No point in getting dressed in dry clothes when so close to bed. I've run out, I'm afraid, so had to borrow some. We're just hoping dinner will be soon as this one's tummy is rumbling. I think his nana is cooking for everyone in England. She's been in the kitchen for hours.'

Kate gave an amused smile. She could well imagine. Grace also didn't like anyone in the way while cooking.

'She might call us soon,' Olivia added, giving Kate her cue to leave.

Kate gave a thumbs-up to show she understood. She would try to hurry things along.

Grace was wiping the moisture from her face with the back of her sleeve. Kate wasn't surprised. The kitchen was like a steam room. But it was worth it. Dinner was ready. The roast chicken looked perfect. The roast potatoes crispy. The dish of stuffing had a crust on top. On the table, knives and forks, napkins torn from a kitchen roll, and a pint jug of gravy. She breathed it all in and felt her mouth water.

'It's ready,' Grace said.

Kate saw the exhaustion on her face and realised she hadn't considered properly how everything was affecting her. Grace loved Mark like a son. She'd witnessed him at his most vulnerable while reading to him in his hospital bed. Yet she had soldiered on to support Kate. After dinner, Kate would make time to talk to her and find out what was wrong, and tell her everything that had happened so as not to leave her in the dark. She would keep the news of the pregnancy in reserve for when she was sure it felt safe. It wouldn't be fair to give her that joy and have it snatched away afterwards. It was kinder to stay quiet about it.

CHAPTER FORTY-THREE

Kate carried the plated dinner wrapped in layers of tinfoil out to Grace's car. She wasn't given the chance to ask her to stay. As soon as the meal was over, Grace was on her feet to fetch the plate of food off the counter. She kissed Jacob's cheek, gave Olivia a cursory farewell, and bundled into her coat. She was on a mission to the hospital to see Mark.

Kate caught up with her mum at the car, her seat belt already on. Instead of putting the plate in the footwell, Kate got in beside her. She shut the car door.

'I didn't know you were going to see Mark,' Kate exclaimed.

Grace turned her head and stared at Kate pointedly. 'Someone has to.'

Kate's mouth dropped open. 'You think I don't want to see him? He won't let me, Mum! Why do you think I'm working again, except to be near him?'

Grace rested her head back and sighed wearily. 'There's a lot of cloak-and-dagger going on. I've never known you to be secretive, Kate, and it's worrying me.'

Kate reached for the hand resting on the steering wheel.

'Turn on the engine and I'll tell you everything. I don't want you getting cold.'

Half an hour later, Kate had given her the complete story and was relieved to see her coping better than expected. She'd winced and gasped a few times, but was able to collect herself. The deeper impact was in her steady blue eyes. She had not missed the seriousness of the situation, not by one iota. She fully understood.

She clasped her daughter's hand. 'I'll talk to him, Kate. He desperately needs you. I'm more worried about his mental health than his physical. I think that nice consultant is keeping him there for that reason. You can tell they're watching him carefully.'

Kate caught her lower lip between her teeth to keep it from trembling. Her voice was shaky. 'Probably, Mum. But I think Julian's also keeping him there to protect him from the police. As soon as he's fit, they're going to arrest him.'

Grace took a deep breath. 'You need to go back in. Olivia will wonder what's keeping you.'

'I'll say I was talking to you, Mum. That I was having a catch-up. Which is the truth.'

Grace gave a smaller sigh. 'I know it's not the best time, and you won't want to hear it, but I'm worried about Jacob.'

Kate went still. There, it was out in the open. It bothered her about her grandson. But why? He seemed happy. 'What are you worried about, Mum?'

Grace turned and looked at her. 'Do you realise he won't answer to his name, and insists he's called JJ. He's different with me, Kate. And it's not me being sensitive. I know my grandson well enough to know his behaviour has changed. He hasn't come to me once today. In fact, I don't think he would have spoken to me if Olivia hadn't taken a shower, leaving us on our own for that one time. He spent every minute with her. Laughing and playing like I wasn't there. He's become distant.'

Kate wasn't sure what to say without upsetting her. It all sounded like the normal behaviour of a small boy. Preferring to play with someone younger and more energetic, out in the snow building snowmen or colouring in books. He had bonded with Olivia – there was no taking that away from him. If Kate had sisters, he'd probably be the same way with them. From Grace's perspective, it must seem too extreme. Only a short while ago she was teaching him to knit, the bond between them like glue. Now Jacob had separated from her and gravitated to someone new. It didn't mean he didn't love his nana. In Jacob's words, he had enough room in his belly for everybody.

'I'm sorry he made you feel like that, Mum. You know he loves you.'

Grace reared back. She was shocked. 'You think this is about me? Have you forgotten who your mother is? You didn't get your common sense from your father. I'm not a fool. I expect my place in his life to change. I want that for him, as should you. The most important job of a mother is to make their child feel strong and independent, so that if you suddenly leave this world they will cope. You don't want them hurting for you, but you also don't want them confused. Jacob is showing attachment to a woman you barely know. Your home is changing, Kate. It might look all very nice, but if anyone makes a change, it should be you. You might think me a fuddy-duddy, but I've moved with the times and I'm pretty good at reading people. No young woman gives up all her time to mind someone else's child unless it's a paid job, or done by a family member. What do you even know about her?'

Kate had to bite back her resentment. She didn't need her mother's opinion about someone she didn't know. Would her mum feel this way if Kate had an au pair? Would she be resentful of Kate getting help from anyone other than her? She felt the pulse in her temples pound. Grace wasn't making this easy on her. But that was her character. All Kate's life Grace had been straight-talking, whether or not her opinion hurt. She wasn't there to be Kate's friend, she was there to be her mother. To tell her right from wrong, guide her morally, make her have a conscience, to take responsibility. No matter how harsh it might seem. She wouldn't sweet talk Kate to make things easier.

Kate calmed her thoughts. Her mother was not possessive. She liked her independence as much as the next person. She enjoyed being a grandparent, but she'd never tried to take over from Kate. All of this had to be from natural concern. With the lives of her daughter and grandson turned upside down, she was bound to be more anxious about further things happening. Kate could hear the anxiety in her voice now.

'Do you want to know what he talked about when we were on our own? He told me that mummies spend time with their children, and play with them. But his mummy isn't doing that. Olivia is, because Olivia cares. Where the hell did that come from? You should be at home, Kate, or else have me take over from Olivia. Jacob needs to know who his mummy is.'

Kate was scrabbling in her brain for an answer and leapt on something that was true. 'He's very bright, Mum. Jacob knows who his mummy is. Not for one second has Olivia replaced me. So please stop making me feel I should worry. Be honest, Mum, how well would we have coped with just us two? The both of us would have collapsed by now. What you have been doing is more than enough – seeing Mark, reading to him. Do you know the first sentence he said was because of you, because of the book you read about Concorde? He quoted a sentence from it.'

Grace jerked her head in denial. Her tone was adamant. 'We would have coped somehow. But that's in the past. I told you my thoughts. What you decide is up to you. I can pack a bag and come back in the morning. You can blame me for asking Olivia to leave. Tell her I want to be the one minding Jacob. She should understand. He's my grandson. It's up to you, Kate. Let me know if that's what you want.'

'I checked her out, Mum. No one had a bad word to say about her. She's good with children.'

Grace gave no acknowledgement. Her lips remained closed.

Kate got out of the car with a hard ball of resentment in her chest. She didn't doubt Grace's concerns were genuine, but addressing them wasn't so simple. Kate wasn't just looking at today because tomorrow could blow up in their faces. Who was better placed with Jacob if Kate had to deal with the fallout of having her husband arrested? His nana, who would be equally affected, or Olivia, who he could laugh and play with?

She let herself in the house. The hum of the dishwasher let her know where all the dishes had gone. Olivia had loaded it while Kate was outside. A look at the kitchen clock showed twenty past seven. She'd been in Grace's car for nearly an hour. She climbed quietly up the stairs. Jacob's door was ajar. Olivia was sitting on the edge of the bed with a storybook in her hands, but the pages were closed. She was talking to Jacob instead.

Kate felt like a traitor standing outside the room trying to listen, but Grace had made her paranoid with the thought that Olivia might poison his mind. She stood completely still and heard Olivia's voice.

'You're right. Peter Rabbit's mummy said they were not to go in to Mr McGregor's garden.'

'But they did,' Jacob replied softly. 'While their mummy was at home.'

'Yes, that's right.'

Jacob raised his voice. 'She looked after them in their little cave and made them dinner.'

Kate saw Olivia yawn. She patted her mouth. 'Oh dear. I'm tired.'

'That's because you're looking after me.'

Olivia angled her head so she looked down at Jacob's face. 'Yes, but only because your mummy is looking after lots of very sick people. She gets lots of people better, because she's brilliant. Not many people can do Mummy's job.'

'Or Daddy's,' Jacob mumbled tiredly.

Olivia eased off the bed, and Kate left her spot quickly and went silently to her bedroom. She sat on her bed, breathing freely, glad she had listened at the door. It wasn't Olivia causing Jacob to say those things. It was Mark's absence, and Kate being hardly at home. It was the longest Jacob had been apart from Mark. She should have noticed Jacob wasn't asking about his daddy, although maybe he was to Olivia.

Kate lay back on the bed in relief that Grace was wrong, vowing to spend more time with her son.

Tomorrow, she would take him to school and pick him up, and be his mummy. To reassure him she was still there.

CHAPTER FORTY-FOUR

Robert drank the sediment from the bottom of the glass. The wine dregs, he knew, showed the quality of the wine. It was his third one, but he saw no reason not to have another. He wasn't going anywhere. He was staying put in his chic and comfortable flat. He couldn't remember another time when he spent a whole day at home. Maybe the day he moved in, sorting out his stuff. Mostly it was a place to sleep or get ready in, or a place to entertain, but that would usually be in the evening.

It was spotlessly clean from the weekly Molly Maid service team of two. Between them and a laundry service, the linen on his bed was changed every Friday even if slept in only once. To break the pattern would put things out of sync, so Robert didn't interfere. His four-year-old fridge and cooker still looked brand new, his bathroom looked like it belonged in a five-star hotel. There was never so much as a crumb left in the toaster. He had no complaints. It was a perfect pad for a bachelor.

He poured some more red. He was drinking mostly to forget. Kate had been on his mind most of the day, with an ache in his heart since the night before when he watched her feelings for him change. He saw it in her eyes. She hadn't been able to hide that brief fear and then the distrust that followed. Over the years he'd seen her eyes light up with laughter and tears, anger and frustration and love, and there'd always been room in them for him. Now she didn't want him near her or her child. He had fucked up large.

He should never have said anything about Mark and Fleur. He had tried to play unfairly and interfere with fate and it had backfired. He should have just waited to see how it all panned out. Now he would be unable to see her or Jacob, who he would miss so much. He had sat close to Robert at the table, eating his pizza and laughing openly at every funny face Robert pulled behind his mother's back.

Robert never normally engaged with children for more than a few minutes, but with Jacob it was different. He asked such real and interesting questions. Why don't the stars fall out of the sky? He asked this after asking why planes don't fall on the ground from the sky? Robert did his best to make his replies interesting and was rewarded by Jacob asking even more.

Kate had been quiet, but it was to be expected with all that was going on. She was full steam ahead since Mark landed in Bristol from Spain. Her life hadn't been her own, and Robert was meant to have helped with that. Now Kate only had Olivia, who wasn't answering her phone to Robert. He wondered what Kate had said to her. Or what the police said. Maybe she'd been told not to have any communication with him. He'd send her a text when he was a little more sober. She was his insight into how Kate was. She'd kept him updated but had now clammed up, it would seem.

He needed her help to get Kate to trust him and want him back in her home. Robert needed to repair the damage as quickly as possible now that Mark was getting better. He needed to be Kate's friend again. Robert wasn't going to prison, but Mark very well could. Kate would then spend the rest of her life without him.

He slugged the wine back, his conscience tormenting him for wishing Mark was out of Kate's life. And for wanting to find fault with him. But he couldn't, really. Mark had qualities to be admired. He wasn't afraid to stand up for his friends or offer free advice. He was courageous facing his situation alone. Robert loved him and probably always would. He couldn't stop that feeling, any more than he could stop his feelings for Kate. The irony was, Mark would want him to be there for Kate. If only he could find a way back into her favour. She liked him before. Nothing about him had changed, so there was no reason she couldn't like him again. Mentioning Fleur had been a mistake, but he could undo that by telling Kate the truth.

He'd only dated Fleur once, and it got all out of proportion. She hadn't even seemed that interested. He hadn't even seen it coming until she kept popping up everywhere he went. Even then he put it down to coincidence. Mark was with him when he found her wish list in his jacket pocket. Robert had been embarrassed at finding it and was less kind than he could have been. He ridiculed her for pouring out her heart on paper, for listing what she desired in a man.

Mark had taken it from him, then taken matters into his own hands by bringing it to the attention of Fleur's manager. Mainly for her sake, Robert always suspected, after hearing him mumble about not liking the thought of her suffering from unrequited love. Robert recalled a look on his face and wondered at the time if there'd been a message somewhere in that for him. They had been friends since before Kate. They were together when they met her. Robert remembered that day well. Spotting her in the car park, looking cross and a little lost. His one chance, he'd overplayed his hand probably coming across ingratiating, instead of his true self. Then Mark stepped in to win the day. To Robert's knowledge, he'd never given away his feelings for Kate. He'd never told anyone how he felt about her.

He didn't understand why she had a hold on him that he couldn't shake off. He found other women desirable. His libido was in no way affected. But while he liked them and enjoyed their company, he felt nothing for them emotionally. He couldn't help but smile. There was one thing he should have said to Sharma – he felt nothing emotionally for the women he bedded.

With Kate it was the complete opposite. He clocked every expression she made. He could look at her open and guileless face forever. She could be sweating, have a greasy face, or food at the corner of her mouth – he embraced it all. There wasn't anything unattractive about her to him. He was thirty-eight and had given up all hope of settling down with anyone else. Which is why what happened in Barcelona was like a poisoned chalice he had to be wary of.

Whether Mark was guilty was down to the police to decide. They now had Robert as a suspect as well. He couldn't play fairer than that. It was giving Mark a chance to get out of the situation. What Robert couldn't understand was why Mark wasn't using his ace in the hole. He must know it would make a difference to his predicament. So why wasn't he trying to set himself free?

He must have a reason. Maybe he felt guilty. Or maybe he was biding his time for someone else to step forward and do the right thing.

For all his intelligence, Mark had too much faith in other peoples' goodness. No one would step forward to take his place if they could get away with murder. They would count their blessings and keep their head down.

Which is what Robert should do. If he wanted her *too* badly, or played unfair games like the night before, he wouldn't win. Whatever happened between him and Kate had to happen without him taking any action to turn things in his favour. If anything, he should actively look for ways to save Mark. He had time on his hands now. It wasn't going to make things worse for Mark, or even any better. But it might make fate, and Kate, see he was trying to make amends.

CHAPTER FORTY-FIVE

It felt an age since Kate was last at the school, standing with the mums and dads as the teachers herded the children into the classrooms. She enjoyed watching all the kisses and hugs. Jacob had introduced her to a little boy's mum as if it was Kate's first time there, which felt a little strange. But Kate didn't come every day, so it might have felt new for Jacob.

She returned to her car, ready to face work. Before leaving home she'd suggested to Olivia that she rest all day, or do something nice for herself. Olivia's reply had come across as strange – she had too much to do.

Kate hoped Olivia didn't think she was expected to clean the house when no one was there. She ought to get Grace to pop over and check Barney was okay after his visit to the vet. It's what she would do if Olivia wasn't there. Otherwise Olivia might think Barney was somehow her responsibility, that Kate had forgotten about him and didn't like to ask who would mind him in the day.

There was so much to think of. So many little details. She was losing hold of her daily routine, which was no one's fault. Having Olivia there had changed things. Going forward, or reverting to how things were, it made sense to use her mum again. Make the break now. Give Olivia time to recuperate before returning to her job.

When she got to the hospital she would give Grace a call and briefly put the idea across. Or tell her mother that she liked her suggestion and could pack a bag. Kate was confident Jacob would adjust to the change. He'd soon be knitting or making crumbles and apple pie with his nana again. And hopefully, soon, he would have something very special to look forward to, which he was certain to love. Kate needed to book in with her GP for an antenatal appointment. She had a feeling she conceived on her birthday, the fifth of December. She hadn't had a period since then, which should make her about six weeks. So still very early days to be getting hopeful yet.

The phone call to her mum got forgotten, as the plan changed after Kate bumped into Sophie walking towards her in the corridor. Sophie's face lit up and she exuberantly hugged Kate. While Kate laughed, it jolted her to realise they were friends again. It felt a little weird, like having an out-of-body experience where her emotions needed to catch up.

Sophie must have caught a look on her face, because she stepped back and appraised her with concern. 'Tell me. Am I too much?'

Her honesty helped. Kate gave a dry laugh. 'Always, Soph. You're like a bundle of electricity.'

She grinned. 'I can't help being a bright spark. Spare me five minutes, please. I already miss you.'

Kate gave in. She had a half hour before her shift started, and she could do with something sweet. Ice cream had been her craving when she was pregnant with Jacob, but she settled on a bar of chocolate, and Sophie drank tea. Kate filled her in on the latest, including her new intentions.

'Sounds a good plan,' was Sophie's immediate response. 'But let me check on Barney. It might be easier if Grace has a problem with Olivia. Give us your keys. I finish at lunchtime. I'll knock, of course, if Olivia's there, and just be natural about checking on Barney. That sound okay?'

It did, and was a better idea than sending Grace. 'Be nice to her, Soph. I'm about to ask her to go.'

Sophie's reply was positive. 'I will be. Don't worry. Just be concerned about Robert.' Her expression quickly changed to concern. She frowned. 'Actually, Kate, do you think this is the best time to ask her to leave? Your mum's hardly a defence if he tries anything. Or is in fact the murderer. I can't believe this woman stalked him. I mean there's the connection.'

Kate's body reacted. She shot out of her seat, alarming Sophie. It was absurd Sophie thinking of Robert this way. She wished now she hadn't said anything about his behaviour with her. It's not like he'd assaulted her. A pat on the head didn't count.

'Calm down, Kate. You need to stay calm for the tadpole,' she said firmly, glancing at Kate's midriff. 'I'll still go over and check on Barney, and say hello to Olivia. You've put her in the picture, so this will look like you care for her, and are checking to see she's okay.'

Kate was regretting bumping into Sophie. She'd be calmer, instead of having to wonder if Robert was a threat. Sophie needed to rein it in. Robert wouldn't overstep the mark. She was pretty sure about that. He wouldn't hurt her, or his friendship with Mark.

From the moment her shift started, Kate had no time to worry or wonder about anything apart from the patient she was attending with sickle cell anaemia. The twenty-year-old was in a pain crisis because he had crescent-shaped blood cells instead of disc-shaped blood cells, which don't move so easily through the vessels and block blood flow to the bones.

Usain's eyes were glazed as he breathed in Entonox, clenching his fists as Kate inserted a cannula. She had treated him before and knew he was a trooper. He just wanted a quick in and out, and for the treatment to be over. Morphine and hydration. It was a disease he inherited and lived with and mostly managed at home. But not today. He was febrile with tonsillitis, which she would refer to ENT.

Eva held his hand over the next half hour while the pain decreased, and Kate then fetched his mother to sit with him. She had come prepared with a small leather case and a reassuring presence. 'How's my sticky-blooded boy?' she asked.

Kate smile at her. 'Better than before. Better for having you.'

Kate finished her shift at two. She had time to go to the ICU before collecting Jacob from school. She identified herself on the intercom and Julian opened the door for her. The quick shake of his head told her the score. He stepped out into the corridor and looked at her regretfully. 'He won't budge, Kate. Your mum's with him, and he's fine with that, but he's refusing to see you.'

Kate felt her eyes prick. She sniffed the pressure from her nose. 'How's he doing?'

Julian rubbed a hand over his head. 'Physio have him walking. Physically he's doing well. Tired, as you would expect, but sharp as a razor otherwise. The biggest problem is he's not talking about anything to do with him. He's not asked why he's here, or what's happened. He can converse no problem at all, but not about himself.'

'What do you think he'd do if I just walked in?'

Julian shrugged. 'I don't know, but it can't happen against his wishes. I'm going to suggest a psyche review. Tell him I think it's in his best interest, and go from there.'

'Do you think he needs one?'

'Maybe. I don't know, Kate, but ongoing treatment will keep him here a little longer.'

Kate understood. She gazed at him gratefully, without

comment. Julian was buying Mark some time. 'Give him my love then, will you?'

'I will do, and hopefully he'll respond.'

Kate hurried back along the corridor, grateful to know Grace was with him. Maybe she'd feed him some of Kate's concerns and prompt him to want to see her. To be reassured that everything at home was safe and that his wife and child were coming to no harm.

Her fists clenched in her pockets at the sudden anger with him. He should have told her from the beginning everything he knew instead of holding things back. She was out here trying to piece it all together like a lost soul. Having to listen to Sophie and even Olivia speculating about Robert. How much did her husband damn well know? Was he sitting on the whole bloody truth? She couldn't fathom his behaviour. Why he would lie about leaving the hotel if his reason was innocent?

CHAPTER FORTY-SIX

Kate livened up for Jacob's sake, and chatted to him all the way home. Donning fleecy joggers, she played with him out in the last of the snow. She'd not even said hello to Olivia yet to make the most of the last hour of daylight.

She used the back doorstep to take off her wellies, encouraging Jacob to do the same before going indoors. Olivia had started dinner. 'Fish fingers okay?' she asked.

Jacob whooped a yippee, clearly happy with the menu. Kate didn't care, she would eat anything so long as it was soon. She shrugged off her jacket and offered to make tea and included a decaf for Jacob.

She was wondering if Olivia was going to mention Sophie's visit. Sophie hadn't let her know how it went. Olivia brought it up after they'd eaten the fish fingers and crinkly chips. She smiled as she placed a chocolate cake and pot of clotted cream on the table. 'From Sophie. She said you needed fattening up.'

Kate glanced at her. 'Was everything okay?'

Olivia gave a firm nod. Her voice was warm. 'Yes. She did a great job checking on me and Barney. She was lovely.'

Kate was glad it had gone well, and relieved she hadn't got

Grace to come instead. She lightly shook her head. 'She's not. She's a cow. She knows chocolate is my weakness.'

To prove it, Kate had two slices, then put the rest away. She was standing at the counter when her phone pinged a message. She retrieved it from her pocket and went still at seeing it was from Robert.

Kate, can we meet? I have something to tell you.

She placed the phone on the table for Olivia to read. Olivia raised her eyes to Kate. 'Sounds mysterious.'

Kate picked up the phone and replied.

You can catch me in A & E tomorrow. I'm there all morning till about two.

Once Jacob was in bed, Kate took a shower and only then noticed the gleaming bathroom. Olivia had minimised all the clutter on the tiled shelf above the sink. She had replaced the plastic toothbrush holder with a stone charcoal-grey tumbler, and a soap dish to match. Jacob's bath toys were now in a pale-grey plastic container held to the wall by suction cups. She stepped out onto the mat and grabbed a towel to take a closer look. The three items looked brand new. She wondered if Olivia was an Amazon shopper and was having things delivered.

Kate dressed in clean pyjamas and went in search of her. She was folding clean washing on her bed. 'You've been buying things again,' Kate called from the doorway.

Olivia sighed, pretending defeat. 'Here we go again. I told you you'd hate living with me. I'll be like this until I leave. Looking to make things tidy.'

Kate wandered into the room. 'I'd love to see your home then. I bet it's like a palace.'

'No. Just quiet. I live on my own.'

Kate glanced at the photograph by her bed, making out it was the first time she'd seen it. 'So this is him,' she said, pointing to it. 'God, he looks so like you.'

Olivia's eyes shone proudly. 'He can be a holy terror sometimes.'

Kate broached the subject. 'Did something go wrong with you and his father?'

Olivia's chin lowered to her chest. Her hair fell like a curtain across the side of her face. She tucked it behind her ear. 'He's with someone else, Kate.'

Kate's mouth shaped to the sound she made. 'Oh.'

'He's with someone, but things between them are not good. I just have to be patient. That's all you can do when you love someone.'

Kate tried to make a joke. 'Well, let's hope she's messy like me and he misses your tidiness.'

Olivia lightly laughed and lifted her face again. 'He's not the sort to notice if a house is clean or tidy. He prefers outdoors.'

Kate liked the sound of him. She changed the subject. 'I'm working again tomorrow. Please don't spend the day cleaning. But if you're here, make sure to keep the doors locked.'

'You're worried about Robert, aren't you?'

Kate shook her head. 'Not really. To be honest, I'm worried about my husband's involvement.'

Olivia stepped back in shock. 'My God, Kate, I can't believe you just said that.'

Kate felt an internal sinking. Her toes curled in embarrassment. She clearly wasn't allowed to be judgemental. 'I'm allowed, Olivia, to have doubts when my husband doesn't tell me the truth. He lied about not leaving the hotel.'

Olivia's voice was cool. 'Maybe he was hoping you trust him enough to not have to know everything. I know I would, if I was married to him.'

Kate resented her tone, and also her very presumptive words. Her support for Mark was now an irritation. When Kate was already irritable with herself. Having decided to never doubt him again, the suspicion had once again crept in. She didn't need Olivia on her case. The woman had to be coming up to thirty. She wasn't an innocent. Yet her reaction was like that of a Victorian, her passivity unable to allow the notion that he might be guilty of something.

Kate's own tone was brisk. 'Well, you're not me. After his lying, I can't just take things at face value.'

Olivia clearly didn't agree, her whole demeanour radiated disappointment. Kate didn't know which way to step. What was she meant to do? Say sorry for being honest?

Kate shifted uncomfortably and made a let's-not-do-this-now gesture with her hands.

Olivia leant forward to pick up an item to fold. Her eyes flickered to Kate, her voice casually blunt. 'It must be difficult for you being loved by both of them. Maybe that's what's clouding your faith.'

Kate's heart fluttered in her chest. Where the hell had that come from? It sounded like an insinuation. Was Olivia thinking she had feelings for Robert? This situation wasn't going to work. Not with Olivia making her feel she was in the enemy camp for simply sharing her thoughts. Tomorrow she would suggest Olivia leave. She had a feeling Olivia wouldn't object. Clearly she was as uncomfortable as Kate.

'I'm going to lock up,' Kate replied, taking her leave.

Downstairs, she found comfort in Barney, leaning into his basket to hug him. He licked her face and then pulled away, struggling to his legs.

'You need a wee, don't you?' she said, and led him outside the front door. 'Go on. Do your business.'

While she waited, she glanced around the garden. They were lucky to have as much land at the front of the house as at the back. The sloping drive up to the side of the property, joining the garden with a path leading to the back and to the front. Jacob could circumnavigate the house on his bike without meeting grass or gravel.

Barney was taking his time, sniffing at every blade of grass. She was about to encourage him inside when his head tilted upwards, teeth exposed, snarling.

She peered in the direction he was looking. The entrance to the drive, screened by low trees and bushes. Barney's snarl now turned into a continuous low-pitched bark. It was likely to be a fox. She dug her phone from her pocket and switched on its torch. She aimed the beam into the wall of foliage, but the lights on in the house made it too weak to show anything. She might as well have lit a match.

Olivia suddenly appeared at her side. 'What's he barking at?'

'Probably nothing,' Kate replied.

'First time I've heard him. He doesn't sound happy. Shall I grab a torch?'

'Yes, please. There's one under the stairs on a hook.'

Olivia hurried indoors. Returning a few seconds later, she switched on a much stronger beam and shone it at the leaves in the trees. Barney was now crawling on his belly, edging away from them.

Olivia let out a gasp. 'Someone's beside that bush.' She stepped in front of Kate and shouted. 'Oi! Fuck off. We can see you. Or I'll release this guard dog from its chain.'

The torch picked up a dark movement. Olivia began running towards it. Kate cried for her to stop, but her long legs carried her quickly across the lawn, her torch bouncing light on the ground. Kate heard an engine start up. A soft roar. She bounded after Olivia just in time to catch the shine of a metallic red. She came to an abrupt halt, gaping into the distance as the vehicle disappeared. She wondered if Olivia had seen it, whether she knew.

Her hand gripped Olivia's. She turned to her with wet eyes, angry tears. 'I can't believe Robert did that. Stand in my garden, watching us.'

Olivia gripped her hand in return and pulled her to the house, where Barney was waiting, looking fairly worn out from all his barking.

A giggle pushed out of Kate's throat at remembering what Olivia said. Once started, she could hardly get her breath, with each second the memory getting funnier. 'A guard dog on a chain,' she spluttered. 'And you're going to release him.'

'He is a guard dog. That was a valiant effort,' Olivia protested, before her own hysterics started. 'That belly crawl would have turned in to a full-blown charge when he was ready. He was just taking his time, as is sensible, before showing off his moves.'

In the kitchen the women had a glass of wine, and Kate gave Barney a treat. Kate wasn't ignoring her pregnancy, she was paying attention to her fear. It was squeezing her insides far too tight and drumming her heart too fast. She needed to calm down for the baby's sake. In the present situation, a cup of tea wouldn't do that. It might work in a hospital situation with a distressed relative, but Kate was more likely to throw the cup at the floor. She was furious at Robert for making her so afraid.

She grabbed out her phone and stabbed at the screen. Sent her message:

What the fuck are you playing at?

'There,' she said to Olivia. 'See how he likes that.'

Olivia took the phone from her. 'Don't, Kate. We don't know what he's capable of. Just tell the police.'

Kate's nod was tentative. Robert's visit had shaken her. She was having doubts about his character. Why did he come and stand in her garden? It was creepy, if not sinister. How was she going to explain this to Mark? He'd be devastated. *She* was devastated. 'I'm not doing it tonight, Olivia. Not over the phone. I'm going to see Sharma and tell him that I'm worried about Robert.'

CHAPTER FORTY-SEVEN

Sharma agreed to see her again at the hospital. Kate didn't let on that she was working. She had changed out of her scrubs back into her clothes for this meeting. She wasn't going to allow Sharma to know more than he needed to about her present situation. Even though she met him outside her husband's ward, Sharma didn't need to know that she had not been inside since Saturday morning when Mark sent her away.

She kicked off the conversation.

'Any update on my husband's hit-and-run driver?'

He shook his head. 'The answer is still no, I'm afraid.'

'Any update on my husband's innocence?'

He looked at her kindly. 'You know the answer to that.'

She folded her arms. 'Actually, Detective Sharma, I don't. I hear you now have a second suspect. So was this a two-man job? Are they both guilty of killing this woman? Or are you just hedging your bets?'

Sharma glanced up and down the corridor. She had ignored the offer to sit at their bench. She'd rather stay on her feet.

'I take it you've spoken with Mr Brennan, then?'

She pointed her chin at him. 'I have. He enlightened me

about a few things. He let me know Fleur O'Connell was stalking him, and that was why you interviewed him again. Have I got that about right?'

Sharma was wearing a white shirt under a buttoned-up navy suit. His black hair was immaculately smooth. He looked completely at ease with what she was telling him. His voice was calm, as if discussing the weather. 'Yes, I would say so.'

Kate was prepared to take a gamble with something else Robert said. 'Robert told me she was a problem that Mark helped make go away.'

He raised his eyebrows. 'My understanding is your husband reported her to the airline for harassing Mr Brennan.' Something shifted in his eyes, possibly regret, as he quickly added, 'That's the only information I can give you, as it's something you are already aware of.'

She hoped her expression didn't give away her surprise. How clever of Robert to have worded it in such a way as to appear to have only recently happened, instead of a year ago. Kate stopped sparring. She needed his support.

'So does this make Mr Brennan a strong suspect?'

Sharma clasped his hands together, the only sign he was not comfortable. 'As of this morning, Mr Brennan is no longer a person of interest. Your husband, I'm afraid, remains the only suspect.'

It took a second to realise what he said, for her knees to start shaking and her feet to stick to the ground. A sense of losing her last desperate hold of him overwhelmed her. Sharma was slipping from her reach. Kate closed her eyes to stop the ceiling spinning. She was going to be sick otherwise.

* * *

Rachel held the glass to her lips for her to sip. Over her shoulder she could see Julian talking to Sharma. Beneath her head was something soft. She drank the water and tried to sit up.

'Slowly,' Rachel advised. 'The wall's behind you. Let me set you against it.'

Kate used her hands to sit up and felt behind her back for the pillow. She found it to be Sharma's navy jacket. 'Can you give it to him, Rachel?'

The nurse didn't need to. Sharma was walking over to them. He crouched elegantly, his wrists lightly balancing on his knees. 'Are you okay?' he asked.

Kate nodded. 'Yes, I'm fine now.' She held out his jacket. 'Thanks for making me comfortable.'

He touched her hand. 'I'm sorry this is so stressful. Please look after yourself.'

Julian took his place as he walked away. His tone was light. 'Doctor Jordan, if you're going to faint, do it in your own department, not outside my door, please.'

Kate mildly glared at him. 'Shut up, Julian, and get me up before I wear out the floor.'

He chuckled. 'Still blazing, I see. That's what I like to hear. Your detective has a soft spot for you. I don't think he likes his job very much at the moment. You're making it hard for him.'

She grabbed onto Julian's arm to pull herself to a standing position. Hearing this made her feel worse. That Sharma was finding this difficult made it more real and something he couldn't stop. Kate let go of Julian and tested her legs. 'I'm fine.'

Rachel protested and said she'd fetch a wheelchair. Kate stopped her. She wasn't going to be wheeled to her department for a second time. She took out her phone and texted Sophie, asking her if she fancied a hot chocolate. The reply came back a few seconds later.

Kate then glanced at Julian and Rachel. 'The cavalry's on the way, so you two can please go away. Believe me, I'm not going to fall down a second time. I have too much respect for my dignity.'

Without giving them a chance to answer, Kate walked away. They watched her progress, her shoulders back and with her hair undone from its clips down her back, catching sunlight through the window in a blaze of colour.

Julian chuckled and shouted down the corridor. 'You're like a lion, Kate. A lion with a red mane.'

* * *

Sophie watched Kate fix her hair. 'You can't go back to work. You're being silly.'

'I'm fine, Soph. I want to be there in case Robert turns up.'

'He won't after the message you sent him. He'll stay away, you can bet. Why didn't you tell the detective when you were with him?'

Kate regarded her with an open expression. 'And say what? I think he was in my garden watching me. I didn't see him. I just got a flash of a red car. No, I want to be here and listen to what he has to say. He can tell me why he's no longer a suspect.'

Sophie took a sip of her orange juice. 'I think you should tell this Sharma about Robert's feelings. And why they should still be looking at him.'

Kate put the last clip in her hair. 'And again, say what? Robert has never confessed to any undying love. I'll look like a coy little wife trying to fight off a suitor. It won't wash. I need something concrete. And the only one I'll get that from is Robert. He hasn't been yet, because I asked a nurse to contact me if he turned up. So I'm going back to work for the next couple of hours in case he does.'

'Okay, but no heroics, and no going off with him on your own,' Sophie warned.

Kate glanced around at the busy canteen. 'I've left a department full of people. It'll be hard for him to get me on my own. The staff are going to be peeved. I've been gone too long. It was meant to be a twenty-minute break.'

Sophie stood up. 'I'm in theatre for the next few hours. Ring me there if you need me.'

Kate promised she would, before hurrying back to her department.

Come two o'clock, Kate had given up expecting him to turn up. Sophie was right – he was staying away. He hadn't responded to her text, which should have told her this already. It was going to be interesting when they next communicated. Their relationship had completely changed. They could not go back to their old ways. After last night, she could not pretend they were friends anymore.

She had to see Mark, even if she had to trick her way in. He owed her an explanation of why his so-called friend was behaving like this. If Mark was protecting him, he needed to stop. He needed to put his wife and son first. He needed to see Robert with open eyes.

That is what she would tell her husband when she saw him. To look at Robert. To look at his friend and tell her what he sees. Was Robert someone he could trust?

CHAPTER FORTY-EIGHT

Grace was at the school when Kate arrived. They'd made no prior arrangement, so it surprised Kate to find her there. She had in her hands a small carton of apple juice and a bag of popcorn. Her nose was pink and Kate huddled closer to give her some warmth.

'This is nice. He's going to be thrilled we're both here. Are you coming back to mine?'

Grace shook her head. 'No, it's just a hello, and then I'll be off.'

Kate tried to break the ice. She looked brittle and unhappy. Not the right face to greet her grandson. 'How did Mark like his dinner?'

Her shoulders shifted sideways, ignoring the question. Kate was trying not to think of Sunday, but this was clearly the issue.

'She's not staying forever, Mum. I'm needing her less and less. Yesterday and today I took Jacob to school and I'm collecting him now. I'm working short shifts. Soon she'll be gone, but at the moment she's making me feel safe.'

Grace turned her head sharply. 'What do you mean?'

Kate glanced at her phone. They had two minutes before

the classroom doors opened and the children were let out to the parents. She spoke quickly. 'It's Robert. I think he's somehow mixed up in what's happening to Mark. The police still think Mark is guilty, but I think it's Robert they should be looking at. He was outside the house last night. Watching us, I think.'

Grace clutched her arm. Whether to support herself or give comfort, Kate couldn't tell. Her shock was obvious in the two-handed grip she had on her daughter. Kate let the information settle and didn't say more until they collected Jacob and let him run around in the playground

'Are you shocked, Mum?' she asked as they sat on a small red bench.

'I've been shocked since you told me, Kate. I've thought of nothing else since. Mark doesn't mention it, but I saw a police officer outside the department on Sunday when I went there and again yesterday. They know he's awake and are standing guard. Am I shocked about Robert? Of course I am. I've known him as long as I've known Mark. He's shown no sign of his character being deranged. Surely they would pick up something like this in a pilot? In all the tests they run?'

Kate blessed her naivety. The only way to tell with certainty if someone was capable of murder is when they killed another human being. 'Well, they think Mark is guilty, and he's shown no signs either.'

Grace nervously fiddled with the collar of her blouse. 'How can they be so sure, Kate? Without concrete evidence?'

'I think, Mum, they have concrete evidence. In fact, they must do. What I'm trying to find out is how they have it. Which brings me back to Robert. I think he stole Mark's watch and planted it at the scene.'

'Mark's watch! The one with his name on? Is that what the police have?' Her voice was anxious.

Kate felt Grace slump against her and looked at her worriedly. Grace's face blanched, but she was breathing all right without needing her inhaler. Kate encouraged her to breathe in and out slowly until the pinkness returned to her cheeks.

'Don't you go fainting as well,' she lightly remarked.

A few moments later, Grace was studying her daughter's face. She gave a small gasp. 'You're pregnant. You fainted when you were pregnant with Jacob. Marks and Spencer, coming down the escalator, you fell on the poor man in front of you and gave us all a fright.'

Kate remembered. She barely nodded. 'Don't say anything to Mark. It's too early. I'm only a few weeks.'

Her mum sat hugging the news to herself, her eyes following Jacob around the playground. 'I don't know how you're coping with everything that's going on. You must be worn out.'

'I'm fine, Mum. I just need to see Mark.'

Grace opened her arms as Jacob ran towards them. 'Don't worry about it. I'll think of something. You go home and rest, and let that kind woman wait on you.'

Kate gave a slight smirk. 'I take it you're liking her more now?'

Grace hugged Jacob to her. 'How have you learned to run so fast?' she asked him.

'My legs have got long, Nana,' he explained sincerely.

Grace gazed sagely at Kate. 'If needs must, it's probably better that she stays.'

* * *

Olivia wasn't there when Kate got home. The house had a settled quietness about it, Barney's snoring adding a homeliness to it. Kate glanced around for a note from Olivia, but couldn't see one. The table and surfaces in the kitchen were clean. On impulse, she went upstairs to check Olivia's room. Her cabin suitcase was laid neatly on the floor. Kate's pregnancy pyjamas were folded on the pillow, and Kate was relieved she hadn't suddenly gone.

She slipped back down the stairs to start tea. Hopefully Olivia had taken her advice and was doing something for herself for a change. In the freezer she found a family size lasagne, which would be enough for the three of them. She'd serve it with some garlic bread. She turned the oven on and left the lasagne to cook.

She found Jacob in his room trying to take off his uniform. He had two small coat hangers ready to hang the clothes on the low hook on the back of his door. Kate would be happy if they just went on a chair, but he liked to do things properly. He seemed more quiet than usual. She helped him off with his jumper and kissed him on his head.

'That was nice seeing Nana?'

'Uh-huh,' he agreed, holding his neck up for her to undo the top button on his shirt.

She undid the first three, then said, 'Hands in the air like you don't care.'

Jacob put his arms up for her to ease the shirt over his head. She turned it in the right way to make it easier for him to pull on in the morning, then helped him into the pyjamas he had on last night. It would be a face and hands wash before bed. He was tired and so was she.

'Do you want to watch some TV?'

'I don't mind.'

His response was wan. Kate glanced at him closely. 'I'll watch with you if you like?'

He surprised her by answering with a question. 'What's a divorce, Mummy?'

Kate wondered where the interest came from. She answered him simply. 'It's when two people who are married don't want to be married anymore. They get a divorce and live in separate homes.'

He nodded solemnly. 'Julie's mummy is getting a divorce. Her daddy's going to live in their caravan.'

'Oh,' Kate replied, assuming this must be a schoolfriend. 'Is your friend Julie sad?'

'I don't know. She didn't say. Is that where Daddy is? In another home because you had a divorce?'

Kate was stunned, and thought to herself, out of the mouths of babes. She kept her voice jokingly light. 'Wow. Poor Daddy in another home. I don't think so. All his clothes are here. His shoes, and coats, and his car. Daddy's just been a long time at work, but he'll be home soon.'

Kate wondered if she was doing damage by lying. If Mark hadn't woken with full capacity, she would have had a difficult conversation with Jacob by now. She would have told him that his father had been in an accident and had hurt his head. But Kate herself had been in a waiting game, and still was, ever since this all began. She'd rather talk to Jacob about the outcome when it happened, without having given him a dummy run of other possible outcomes that had come and gone. If Mark wasn't coming home, she only wanted to tell him once.

CHAPTER FORTY-NINE

Hours later, Kate was looking out of the windowpane when she saw the headlamps of Mark's car. She came away from the window, not wanting to get caught looking out. She sat on the sofa and picked up the book beside her, pretending to read.

Olivia spotted her from the hallway. She came in to the room and frowned at the book in Kate's hands. 'Have you mastered how to read upside down?'

Kate stared at the pages and gave a sheepish look. 'Didn't want to look like a worrywart when you came in.'

Olivia put a hand to her mouth. 'I didn't think! Have you been sitting here waiting for me to come home?'

'Pretty much.' Kate stared with a fixed grin to keep her emotions at bay. 'Never mind. Tell me about your day.'

Olivia sat down beside her and picked up Kate's book to hit herself on the head. She sighed heavily. 'Why didn't you text? I would have let you know where I was straight away.'

Kate felt foolish. She should have thought of it herself. She took the book from Olivia and gave the same punishment to her own head. 'Because I'm an idiot. That's why.'

Olivia pushed off her trainers to reveal a pair of Mark's

socks. Kate didn't comment. Her feet were bigger than Kate's and might have felt squashed in her size four to seven's. 'No, you're not. I get that title for not seeing what was in front of my nose. I've been staking out Robert's place.'

Kate's face turned in alarm. 'What?'

'It's okay, he wasn't there.'

'How long were you there?'

Olivia counted on her fingers. 'About seven hours. Apart from a quick pee in a Chinese restaurant.'

'You're mad,' Kate pronounced.

'I am, but I also have new information. I phoned my cabin crew colleagues to see how they were and had an interesting chat with one of them. She's new. Her name's Kerry. It seems Kerry saw Robert leaving the hotel not long after Mark left. The purser persuaded her to report it to the police.'

Kate's eyes opened wide. 'He never told me this. He was out the same time as Mark. So how come the police aren't still interested in him?'

'I don't know, Kate. I can't fathom it. Has he been in touch at all?'

Kate shook her head, then realised she hadn't looked at her phone once since being home. 'Let me check.'

She fetched it from the charger in the kitchen. Olivia had followed and was filling the kettle. There was a message sent an hour ago, at nine p.m.

Sorry if I scared you. Was just making sure you were safe. You don't need to be afraid of me, Kate.

'What the hell?' Olivia said as Kate showed her the screen. 'What is that meant to mean?'

Kate felt her insides cramp. His message was having the opposite effect. Of course she'd be afraid with him standing in the dark in her garden. How was that supposed to make her feel safe? 'I'm changing the locks. In case he's made a copy of my keys.'

Olivia looked undecided. 'He hasn't had them, not since you gave them. They've been with me the whole time.'

Kate had made up her mind. 'I'm not taking chances. If he comes here again, I'm ringing 999. He can fuck off with his *didn't mean to scare me* and tell it to them. I'm not playing his game. Maybe it wasn't Fleur O'Connell doing the stalking, but the other way around. I wouldn't put anything past him now. I don't know what he's capable of anymore!'

Olivia cupped Kate's shoulder and gave a reassuring squeeze. 'At least it's helped you trust Captain Jordan again. You don't think anything bad about him now.'

Kate leaned against her for a few moments in response. It wasn't fair to share her doubts about Mark. Olivia wouldn't understand the troubling thoughts Kate still had about her husband. Like, why wouldn't he see her? Was it just to distance her from what was about to happen? Or were there ulterior reasons for keeping her away? Perhaps he didn't want her asking again for the truth? He was smart and would know she wouldn't settle until he told her what really happened. He could avoid that by not letting her see him, or talk to him.

She glanced at her phone. Mark's mobile was upstairs in the bedroom. He did not have it on him when he was knocked down. Which helped Sharma's theory. He left all his identification behind when he walked out of the house that day, ostensibly to go for a walk. But maybe he emptied his pockets to leave his life behind? Kate didn't want to believe this was what happened. It was just another annoying factor to consider. To leave her in the dark with all the other murky thoughts. He had done a good job of leaving her to fathom it all. She just wanted to ask why. Why couldn't he have trusted her with the truth from the very beginning?

Was she difficult to talk to? Had her distrust in the past tied his hands, so he feared mentioning any involvement with any woman he came in contact with in case it kicked things off again? Had she made this part of their marriage awkward so he couldn't talk about normal happenings, like losing his watch, in case she jumped to conclusions? He would know that she was hanging on to his brief indiscretion in the bathroom, when he let her down. Only he hadn't. He wasn't attracted to Sophie.

God, she felt pious. That she should even expect a perfect marriage for all of her life? It must have been so boring trying to live up to her standards. It's a wonder he hadn't walked away.

'What's going through your mind? I can feel the tension in you,' Olivia asked.

Kate sighed and gave a watered-down version of her thoughts. 'Only that I'm boring and stupid as well.'

Olivia clasped Kate by the shoulders, this time to give her a reassuring hold. 'I don't think so. If that were true, Captain Jordan wouldn't be with you.'

Kate smiled dryly at the backhanded compliment. It was nice to know where she ranked in Olivia's estimation. She clearly had Mark on a pedestal. Kate could cope with that and wouldn't want to knock him off it. He was Olivia's captain. It was best leave it at that.

CHAPTER FIFTY

Kate was wearing out the corridor with her repeated pacing. Now so familiar, she recognised the cracked paint lines in the walls, and had memorised every noticeboard along the way. She had come up with a plan she hoped would work, having confirmed Julian was unavailable to speak to her because he was off the ward.

Before leaving home this morning, she put Mark's mobile in her bag. It would be the reason for her visit, as he would want it with him. All she had to do was get on the ward. If he refused to talk to her, she had a letter ready for him she wrote after finishing her shift. It wasn't long, but was explicit enough to cause him concern. She was afraid of Robert.

It was quarter past two. She hadn't given herself much time. It might be wise to ring Olivia and ask her to collect Jacob from school. That way she'd be under no pressure. She tried calling, but Olivia wasn't picking up. She wrote a text, apologising for the short notice and favour, and hoped for a response soon.

She raised her hand to press the intercom as a doctor leaving the department opened the door. Kate smiled at him and said thanks as she passed through the opening, acting like it was normal to be let in. She walked to a second door and looked through a window at Mark's bed.

Her heart skidded to a halt. Her brain couldn't assemble what she saw. Jacob was sitting on Mark's bed. Mark sat in the chair beside it.

She couldn't understand how this could be happening. Jacob should be in school. How had he got here? His small hands were clasped, his shoulders hunched up around his ears. Kate's eyes fixed on her phone as it pinged a message.

No worries. On the way.

Kate peered again at her son. In that moment, Olivia appeared, joining them and sitting in a chair beside Mark, her phone still in her hand. Seeing her through the window, Kate felt the treachery press in on her. Olivia had just lied to her horribly. She had taken a liberty with this unwanted intrusion into Kate's life.

Kate backed away from the door. She reached the outer door to the department and fled back the way she came. A couple walking towards her jumped out of the way. She felt a loss of her bearings. How had she let this happen? Every day she had trusted Olivia and this is what she did behind her back? She had taken Jacob out of school to bring him to the hospital see his father. Everything Kate had done to protect Jacob from knowing why his father wasn't home, Olivia had undone, and also broken Jacob's trust in his mother.

She reached her car shaken to the core. Once inside, she leant her head against the steering wheel. She'd been doing her best to keep everything from falling apart, to keep her fears at bay. And all the while Olivia had not had her back – she had taken matters into her own hands and completely destroyed Kate's trust.

She felt a hammering in her forehead. Her poor little boy.

What a shock it must have been to see his daddy in hospital. It would stir his fear at the thought of leaving his daddy in the hospital when Olivia and him had to go. He would lie awake worrying about when Daddy would come home.

She raised her head. Forewarned was forearmed. She would take on the caring for Jacob from now on. Olivia could pack her bags. When Jacob arrived home, Kate would be ready if he tried to push her away. Her usual mothering style would soon sort that out, the same as it did when he was ill. Treat every symptom when it occurred. When hungry she'd feed him, when bored she'd play with him, when sad she'd stroke his hair. It wouldn't take long for him to trust her again. She would start by being honest and tell him she knew he had seen his daddy. Mummy had lied only because she loved him and didn't want him to worry. The important thing to impress on him was that he had his mummy and Barney and Nana at home with him. And then he could forget Olivia.

* * *

On the surface, everything seemed unchanged. The two came through to the kitchen as if everything was normal. The only giveaway was Jacob, who avoided looking at her. Kate took the initiative, not giving Olivia a chance to hoodwink her further. She went over to Jacob and pulled him into her arms.

'I know you've been to see Daddy. I'm sorry I didn't tell you where he was, but I didn't want you to worry.'

Kate heard Olivia gasp, but focused her attention solely on Jacob. 'Can you understand why Mummy told you a lie? I didn't want you worrying about Daddy.'

Jacob was resisting her hug. His small hands lay curled between them, not attempting to hug her back. Kate eased back to look at his face. His eyes were closed. She nuzzled his cheek and tasted the salt of a tear. She hugged him closer. 'How about you and me snuggle up in Mummy's bed with the iPad and look for dinosaurs? We can have a picnic in bed?'

She felt his head move against her chest and picked him up. She carried him up the stairs and on to her bed. She settled a pillow behind him, and found the iPad, putting on a dinosaur programme for kids.

She waited until she saw him engaged in the programme. 'I'll be back in a minute with our picnic,' she whispered.

Olivia hadn't moved from her spot in the kitchen. Kate ignored her, hoping she'd get the message and leave. She put some snacks on a tray with a carton of juice and was heading back out the door when Olivia spoke.

'I had to take him, Kate. He thought his daddy was dead.'

Kate turned and stared at her. Olivia's face was pale, her stance rigid with resentment.

'How would he think that?' Kate asked coldly.

Olivia stepped forward. 'Because he heard your mum talking on the phone about him being brain dead. He's had it in his head, probably since the accident, that his daddy is dead. The school phoned your landline and said Jacob had a tummy ache, and could we pick him up. When I got him in the car, he was upset. He said his tummy kept hurting because his daddy's brain was dead. I asked him what he meant, and he said Nana had said it on the phone.

'What was I meant to do, Kate? Ignore it? Or try to help by putting his mind at rest. You said you couldn't visit Captain Jordan, so I took him, hoping it would help you and your situation. And I'm not sorry I did, after seeing the relief on his face. I would have told you when we were on our own. I really thought it would help you. Not that you'd see it like I'd done something wrong. For that, I'm sorry. For that reason, I'm going to get my things and leave. I've clearly outstayed my welcome.'

She was halfway up the stairs when Kate called her back.

She turned with overly bright eyes. 'I'm sorry if what I did hurt you.'

Kate set down the tray. Her heart was racing. Was she in the wrong for reacting this way? The lie Olivia had texted rankled. Why say *On the way* when she was sitting right beside him, making a fool out of her? It was the small things as much as anything that hurt her. But what did she do now? Let Olivia go on her way, or try to make amends? Should she even bother? In the first place, Olivia should have told her about the school calling and let Kate collect him instead.

She rested her hand on her neck, feeling frustration at beginning to feel guilty. Olivia had been trying to help by saving Kate the journey. What Jacob had told her, she couldn't have foreseen. If their positions were reversed, in the same circumstances, Kate might have done the same to help a child in distress.

'Can we start again?' she asked quietly.

Olivia sat down on the stairs. She rested her head against the wall. She gave her a long look. 'What did you say about you being boring? I wish.' She sighed. 'Let's say we start again tomorrow. You give your boy his picnic and hugs. I'm going to take Barney for a walk around the garden, and then have a long bath. We probably both need a night to just chill.'

By the time Kate collected the tray, Olivia had disappeared to her room. They didn't see one another again that night. Kate let Jacob sleep in her bed, only leaving the room to use the bathroom. She lay by her sleeping son, thinking into the early hours. Had Jacob's visit changed Mark's decision? Would he now see her after so long? She hoped seeing Jacob had pricked his conscience, that while he was there, she was at home waiting, worried.

CHAPTER FIFTY-ONE

Kate peeled the bloodied gloves off her hands and dropped them into a biohazard bin. The patient was admiring Kate's handiwork. It was not the first time she had put stitches in Kitty. The slash along the length of her forearm made with a Stanley knife had missed arteries and tendons, as was the intention. Kitty had learned to cut her skin deeply enough to be extremely painful, but without losing the use of her limbs. She cut or burned herself to cope with the emotional pain, and afterwards was always so grateful for the care received.

Kate was transferring her to the Obs ward where she would be seen by the Psychiatric Liaison Team. It depressed Kate, though she would never show it, that this beautiful twenty-three-year-old responded to severe emotional distress by self-harming. She wished the world could feel a better place for her, so she would stop what she was doing. Kate found it hard to conceive of hurting oneself so violently. She didn't judge Kitty. She couldn't. The nearest she could come to understand was the thought of digging out a deep splinter from her own skin, especially if she drew blood and had to keep digging, and the sweet relief when the splinter was out. She would be hurting herself to stop the pain. Which was what Kitty was doing with a different kind of hurt – cutting to find relief.

Kate went to the loo and washed her face. She was tired after a sleepless night. On the plus side, Jacob had woken curled to her side, smiling. She would ensure it continued, no matter what the outcome with Mark. His son deserved a happy life.

Eva was waiting to see her when she came out of the staffroom. 'There's a man waiting to see you. He's not a patient.'

Kate immediately thought of Robert. She must have looked anxious, because Eva asked if she should send him away. 'I can say you're busy.'

Kate shook her head. 'Where is he?'

'In the waiting room, standing near reception. He's wearing a green jacket, and has a bald head.'

Kate frowned in surprise. Whoever it was, it wasn't Robert. 'If I'm not back in ten, come rescue me. It's probably a thank you or a complaint.'

Kate headed out to reception. Her surprise turned to genuine pleasure when she saw her visitor. Abe Grier was a pilot, due to retire soon. He had visited Kate on Christmas Eve to deliver a present for Jacob and had told her then he was giving up his wings.

She approached him, smiling. 'What are you doing here?'

Abe touched his forehead with a brief salute. 'Been visiting your man upstairs. Cheeky swine said I needed a haircut.' He gave a self-deprecating smile, before turning more serious. 'I was scared to come. I didn't believe it when they said he was all right, but he's as right as rain to look at him.'

Kate wasn't so sure. When she saw him yesterday, sitting in the chair, unshaven, he'd looked grey and the spark gone from him. 'So you thought you'd pop in and say hello to me while you're here?' Kate remarked.

'That, of course. And to ask for some help as well, if you've got a second. I'm trying to track down Robert. Mark said I might find you here.'

Kate wondered if it was Olivia or Grace who told Mark she was back at work. It didn't really matter either way. It wasn't a secret.

'I've no idea where Robert is. I've got his phone number if that helps?'

He shook his head. 'No, I've tried it. I've tried several times. He's not answering.'

'What about his home? Have you tried visiting?'

His expression livened. 'Blast, I should have asked Mark his address. Do you have it?'

Kate didn't. She had a rough idea of where he lived in Bristol. She'd never been there, but she knew someone who had. She fished out her phone and asked Abe to get ready to take a number. 'I'm sure she won't mind. She's a colleague of yours. Just tell her I gave it to you.' Kate rattled off the number while Abe added it to his contacts. 'Her name's Olivia. She knows Robert's address. I'm sure she'll give it to you.'

'Thanks, Kate. Appreciate it. I'll not keep you any longer.'

His departure was swift. Kate wondered at the hurry, and at the words he had used. Trying to get a hold of someone sounded more friendly than trying to track down someone. It sounded less like a hunt, more a desire. Though maybe only to her. She was being fanciful in her thoughts about Robert, making Abe's intention dark when it probably wasn't.

She was still standing in a world of her own when Eva came to the rescue. Eva looked about and stated the obvious. 'Well, it looks like he's gone. Did he leave you under a spell?'

Kate gave a short laugh, turning to lead the way back to the patients they had left behind the closed doors.

'I spoke too soon. He's back,' said Eva.

Abe came towards them in a hurry, his affable expression

replaced by a serious look. He got straight to the point. 'Kate, I need to talk to you privately.'

Kate felt a swirl of anxiety wrap around her chest. Abe probably wanted to discuss something personal, but her mind was on hyper alert, in case it was to do with Robert or Mark.

'I finish in twenty minutes. Can it wait till then?'

He looked undecided for a moment, before nodding. She noticed the small hesitation and pressed her hand against her stomach to settle her nerves. She longed for the day this terrible uncertainty would leave her. Its constant shadow blighted every moment of happiness, like it was a living creature with a dark heart feeding on her fear. Waiting... waiting... waiting... To drag her all the way down.

CHAPTER FIFTY-TWO

Kate realised she wouldn't be able to see Abe and still have time to collect Jacob from school. She rang Olivia and asked her to do the honours, which she was clearly eager to do to get back on the right footing. Kate was relieved. She didn't like falling out with anyone, especially with Olivia, after she had been so kind. It would have been a horrible ending to the relationship. She had felt a genuine shock at seeing her with Jacob and Mark. It was difficult to get that image out of her head. Thankfully, overnight, logic had prevailed – that visit had done Jacob good. He now knew his father was alive, and his tummy could stop hurting.

Kate passed through the A & E waiting room, keeping her head down, glad she had changed into civvies. Any scent of a doctor or a nurse would have these patients pounce on any of them trying to escape. She joined Abe as he was lighting a cigarette and moved him quickly away from outside the department.

'I thought you'd given up,' she scolded as they crossed the road to stand away from the building.

'I have,' he replied, taking a puff. 'I only have the odd one when stressed.' He eyed the cricket pitch beside them and nodded at the clubhouse. 'Do you think they'll be serving?'

She pointed to a gate in the hedge, and they went through and walked around the boundary rope to the clubhouse. A couple of old boys braved the cold sipping pints outside the club. She beat Abe to the bar and asked him what he was drinking. He ordered a half pint of bitter to go with her orange juice and put the money on the counter before she could.

The place was empty apart from the landlady. They took their drinks to a table by a window and sat down. Abe drank a third of the beer and wiped his top lip before she had taken a sip. He then looked at her with reluctance.

'Olivia Vaughn,' he stated quietly, making Kate sit up, alert. 'I recognised her voice, but she confirmed her name for me. She gave me Robert's address. Do you know much about her, Kate?'

A surge of anxiety spasmed in Kate's chest. It would be ludicrous to say she only now knew her complete name, thanks to Abe. She gripped her glass tightly to hide her trembling fingers, hoping to press the tremor away. She spoke in a breathless rush. 'Not much. She works for the airline. Robert introduced her. She has a little boy who doesn't live with her. She's helping me mind Jacob.'

'So nothing else?' he asked.

Kate's hand wobbled the glass. She let go of it and laid her hand on her lap. Her eyes fixed on his face. 'Abe, you're scaring me.'

He winced. His expression showed concern. 'I don't mean to, Kate. Has she mentioned why she's not with her son?'

Kate lamely shook her head.

'She should have,' Abe said firmly. 'I don't know the full story. Only that Olivia Vaughn's husband has full custody, and she's not allowed to see the child anymore. I'm not suggesting Olivia's a danger to children, otherwise she wouldn't be in the job she's in, but the fact she's not allowed contact with her own child concerns me. You should get her to tell you, Kate. Or reconsider your childminding arrangements while you find out if she's suitable for the job. I had to tell you, in case you didn't know.'

Kate felt the blood drain from her face. The enormity of what she had done suspended the breath in her throat. She had trusted someone with her son without properly checking them first. She asked Diane if there were any skeletons and was waiting to hear back. And in the meantime, ignored Grace's concerns.

He's become distant. He won't answer to his name.

She had left Jacob with a mother who wasn't allowed to see her own son.

The room tilted as her heart rate soared in her chest. She reached for the orange juice and gulped it down, staving off a second faint. She wiped her mouth with her sleeve. In a shaken voice she asked Abe, 'Does Mark know this? Only she visited him yesterday.'

He raised his heavy brows. 'In that case, no. He would have mentioned it to you otherwise. I don't think many people know. The only reason I'm aware is she got blotto on an overnight stop and wasn't fit for duty. She couldn't sit up properly at breakfast, so I had to have a word. She spilled it all out. Her husband got custody of her child. He didn't think her a very good mother. From my limited experience, though thankfully me and June co-parented our kids, a father getting full custody has to be rare. He would have to have proved he was the only suitable parent. The courts would have considered the welfare and best interests of the child for it to have happened.'

Kate waited until the shakes subsided before getting to her feet. She couldn't pretend nothing was wrong. The burning question in her mind – why wasn't Olivia allowed to see her son? She needed to leave quickly, leave Abe sitting there while she rescued her own son. Sophie's words were coming back to haunt her. Why is an attractive young woman giving all her time?

Kate could think of only one reason – Jacob.

And she could think of only one person who would know what to do. Outside the clubhouse, she called Sophie. Kate held her head in her hand while she relayed her concerns. Sophie cut her off. 'Give me ten minutes. Buy some time. Call her and tell her you're going to be late. You can't wade in knowing only this.'

Sophie was true to her word and shortly joined Kate in her car. Getting in the passenger's side, she showed Kate a piece of a paper. Kate's eyes widened at the name above the written address.

'Did you call her?' Sophie asked.

'I'm just about to try again,' Kate replied. 'She didn't pick up.'

Sophie nodded. 'I'll just sit here quiet then.'

When Olivia answered, Kate didn't give her a chance to speak. 'Why didn't you tell me you can't see your son?' she asked in a snippy voice.

Olivia gasped in Kate's ear. 'How do you know that? Who told you? Can you let me explain? I would have told you. Just give me a minute and I'll tell you. I just need to pull over.'

Her quivering voice cut in and out at the rapidity of her speech. Kate could hear the panic and instantly regretted making the call. It was stupid of her when the woman was driving. Calling her out of the blue and challenging her about her past was not brilliant. Jacob was with her and would pick up on her distress.

A few moments later, her voice still quivering, she informed Kate she was parked.

Kate now had to calm her and control the situation. She made herself smile, knowing it would alter her voice to sound friendly and warm. 'Olivia, please don't get upset. I'm not angry, I promise. I was just surprised to hear about the situation with your son. I would have preferred to hear it from you, and not some nosy parker.' She gave a deep, weary sigh. 'I'm beginning to think I'm an ogre. My husband can't even talk to me. And now you. Am I that unapproachable?'

'You're not an ogre, Kate. It's just... it's embarrassing.' Her voice wobbled, like she was on the verge of tears. And now Kate could hear Jacob.

''Livia, 'Livia, are you okay?'

Kate's heart squeezed. His concern was endearing. She spoke loudly in the hope he could hear her voice through Olivia's speaker. 'Give her a hug, Jacob, she needs one. A big one.'

She heard Olivia reassuring him. 'It's okay, JJ. I've just got a bad cold.' She then spoke to Kate in a subdued tone, 'I'm fine, now. I was just shocked.'

Kate bet she was. She had not expected Kate to say what she had, but the conversation should have happened when Jacob was out of earshot. It was not a subject for his ears. She kept her tone light. 'I'm going to do a food shop. Is there anything you both fancy for tea?'

The change of subject worked. Kate could hear her talking more normally to Jacob. 'She wants to know what we fancy for tea.'

Kate pulled a face at the phone at being referred to as 'she'. Olivia could have called her Mum or Mummy instead, like most people would when talking to the mother's child. They came to an agreement and Olivia announced their choice. 'Sausages and mash, which I can start cooking when I get back as you already have potatoes, and there are sausages in the freezer.'

'Thanks. That would be great. So, see you in a bit.'

Kate had no intention of going shopping. She only said it as an excuse for not going straight home, because Sophie had found an address for Luke Vaughn. She didn't want Olivia wondering why she was late.

Sophie was eyeing her as she put away her phone. 'I heard most of it. I thought she was going to cry. I feel bad now for finding this.' She waved the piece of paper. 'Maybe we should leave it. Let Olivia explain. You don't want to do this.'

Kate shook her head in annoyance. 'I have no choice. I didn't even know there was a husband until Abe told me. You sure it's him?'

'Has to be. He's down as next of kin for an Olivia Vaughn. It must be her, because it's the only one I found around her age. She's thirty-one. Not as young as I thought. Born 1991... Kate, she might tell you, if you give her the chance.'

Kate's voice was scathing. 'Why should I? She made out it was her job why her son was living with his dad.'

'Calm down, Kate. I just don't want you to have more stuff to deal with. You've got enough on your plate already. It's just a shame you had to be told when things were going well. Even I liked her the other day.'

Kate was on the verge of asking Sophie not to come. That, or challenge her about what she said. Her comment was a little too close to home. If Mark had never told her about him and Sophie in a bathroom, would Sophie have kept stumm because it would be a shame to tell her when things were going well? But even worse, she was suggesting Kate should stick her head in the sand and ignore the problem.

'No, you're right, I'm sorry,' Sophie said. 'It's all a bit whiffy. She's too good to be true.'

Kate gave her a hard stare. 'Are you sure now? Do you want more time to think about it? Do you want to call a friend? Do you want to use fifty-fifty to help you with the answer?'

Sophie's eyebrows rose dramatically up her forehead. 'All right, you ogre. No need to show your age. Your face does that already.'

Kate sighed in fond exasperation. Sophie could be such a

clown at times. She wore Kate out. She switched the engine on while Sophie put the postcode into Google Maps.

'It says it'll take thirty-five minutes. We need to head towards Saltford for Long Ashton. We'll be on the Bath Road for most of the way. Now let's just hope he's in.'

CHAPTER FIFTY-THREE

Luke Vaughn opened the front door to the terraced house, wearing work trousers covered in dried plaster and a black T-shirt that had seen better days. His thick wavy hair was in need of a brush. He had an angular face and an intense stare, his tone clipped as he gave warning. 'If you're collecting, I have no change. If you're preaching, I'm cooking dinner.'

'We're here for neither,' Kate confirmed. 'We're both doctors. I just wanted a quick word, if I may?'

A wariness came over his face. He looked them up and down and then ushered them in. An archway separated a kitchen-cum-dining room from a snug sitting room. A boy was sitting at a small table with a plate of fish fingers, peas and mash, which he had yet to start. A second plate of dinner was on the worktop. She apologised for interrupting.

Luke waved the apology away. 'Don't worry, I'll microwave it.' He filled a glass with water and placed it next to the boy's plate. 'Josh, eat up or it will get cold.' He ruffled his son's hair and smiled as the boy craned his neck to feel his father's palm against his head. 'Stop it or I'll start noticing I need to wash it.' A look passed between them that showed a strong bond.

Josh smiled shyly as Kate caught his eye. She felt terrible for only just learning his name. He looked exactly like his photo, so it must have been taken recently. The room was uncluttered, the two-seater sofa unadorned with cushions, the walls bare apart from two school photographs of Josh. On a coffee table, an old ice-cream tub filled with pencils and felt tips, sat beside a stack of plain paper and colouring books. A footstool, a little lower than the table, was probably Josh's chair when drawing. There were no toys, she noted, not a single one in the room. She glanced at him. He held his small knife and fork properly. Someone had taught him well. He was five, the same age as Jacob. Still only baby years.

She looked at Luke Vaughn and saw he was waiting for her to speak, his expression still wary. It occurred to her he assumed they were there for some sort of inspection, which was why he invited them in and was being patient. She had introduced themselves as doctors. She felt mortified.

'Thanks for letting us in. I'm here on a delicate matter about Olivia.'

When he realised they were not there in some official capacity, his expression turned instantly cool. His voice lowered as he bluntly ordered them back to the hallway. He closed the door softly behind him before speaking his mind.

'That was bloody rude, coming into my home under a false pretext. Who do you think you are? Josh receives support from a counsellor. She's satisfied with how he's progressing. Did Olivia put you up to this? Get you to pretend to be doctors just to worry me?'

Sophie's mouth had dropped open. She was as appalled as Kate. Kate looked at him in dismay.

'Mr Vaughn, I am so sorry for causing this upset. I promise you we really are doctors, and Olivia doesn't know we're here. If I can quickly explain? My husband is a pilot. Olivia works with him. Recently he was involved in a serious

accident, putting him in the hospital. Another pilot introduced Olivia to me, and since then she's been living at my
home minding my five-year-old son, Jacob. Today I heard
something about her circumstances that had me worrying if
my son was... if he's...'

'Safe is the word you're looking for,' he answered in a
disparaging tone, making Kate flush. 'Did you know my ex-wife
before?'

'No, like I explained—'

'Did you ask for references?'

Kate jutted out her chin. 'No! My husband was in intensive
care. She offered her help. I accepted.'

His attention turned to Sophie. 'So she just let a stranger in
to mind her kid. Is that right?'

Sophie shook her head. 'No. Her husband's friend introduced your ex. Kate took that as reference enough.'

He looked back at Kate. 'And now you're worried, is that it?'
He leaned against the hall wall, pulling his hands through his
hair, causing a flurry of plaster dust in the air. He glanced about
him. 'Sorry, I haven't had a chance to wash.' He waited a beat,
then sighed. 'Look, you'll have to forgive my curtness, but I'm
particularly fierce when it comes to child protection. I don't
accept excuses for not taking precautions. You can never be too
careful. You hear that expression bandied about, but people
never pay it proper attention. I nearly lost that boy in there
because I didn't.'

Kate felt her insides lunge. She unconsciously put her hand
out to Sophie. Sophie gripped it and gave her a warning.
'Breathe, Kate. Right now. Jacob's fine! Just stand still and
breathe.'

Luke moved in front of her vision. 'Is she all right?' he asked
Sophie. 'Does she need some water?'

'Please,' Sophie answered.

He disappeared through the door and returned with a pint

glass of water and a chair for Kate to sit on. Kate drank half the water.

'Sorry for all the trouble,' she said as she handed back the glass. 'We'll get out of your way soon. I just want to know if I should be worried.'

He hunkered down and rested his back against the wall so she didn't have to look up. 'Probably not.' His voice had gentled. His face transformed with this small amount of kindness. The sharpness had gone.

'After Josh was born, Olivia seemed like a normal, happy mother. She threw herself into all the baby things. Toddler groups, baby gym, soft play. She was a natural. I couldn't have asked for a better mother for our son. Josh was around three when I began to notice things. He'd get startled if she laughed too loud. He'd flinch at sudden noises. When I came home from work, he'd sit in the chair beside me, quietly trembling, like he was trying not to be noticed.

'I went down the route of thinking it was autism, without really knowing anything about it. The health visitor was inclined to agree. By that time I was focusing hard and noticed his behaviour was only affected when his mother was in the house. I studied him. He would stiffen when she spoke, even when her voice was soft, which is when I realised he was afraid of her.'

His eyes drifted to a corner of the hallway, his mind somewhere else for a moment. 'I didn't want to leave him on his own with her. If I voiced it to anyone, it could have been me out of the door. Not that there was anyone I could talk to. I've a brother in the army and my parents live up north.

'There were no physical signs. He was immaculate, beautifully dressed, his nails carefully clipped and his hair shiny clean. This was what people saw, what was on the surface. Then he'd sit beside me and I'd feel him shake. It was the one constant behaviour. I'd tuck his icy hands in mine, even though the house was warm. The only time I felt his body relax was when she wasn't there. He remained guarded even then. I tried talking to him, touching on subjects that he might find scary. The dark, loud noises, shadows on the wall, dogs barking, daddy-long-legs. He denied fear of any of it.

'We were at the supermarket when I saw Olivia pass the window, coming to join us. I said, "Hey Josh, Mummy's coming." He looked up at me with his enormous eyes, rooted to the spot, and wet himself. I knew then something was seriously wrong.

'It was agony knowing he must be more afraid when I wasn't there, and agony not knowing what she was doing to him to make him so scared. I started looking for nurseries he could go to full-time. Olivia wouldn't agree to it. She said it was too expensive, and why would we need it when she was at home when not flying? I had to be careful that she didn't become aware I was suspicious of her.

'Then a job came up and I found someone to listen. I poured my heart out to the poor woman all in one day. And for free.' He smiled at Kate. 'When I came to a full stop, she told me she's a solicitor in family law. She then gave me some hard facts. If I felt my child was legitimately afraid of his mother, I needed to take the issue seriously. And I was going to need evidence.'

He laughed harshly. 'In one night, after just a few hours of research, I knew getting full custody was beyond my reach. I'd need to separate from her first. It would be me who would have to leave. But the biggest hurdle was getting evidence. I couldn't present them with domestic violence, drug usage, alcoholism, or mental health issues. I could only go on Josh's behaviour, which could be attributed to other factors. That night, I seriously thought of taking him far away. What happened next, I will deny as far as the law is concerned. I don't ever want it on record for Josh to one day read what his mum did.'

He gazed at Kate. 'Olivia doesn't know what I have on her. She thinks I only witnessed it with my eyes. If she hadn't agreed to leave and give me full custody, then and there, I would have called the police before another hour passed.

'I had my solicitor friend draw up the papers. Olivia agreed to me divorcing her on grounds of unreasonable behaviour. She agreed to abandon Josh to my care, so I could later apply to the court for legal custody. She knows I will never let her see Josh again.'

Sophie's fidgeting caught Kate's eye. She had a look on her face that Kate knew well. Chin pressed to her chest, eyes wide, mouth partially opened. Her huff caused Luke to glance at her.

'Did you want to say something?'

She shook her head, while her expression told the opposite, her arms folded and shrugging her shoulders. Kate hoped she would stay quiet. She needed to hear what else he had to say.

'Well, actually I do,' she announced, causing Kate to grind her teeth as it was too late now to shut her up. She had Luke's full attention.

'Go on then, I'm listening.'

She took a deep breath. 'You say she was a normal, happy mother. You couldn't have asked for a better mother for Josh. Then her behaviour changed. I mean, you basically blackmailed her into handing over her child. You considered autism where your son was concerned. Did you consider postnatal depression may have been the problem for your wife? Did you explore any reasons she might have changed? I mean, come on. You just don't take a kid away from his mother!'

He lowered his head and shook it slowly from side to side, as if in defeat. Kate wished Sophie had restrained herself until he had finished talking. He reached into a pocket in his trousers and pulled out his phone. He wiped some dust off the screen and tapped a finger on the glass a few times. He then handed the phone to Kate. He pointed at the stairs.

'Sit at the top. I don't want Josh hearing it. Just press play. When you're done, leave my phone behind and go. I'm done with talking. Make your own minds up.'

He got to his feet, and without looking at them again, went back through the door to his son, leaving Kate and Sophie in the hall with his phone.

Kate felt dizzy. She was afraid of what she would see, but conscious that every minute they were there, Jacob was alone with Olivia. She still didn't know if she should be worried. Luke had said probably not. Yet he'd taken full custody and would never let Olivia see her son again.

CHAPTER FIFTY-FOUR

They sat side by side on the top stair. The three doors on the landing were open. Kate could see into Josh's room. It was tidy and well organised. Low and high shelves on pale blue walls held dozens of different dinosaurs. On the floor, a large wooden farm filled with a large assortment of animals.

Kate settled the phone on her knee. She glanced at Sophie, then pressed play. Luke had taken the video from where they were sitting, except it was daylight. It was shot through the open door to the bathroom and took in the white bathroom suite and the window. Josh was standing in the bath. He had his back to the camera, legs jammed together, arms around his chest, either shaking or shivering. 'Can I get out now, Mummy?'

Kate had to bite her lip at the sound of his voice. He was politely asking.

'No, JJ. Another ten minutes,' Olivia's voice called from another room. 'Just sit there and be quiet. I'm tidying.'

Kate felt her eyes smart. Both at her reply and hearing her call him JJ.

He put his hand on the wall and bent his knees to lower

himself. He leaned forward to reach a tap. He cast a look over his shoulder before turning it on.

Olivia instantly shouted, 'Turn that tap off! Otherwise you'll sit there even longer.'

He quickly complied. His shoulders hunched over, his voice now a small plea, he said: 'But it's melted, Mummy. It's all melted.'

The video showed a pair of feet walking on the carpet on the landing to the bathroom door. On the lino floor were what looked like crumpled plastic bags. A foot stepped on one of them and the sock came away wet. The camera then captured a brief shot of shallow, clear water in the bath, and Josh's naked torso and blue-lipped face, before the phone was put in darkness in a pocket.

The screen on Luke's phone was now black. Sophie raised her eyebrow to ask if it was over when Luke spoke. 'Hey, buddy, let's get you out.'

Then Olivia's surprised voice: 'I didn't hear you come in.'

'I bet you didn't,' he whispered. Then: 'Hey, Josh, I'm going to make you some hot chocolate downstairs while Mummy picks up these bags from the floor. She's got to go to work, so she needs to pack some things.'

'Luke, wait!' Olivia demanded. Her voice sounded controlled. 'This is healthy for him.'

'Tell it to your lawyer, Olivia,' Luke replied. 'Because I'm more than happy to argue otherwise.'

Then, the sound of his quickened breathing as he descended the stairs carrying his son, a door closing, and then a discordant noise from his throat like a held-back cry. 'Sorry about Daddy's smelly T-shirt, but it's warmer than that towel. There, let's get that hot chocolate now so we can snuggle up. You can watch the telly while Daddy makes it.'

A minute later, Kate heard *PAW Patrol*. Then, the camera showed Luke's feet as he took the phone back out of his pocket.

Either from clumsiness or the intention to have himself recorded, the view switched to the selfie camera. Luke was looking at the screen, his eyes awash with tears as he switched it off. A still image of his distress brought the video to an end.

Kate rose to her feet and went down the stairs. She placed the phone on the bottom step, then carried on to the front door. Sophie walked behind her.

In Kate's car, Sophie spoke first. 'Do you want me to drive?'

Kate turned on the engine and drove out of Luke's road. She waited until they were heading in the right direction before she spoke. Her voice full of despair.

'What was I thinking?'

Sophie drew in a deep breath. 'She may have genuinely thought it was healthy. After Covid, mums were worried their kids had a lower immunity. She may have thought this would strengthen him.'

Kate's voice was scathing. 'What? Stick him in an ice bath?'

Sophie gave a sigh. 'Some cultures believe cold baths help their babies sleep.'

Kate gripped the steering wheel and ground her teeth hard. Sophie was an excellent doctor, but she dealt in a speciality that was mostly away from all the shit people did to each other. She didn't have to see the cruelty, sometimes deviously hidden, as they gave explanations of an arm break, a serious bruise, a snapped leg, a fall off a bed, off a chair, down the stairs. Had Sophie not heard his small plea?

But it's melted, Mummy. It's all melted.

He'd lowered himself in the water like an obedient lamb.

What Olivia did was neither loving nor normal.

As a doctor, Kate could agree with Sophie. Olivia may have been experiencing delayed postpartum depression, or some other psychological disorder, and should have been receiving help. As a mother, Kate wanted to rip her hair off her head for what she did to her boy. She couldn't forget or forgive what she had seen in the video.

She put her foot down on the accelerator, ignoring the speedometer, thinking how she was going to handle the situation. It wasn't in her nature to physically hurt anyone, or verbally attack them, either. She was a seether, not a shouter. She would just tell Olivia to leave. She wouldn't use the excuse of her mum wanting to take over the role, or that she had decided to stay home. She wouldn't give her any reason, true or false, but just tell her to go.

Kate parked, leaving enough room for Olivia to do a three-point turn. She would let her use Mark's car to get to wherever she lived and arrange for it to be brought back by a garage. Rather that than have Olivia waiting around for a taxi. Kate wanted this over and done with as quickly as possible. She would pack Olivia's few belongings and bring them down the stairs. She didn't want her going anywhere near Jacob's room.

She turned to Sophie to brief her. 'When we get in, you take Jacob to his room. Say you're going to read him a bedtime story. Don't come out until I give the all-clear.'

Sophie gave a faint nod.

Her stomach muscles clenched with anxiety as she unlocked the front door. She went into the hallway, letting Sophie close it behind them, then listened to the silence.

Kate called out a soft hello in case Olivia was putting Jacob to bed. She poked her head into the living room and saw it was empty, with only Barney asleep in there.

'I'll pop upstairs,' Sophie suggested. 'If she's with Jacob, I'll send her down.'

She padded up the stairs while Kate went to the kitchen. It was clean, with no smell of recent cooking. In the silence she could hear the clock on the wall ticking. Her nerves were jangling with the wait. She heard footfalls and crossed the kitchen floor, back out to the hall, and looked up the stairs. Sophie was coming down, her face worried.

'Have you checked down here, Kate? I'll go check the garden.'

She flew past, leaving Kate to open the doors to the utility, to the downstairs toilet, to the cupboard under the stairs. What did Sophie imagine them to be doing? They were not playing hide and seek. She came back through the door to the kitchen, with no one following behind. Her eyes fixed on Kate as she shook her head.

'Has she left a note anywhere?'

Kate didn't answer. She took out her phone and went up the stairs instead. A glance in each room assured her they were not mistaken. Olivia and Jacob were not in the house. They were not in the garden. They were not anywhere.

CHAPTER FIFTY-FIVE

The response time was extraordinary. The number of vehicles parked on her drive, and the officers in her home, was testimony to how serious the police were taking her call. But they would for a child abduction. Kate had stated it starkly. Her son had been abducted from his home.

The officer, who had taken her account of the situation on arrival, now joined her in the sitting room. She was wearing civvies. Her name was Sergeant Maureen something, Kate couldn't remember her surname. Her expression was neutral. She sat on the opposite sofa.

'Do you mind if I call you Kate?'

'I'd prefer it,' Kate answered.

'Great. Your friend Sophie is making you some tea. She's been answering questions in the kitchen. Do you mind if I give a quick summary to be sure we've not missed anything? The more accurate the information, the better we will be able to help get your son home.'

'Please do,' Kate replied. 'I want you to be sure.'

Maureen took out a notebook and rested it on her knee. 'So I have Katherine Jordan as mother. Mark Jordan, father, presently in hospital after sustaining injuries from a hit-and-run driver. Jacob Jordan, five years old, light-brown hair, small for his height. Possibly in school uniform – white shirt, grey jumper, blue tie with gold stripe. Then there's Olivia Vaughn. Cabin crew with the same airline as your husband, who has been staying here since the tenth, so nine days, minding your son while you visit your husband or work at the hospital. You spoke to Olivia at 14:40, and then again at 15:15. The first call was to ask her to collect Jacob from school. The second call was to tell her you'd be late, as you were going food shopping. In the second call, you heard Jacob with her. You then arrived home at around 18:50, in the company of Sophie Willis, where you found your husband's car on the drive, but Olivia and Jacob gone.' She now paused and looked at Kate for a couple of seconds before continuing. 'Is this the complete account? Have I missed anything out?'

Kate nodded. 'No, everything is accurate. I checked my phone for the times. And I'm thinking he's in school uniform because it's not upstairs. Jacob always hangs it on the back of his door.'

'Well done, good thinking. So when you got home, what did you do first?'

'I looked downstairs, while Sophie checked upstairs, and then in the garden. We both looked around for a note telling us where they'd gone. We didn't find one. That's when I rang the police.'

'You've tried calling her, I take it?'

'Yes. It said the number was no longer recognised.'

'Have you given thought to how they would have left? I mean, with your husband's car being here, what transport might they have taken? We've checked taxi firms in the area and none have taken a booking for this address. We're checking the bus routes. Thankfully, it's only nine twenty, so we're still able to talk to people. I notice there's a small field at the back of your garden. Might they have set out on foot, do you think?'

Kate frowned. How was she meant to know that? She wasn't here. 'There's a lane on the other side of the field. If you turn left and walk about a mile, it takes you to the viaduct. Turning right will lead you to Pennyworth Farm, about a two-and-a-half-mile walk, to where my husband was knocked down. There's no bus route through there.'

'Did you put away the shopping while you were waiting for us to arrive? Or is that still out in your car?'

Kate didn't like the question. It sounded like the sergeant was trying to trip her up. 'I didn't go in the end. I was too tired after work.'

'I see. So you came home and when you didn't find your son here, you concluded he'd been abducted by Olivia? Why do you think that?'

Kate spread her arms. 'Well, because all her clothes have gone. All her belongings have gone from the spare room.'

'I see,' she said, again. 'So there's no other reason? You didn't have words, perhaps?'

Kate felt her cheeks redden, heat crawling up her neck. 'Well, yes, we did. Things weren't working out. I was worried Jacob was becoming too fond of her. Getting too attached. Olivia has a son who doesn't live with her. I think Jacob was becoming a substitute.'

'So you think this is the reason she's taken him?'

Kate gave a faint nod.

Maureen gave a small shake of her head, as if trying to align her thoughts. 'I'll go along with it for the moment, but it seems rather extreme. Might it be possible they're simply lost? Or she's lost track of the time? Could they be at the cinema or eating out somewhere? Might she have taken him to see someone, a friend or a family member?'

Kate shook her head in frustration. 'My mother is visiting

my husband at the hospital. That's my only family. I know it's not late, but her suitcase has gone. She's not going to take it with her to the cinema, or to visit a friend.'

'She might, if she intends staying with them,' Maureen stated. 'There's also the possibility she might have taken Jacob to her home to get a change of clothing. You haven't been able to supply her current address. We're hoping her ex-husband can help with that. His home is down as her last known address. An officer is paying him a visit. Failing that, we'll get it some other way.'

Sophie appeared at the door with two mugs on a tray. She carried it over to the blanket box. 'Are you sure you wouldn't like one?' she asked Sergeant Maureen.

'I'm fine, thanks. Kate and I were just finishing. I'd say try not to worry, but I know that's not possible. A liaison officer will stay with you. He should be here soon. If you hear from Olivia, let him know. Or if you think of anything else that might help. In the meantime, could we have the keys to your garage? It's the only place we haven't looked.'

'Where are they, Kate? I'll fetch them,' Sophie offered.

'It's in the bowl in the hall with other keys, on a red tag.'

Sophie disappeared, leaving Kate and Maureen alone. When the sergeant stood up from the sofa, Kate saw she was very tall. Her dark, cropped hair suited her narrow face. It was hard to tell her age, possibly early thirties, as her eyes were wise. She gazed keenly at Kate.

'If there's anything you wish to add, anything at all, it's not too late. I find with these situations usually there is something missed out. Mostly to save embarrassment or for fear of having told small lies. It's always better to admit to these as soon as possible to save wasting time, especially if someone might be truly in danger.'

Kate held her gaze steady, her voice strong. 'I agree, I find the same in my work as a doctor.'

The sergeant slowly nodded while her eyes pinned Kate to her chair. 'Then you'll understand the importance of what I'm saying. Time is of the essence if Jacob is in danger.'

Kate watched in a daze as she turned and walked to the doorway. One more step and she would disappear. Her heart pounded in her chest. The reality hitting her. Jacob's life was at stake and she hadn't told her everything. She had to stop her and tell her before it was too late.

'Sergeant! I went to see Olivia Vaughn's husband. I told Olivia I was going shopping. He has full custody of their child. He's the same age as my son. She doesn't see her son, because he's afraid of her. She did something to him. I only discovered this this evening. And when I came home, Jacob was gone. I didn't mention it because he's trying to help his son recover but you have to know. Please take this seriously. She's taken my child.'

The sergeant gazed at her keenly. 'It's as well you spoke up, Doctor Jordan. This puts a different spin on things. It helps for us to understand the gravity of the situation.'

'Find him, please,' Kate cried. 'Don't let her take him away from me.'

CHAPTER FIFTY-SIX

The time on her phone said 03:14. Kate got up from the bench in the kitchen and put the kettle on again. She was surviving on mugs of coffee every hour. Her tongue felt furred, her breath probably stank. She left the kettle to boil and went upstairs to the bathroom, where impulsively she stripped off her clothes. She turned on the shower, grabbed her toothbrush from its new holder, and stepped into the cubicle before it was warm.

The iciness woke her. She opened her mouth and scraped her tongue. As the water turned tepid, she turned the tap to make it cold. It was bearable. She had the choice to turn it to warm or step out of the cubicle. She wasn't five years old. She wasn't being forced to sit in a freezing bath.

Her breast heaved with painful sobs. She prayed to God Jacob was safe and not suffering the way Josh did. She had heard no word from Sergeant Maureen, and the liaison officer had gone, persuaded by Kate to leave as she had Sophie with her. But even Sophie was now gone. She had surgery in the morning, an eye operation to perform. Kate had reassured her she was perfectly safe and would prefer to be on her own. Which was true. She couldn't think with others around.

She dragged a flannel across her face to stem her tears, then turned the shower off. She dried quickly, and still damp, dressed in her travelling tracksuit – the black sweatshirt with matching pants washed after her trip to Barcelona. It seemed crazy that the last time she wore it was only a week ago, and in the interim she had allowed a woman to take over her home, her life, and now take her child.

How had she missed the seriousness of Olivia's instability? What she had done was insane. She had taken her son like it was nothing, leaving her in despair. Was she punishing her for looking into her past? She would prefer to think that than what she truly feared, that Olivia had planned it all from the beginning.

Back downstairs, she picked up her phone, debating whether to call Robert. She could think of no one else who might know where Olivia had gone. Could she risk asking for his help when he was a potential murderer? Would he put aside what he had done in order to help Kate get her son back? Right now, she feared him less than she did Olivia.

She stared at his name in her contacts, then thought of another way to elicit his help. She would call Abe. Abe answered on the fifth ring.

He sounded groggy. 'Hello.'

'Hi, Abe.'

His voice became instantly alert. 'Has something happened? Is it Mark?'

She forced the lump from her throat. 'It's Jacob. Olivia Vaughn has taken him.'

She heard him gasp. 'Where are you, Kate?'

'I'm at home on my own. Waiting to hear from the police.'

'I'll be with you in thirty minutes. Stay calm. I'm on my way.'

* * *

By half four, he was there in her kitchen, his T-shirt on back to front. Kate made him coffee as soon as he arrived. He ignored the mug, instead asking how he could help.

She pushed it across the table, encouraging him to sit down. In front of her was a glass of orange juice. 'Did you contact Robert?'

The question surprised him. 'No. I went to his home. He wasn't there. I've emailed, texted, rung him. He's off the radar. I've left him an enlightening voice message. Why do you ask?'

'I was hoping he might know where Olivia is. The police don't have her current address. But Robert drove her home to fetch clothes for her to stay here. So he must know where she lives.'

He frowned. 'And you don't know where this is?'

An overwhelming feeling of inadequacy engulfed her. Her slumped shoulders gave him his answer. He reached across the table and patted her hand. 'What's done is done. What's important is what we do now. Let's use that excellent brain of yours to come up with a solution. Is she running or hiding? I'm going to make a few calls. Good job I'm not retired yet. I still have some pull with the big bosses.'

She glanced at him gratefully. 'What should I do? I don't know anything about her.'

'Search social media. You probably know more than you realise. You know her job, where she works. She's divorced and has a son. You're bound to find something. Even if it doesn't help, it might lead to somewhere else.'

At five thirty they crossed paths in the kitchen. Abe was putting the kettle on. 'I'm making tea. It's better for my ticker. I'll make you one as well. And you better eat something. You look like a sickly ghost.' He covered his mouth to yawn. 'I'm waiting on some calls. I struck lucky getting hold of a purser. Martin Samworth has a sensible head on his shoulders. He's asking other cabin crew for information on her. He knows one or two who were close. I've also let the big guns know she might try to leave the country. They suggest we check Jacob's passport hasn't gone.'

'Christ, I never thought,' Kate whispered. 'She might have gone already. It might be too late.'

He crossed the kitchen to her and placed his hands on her shoulders. 'Calm, Kate. His passport will be here. Go and look for it.'

She hurried from the room and upstairs to the drawers in her bedroom. Her passport was there, back in its place after returning from Spain. Mark's was in his flight bag. Jacob's was missing. She always kept it with hers in the drawer. It would be visible if it was there. She rummaged through the contents of the drawer. It was not hiding beneath anything. She took out the drawer in case it had fallen down the back. She pulled the other two drawers off the runners and placed them on the bed. She checked to be sure it hadn't gone in them by mistake, before checking the floor in the carcass. The carpet was clean, apart from two hairgrips.

Panicking, she checked the overnight bag she'd taken to Barcelona. The passport wasn't in it or in any of its pockets. She dropped it to the ground and flew back down the stairs.

'It's gone!' she cried. 'She's taken it!'

She was stricken by fear and incapable of calming herself. The terror cut off her ability to breathe, her words taking up all the air in her lungs.

'What am I going to do? What am I going to do? What do I do? What do I do? Oh God, please help me. What am I going to do?' Her scream for Jacob brought her to the floor.

She couldn't breathe in properly. She couldn't slow her heavy panting, and was shocked at the high-pitched stridor in her throat. She couldn't get up off the floor. Her head flopped back, her arms felt weak by her sides. She needed Abe to take control, and was relieved to feel her legs being raised. She needed to lie there for however long it took to get her breathing back to normal.

Minutes passed. She didn't try to talk. She had learned her lesson. Her panic attack had gone out of control. She had felt like she was suffocating. She breathed in, relieved to be feeling calm again.

Abe's face appeared in her vision. He smiled gently. 'Good bloody job I've dealt with loss of cabin pressure. If a mask had dropped down, I'd have stuck it on your face. I'm going to raise your head a bit, then get you some water. Don't get up.'

She sat at the table a short while later with a mug of sweetened tea and thickly buttered toast, and was surprised to find she was enjoying both. It was years since she'd taken sugar in her tea, but she wasn't about to complain. Abe had looked after her well. More importantly, he put her mind at rest – Olivia Vaughn's name wasn't on any passenger list flying out from the UK yesterday.

He splashed water on his face at the kitchen sink and dried it with a tea towel. His good-humoured face turned to her. 'Best thing to wake you up. That, or have someone nearly die on you. That does the trick as well. Are you feeling better?'

She nodded while she munched her toast. She felt absolutely fine, better than she had in a while. Abe's calming manner had a lot to do with it. She felt she was in safe hands.

He rested back against the sink. 'Good, because I've heard from Martin. He's been able to dig up a possible address. The home of her parents. The colleague he spoke to went there once, a few years ago. Olivia said it was where she grew up, that her parents were both dead. It may be a dead end, it might have been sold by now, but it would be worthwhile checking. What do you say? Are you up for it? Or shall we pass it on to the police?'

She finished her tea, drinking the last mouthful, before standing up. 'Let's not tell the police yet. We don't want sirens alerting her. If it's not far, it might still be dark when we arrive and we'll catch her in bed.'

Abe didn't seem surprised. He patted his pockets and took out his car keys. 'It's just outside Wookey. We'll be there by seven thirty. Before sunrise.'

'Okay, well let's go then.'

Her quick response raised his eyebrows. 'Are you sure? It could be dangerous, Kate.'

She returned his gaze steadily. 'I'm sure, Abe, for that very reason. It could be dangerous for my child.'

CHAPTER FIFTY-SEVEN

The satnav took them off the beaten track for the last mile, the road surface testing the vehicle's suspension. More suited for a tractor or quad bike, it was not a smooth ride. The verges and uncut trees and hedges lining the track were not pretty in the dark, and Abe's Mondeo was getting badly scratched. Kate could hear the metal scraping as the car rocked side to side, brushing the hedgerows. She would pay for the damages, of which she was sure there would be many.

The house came into view. A squat, one-storey building with a disproportionately large roof, so maybe with an upstairs. They were plunged into darkness when Abe switched off the headlights. Kate had her phone ready and switched on the torch. She got out of the car. Her feet hit a smattering of gravel on hard-packed earth. She'd barely gone a yard when Abe grabbed her jacket to pull her back.

'What?' she whispered harshly.

'Don't go wandering off. Stay by me. We check this together. Let's look around the back first to see if there's a car.'

A beam at her feet directed her. Abe had a proper torch. They stayed away from the windows and walked around the perimeter of the garden, which was just more packed dirt and gravel. After a full circuit and no sign of a car, they reached the front door. Kate tested her theory and knocked on it hard.

'There's no one at home,' she said in an overly loud voice.

They stood there for a minute, contemplating what to do.

'It's getting light,' said Abe. 'Let's sit in the car until we can see in the windows. We might as well have a look inside to see if she's been here.'

Back in the warmth, Kate shivered a little. She stared in surprise at the flask in Abe's hands. It was hers and was normally in a cupboard in her kitchen. She smelled the drink as he took off the lid.

'Hot chocolate,' she exclaimed.

Abe chuckled. 'I like to come prepared. You never know when you might get stuck somewhere. Or have someone faint on you.'

She took the drink gratefully. Then blurted out her secret. 'I'm pregnant, Abe.'

He surprised her with his answer. 'So that's what it is. I saw a bit of something different in you yesterday, a scattiness, for want of a better word. Even given what's going on, you're not the calm Kate I'm used to seeing. You're usually unflappable. Nerveless.'

She eyed him over the brim of the plastic cup. 'That makes me sound cold.'

He nodded in agreement. 'Well, you are. But in a good way. Cool-headed, when needed. While the rest of us fall to pieces.' He closed his eyes as he shuddered.

She knew he was remembering what happened to his daughter. Kate had performed an emergency tracheostomy in Abe's back garden after a Heimlich manoeuvre failed to dislodge a pen top from ten-year-old Tanya's throat. She'd been lounging on a chair with cute sunglasses on, sucking the lid of a pen as she filled in shapes in a colouring book, when she began choking. Kate reacted instinctively as the girl lost consciousness. She grabbed the plastic straw out of the beaker Tanya was drinking from and doused it with her own bottle of water to clean it of Coca-Cola. She then grabbed the slicing knife that Abe had used at the barbeque, wiping it with her top, before pouring neat vodka over it and using it to make the incision.

The small scar had faded over time, while the memory was still clear. Kate may have looked cool-headed, but she remembered the icy terror she'd felt in fear of Abe's child dying.

'It's daylight,' Abe remarked. 'Let's go take a look.'

Kate was staring through a dusty window when she heard glass smashing. She turned and stared at Abe, standing a few feet away at another window.

'You broke it,' she whispered in astonishment.

He shrugged. 'Only one small pane to get my hand in. I'll patch it before we leave.'

Emboldened by his behaviour, Kate didn't hesitate to climb in through the window once it was open. She let Abe in the front door before looking around her.

She imagined a cottage in the woods should have character, with creaky floorboards. Instead, the floor was covered with a boring beige carpet. Kate stood in the hallway. To her left, the door to the kitchen, with cabinets on walls and a very dark-brown worktop. The door on her right showed a room with a chintzy sofa and armchair. On the mantelpiece was a china shire horse with ornamental harness, and in a glass cabinet a collection of china figurines. Straight ahead, a modern pine staircase, which was where Kate wanted to look.

'Check the kitchen for any food,' she suggested to Abe. 'I'm going to have a peek upstairs.'

On the landing, she found creaking floorboards covered with a narrow rug. The bathroom suite was pastel yellow with small, busy tiles on the walls. She carried on to a small bedroom with a single divan, and then a double room with two pillows on each side of the bed. A small photo gallery hung in frames on the wall. One showed a couple on their wedding day – her parents, she presumed.

A photograph by the bed caught her attention. She took a step towards it, then another, while her lips parted and the hairs on the back of her neck sprang up. She dropped onto the edge of the bed and reached out a shaking hand to pick it up. She touched a trembling finger to the glass, tracing the outline of his face, before releasing a gasp.

Olivia had been here recently. The photograph of Jacob had been in Kate's house, on the windowsill in her bedroom. She hadn't noticed it was missing. Maybe because Olivia hadn't taken the frame, as she already had one. Kate turned it over and used her nails to pry up the metal tabs at the back. The board, the photo, and glass dropped out. She lifted the glass and took back her photograph, pressing it gently to her breast, whispering his name.

Her heart was beating fast, but she refused to let her anxiety get out of hand. Jacob needed her to be strong to find him. She took a breath, then another, and stood up, shaken but not beaten. She had proof that Olivia was unhinged. She had no qualms about telling the police she had broken in. The woman had abducted her child. Despite Sergeant Maureen initially thinking otherwise, Olivia Vaughn was dangerous. She had taken Jacob's passport to take him away.

Then it was as if the entire world had stopped turning. She couldn't breathe as her eyes fixed on the photograph that lay beneath Jacob's. An image of Josh, smiling sweetly. Hidden beneath the image of another boy. Like she had discarded him.

Kate cried out for Abe. Fear rooted her to the spot. Would she ever see Jacob again? Olivia had intentionally covered the image of her son with a permanent replacement. She no longer had need of him. Jacob had replaced him.

CHAPTER FIFTY-EIGHT

Kate resisted the urge to leave the cottage in the hands of the police, afraid that their presence would warn Olivia away if she came back. She wanted to hide in the woods and keep watch for her while they carried out their search for clues. Their world frightened her. Their white hooded suits hid face and form as they made this place their own, inaccessible to outsiders. It was now a crime scene.

'Do you think he's safe?' she asked, throwing Abe a harrowing look.

Abe tried to smile at her in reassurance. 'Yes, Kate, I do. She'll look after him. I don't think she has any intention of harming him.'

'Only taking him,' she breathed.

Abe reached for her hand. 'Come on. We've got work to do.'

They visited Bristol Airport where Abe introduced her to several airport personnel. After a brief awkward silence, he sat her in a chair and deep discussions went on around her. She was in a part of the airport normally off-limits to the public. Abe's clearance had got her in. And now, Abe's influence led to her being offered food.

The sandy-haired woman regarded her with sympathy as she placed a tray on a low table by Kate's knee. 'Breakfast. Abe said you're starving and you're to eat it all up.'

The bowl of chopped fruit looked inviting. The croissant was plump and fresh. The large cup of frothy hot chocolate had double handles like the ones in Costa. She looked across at Abe to thank him, but he was talking with someone. She thanked the woman instead and was then left alone again to sit and eat.

The dishes were clear and the cup almost empty when Abe returned. 'Let's get you home. You must be shattered.'

In the car park, she noticed the deep scratches on the paintwork. The car was no longer a uniform blue. Abe opened the passenger door and ushered her in. 'Stop worrying, Kate. It's nothing a bit of T-cut won't put right.'

He got in beside her and fastened his seat belt. 'Okay. Home? Or my place?'

'Home, please. I need to check on Barney.' Kate glanced at him. 'You don't need to stay when we get there. I'll be fine on my own.'

His head pulled back as if truly surprised. 'Are you mad? I wouldn't dream of leaving you alone. No more would you if it was me in this situation. Now, no more nonsense, please. Besides, I'll be at the end of the phone for updates. All airports are on alert in case she books a flight. We're hoping she does, because airport police can nab her at a gate. DS Dean will have done the same, but we have the advantage of knowing her well. Hair up, hair down, someone will recognise her. She's worked for the airline for eight years. She won't be able to disguise who she is.'

Kate nodded her head gratefully. Then, confused, she asked, 'Who's DS Dean?'

Abe gave her an amused smile. 'The woman in charge of finding Jacob? Detective Sergeant Maureen Dean. Who you've been talking to.'

'Oh, so that's her name. Now I know.'

Abe settled back in his seat and started the car. 'I think you should sleep,' he suggested. 'I'll wake you when we're there.'

Her mobile phone rang, sending sleep out the window. Julian's name appeared on the screen. She answered in an empty tone. 'Hi, Julian.'

'Hi, Kate. From your voice, it sounds like you might already know.'

She sat up, alert. 'Know what, Julian? What's happened? Has Mark...?' Her voice rose. 'Just tell me quickly.'

'The police. They're coming to arrest him. I'm breaking protocol, letting you know. The only reason I know about it is because we have to physically let them in the ward. The detective seems to care that this is done with dignity. He doesn't want patients scared.'

Kate clutched her stomach to calm the somersaults. 'How long till they're there?' she asked.

'They didn't give a time. But soon, I suspect.'

'I'm on my way, Julian. Please don't let them in. Say he's having treatment. Say anything to delay them. I'll be there as fast as I can. Please, I won't ask for anything else.'

He sighed heavily. 'I'll do my best. Just drive safely. I'll see you soon.'

'Christ,' Kate whispered as Julian got off the phone.

Abe threw her a concerned look.

'Straight to the hospital, Abe. They're going to arrest Mark. I have to stop them.'

* * *

Her frantic running through the hospital corridors startled people into stepping aside. People don't run in hospitals, they hurry. Kate's legs and arms were moving like a sprinter, the slap of her trainers and loud gulps of air the only warning people got. She had left Abe far behind, not heeding his calls to slow down. She would rest when she got there.

She turned onto Mark's corridor and saw uniforms at the other end. They were coming towards her. She would beat them to the door, and chain herself to it if necessary. DS Sharma pushed through to the front of the officers, and Kate stumbled to a halt. She tried calling his name, but her throat only produced a wheeze.

Stupid for getting in a state, again. She couldn't talk.

'Doctor Jordan,' he called with concern. He reached out a hand to steady her. She looked into his eyes before she bent over to catch her breath. His hand rested on her shoulder while she stared down at his brown shoes, the leather polished, the laces in neat bows.

She took a deep, steadying breath before standing up straight. They stood only inches away from one another.

'I caught you, just in time,' she uttered with relief. 'Please don't arrest him today. I'm begging you.'

She was so close she could see the pity in his eyes. She had to make him understand that this was about more than the arrest. Mark would have to be told something much worse if they went through with it.

'Please, just not today. Our son is missing. He's been gone since yesterday. He's been abducted from our home. The police are looking for him. But this woman has his passport, and I'm terrified we won't get him back. I cannot tell my husband yet. I don't know what it will do to him. I don't know if his heart will take it. It already stopped once. I can't take the chance that the shock will stop it again.'

Kate heard a sob from behind her. She turned and saw Grace standing there as white as a sheet. Kate grabbed hold of her arm. 'Mum, I'm so sorry you heard this way. You were right. I should have listened.'

Grace gave little attention to her daughter. 'We'll talk about it in a moment. Right now, I need to speak to this young man. Someone needs to make him see sense. My name is Grace Shortman. I'm Kate's mother.'

Whether from concern for the white-faced woman before him, or the memory of her daughter fainting, Sharma sat them down on his and Kate's bench. Grace only sat for a moment before getting back to her feet. The top of her head barely came up to Sharma's chest, but she didn't let this get in the way of a fight.

'My son-in-law is not guilty,' she stated firmly. 'Whatever evidence the Spanish police have, the person you should be looking for planted it. Robert Brennan. Mark tells me no one from the airline has been able to get a hold of him. I'd say he's on the run.'

Sharma put his hands up to object. 'Mrs Shortman, I'm sorry this is stressful, but we've already looked into Mr Brennan. He's not a suspect.'

Grace stamped a small foot, her rubber-soled ankle boots making little noise. She folded her arms firmly against her chest. 'Well, he should be! He's the only one who could have known how to frame Mark. He was present at Mark's birthday when he received that watch. He knew Mark's name was on the back!'

Kate saw the surprise in Sharma's eyes, and knew for sure it was the watch they had as evidence. He was about to speak, but Grace wasn't done yet.

'Robert has dark hair and is taller than Mark. He fits the description given by this witness just as much as Mark does. And if you're looking for motive, she's sitting right there. There's his reason for framing his friend.'

Sharma looked at Kate for an answer, but Grace was more than happy to supply one. 'Robert has been in love with Kate for the past ten years. Everyone seems to see it, apart from her. The only way he can get her is by framing Mark for murder.'

Sharma met Kate's gaze. His lips pulled back in a grimace, probably to hide his surprise. She knew he had met with Robert and seen a very handsome man, and was now expected to believe he'd commit murder to be with her. Kate didn't need a mirror to know she looked her very worst, but even at her best she was just averagely attractive.

Grace harrumphed. 'I can see you're not persuaded, Detective Sharma. Maybe this will do it. Robert was in Kate's garden the other night, standing in the dark, watching her home. He frightened her half to death, hiding in the bushes, before driving off. Does that sound like the behaviour of a normal person? When he's meant to be their friend?'

He frowned, then turned his gaze on Kate. 'Did you report this?'

Kate shook her head. 'No. I would have if he'd done it again.'

His eyes narrowed. 'And you're sure it was him?'

She nodded firmly. 'I'm positive it was him. I sent him a message asking him what he was playing at. His reply said sorry if he scared me. I didn't need to be afraid of him.' Kate stood up. 'But I am afraid. I don't know what he's capable of anymore. Someone I've known for ten years is like a stranger to me now. He's involved somehow. I know he is.'

Sharma came to a decision. 'Okay, please sit here and wait while I talk to my boss. I'm not promising anything. One thing you should know, though, is if we arrest your husband, we're not taking him away today. An officer will stay with him here.'

Kate sat with her mother, neither one saying a word, both praying for the same thing. For Jacob and Mark to come home. Seeing tears leak from Grace's eyes was another first for Kate, after hearing her mother swear for the first time in her life. She felt guilty for making both happen. She'd ignored her mother's warning about letting a stranger into her house. And now Jacob was gone.

They waited half an hour for his return, but it was worth it. Sharma had good news. 'It's been agreed. We'll postpone the arrest. In the meantime, Doctor Jordan, we'd advise you to avoid contact with Robert Brennan. If you do hear from him, notify the police immediately.'

Kate rose to her feet. The anguish in her eyes made room for gratitude.

He smiled benignly, before reminding her that this was only temporary in view of their current situation. 'Finding your child is what's important. I can imagine how worried you are.'

Kate saw sadness in his brown eyes and wondered if he had children. There was something about him: a sincerity she wanted to believe in. But more than that, she wanted to believe he would do his best to find the truth.

'Thank you,' she murmured. 'Your kindness means a lot.'

CHAPTER FIFTY-NINE

Abe paved the way for her to visit Mark. She warned him not to say anything other than that she was here. He took Grace under his wing so Kate could see her husband. It was going to be hard to face him without revealing her fear over Jacob. But she'd meant what she said to Sharma – she couldn't tell him yet. Once Mark knew, there would be no stopping him from trying to find his son, and he would then be a fugitive. He wouldn't get far, and the shock of knowing Jacob was missing and he was unable to help might be too much for him. Kate would rather keep him in the dark and at least know one family member was safe.

He looked clean and shaven in a pair of pyjamas she didn't recognise. Probably a gift from his mother-in-law. He was sitting on the bed, ankles crossed, with Grace's book in his lap. She wished she'd taken the time to tidy herself. The knees of her tracksuit were dirty from climbing through a window, the palms of her hands grubby, her hair – every grip and tie gone – falling around her face.

He looked up and saw her. His eyes widened. He pushed the book from his lap, and in one movement he was off the bed.

His arms around her, pressing her close to his chest, he whispered in a broken voice, 'I'm sorry.'

Someone drew the curtains closed around them while Kate cried. He kept hold of her as he pulled her beside him on the bed. Her hand now held in his, her head resting on his breast, her body reassuringly hugged. 'I'm sorry,' he whispered again. 'For what I've put you through.'

Kate kept her eyelids closed. The hot tears stung her skin. She wanted a cold flannel to soothe them but settled for the softness of his top pressing one side of her face. She was too tired to move, too afraid to let go of this temporary haven. Her boy was missing. Her sweet, sensitive child was out there. Terrifying thoughts flitted through her mind of other children who had gone missing. She closed her eyelids tightly, trying to make the images go away. Jacob would not become one of them. They would find him. He would not be a child who stayed missing for ever.

She felt the soft rumble through Mark's chest wall as he talked.

'I couldn't have you here. I couldn't bear for you to see it happen. I didn't want you witnessing my arrest and have that image in your head. I'd rather do it alone, Kate. And if I go to prison, I want you to forget about me and make a new life.'

She squeezed her eyes tighter, ignoring the sting. She had waited for so long to see him and she was hearing nothing new. All her digging into this mess – her mad rush to Barcelona, her stay at the hotel, meeting Mateo, Valentina, then Paulo and Perez, the superintendent in charge of the case – it had all been for nothing. He knew none of this. He didn't know about her meeting his friend, finding his bar, and seeing all his children's artwork on the walls. About finding a green parrot drawn by Paulo's grandson. He knew none of this. She had told him while he was sleeping.

Kate could only ask one question. She raised her head and peered at him. 'Are you innocent, Mark?'

He tucked her head gently down and shushed her. 'Don't go there, Kate. It doesn't help.'

She felt a current of resentment shoot through her body. She wanted to curl her hand resting on his chest into a fist and beat him with it. It was his evasiveness that didn't help. His close-lipped hold of the truth. God damn it, if he wasn't guilty, who was he protecting? Because it wasn't her and it wasn't Jacob. He had left them to fend for themselves. Who did he love more than them? For who else would he walk away and give up his life?

A moan escaped her. It had to be Robert. Mark must know he was guilty and was prepared to cover it up. Until this moment, she hadn't been sure. She had allowed her mother to try to convince Sharma. She had wanted it to be him who was guilty rather than Mark. Why wouldn't she, if it meant saving her husband?

She had to find a way to break down his loyalty. The letter she had written to him was still in her bag. It was her backup, in case he wouldn't talk to her, but never given after seeing Jacob and Olivia at his bedside. He didn't know that she'd been afraid of his friend. That he'd come into their garden and frightened her. She should have noticed that not once during the period before his accident had he mentioned Robert's name. Not mentioning he was his co-pilot, even though Kate knew. Not saying they had a drink on their first night stop, or that he was there or they were together. Not mentioning him when he came home after being met by the police. The most natural thing would be for him to say, I'll call Robert, I'll see what he says. I'll get him over to see what he knows. I'll call Robert, because he's my friend.

Robert had disappeared completely from his vocabulary, and Kate hadn't noticed. What she didn't understand was why

Mark would take the fall. He wouldn't want someone to be free after unlawfully taking a life. He wouldn't want them free to do it again. So why was he taking the chance with Robert? It didn't make sense in any shape or form unless Mark was guilty. Or? A new thought skidded her heart to a stop...

Her mouth turned bone dry. It didn't make sense unless Mark was guilty as well! Could it be both of them? Not just Robert. Maybe one more than the other. Maybe one of them intervened. A struggle ensued, a blow got landed, a woman was dead. Either way, there was no point in them both facing jail. Only one of them needed to take the fall. And it looked like Mark had decided it would be him.

He had decided for them all. Perhaps because he had already experienced having a family, and Robert hadn't. Robert hadn't had children. Perhaps through some misguided guilt, he felt responsible for Robert never marrying. Mark's character was watertight, with many honourable traits. He would see it as doing the honourable thing. Fall on his sword for the sake of another. Or killing himself as proof of his guilt by stepping in front of a car. Case closed. Game over. Robert wins.

CHAPTER SIXTY

Robert put his phone back in his pocket. He glanced at Jacob sleeping on the sofa, then turned to Olivia. 'Should he be sleeping so long? He'll be awake at bedtime.'

Olivia shrugged. 'He's had a busy day. He needs his sleep.'

Robert wasn't so sure. 'What about his dinner? He's not been fed yet.'

'He'll survive,' she muttered, her green eyes looking past Robert as if his presence was irritating.

'Oh well.' He sighed. 'Just you and me, then. Do you want me to bring you a bowl in here?'

She shook her head. 'I'm not hungry, Robert. I'd like a drink instead.'

His eyebrows raised at her short tone. She was on edge because he was there. He wasn't surprised. She'd seen him in the garden and been questioned by the police again, and was probably wondering if she was safe with him. He'd let her stew. He no longer trusted her. The atmosphere in Kate's home was different from the last time he was there with Olivia. She'd been helpful and kind then like nothing was too much trouble for her. She'd looked shocked to see him turn up on the doorstep with a bag of food and a bottle of wine and make himself at home. She was a smart cookie, he'd give her that, worming her way in here. What was her agenda, he wondered?

He gave a slight bow from the hip, his head down. 'Your wish is my command. I'll fetch the bottle.'

He stopped at the doorway to look back at her sitting comfortably on the sofa, admiring what she was wearing. 'Is that Kate's dress you have on?'

'Yes,' she said, sounding annoyed. 'It's the only one that comes to my knee. Kate is short.'

He continued to regard her with amusement. 'Why? Have you run out of your own clothes?'

'Leave it, Robert. I'm not in the mood for your jokes. I have no clothes here.'

He chuckled. 'Well, you arrived with some. I carried your bag in myself.'

She scowled. 'Why are you here? Kate won't want to see you.'

He watched her for a moment – hands tucked in her lap, knees drawn neatly together, feet wearing sensible cabin shoes – and realised his presence threatened her. She wanted him gone so she could be alone. He didn't know her at all. She had hidden layers to her character he hadn't spotted. He'd seen proof of that before knocking on the front door.

'Are you speaking for yourself or for Kate?'

She gave her head a little shake. 'I think you should leave. Kate's going to be cross finding you here.'

He raised his eyebrows again. 'My, my, you've become quite the friend. I'd like to be a fly on the wall to hear what you have to say about me.'

Her chin jutted out. 'You should leave. Stalking her from the garden didn't go down well.'

He folded his arms and leaned in the doorway with his head against the wood. 'And miss out on all the fun?'

'You're not going to be here!'

He tutted mildly. 'I'm not going anywhere. Maybe it's you who should leave. I think it best if I explain it to Kate.'

'Explain what exactly, Robert?'

'That you're coveting her child.'

Her mouth dropped open. He had stunned her, rendering her silent, which he used to his advantage. 'I didn't know you weren't allowed to see your own child. It must be for a serious reason. Did you smack him? That's frowned on. Or did you use a naughty step? I favour neither, to be honest.'

Her mouth was moving. She finally spluttered: 'I never smacked him. I know how to look after a child!'

He smiled at getting a rise out of her. 'Ah, getting to the heart of it, I see. Do you think you can do better than Kate?'

Her face and voice hardened. 'I do a better job at it than her! Children need structure, routine, and a mother who's always there.'

'So why aren't you with your son?' he answered mildly.

Her hands clutched the material of Kate's dress, stretching the skirt hard across her knees. She gave him a look of dislike and flashed a scornful smile. 'Because his father is a softy. Luke spoiled him. Always hugging him, and kissing tiny grazes that weren't even there. He objected to me trying to make our son strong.'

Robert was curious to know her method. 'What did you do? Take him off hunting? Teach him how to live off the land? Or something more mundane, like stand him in a corner to discipline him?'

Her nostrils flared. She spoke through her teeth. 'I didn't need to discipline Josh that way. He did as he was told until Luke's leniency got in the way. One day he said no to me when it came to his bath time. Luke let him get away with it. I didn't. Next day, he had a cold bath instead. He responded well, so it became part of our routine.'

Robert's eyes widened. 'Wow. So, not like taking a cold shower to dampen one's ardour then? A cold bath makes you strong? I must try it.'

Her lip curled. 'Why do you have to debase everything? Cold baths are good for endurance. My mother bathed me in cold baths for years, and it did me no harm.'

Robert gave a polite cough, provoking a frown from her. His tone was kind. 'From an outsider's point of view, I'd say that's debatable. I suspect it probably did do you harm. But hey, if you say different, I believe you.' He paused while he glanced at Jacob, shoes on, without a care in the world, fast asleep. 'What say I put him to bed?'

Olivia put a hand across Jacob's legs. 'Leave him. It's early yet.'

He shrugged. 'Fine. We'll let Kate put him to bed.'

'Actually, it'll be me.' Her tone was smug. 'I don't think she'll be back for hours yet.'

Robert gave a small smile. 'Well. That's where you're wrong. I suspect she'll be home any minute.'

Olivia went still. She stared at him. 'What makes you say that?'

He pulled a guilty face but his voice was triumphant. 'I texted her to say Jacob was asleep on the sofa at home.'

CHAPTER SIXTY-ONE

Kate read the message again. Robert was with Jacob. He hadn't been in contact since his text on Tuesday, three evenings ago, and now he was at her house with her son. Like nothing had happened, like it didn't matter that he had scared her by lurking in her garden.

Her head buzzed with alarm. Where was Olivia? Was she in harm's way? Like Sergeant Maureen Dean, she wondered how Olivia had left the house. If not in Mark's car, and not by taxi, had she been picked up? Had Robert taken her and Jacob to the cottage in the woods and then returned them to Kate's home? Or had Olivia seen Robert arrive and run with Jacob to protect him? Nothing was making sense.

Perhaps Sharma had been in touch with Robert. Would he have revealed Kate's concerns? If so, Robert must now be aware she thought him guilty of murdering Fleur. She had a horrible feeling he sent his message to taunt her.

Jacob's asleep on the sofa at home.

It sounded so innocent, and something she had been

desperate to hear. Yet the very fact he worded it so simply put the fear of God into her. Where was Olivia? Was she with him? Was Jacob even there? Was it a ploy to get Kate alone? To corner her in her home?

She eased off the bed, careful not to disturb Mark. She grabbed her bag from the floor and made her escape without talking to anyone. Out in the corridor, she allowed her anxiety the freedom of pacing the floor. What should she do? Who should she call? The police would get there quicker than her, but at what price? She was between a rock and a hard place. God forgive her, but she wanted to kill Robert.

The damage he had done to her family made her feel sick. He had been there at every special occasion. Best man at their wedding, godfather at Jacob's christening. At special birthdays. He had shared ten years of their lives and was now ripping it apart. Did he truly expect her to love him after this? If this was what it was about, she would leave him in no doubt of her feelings. No one used her child to get what they wanted.

Her mind made up, she started walking. The advantage of going alone was she could arrive without alerting him. Her car was still in her drive after returning from Luke Vaughn's home. Abe had driven her in his car this morning. She could get an Uber and ask the driver to drop her away from the house. There were no security lights in her garden. She could walk to the front door undetected.

Her phone still in her hand, she tapped the Uber app. By the time she reached the exit, there was a taxi waiting. She hopped in and sat quietly for the entire journey. In the silence, she was surprised the driver couldn't hear her fear. Her heart was kicking up a racket in her chest like a volleyball slamming against a wall. Its beat literally hurt her ribs.

In the back, her eyes adjusted to the gloom. As with her fear, it was just as well the driver didn't notice. The glitter of malevolence might have made him stop the car.

CHAPTER SIXTY-TWO

Robert checked his phone for a reply from Kate. She was staying quiet. Probably angry, like Olivia said. He understood. He had a list of messages sent to him he hadn't answered. Several of his colleagues, including Abe Grier, had contacted him. He'd been in no mood to talk to anyone. They all wanted to know the same thing. What was he doing to help Mark?

He was doing a lot, but he suspected people wouldn't see it that way. They would see it as feathering his own nest. It was partially true, but not all of it. Some of it was down to plain old curiosity. He wanted to know if he'd been taken for a ride. Had Olivia engineered a lift with him that day to come to Kate's? From the moment she jumped into his car, it all seemed to happen so seamlessly. He'd driven her to fetch some clothes, expecting to drive her home. Instead they'd gone to the airport to pick up her packed suitcase that she said was always kept ready. Then she quickly worked her way into staying in the house. Was she just trying to make amends for what he suspected her having done? Or was she there with a more sinister agenda?

Out of the corner of his eye, he saw her and turned. He put his phone away.

She glanced around the kitchen, at the set table, and laughed sneeringly. 'I can see through you, Robert.'

Robert moved towards her, his expression mildly curious. 'Can you? What can you see?'

She gestured at the table, at the pan on the stove. 'Here to save the day, and have Olivia gone.' She eyed him coolly. 'But there's one thing you've forgotten. They haven't arrested Mark yet. You'll have to wait a bit longer before you're on the homeward stretch.'

He supposed she had a right to look smug. She was more canny than he'd realised. He gave an appreciative pause. 'Sounds like you've been studying me.'

Her lips curved into a thin smile. 'Hardly. You're transparent. Do you know how many times over the years at work we heard you mention her name? Just about a zillion times. You prefix her name with the same opening: Mark's wife, Kate. Like it gives you permission to say it. Even Fleur noticed it on her date with you. Why don't you try a spritzer? Mark's wife, Kate, likes it.'

Olivia looked at him with disdain. 'Poor girl wanted a Jägerbomb, not a fucking spritzer. She didn't want to be reminded of another woman's name, either. You can be a real shit, Robert. For all your clever talk, it's a wonder you haven't learned better how to disguise your feelings.'

Robert felt a sharp surprise at Olivia knowing about his date. He thought only Mark knew he had taken Fleur out. He wondered what else she knew. Did Fleur share any other titbits with her? About the encounter in the car park on the day she left the airline, perhaps?

Fleur had been waiting for him by his car. She made out like it was *him* causing *her* problems and not the other way around. That it was him who was the stalker and not her. Her lunge at him had taken him by surprise. He'd had to hold her off from doing damage with those sharp little nails. Then her fit of crying because he didn't understand showed how unhinged she was. It didn't surprise him she turned up in Barcelona. He'd known one day she would rear her head again. But he hadn't expected her to end up dead.

He didn't know Olivia knew Fleur that well. Is that why she came with him to Kate and Mark's house? Did she think the same as Kerry Hall, that it was him who murdered Fleur? Was she spying on him?

He wanted to turn tail and leave Olivia standing there. She saved him the trouble, giving a tinkling laugh as she walked out of the kitchen. He stood there and breathed in, annoyed with himself for letting her get to him.

His name was in the clear. The police would not be coming after him. He was a hundred per cent certain of that.

He stared up at the ceiling as he heard her footfall. She was in Kate's bedroom. She had no business being in there. He stepped into the hallway and looked up the stairs, then quietly stepped up them to see what she was doing.

CHAPTER SIXTY-THREE

Kate walked past four cars parked in her drive. Her own and Mark's, Robert's Mazda, and a grey Fiat. She turned the key in the latch and heard sounds of normality from the kitchen. A clash of metal as cutlery went in a drawer. She closed the front door quietly and tiptoed to the sitting room door. She peered around the door frame, afraid he wouldn't be there. But his small form was fast asleep on the sofa, just as Robert said.

She hovered by the doorway while the noise in the kitchen continued. Barney was asleep in his basket. She couldn't take the chance that he might bark if she roused him. She had her car keys in her jacket. The Mazda and Fiat were blocking her in, but if she drove onto the lawn, she could get past them and be gone with Jacob before anyone knew she was there.

She nipped back to the front door to open it so she could leave quickly. She crouched beside Jacob and slipped her arm beneath his head, expecting him to stir, but he was sparko, and still wearing his school uniform from yesterday.

She blinked back tears, prepared to stand, then stayed still at the sound of rustling material behind her.

'I was about to put him to bed,' Olivia announced in a chippy voice.

Kate had no desire to talk to her, but she wasn't a coward. She stood up and turned to face her. 'It's okay, I'm home now.'

Kate was surprised to find her so calm. Her worries about her safety unnecessary. She didn't seem at all perturbed by the last twenty-four hours. Her hair was neatly brushed and flowing. She had on Kate's Karen Millen green dress that Kate wore on Christmas Day. It had long sleeves and on her it lengthened her silhouette. On Olivia, the hem fell above her knees.

The image being presented was not the one she'd envisaged. She had thought she would either have to save Olivia or find her not here, having being hidden away by Robert. Instead, she was standing there as if everything were normal. Kate needed to decide whether to call the police. It would be the sensible thing to do. Olivia had taken Jacob from his home. It was irrelevant that she had brought him back. It didn't put right what she had done wrong.

She sighed wearily. All she wanted was for Olivia to be gone and to hold her son. She didn't want a fight with this woman. She'd be happy just to let her go. She might, though, need some help. Her behaviour was off. She had committed a crime, but it didn't seem to have registered with her.

'Where's Robert?'

Olivia waved a hand towards the door. 'He's gone. I told him you wouldn't be happy with him here.'

Kate frowned. 'But his car's on the drive.'

'Well, he must be walking then. He went out the back door. He turned up with a bag of food and wine and just started cooking. Like the other night didn't happen.'

Kate shook her head in astonishment. Talk about the pot calling the kettle black. Had she no perspective on her own actions? Kate had heard enough. 'Olivia, you're hardly in a position to criticise someone else's behaviour. I think it best we don't say anything more.'

'Fine,' she replied in a docile tone. 'If that's what you wish. Can I ask what you'll do?'

Kate sighed. 'The only thing I intend to do is let the police know I found my son, so they can stop looking.'

'Fine,' she repeated. 'I'll just fetch the suitcase.'

As she exited the room, Kate stared after her in amazement. Had she really put her case back upstairs like she was there to stay again? She seriously needed some help with her behaviour. While she was gone, Kate gazed at Jacob. He hadn't stirred. She would wake him as soon as Olivia left. The grey Fiat, she realised, must be hers.

Olivia returned with a large suitcase. It was Kate's, the one she took on holidays that were more than a week long. Why was Olivia taking it? Was this a joke? She was wearing Kate's dress. Was she taking other clothes as well? Kate waited for an explanation.

Olivia took a step towards her, biting her lip like she was worried.

'Maybe you could stay with Grace until you find somewhere else.'

Her words skittered around Kate's brain like roaring traffic. Had Olivia just suggested she leave her home? Was the woman completely mad?

What the fuck was going on? Kate stormed past her into the hallway. Olivia calmly followed. Dread, like a boulder, settled in the pit of Kate's stomach. She turned to Olivia.

'Where is Robert?'

Olivia sighed and gave a reluctant look towards the stairs. 'He's staying out of sight, packing the rest of your things.'

Kate let the answer sink in. She clicked a button in her mind to replay the words. With a menacing expression she pointed an angry finger at Olivia. 'You stay there. Don't fucking move until I come back.'

'As you wish,' came her docile reply, making Kate want to rip her head off.

She mounted the stairs two at a time and rushed into her bedroom. Robert wasn't there. Then she saw his feet sticking out from the other side of the bed. Was he hiding? She stepped closer, then it was too late to double back or unsee Robert's dead body on the floor. Kate froze, while shock filled her eyes with tears. All her experience as a doctor told her he was dead. She didn't need to listen for breath or try to start his heart again. The waxy skin of his hand and face, the flaccidity of his body, told her she was looking at death.

The handle of the blade sticking out of his neck belonged innocently downstairs with all the other kitchen knives. Kate had used it for so many useful things. Paring an apple, eyeing potatoes, peeling, slicing, coring. She had held it so very recently, while cutting slices of pizza.

Trying hard to get a grip, she looked at the phone by her side of the bed, relieved she wouldn't have to walk by Robert's body. She picked up the handset from the cradle. It was dead. There was no dialling tone. She slotted it back in the cradle, hoping the action would make a connection. There was no beeping sound and no light on the panel. She checked the cable was plugged in to the phone, then pulled the other end. It came freely to her, the end of the grey cable cut, the plastic connector probably still in the wall.

Fighting down a rising sense of panic, she looked around for a weapon. The lamps on each side of the bed were too big to hide, her jewellery box was made of leather, a coffee mug on the drawers would do too little damage.

Her eyes fixed on the knife in Robert's neck. She couldn't. She couldn't. She couldn't take that out of his body.

She needed to find something else. She had been upstairs

too long and would have to go back down before Olivia came up to look for her. She descended the stairs silently. The hallway was empty. The front door had been closed. The second house phone was on the slim console table against the wall, beside a bowl of keys and loose change from emptied pockets. If she could get to it undetected, she could go out the back door in the kitchen and call the police. She needed only a few seconds. Just three digits to press. Even if she did just that in the hallway and could do nothing else, it would raise the alarm.

Her eyes fixed on it, then automatically glanced at the skirting. Fuck. She had cut this cable too.

Kate stretched the muscles in her face, opening her eyes wide, to relieve some of the tension. She had to appear unconcerned when she went through to the sitting room door. She had to fake it for Olivia to believe it, act as if she hadn't seen Robert's body upstairs.

She held her forehead as if confused as she walked into the room. 'I looked upstairs. There's no clothes on the bed. Where has he bloody gone?'

Kate didn't dare look up and see if her ruse had worked. She listened instead to Olivia's response, the light rise in her voice showing surprise. 'Well, I could have sworn that's where he was.'

Kate spread her hands out as if exasperated. Her tone irritable. Her eyes were steadfast on the woman standing by Jacob's sofa, a foot away from Kate's bag which held her mobile phone. 'Look, I don't know what's going on. You might be having a mini breakdown, Olivia, but this is nonsense and it has to stop. Robert's up and left. I'd like you to go as well.'

Olivia shook her head. She sat down on the sofa, only just missing Jacob's legs. She gazed at Kate.

'Fleur was my friend. We told each other things. She put a wish list in Robert's jacket. He ridiculed her for it. I heard him telling Captain Jordan, making fun of what she wrote on a piece of paper. That wasn't kind or fair. It's so easy for someone to make fun of you for carrying a checklist for finding the right man to marry.'

Kate needed Olivia to tell this to the police. Sharma needed to hear all of it.

As shocking as it was with Robert lying dead upstairs, she felt some sympathy towards Olivia. Perhaps it wasn't Olivia who cut the cables. She was beginning to think Olivia might be in shock. She was behaving bizarrely, denying Robert was dead. 'I'm sorry for the loss of your friend,' Kate murmured.

She moved towards her, intending to get her bag. Olivia stopped her in her tracks as she posed a question.

'Supposing Fleur wrote to Mark?'

Kate felt like she was in a maze with this woman's thoughts. At the eleventh hour, she decides to stop calling him Captain Jordan and call him Mark. Kate wanted facts from her, not wishy-washy thinking.

Olivia stood up abruptly, shaking her head hard, gripping her hands together.

'She should never have stolen it from me. She scuppered herself by doing that. She put it in the wrong jacket, would you believe? As if I'd look at a man like Robert!'

Her anger unnerved Kate. She was worked up about Fleur. But why? Kate tried recalling what Olivia told her – she was stalking a pilot, making his life difficult, leaving a wish list in his jacket. And now this: *She should never have stolen it from me.*

Kate gasped. The wish list wasn't Fleur's. It never belonged to her. She had stolen it from Olivia.

CHAPTER SIXTY-FOUR

Kate was trying to piece things together when Olivia offered her a drink, as if it was *her* home, pouring her a glass of wine from a bottle on the blanket box. She then casually walked around the room, stopping at Barney to stroke his head, looking curiously at Kate, before giving a pointed stare up at the ceiling.

Kate acted dumb, pretending she hadn't noticed. She took a sip of the wine. She was wrong. It wasn't shock she was seeing. It was abnormal behaviour. She was conscious of Jacob lying there unprotected. She needed to wake him. He would then come to her naturally, and she could walk him out to her car. She called his name. Then called him again. He didn't stir.

Olivia tutted and stood over Jacob. She leaned down, her head almost touching his, and spoke into his ear. He didn't move. Not even so much as the flicker of an eyelash. Kate waited with bated breath, her frightened eyes staring at Olivia.

Olivia perched on the edge of the sofa, her hand resting on Jacob's chest. She glanced at Kate and shrugged, then sighed impatiently at Kate's imploring look. 'Oh, for goodness' sake. Stop worrying. It's only a sleeping pill.'

Kate reeled at her blasé explanation, more terrified of this than of anything else Olivia had done. She became acutely aware of the danger right in this room. Robert's body upstairs, even Jacob being taken, hadn't touched the core of real fear way down inside of her body until this moment. She had allowed herself to be distracted by thoughts of how she would deal with everything. She should have just looked at Olivia. Really looked. A woman who believed she had done no wrong could only be a psychopath.

Kate focused on the now. 'What have you given him?'

Olivia tutted and shooed the question away with a flick of her hand. 'Oh, don't go all doctor on me. It's just nitrazepam.'

'What dosage? What dosage, Olivia? How much has he had?'

'Five milligrams. And five milligrams this morning,' she answered sullenly.

Kate calculated the correct dose for Jacob's body weight. If it was being used to treat epilepsy, he should have had only 2.5mg. She glanced at his face for signs of a rash, a less common side effect, but his skin was clear. She was relieved he was on his side, as an overdose could lead to respiratory distress, or even sudden death.

She watched Olivia's hand smooth Jacob's hair and wanted to yank it away.

Olivia glanced over at her. 'Look, it was better to keep him sedated while this was all going on.'

Kate stared at her aghast. What the hell was she referring to? Taking Jacob? Hiding him somewhere? Coming back here and putting on Kate's clothes? What did Olivia think she was going to do with the body upstairs? Keep Jacob sedated forever so he didn't see it? Kate was stunned. Even at the cost of being injured, she needed to confront her, provoke her with the one thing she was sure about.

'It was your checklist, wasn't it? Who's jacket was Fleur meant to have put it in?'

Olivia sighed. 'Look, it was a mistake. It wasn't meant to have gone in any jacket.'

Kate pushed the question again. 'Yes, but whose jacket was it meant for?'

'It wasn't hers to take,' Olivia snapped. 'The thing about having a friend is they think they know everything. What's worse is when they start meddling. She thought it was Robert. She felt guilty for going on a date with him. So to make amends she puts my private thoughts that I wrote on a sheet of paper in his jacket without consulting me. I'm ignorant to what's she done and tell her the man I have chosen. Fleur instantly disapproves. I think she thought I was going to try and baby trap him or something. Realising her mistake, she tries to warn Robert. So I turned the tables on her. I let her overhear where he'll be, and off she'd go running. Never quite getting there on time to actually talk to him, because he's been alerted that she was coming. The same trick done a few times starts a rumour. After she put that piece of paper in his pocket, and then kept popping up everywhere, all that was needed was to point out that maybe she was stalking him.'

Kate looked for shame in her eyes but there was no shame there. She shook her head in dismay. 'You were the one who started the rumour. You set her up. She was your friend. How is my husband involved in all of this? Did you implicate him in a murder?'

Olivia gaped at her. 'You really have not been listening, or else you're not very bright. Robert killed her. He obviously enticed her to Barcelona. Fleur would have seen it as a chance to tell him he was wrong – that she hadn't stalked him. She was trying to tell him the checklist wasn't for him.'

Kate was bright, but she couldn't grasp the full meaning of Olivia's words. All she wanted was to hear Mark was innocent. She refrained from screaming, and instead spat out the words through gritted teeth. 'You're right. I'm not very bright. So spell it out for me so I understand. How do you know Robert killed her? What proof do you have? And more to the point, why did he?'

'I'd say that was down to you, Kate.'

Her regretful tone raised Kate's head. 'What?'

'Well how else was he going to get Captain Jordan out of the picture?'

Her words sent a huge shiver up Kate's spine.

'He would kill someone for that reason?' she uttered in a hollow voice. 'Frame his best friend? I think I'm going to be sick.'

She gulped in air, trying to stop the wave of nausea. She let the glass fall from her hand, focusing on various parts of the room while she tried to take it all in. She interlocked her fingers to cradle her forehead. 'So, killing Robert. Was that for killing your friend? Retribution for Fleur?'

Olivia got to her feet and came towards her. Kate stood her ground. She wasn't going anywhere. Not until she had the truth. She kept her focus on Olivia's empty hands.

'Oh, so you did see his dead body?' She challenged Kate with a glare. 'But no, not for retribution. That was because he was taking photographs of my car.'

Kate stared out of the sitting room window, her thoughts like broken pieces of a jigsaw. What the hell was she on about now? What had Olivia's car got to do with any of this? She could hear the creaks of her home as Olivia paced the floorboards behind her. She felt numb, almost disassociated from the reality of what was happening around her. If not for her child lying asleep and innocently unaware, she'd walk out of the room and out the front door. She took a moment to focus again.

'You've lost me, Olivia. What has that got to do with you killing him?'

Behind her, Olivia gave a hollow laugh. 'Robert was quite the detective, you know. Quietly working things out. Like why I didn't bring my car back with us that day, when we went to fetch my things. I said it was in the garage. I saw him from JJ's window, when he arrived, taking photos with his phone. He'd seen the dent in the bonnet. Not very big, but noticeable. He came up the stairs and asked if I had knocked Mark down. What could I say? I was following him? It's not something he would understand.'

Kate turned around in shock. '*You were following Mark!* Why were you following him?'

Olivia stared at her petulantly. 'It isn't what you're thinking. I just wanted to see how he was coping. If he'd stepped to the side, I would have just driven by. But he slowed down and was starting to turn around. It would have been impossible for him not to see me. He would have wondered why I was there. I reacted instinctively. It was a nightmare. I had to find somewhere to hide the car. A derelict barn. I had to walk for miles before I could call for a taxi. I thanked God after that he wasn't dead. I never expected it to put him in hospital, but you have to admit it delayed his arrest. And it allowed me to be in his home and mind his son.'

Kate's mouth had gone dry. She had no spit to swallow. This was madness. Complete insanity. She ground her teeth, trying not to lose control. She thrust her legs forward, forcing Olivia to step back sharply, and took some relief at being able to do that.

'You have to understand. I couldn't let Robert or Fleur take away my dream.'

Kate was trying to remember Olivia's bloody dream. She couldn't recall Olivia telling her about it, apart from saying it was always the same one. She shared with Kate her hopes of being with her son's father. He was with someone else. That things between him and his partner weren't good. She had hope that one day they'd all get to live together.

Kate couldn't take much more of her riddles. She just wanted to lie on the sofa and put her arms around her son. She stared at the suitcase by the door. She'd forgotten it was there. 'You still haven't answered the question. Why were you following my husband?'

Olivia came a step closer and Kate stiffened. She spoke slowly, making sure Kate heard every word. 'Because I love him. He's the right one. And more. He has a son. My son now. You realise that now, don't you, Kate? This is no longer your home. Mark and JJ are no longer your family. They're mine now, Kate.'

CHAPTER SIXTY-FIVE

Kate's harsh cry rang through the sitting room. 'Are you for real? Do you think my husband is going to just let you take my place? You're deluded, Olivia. Why don't you just get in your car and go before I call the police? You've known my husband was innocent, and you knew it was Robert who killed her. My husband's on the verge of being arrested and going to prison!'

Olivia turned away. 'Don't be so dramatic. That's not going to happen. It's not part of the plan. I wasn't going to leave him in trouble. What you have to understand is, I had to put him in a difficult situation in order to save him. He needed to see for himself he was with the wrong wife. A wife who didn't trust him, who would easily believe him guilty of something bad. He had to be shown what you were like. Because, let's be honest, you did believe your husband could be guilty of murder.'

Kate's body twitched in shock, stilling the air in her lungs. She felt as if she had just walked off a plank and was falling through the air.

Olivia heard her cry and faced her again with a pitying look.

'Like you just believed Robert was guilty. You're gullible, Kate.

Feeding you lies is like taking candy from a baby. I've had to worry about Fleur for a whole year. All she had to do was write to Mark. I couldn't risk that happening. I knew she'd come if Robert sent her a Christmas card. A chance to tell him he had to save Mark from little old me. All I had to do was bring the characters into play. Fleur was expecting Robert. She got me instead. Poor thing was embarrassed.'

Kate looked up at the ceiling, fighting back the tears that were trying to take over for her overwhelming guilt. Her senses reeled. Everything said earlier had been a monstrous lie. All of it lies. Robert was dead, and she hadn't given one thought to whether he'd suffered or felt fear. His standing in the garden had been to watch over her.

She was terrified. Olivia was sharing the real truth. She could have hidden her involvement. There was enough in her story for her to have got away with it. Robert had dated Fleur, then ended it. There was worrying history between them. Add that to his obsession with her, the description of the man given to the police, and Olivia could have stuck to the narrative that it was him. Even blame him for Jacob's abduction. Instead, she had packed Kate a suitcase and told her the truth. Robert was innocent.

Kate dug her fingernails into her palms to stop the shaking. 'You're the witness,' she whispered her revelation. 'You murdered her, then reported seeing a man. You got Mark to leave the hotel.'

Olivia shook her head. 'A housekeeper let me in while he was in the shower, believing I'd left my key card inside and I took his watch. On my way to meeting Fleur, I saw him in a bar searching for it. It was perfect. That he chose then, that time of night to go out looking for it. Otherwise I would have had to think of something to get him to leave his room, but he saved me the bother.'

Kate couldn't understand why she would do such a thing if

she loved him like she said. 'But why set him up? Why not just let Robert take the blame?'

'You really haven't been listening. I needed to show him he didn't need you. I figured out what type of woman you'd be from hearing Robert praise your glory. High standards. High achiever. A perfect wife. You had a pinched little look on your face in a photograph I saw of you. Like nothing was good enough. I couldn't leave him with you.'

Kate's mouth twisted in a contemptuous smile. 'But you were happy to leave his watch at the scene. You sad woman. Surely you would have been better off choosing someone who was single? There must be plenty of men out there more attractive. Younger even. I love my husband, Olivia, but he's not perfect. I'm sure he didn't tick every box on your checklist.'

Olivia's cheeks turned red. 'That's where you're wrong. He ticked boxes I only dreamed of. He had a son. The same age as my son. Nearly with the same name. I knew then he'd be the one. He saw how good I was with JJ. He would eventually see I was the right mother JJ needed. All I had to do was work out how to save him.'

'Save him? Save him from what? Save him how?' Kate ridiculed with open scepticism. 'The police are about to arrest him. They have his watch as evidence. Your plan. Your devious murderous plan is a convoluted fucking mess. How did you expect it to end? You and Mark going off into the sunset? You made him a suspect in a murder! Has that not registered?'

Olivia laughed at her. That she could laugh about anything after what she had done sickened Kate. The irritating sound ceased. She jutted out her chin.

'It's on my agenda to fix it. I'll contact the Spanish authorities and say I remember the man I saw had a bandage on his hand. I already told them I thought it was a pilot I saw at the airport. Robert had plasters on his knuckles. Everyone knew he liked to go out running at night. It was always going to be him that was guilty.'

Kate gave a scathing look. 'Do you think the police are fools? You obviously made an anonymous call. They'll have to verify who you are.'

Olivia was unfazed. 'They know who I am, Kate. I'm a student, studying in the US. I'm at Boston University. I couldn't hang about after what I witnessed. I had to fly home. I think it will take them a while, if ever, to find me.'

Kate wasn't sure how much longer she could stay upright. She was lightheaded from so many shocks. She needed to shut out Olivia from her mind, grab Jacob and run while she still could. Olivia might not be as keen for her to go when she realised what she had shared.

She glanced at the wine bottle on the blanket box and wished it was full and heavy, instead of nearly empty, so it could do some serious damage. The best it would do was to stun her. She'd be better off throwing it at a wall to distract her while she grabbed Jacob and ran. She should keep talking. Maybe her voice would wake Jacob. Olivia wouldn't want him to hear anything. Her gaze went to Barney. He hadn't stirred the whole time she was there, not even when stroked. Olivia must have sedated him as well.

'And how do you explain Robert's now dead with a knife in his neck?' she asked scornfully.

'Self-defence, Kate. He came here looking for you. I confronted him about Fleur. He went for me, but I grabbed the knife before it went in to me.'

The coldness of her lie made the tears flow. Kate couldn't stop them. She hesitated to ask, to get her to confess to the real truth. Her mouth trembled. 'And what really happened, Olivia? Did he attack you?'

She gave a slight shake of her head. 'He came into the bedroom and saw Mark's cupboard open. He walked over to close it. He asked me if it was my car that drove into Mark. I went behind him. He didn't notice what I was carrying. He didn't see it coming. He just went down.'

Kate closed her eyes, and saw Olivia with a knife in her hand, casually standing there waiting to use it on him. Robert never had a chance.

'And what about me, Olivia?'

Olivia stared at her. Her eyes quite mad. Kate couldn't bear to spend another minute in her company. She looked at Jacob's position on the sofa, working out the safest and quickest way to move him, the best route to take. The obstacles to avoid. The blanket box between the sofas. She'd need to walk sideways, bend and lift him in her arms, and carry him through the door this way, to avoid hitting his head against the frame. In the hall-way, she'd throw him over her shoulder so she could open the front door.

She needed to pick her moment. Olivia was younger, taller, bigger. She would try to stop Kate, so she had to show she was unafraid. This was her home. She had every right to pick up her son and carry him out of the house. She breathed in, watching out of the corner of her eye as Olivia strolled to the far end of the room. She made her move.

She released her deep breath explosively in a gasp of surprise. One step forward was as far as she got before Olivia slammed her to the floor. Swift and hard before Kate could even think. Straddling her chest before she could even move. Olivia's hands were around her throat, squeezing. Kate couldn't get up. Olivia's knees pinned her arms to the ground. The face staring down at her was bright red, spittle forming on the lips, teeth bared. Voice hard.

'You shouldn't have asked that question, Kate. You shouldn't have put thoughts in my head. Giving me a better solution. Mark will have to hear Robert killed you. Then I had to kill him to save myself.'

Kate bucked her hips, then raised them to dig her knees into Olivia's back. She couldn't make contact. Her thighs were too short. She couldn't roll her hips high enough because of the weight on her chest.

She twisted her head to try to evade the hands and saw Jacob's face, eyes asleep. She prayed they didn't open to see her death. It was happening right now. She could do nothing to stop it. Her lungs and brain were being starved of oxygen. Olivia was killing her. She remembered what Olivia said about her son's father.

He's with someone else, but things between them are not good.

She'd been talking about Kate's marriage.

She could feel pins and needles in her left arm. It felt floaty. The shine of amber glass caught her eye. How ironic that she was leaving this world with her one last image being a gift from Olivia. She raised her hand in defeat. She had no breath to hold and no more to come. Her lungs burned from starvation.

She stared at her hand in the air. Floating. Weightless. Maybe she was already dead. She raised it higher. Then let her fingers rest on the rim of the cool glass. It was a splendid gift. A beautiful bowl. Her fingers spread into the smooth irregular dips in the rim.

She gripped it for comfort, her thumb wide along the curve of the rim. She gripped and lifted and felt the weight bend her wrist. Its heaviness would pull her arm crashing to the ground. She was going to die holding Olivia's gift. She peered through her lids at the blurring face above. All red. She could feel Olivia's breath – breath she couldn't breathe in. It wasn't fair that she was leaving her boy with his mother's murderer. It wasn't fair that he would never get to meet the brother or sister growing inside her. It wasn't right.

Her wrist was bending like a twig. She needed to be like a tree, a sturdy branch. Stretching up toward the light, where there was air, Kate raised her arm as high as it would go. Right up to the sky. Then brought it back to earth with the fastest fall. It made a dense solid sound like the earth had cracked. She didn't care.

She could finally breathe.

She rolled the weight from her chest. Kate had no energy to help her. Olivia had taken all of it away.

EPILOGUE

Kate stared at her hands as she washed them in the sink. A habit that will chip away at her sanity if she lets it. The counsellor said she must try not to see them as having done harm. They had saved her life. As a doctor, Kate found that difficult to accept. She had used them to take a life. She relives those minutes, those last few seconds, most days. She knows it is her mind and not her hands that saved her. Her hands were merely a tool.

She often finds herself staring up at the ceiling in the kitchen, at the expanse of white paint above four of the wall cupboards. Another habit. Robert's body had lain on the floor above in that exact place. It wasn't until the following day that they took his body away. Saturday the twenty-first of January. Nineteen days from when it all began, on the third of January, the day she opened the door to Sharma.

That period had felt like a lifetime, while the last three months had flown by. February, March and most of April had passed in a flash. Days and weeks just gone.

She has no sense of how long she lay on the floor beside Olivia's body, but at some point she had moved herself to climb on the sofa beside Jacob. The seat cushion under her hip was wet with his urine. All she cared about was feeling his breath on her face.

It was Abe who found her. She had a memory of his worried face staring down at her, then the warmth of a cover being put over her and Jacob. At the hospital, her consultant, John Brown, fixed things so that she and Jacob were together in the same room. Grace sat between their beds, alternately holding Kate's hand and then Jacob's. If her arms had been long enough, she'd have held both at once.

A CT scan and an MRI of her neck had shown soft tissue damage to the larynx from manual strangulation. Her voice was hoarse for weeks. They took blood from Jacob without a murmur as he was still drifting in and out of sleep. She hadn't been able to close her eyes until she heard him talking to Grace, and then Grace reading him a story. Her eyes opened again when Mark took hold of her hand. Standing behind his wheelchair was Julian, looking a little worse for wear. His comment about her, directed more at Mark, was that she was 'plucky'.

She regarded them both with energy lasting only long enough to keep her eyes open while her mouth curved in a brief, tired smile. Three weeks of very little sleep, and endless hours of fear, had beaten her into a state of exhaustion.

Sharma visited the next day, and the day after. Allowing her to rest her voice frequently, he recorded what she said, and didn't ask her to repeat things. She was able to read her statement afterwards to see if she had missed anything. When she got to visiting Luke Vaughn, Kate had silently indicated to Sharma that he stop recording. He complied, and listened to her concerns about what she had seen on Luke's phone. He suggested he would treat it as a separate incident and would visit Mr Vaughn to let him know that if he wished to discuss matters about his son, his door would be open.

Luke sent a card to her address two weeks after Olivia's

death, addressed to Doctor Jordan. She had opened it when on her own and taken comfort from the words.

> *If we do only our best, we are bound to get some of it right. All we can do is correct what has gone wrong with time and love and patience. Luke.*

She hid the card after she read it. She had witnessed a father's pain at seeing his child hurt and knew he would not give up, only giving his best to make sure Josh wasn't hurt again.

Kate looked out of the kitchen window at Mark directing where the For Sale sign should go. She had mixed feelings about the decision to move. It was Barney's home, for however long he had left. His amble out the front door every day, and more often than before, seemed to bring him to life as his nose pushed into bushes and swept along the lawn. She had kept up the supplements Olivia had found, as they were clearly doing him good.

It was Jacob's home, the only one he'd known. He had special places for his toys. Sometimes lined up down the stairs, or along the hallway. Now, out in the garden on a low wall, dinosaurs in an imaginary world. It was Grace's second home. She had her own room upstairs. She knew how Kate's home worked – the back door lock a little stiff, the electricity distribution board under the stairs, the fan for the cooker, not normally used because of the noise. It was Sophie's new place to visit to get to know her godson, and to irritate Mark about too much lifting when he should be resting.

Then there was Mark. He had helped build the house. He had spent more than a year patiently restoring it, before turning the garage into a workshop where he could tinker. But more than just tinker. Kate knew some of his projects were the stuff of dreams and expected one day to see a patent for one of his inventions. Every tool and piece of machinery would have to be found a new home. Shelves upon shelves of organisation would have to be dismantled.

Kate was on the fence. Undecided whether to stay or move. She had changed none of the improvements Olivia put in place, she had no motivation to think about her home. The glass bowl was gone, of course, taken by the police. But she could honestly say that she had not gone in her sitting room once without seeing Olivia on the floor, wearing her green dress.

Many of these memories she had not shared with Mark, because she didn't want to put detailed images in his head. It was enough having to cope with his own memories. Being a strong suspect in a murder case had shaken him. It had taken several more days before the pressure was finally lifted. Following the examination of the knife in Robert's body, the dent in Olivia's car, the voice recording of a woman giving an account of the man seen with Fleur O'Connell. Footage of Olivia, not previously searched for, saw her being let in to Mark's room by a housekeeper and emerge a few seconds later with something in her hand.

Knowing Fleur O'Connell had been murdered by Olivia woke him in the night. Should he have spotted something to tell him this would happen? Should he have noticed Olivia more?

Losing Robert had affected him badly. The way he saw it, his death happened in his home while Robert was looking out for Mark. It was a burden he was carrying. She suspected this, more than anything, was his reason for wanting to sell up and leave. For Kate, if there was anything that would persuade her to stay, it was all Robert.

Robert had helped build the house. There were memories here of his laughter. That he had strong feelings for her was no one's fault. For him, it must have been a burden that stopped him from being truly happy. In the ten years he'd known her and come to their home, he'd only ever treated her with respect. That one minor lapse in behaviour, where he'd revealed feelings for her, was easily forgiven. Less so, and possibly never to be forgiven, were her thoughts about him in his last week. She couldn't share that with Mark. She couldn't share that she'd thought his best friend had betrayed him. That she believed he'd committed a heinous crime just to set Mark up.

Mark would find it difficult to bear if he knew Kate had had hatred in her heart for someone he'd loved. He'd find it painful to think of Robert knowing this and feeling alone in the days before his death. Kate couldn't tell him. She'd rather carry the guilt on her own.

She dried her hands and placed them against her stomach. She was at eighteen weeks and the pregnancy was hardly visible. It concerned the midwife that Kate was not gaining weight. The baby was growing and its heartbeat was strong, while the rest of Kate's body was withering. Her face and neck and limbs were shrinking. She wasn't eating nearly enough, and any nutrients were going straight to the baby.

She dropped her hands when Mark walked into the kitchen. She hadn't told him yet. It didn't feel right to share the news, and bring him joy, while she hid something so bad. It felt wrong to salvage happiness while so much damage had been done. It would be like trickery to take care of the guilt.

They hadn't made love since before he went into hospital. She had wondered if it was the fear of increasing his heart rate that stopped him from reaching for her. He would know that most people who experience cardiac arrest don't survive. He was one of the lucky ones who took hardly any time for his heart to beat on its own again. He'd made an early and good recovery. His six weeks of cardiac rehab had come and gone, and he didn't need to see a cardiologist again for a year.

At home he was walking five miles a day, and was in talks with the airline about a return to work, requesting a medical examination by the company. He would need to show he could pass through the special insurance process, which meant he would be free of coronary artery disease and have no evidence of ischemia. He had no fear of flying again. So maybe making love to her was more down to his mental state, still overwhelmed with emotions. He didn't appear angry or anxious or confused, just sad. Grieving, no doubt, for his friend.

He came up behind her and leaned his chin on her shoulder, his hands resting lightly on her hips. 'Well, it's up. Now we have to wait and see.'

She glanced at the For Sale sign and sighed.

He spoke gently near her ear. 'You don't seem sure.'

She shrugged, keeping her back to him, not wanting him to see the tears in her eyes. The closest she had come to crying since Robert's death was on the day of his funeral. The turnout of so many colleagues from the airline, all wearing uniforms matching the colours of all the flowers they sent. The stark beauty of their gathering to mark the event of a fallen colleague had got to her. Mark's opening words of his eulogy brought an ache to her throat.

Robert was my friend. To know him was to love him. To understand was to forgive him.

'I am, if you are,' she replied.

'You don't talk about it, Kate, the effect this house is having on you. You witnessed what happened here. I can't imagine how hard that has been. You're like a lost soul walking around. I'm worried this house is making you ill. Losing your happy place is eating you up. Talk to me, Kate.'

He pulled her back against him, keeping his hands on her hips. Kate's head bent forward as she began to cry. The release of the tears was a relief. She would stop crying in a moment and reassure him.

'Talk to me, Kate. Tell me why you were afraid of Robert?'

She stiffened in shock. How had he found out?

His arm came around her to hold her closer. 'Just before the estate agent arrived, I found a letter in a drawer upstairs, addressed to me. I only just read it.'

She shuddered. 'Don't ask, please. It was foolish. You don't need to know.'

He gave her a gentle shake. 'Hey, nothing you tell me will shock me. I promise.'

Kate could feel her hands shaking and held them tightly together. 'I thought he murdered Fleur O'Connell. I thought he framed you. I thought he took your watch. I thought he did all of that to get me.' She inhaled a shaky breath, before saying worse. 'But I also thought it might have been you. Or that you were in it together. You wouldn't say where you went after you left the hotel, so I thought you must have been there.'

She felt the heave of his chest against her back. 'Oh, Kate, I'm so sorry. I should never have left you in the dark. I should have told you everything. I should have said why I couldn't talk.' He inhaled another deep breath. 'I was protecting Robert. I left the hotel to look for my watch, thinking I'd dropped it at Paulo's. Crossing the road, I saw Robert coming out of the hotel. I didn't give it much thought at the time, assuming he was out for a run.

'The next day, I'm greeted by the police and informed a witness had given a description of someone resembling me, which of course also resembles Robert. An instinct decided me to keep quiet about seeing him. I loved the guy and saw no reason to put him in the frame. I kept quiet about leaving the hotel. Then, when I discovered the woman's name, I didn't know what to think. This was the woman who stalked Robert, who I reported. I knew there was no way Robert had killed her, but this would be a motive. I couldn't say anything, Kate. He was as innocent as me. I didn't want to go free at the expense of Robert taking my place.'

Kate felt the tears sting her eyes. Mark had risked his freedom, because he'd cared more about Robert than he did for staying with her. Her lips trembling, she made herself ask, 'If you knew he couldn't kill someone, then why not let him prove that to the police himself?'

She felt him shudder. 'I couldn't, Kate. The police were going to have one of us. My watch was found in Fleur's hand. They found hairs from my wrist caught in the strap. Why give them both of us?'

She heard him gulp, and knew he was struggling.

His voice was strained. 'I owe Robert everything I have. The day I met you would never have happened. Robert saw you and wanted to help. I was impatient to leave. He'd just dragged me around shops, trying to make me more trendy. Needless to say, not my thing. I came over just to speed things up.

'This is going to sound crazy, Kate, but you need to listen carefully. I knew if you'd chosen him, I would have been all right. It doesn't mean I'm not glad with every fibre of my being that you loved me, and I'm so grateful that his loving you never impacted on our relationship, but it was selfish of me, Kate, to have kept him as a friend, as well as keep you. I've known from the moment Robert met you, he was in love with you. Knowing how he felt, I should have helped him walk away. I couldn't put myself before him, Kate. I did that once already. So I said nothing. But I should have told you and not let you suffer.'

Kate turned in his arms to wrap hers around him, wanting to hold him as close as she could. They kissed gently, then passionately, for the first time in months.

'We don't have to leave here,' she whispered. 'I still love our home.'

He gazed down at her. 'Do you want to think about it first? You don't have to decide now. I'll go wherever you're happy, or stay if that's what you want. It's only bricks and mortar.'

She shook her head. 'You're wrong. You and Robert built this house. All those beers you shared up on the roof when you didn't think I knew? Behaving like lads until you saw my car? Those are the memories I want to cherish.'

His eyes watered. She placed her hand against his chest. She could feel his heart pounding.

She nodded reassuringly. 'It sounds strong.'

He squeezed her hand in a macho way, with a self-conscious grin, keeping his voice low. 'I'm as strong as a fucking bull, I'll have you know.'

Kate grinned back. Then a tender, deeply caring look came into her eyes. 'I have something to tell you.'

She pushed his arms away from her to take hold of his hand. She placed it beneath her shirt against her stomach to let him feel the little bump.

'I'm pregnant, Mark.'

A LETTER FROM LIZ

Dear Reader,

I want to say a huge thank you for choosing to read *My Husband's Lies*. If you did enjoy it and want to keep up to date with all my latest releases, just sign up at the following link. Your email address will never be shared and you can unsubscribe at any time.

www.bookouture.com/liz-lawler

I hope you loved *My Husband's Lies* and if you did I would be very grateful if you could write a review. I'd love to hear what you think. I was inspired to write this story after working as cabin crew for an airline. Several of my siblings had made this a career and I wanted to join them. As a trained nurse I was welcomed, as many medical problems can happen during a flight, and often I was called on to assist with an unwell passenger. During one particular occasion, a woman in her forties was having a panic attack. She was frightened and I sat with her until her anxiety subsided. She then told me a sad story. Her success as a business woman had allowed her husband to bring up their children, and now he wanted a new wife. She hadn't seen this coming and had thought their life perfect. She had thought him an ideal husband and was incredibly sad that somebody else would be taking her place in her home.

My heart went out to her. I didn't of course know her situation, and I didn't know how she would deal with it, but rightly or wrongly a germ of an idea began to weave its way through my imagination and I began to think of what some people might do given similar circumstances. And so this story began!

I love hearing from my readers – you can get in touch with me through social media or Goodreads. If I'm late in responding please never think it's because I don't care or that I've ignored your name. It's only because I'm absent for a little while writing.

Thanks,

Liz Lawler

facebook.com/liz.lawler.90

x.com/authorlizlawler

ACKNOWLEDGEMENTS

Thank you to Barcelona – a city I fell in love with. It became the natural place to set this story, as the idea began there. Thank you for your wonderful hospitality.

When I read this story back, I see all the hardworking and talented people who helped me write this book. All their special inputs written in the pages. But mostly their continued unwavering support. My deepest gratitude to all of you!

To Rory Scarfe, to Hattie Grünewald, and everybody else at The Blair Partnership. You are always there to root me on so that I continue to grow.

My editors, past and present, Cara Chimirri, Natasha Harding, Jayne Osborne, for teaching me along the way, and for squeezing out every last drop of each story with your gentle guiding hands.

The brilliant Bookouture publishing team. I said it before and will say it again. Capability should be your byword...

Research is a favourite part when embarking on a new novel. I am deeply indebted to the experts.

To Dr Peter Forster MBBS FRCA. My endless gratitude for casting your expert eye over this one. Once again you make it all better! Any mistakes are of course mine.

To Detective Inspector Kurt Swallow. My sincere gratitude for reading this through a policeman's eyes, and spotting my mistakes! I'm indebted to you, and hope you'll be with me to catch the next one!

My thanks to Martyn Folkes for keeping me honest. My

brother-in-law Kevin Stephenson and sister Bee Mundy for reading the first draft! Bradley Gould for my IT support. Harriet, my daughter-in-law, for reminding me to press send!

To my husband Mike who cheers me on. Which is all I need!

To the loves and lights of my life – Lorcs, Katie, Alex, Harriet, Bradley, Darcie, Dolly, Arthur, Nathaniel. It's about time we all went out to play...

To my parents, my constant inspiration...

Finally, my thanks to you, the reader, who have taken the time to read my stories. Your encouragement makes it all worthwhile. I hope you enjoy this one.

Milton Keynes UK
Ingram Content Group UK Ltd.
UKHW040815161123
432684UK00004B/180